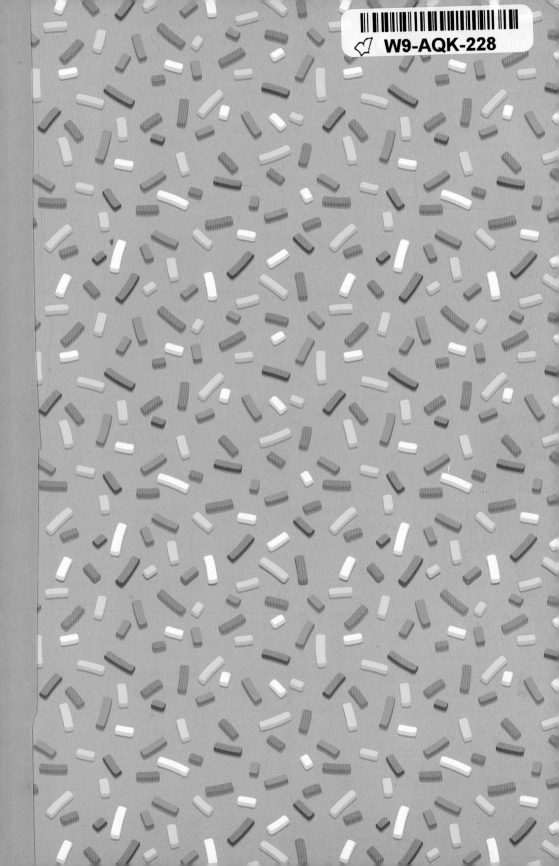

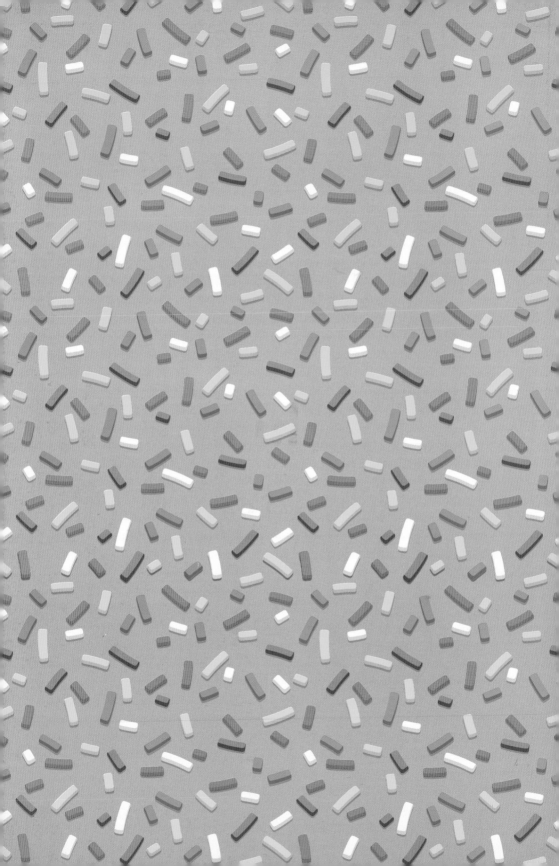

Emma
on
Thin
Icing

This book is a work of fiction. Any references to historical events, real people, or real places are used fictitiously. Other names, characters, places, and events are products of the author's imagination, and any resemblance to actual events or places or persons, living or dead, is entirely coincidental.

SIMON SPOTLIGHT
An imprint of Simon & Schuster Children's Publishing Division
1230 Avenue of the Americas, New York, New York 10020
This Simon Spotlight edition January 2023
Copyright © 2023 by Simon & Schuster, Inc.
All rights reserved, including the right of reproduction in whole or in part in any form.
SIMON SPOTLIGHT and colophon are registered trademarks of Simon & Schuster, Inc.
For information about special discounts for bulk purchases, please contact Simon & Schuster
Special Sales at 1-866-506-1949 or business@simonandschuster.com.
Text by Tracey West
Cover and Character Design by Manuel Preitano
Art by Giulia Campobello at Glass House Graphics
Assistant on inks by Marzia Migliori
Colors by Francesca Ingrassia
Lettering by Giuseppe Naselli/Grafimated Cartoon
Supervision by Salvatore Di Marco/Grafimated Cartoon
Designed by Laura Roode
The text of this book was set in Comic Crazy.
Manufactured in China 0922 SCP
10 9 8 7 6 5 4 3 2 1
ISBN 978-1-6659-1656-1 (hc)
ISBN 978-1-6659-1655-4 (pbk)
ISBN 978-1-6659-1657-8 (ebook)
This book has been cataloged with the Library of Congress.

CUPCAKE DIARIES

Emma on Thin Icing

By
Coco Simon

Illustrated by
Giulia Campobello
at Glass House Graphics

Simon Spotlight
New York   London   Toronto   Sydney   New Delhi

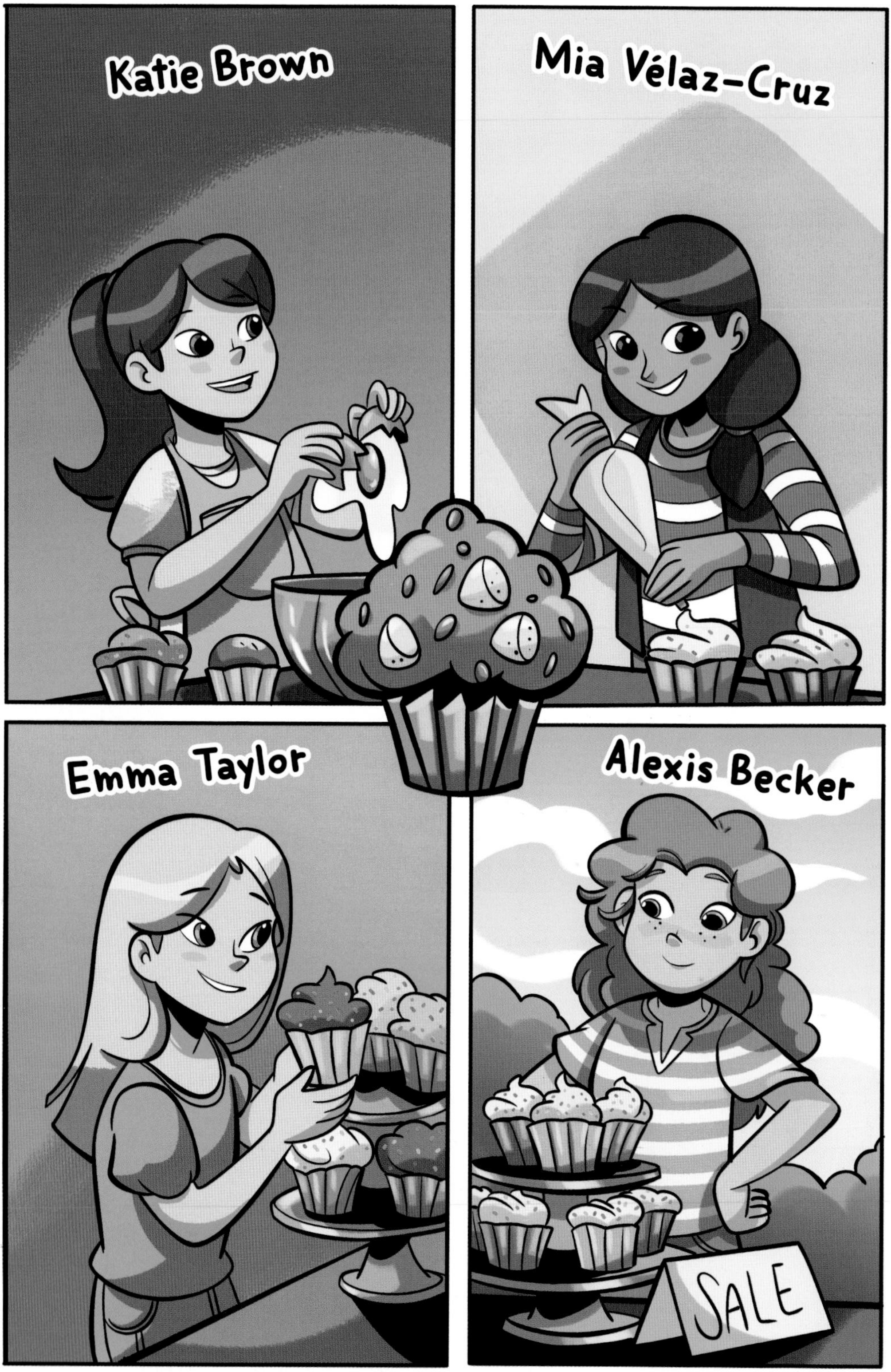
Katie Brown
Mia Vélaz-Cruz
Emma Taylor
Alexis Becker
SALE

Chapter 1

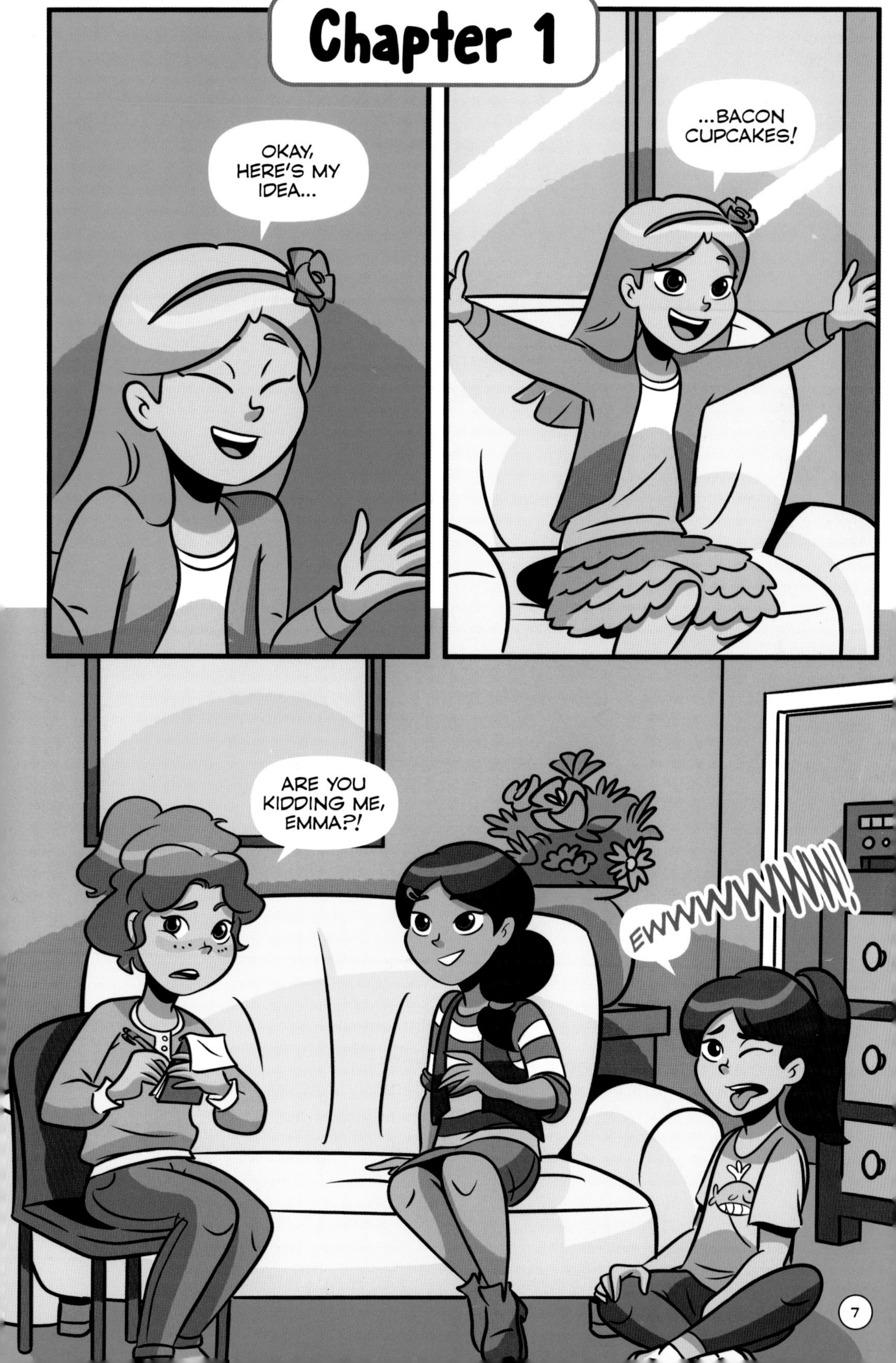

OKAY, HERE'S MY IDEA...
...BACON CUPCAKES!
ARE YOU KIDDING ME, EMMA?!
EWWWWWWW!

I MADE THEM LAST WEEK, AND MY BROTHERS LOVED THEM. THEY'RE SALTY AND SWEET. JUST THINK ABOUT IT!

COME ON, KATIE, AREN'T BAKERS ALWAYS MAKING CANDIED BACON AND STUFF ON THOSE COOKING SHOWS YOU MAKE US WATCH?

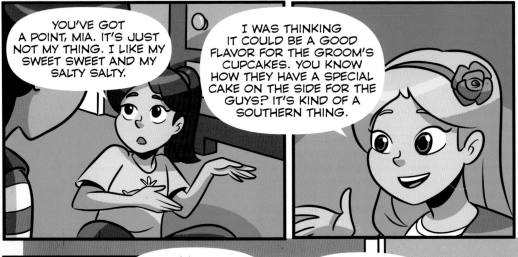

YOU'VE GOT A POINT, MIA. IT'S JUST NOT MY THING. I LIKE MY SWEET SWEET AND MY SALTY SALTY.

I WAS THINKING IT COULD BE A GOOD FLAVOR FOR THE GROOM'S CUPCAKES. YOU KNOW HOW THEY HAVE A SPECIAL CAKE ON THE SIDE FOR THE GUYS? IT'S KIND OF A SOUTHERN THING.

SO, WE'D DO THEM ALONG WITH THE MAIN CUPCAKES WE'RE MAKING FOR THE WEDDING. THE GROOM'S CUPCAKES WOULD BE SPECIAL FOR EDDIE?

YEAH. NOT THAT I'M TRYING TO MAKE YOUR MOM PAY FOR EXTRA CUPCAKES.

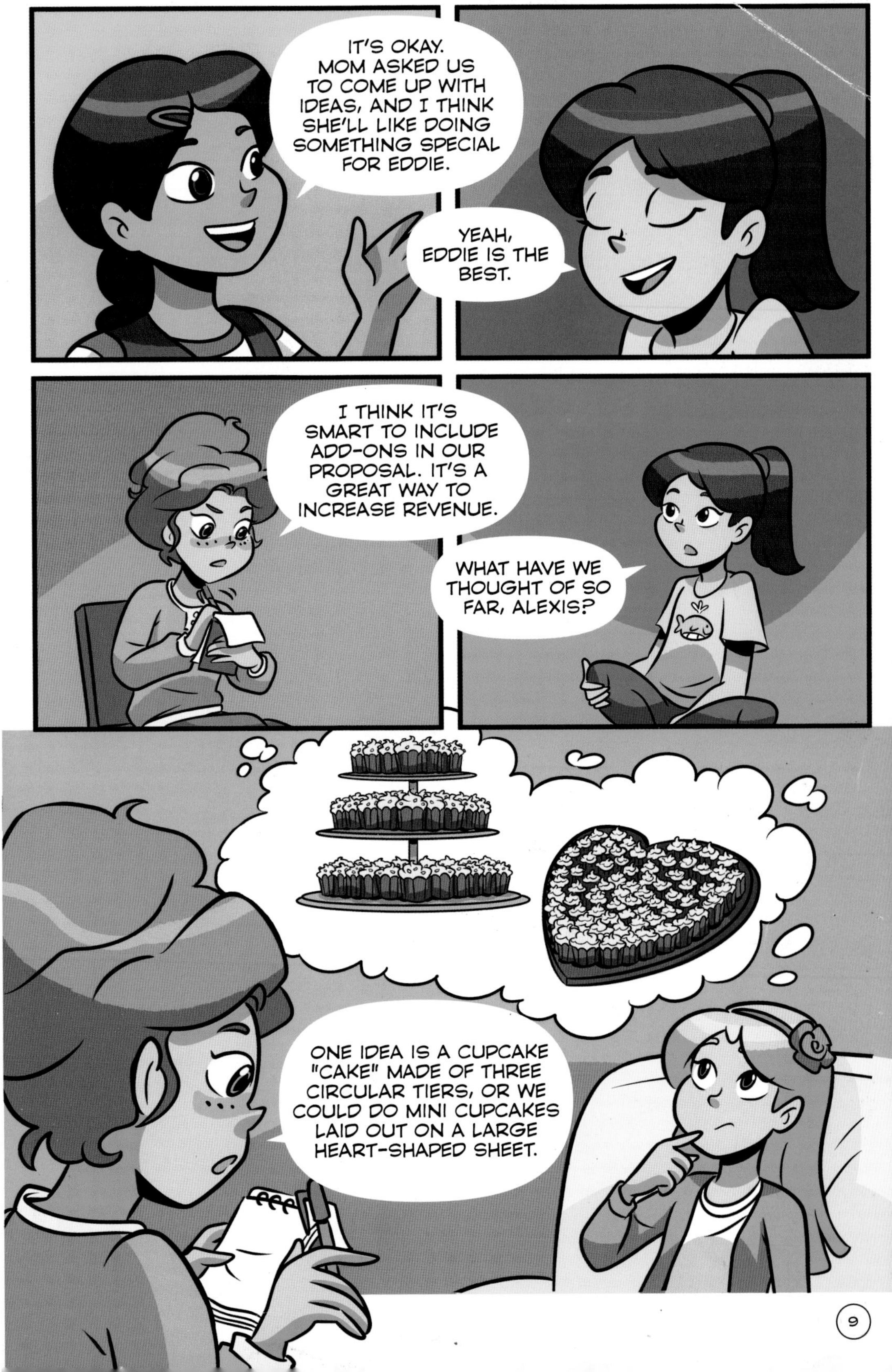
IT'S OKAY. MOM ASKED US TO COME UP WITH IDEAS, AND I THINK SHE'LL LIKE DOING SOMETHING SPECIAL FOR EDDIE.
YEAH, EDDIE IS THE BEST.
I THINK IT'S SMART TO INCLUDE ADD-ONS IN OUR PROPOSAL. IT'S A GREAT WAY TO INCREASE REVENUE.
WHAT HAVE WE THOUGHT OF SO FAR, ALEXIS?
ONE IDEA IS A CUPCAKE "CAKE" MADE OF THREE CIRCULAR TIERS, OR WE COULD DO MINI CUPCAKES LAID OUT ON A LARGE HEART-SHAPED SHEET.

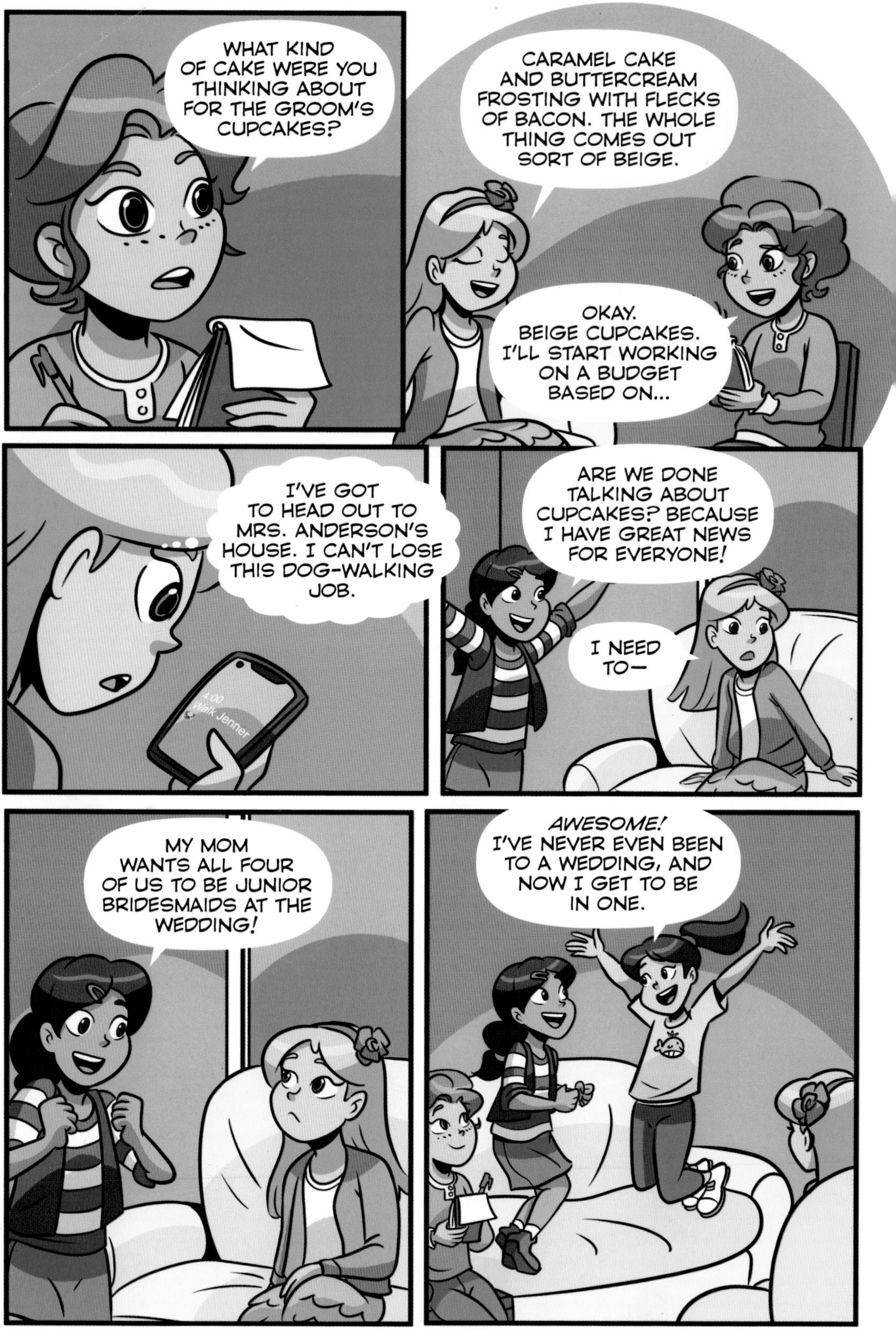
WHAT KIND OF CAKE WERE YOU THINKING ABOUT FOR THE GROOM'S CUPCAKES?
CARAMEL CAKE AND BUTTERCREAM FROSTING WITH FLECKS OF BACON. THE WHOLE THING COMES OUT SORT OF BEIGE.
OKAY. BEIGE CUPCAKES. I'LL START WORKING ON A BUDGET BASED ON...
I'VE GOT TO HEAD OUT TO MRS. ANDERSON'S HOUSE. I CAN'T LOSE THIS DOG-WALKING JOB.
4:00
Walk Jenner
ARE WE DONE TALKING ABOUT CUPCAKES? BECAUSE I HAVE GREAT NEWS FOR EVERYONE!
I NEED TO—
MY MOM WANTS ALL FOUR OF US TO BE JUNIOR BRIDESMAIDS AT THE WEDDING!
AWESOME! I'VE NEVER EVEN BEEN TO A WEDDING, AND NOW I GET TO BE IN ONE.

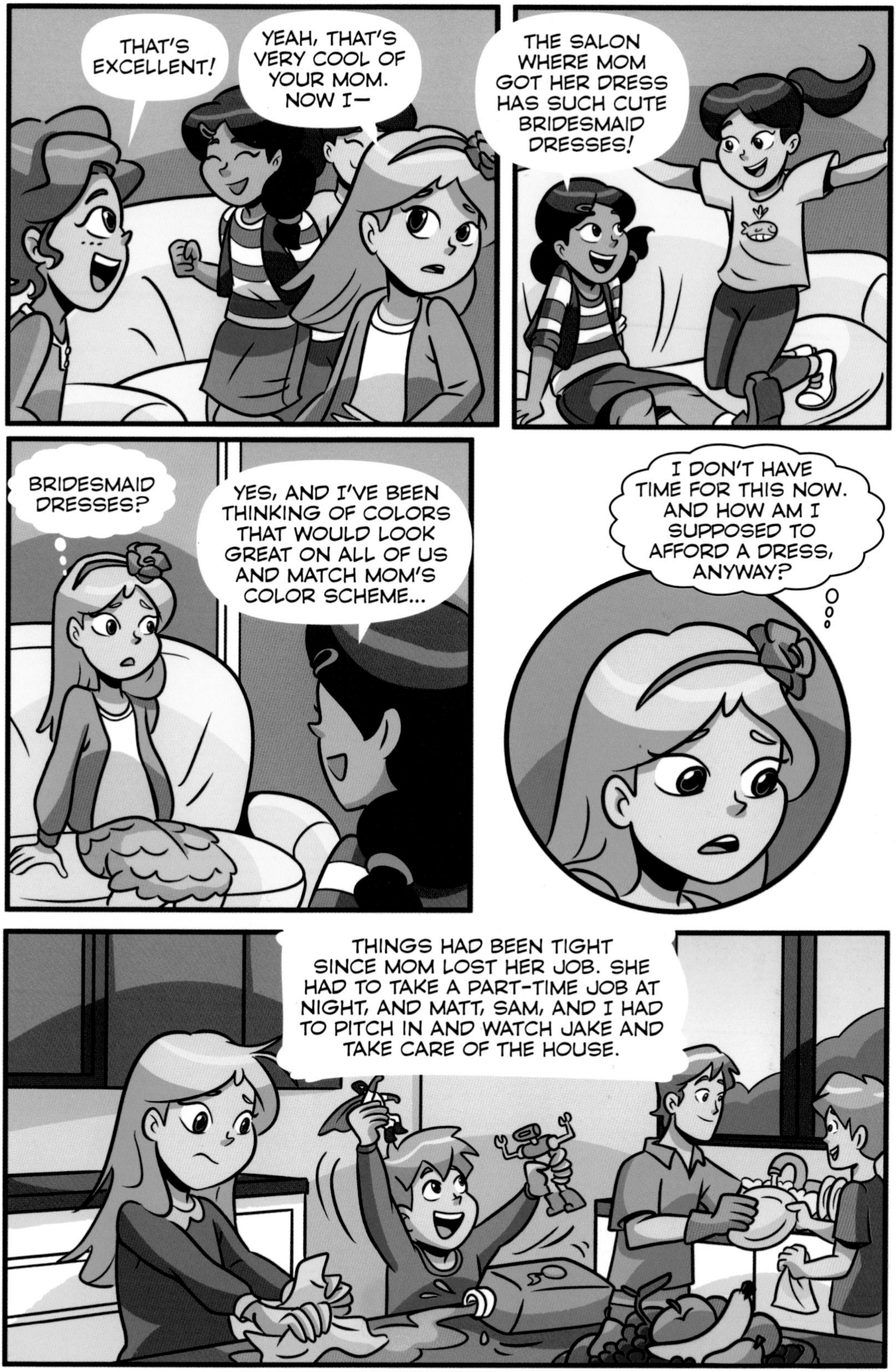
THAT'S EXCELLENT!
YEAH, THAT'S VERY COOL OF YOUR MOM. NOW I—
THE SALON WHERE MOM GOT HER DRESS HAS SUCH CUTE BRIDESMAID DRESSES!
BRIDESMAID DRESSES?
YES, AND I'VE BEEN THINKING OF COLORS THAT WOULD LOOK GREAT ON ALL OF US AND MATCH MOM'S COLOR SCHEME...
I DON'T HAVE TIME FOR THIS NOW. AND HOW AM I SUPPOSED TO AFFORD A DRESS, ANYWAY?
THINGS HAD BEEN TIGHT SINCE MOM LOST HER JOB. SHE HAD TO TAKE A PART-TIME JOB AT NIGHT, AND MATT, SAM, AND I HAD TO PITCH IN AND WATCH JAKE AND TAKE CARE OF THE HOUSE.

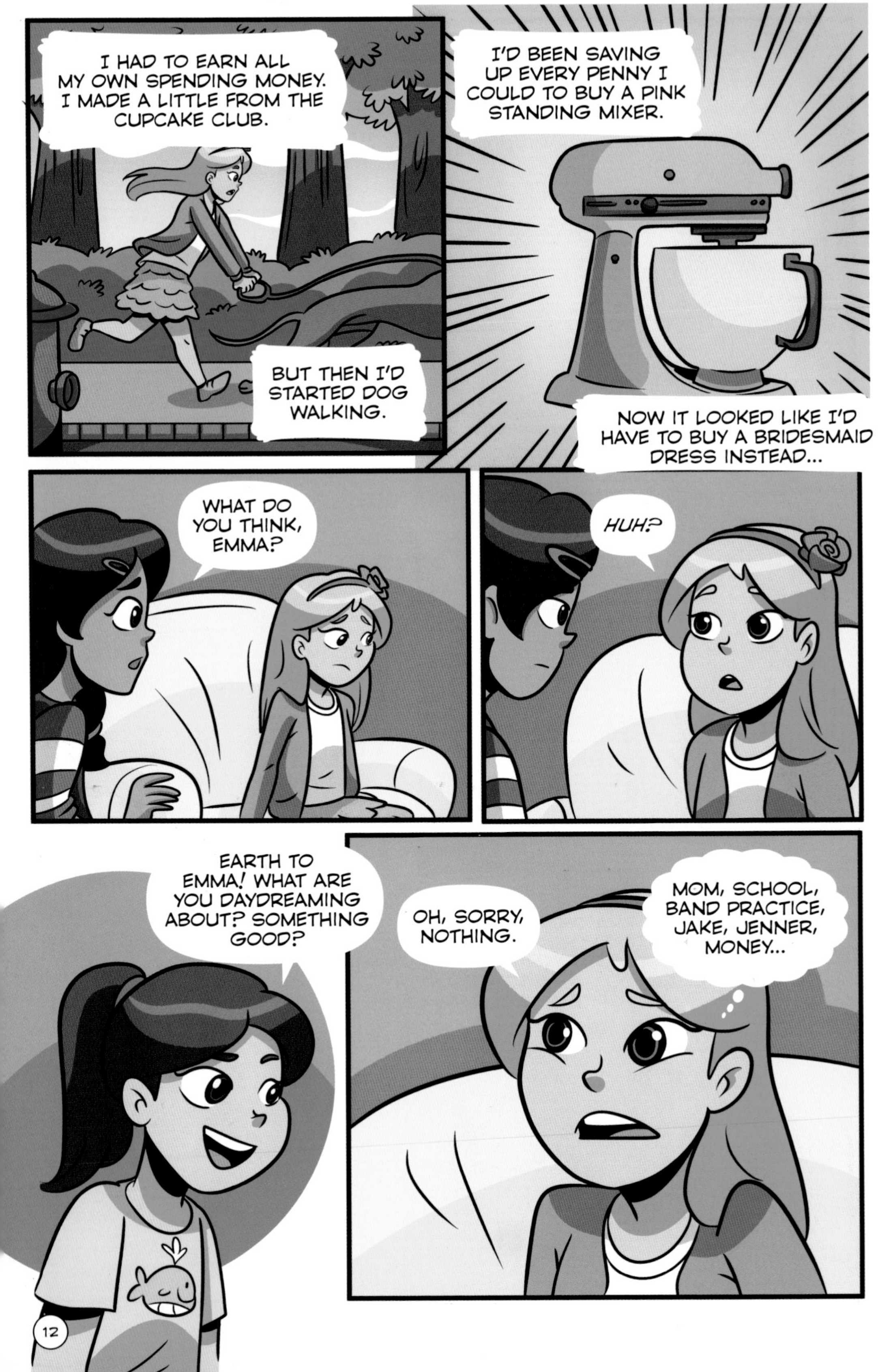
I HAD TO EARN ALL MY OWN SPENDING MONEY. I MADE A LITTLE FROM THE CUPCAKE CLUB.
BUT THEN I'D STARTED DOG WALKING.
I'D BEEN SAVING UP EVERY PENNY I COULD TO BUY A PINK STANDING MIXER.
NOW IT LOOKED LIKE I'D HAVE TO BUY A BRIDESMAID DRESS INSTEAD...
WHAT DO YOU THINK, EMMA?
HUH?
EARTH TO EMMA! WHAT ARE YOU DAYDREAMING ABOUT? SOMETHING GOOD?
OH, SORRY, NOTHING.
MOM, SCHOOL, BAND PRACTICE, JAKE, JENNER, MONEY...

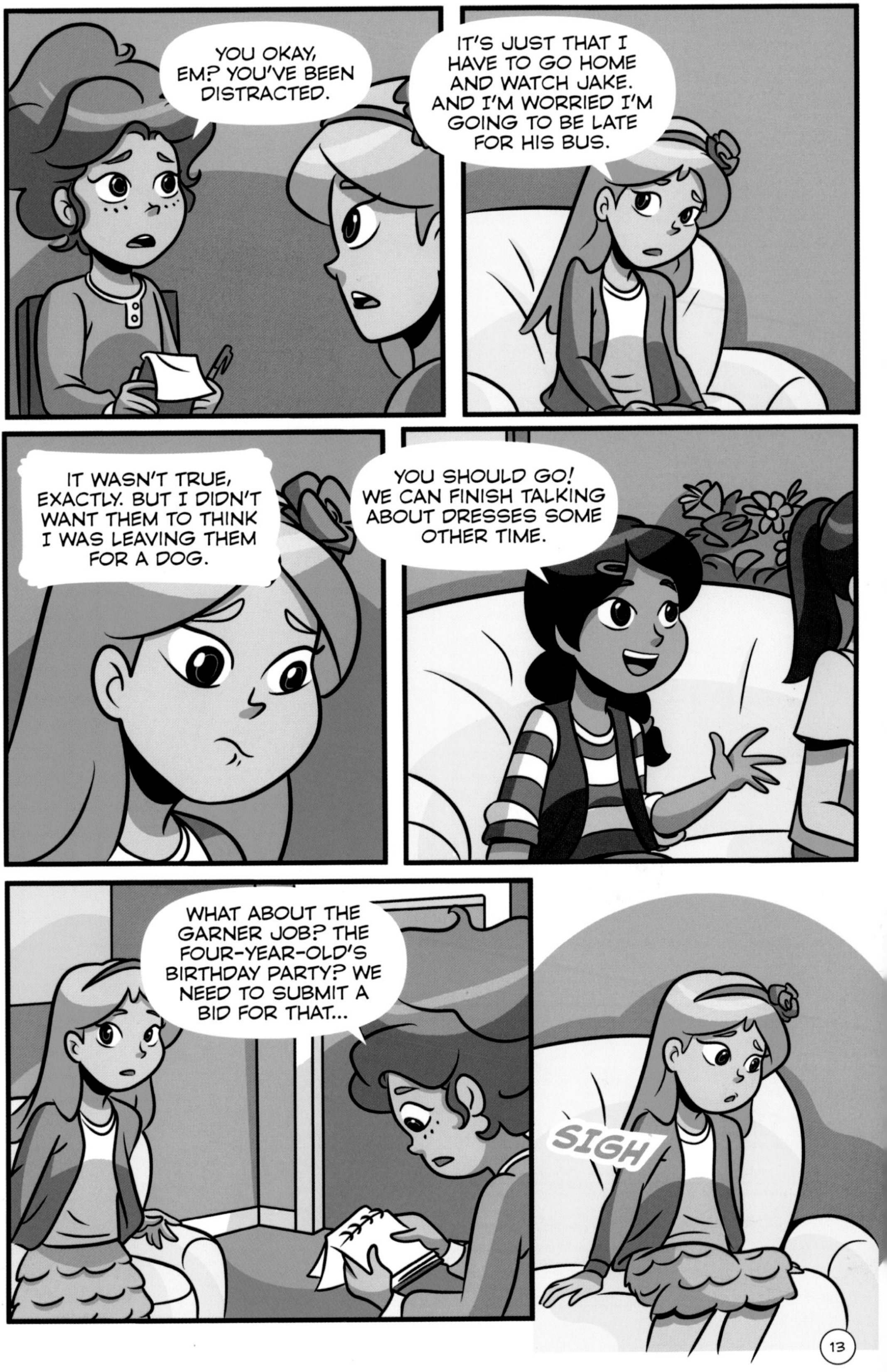
YOU OKAY, EM? YOU'VE BEEN DISTRACTED.
IT'S JUST THAT I HAVE TO GO HOME AND WATCH JAKE. AND I'M WORRIED I'M GOING TO BE LATE FOR HIS BUS.
IT WASN'T TRUE, EXACTLY. BUT I DIDN'T WANT THEM TO THINK I WAS LEAVING THEM FOR A DOG.
YOU SHOULD GO! WE CAN FINISH TALKING ABOUT DRESSES SOME OTHER TIME.
WHAT ABOUT THE GARNER JOB? THE FOUR-YEAR-OLD'S BIRTHDAY PARTY? WE NEED TO SUBMIT A BID FOR THAT...
SIGH

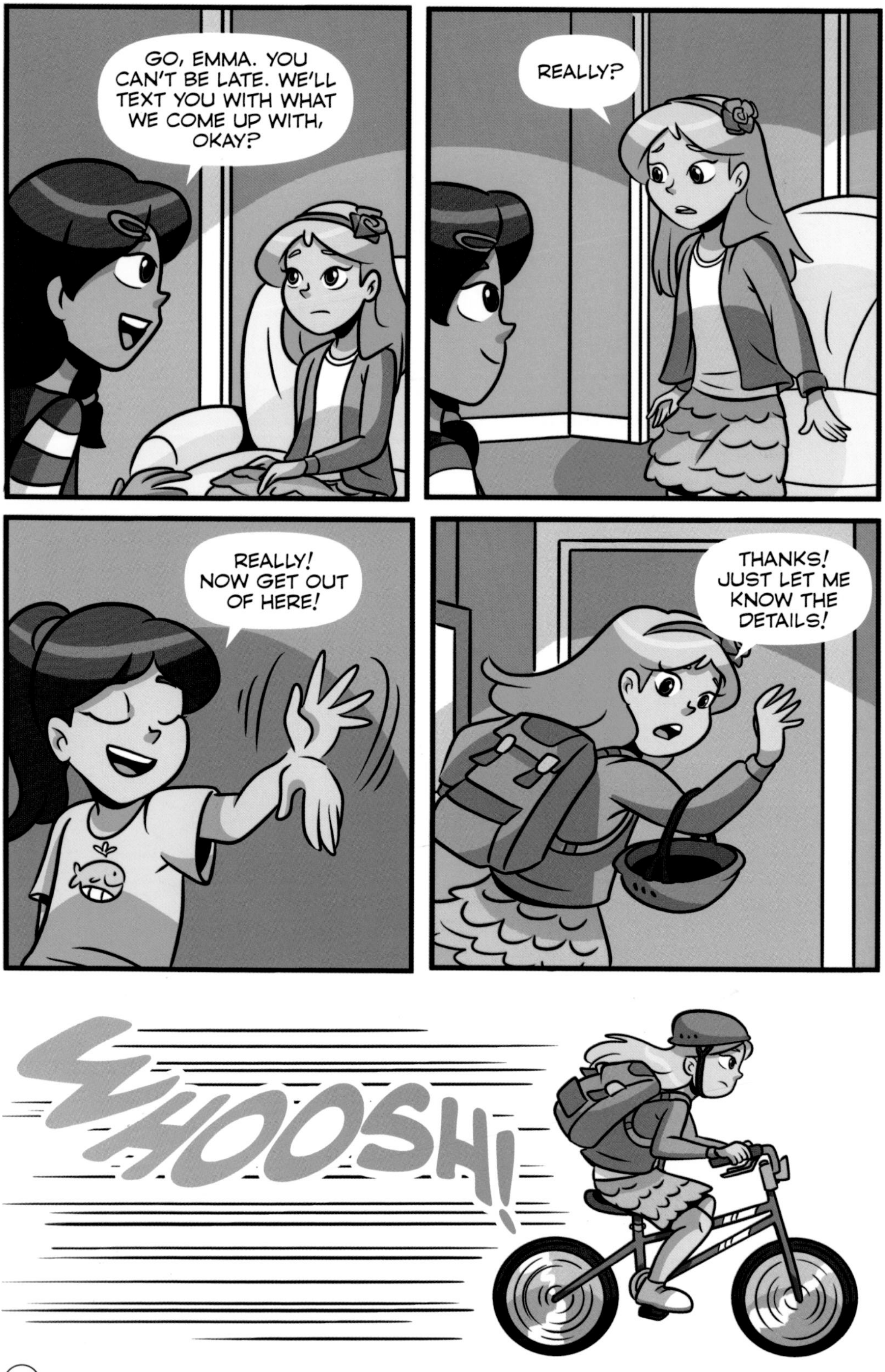
GO, EMMA. YOU CAN'T BE LATE. WE'LL TEXT YOU WITH WHAT WE COME UP WITH, OKAY?
REALLY?
REALLY! NOW GET OUT OF HERE!
THANKS! JUST LET ME KNOW THE DETAILS!
WHOOSH!

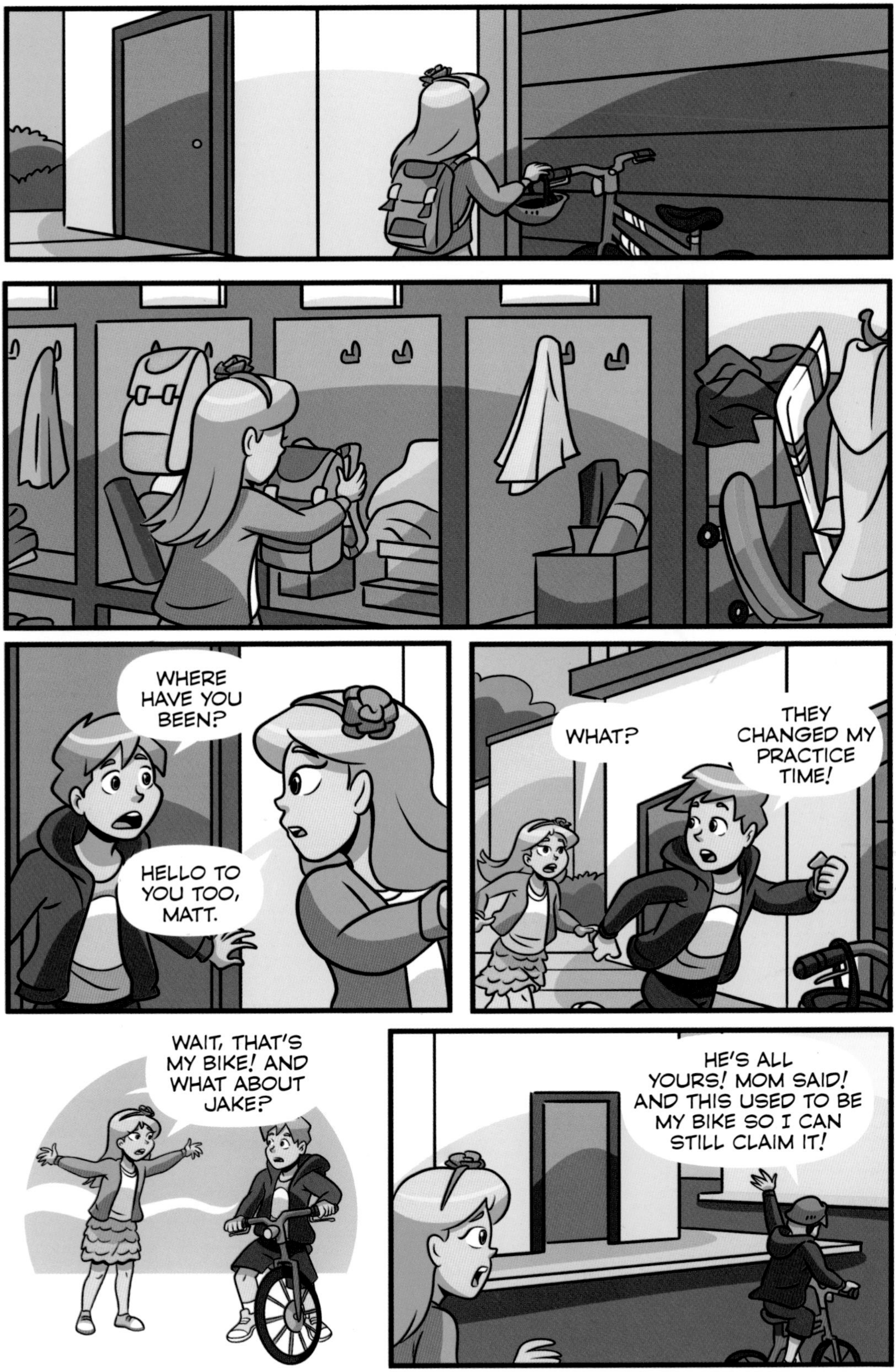
WHERE HAVE YOU BEEN?
HELLO TO YOU TOO, MATT.
WHAT?
THEY CHANGED MY PRACTICE TIME!
WAIT, THAT'S MY BIKE! AND WHAT ABOUT JAKE?
HE'S ALL YOURS! MOM SAID! AND THIS USED TO BE MY BIKE SO I CAN STILL CLAIM IT!

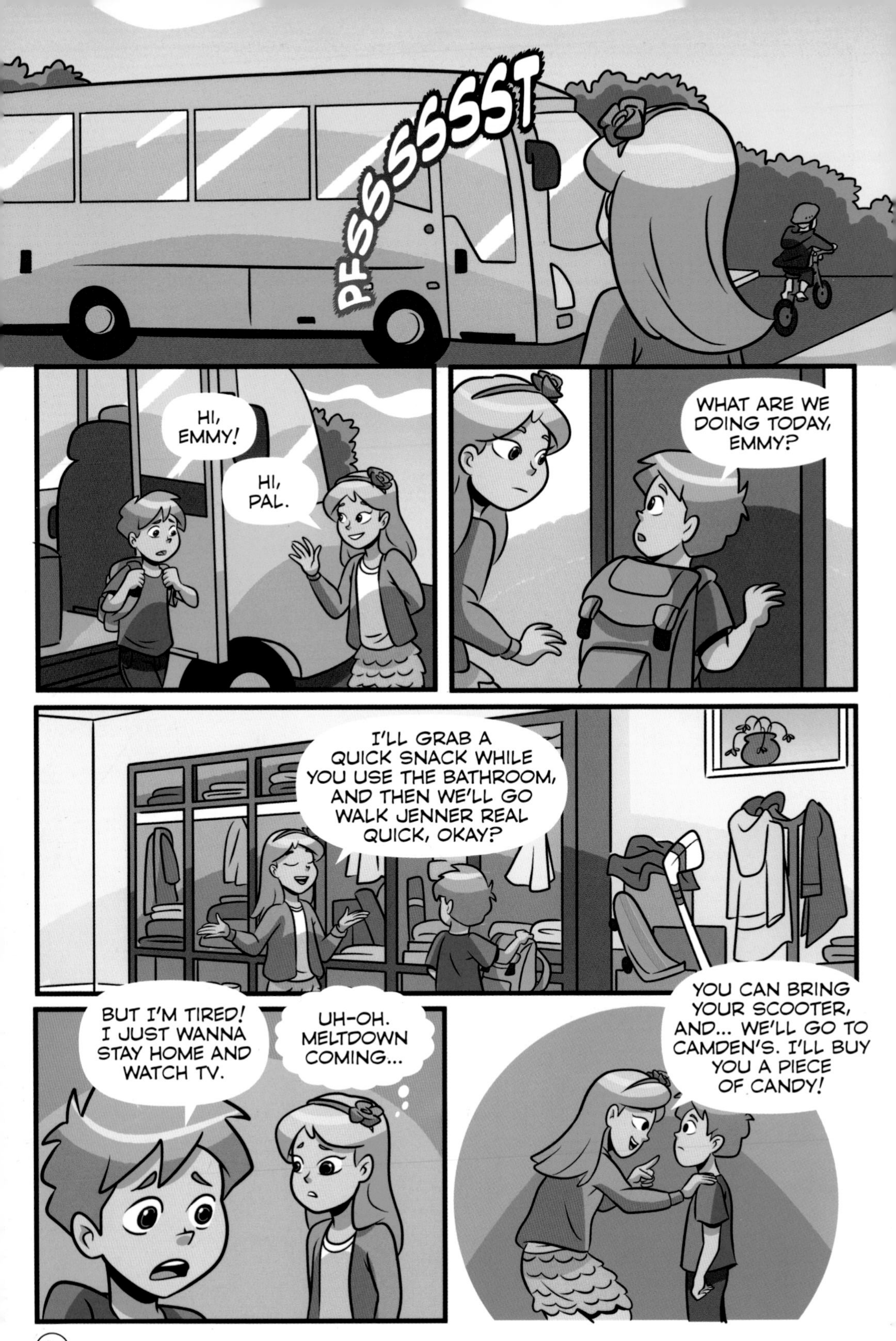
PFSSSSSST
HI, EMMY!
HI, PAL.
WHAT ARE WE DOING TODAY, EMMY?
I'LL GRAB A QUICK SNACK WHILE YOU USE THE BATHROOM, AND THEN WE'LL GO WALK JENNER REAL QUICK, OKAY?
BUT I'M TIRED! I JUST WANNA STAY HOME AND WATCH TV.
UH-OH. MELTDOWN COMING...
YOU CAN BRING YOUR SCOOTER, AND... WE'LL GO TO CAMDEN'S. I'LL BUY YOU A PIECE OF CANDY!

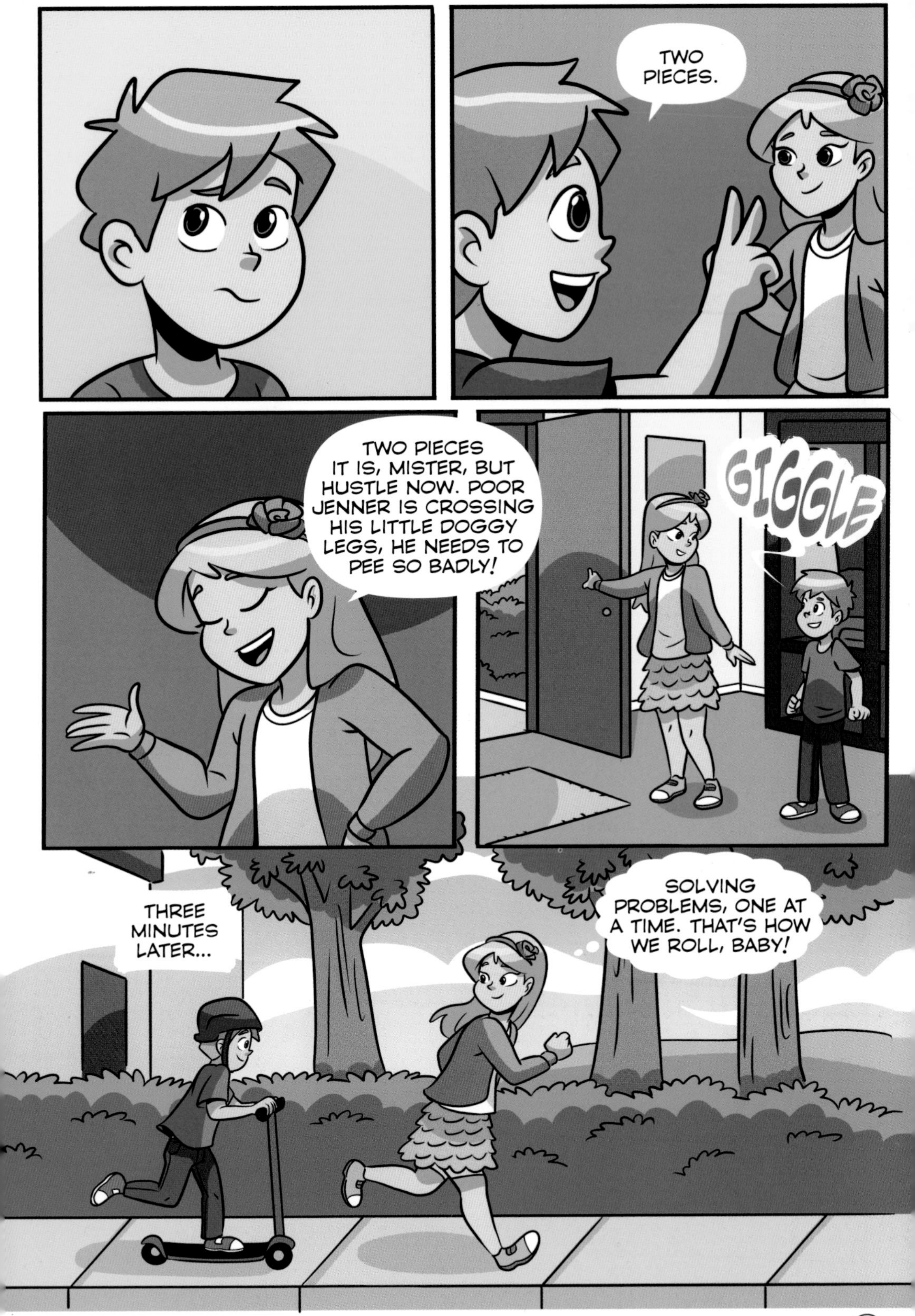
TWO PIECES.
TWO PIECES IT IS, MISTER, BUT HUSTLE NOW. POOR JENNER IS CROSSING HIS LITTLE DOGGY LEGS, HE NEEDS TO PEE SO BADLY!
GIGGLE
THREE MINUTES LATER...
SOLVING PROBLEMS, ONE AT A TIME. THAT'S HOW WE ROLL, BABY!

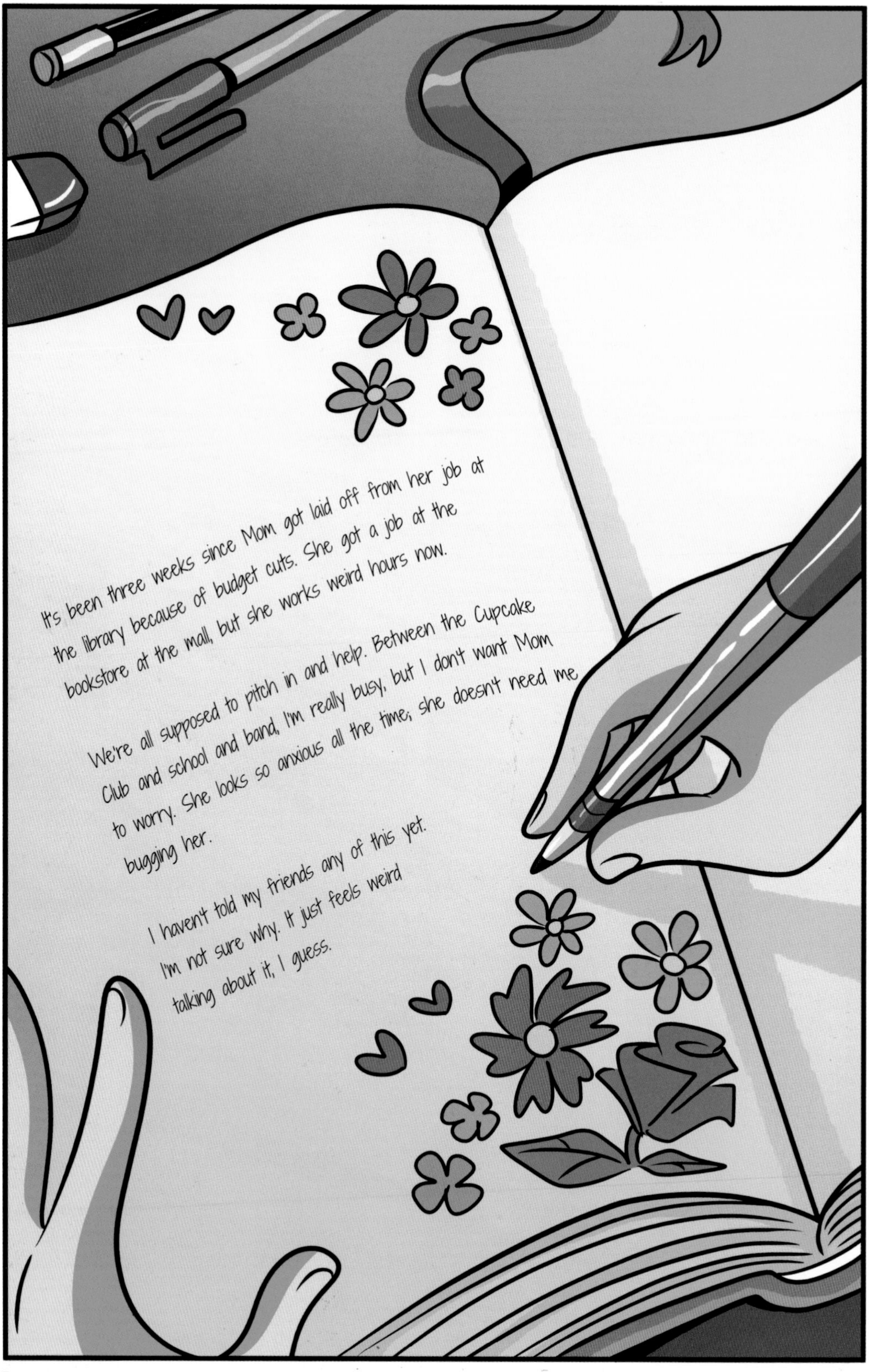
It's been three weeks since Mom got laid off from her job at the library because of budget cuts. She got a job at the bookstore at the mall, but she works weird hours now.
We're all supposed to pitch in and help. Between the Cupcake Club and school and band, I'm really busy, but I don't want Mom to worry. She looks so anxious all the time; she doesn't need me bugging her.
I haven't told my friends any of this yet. I'm not sure why. It just feels weird talking about it, I guess.

Chapter 2

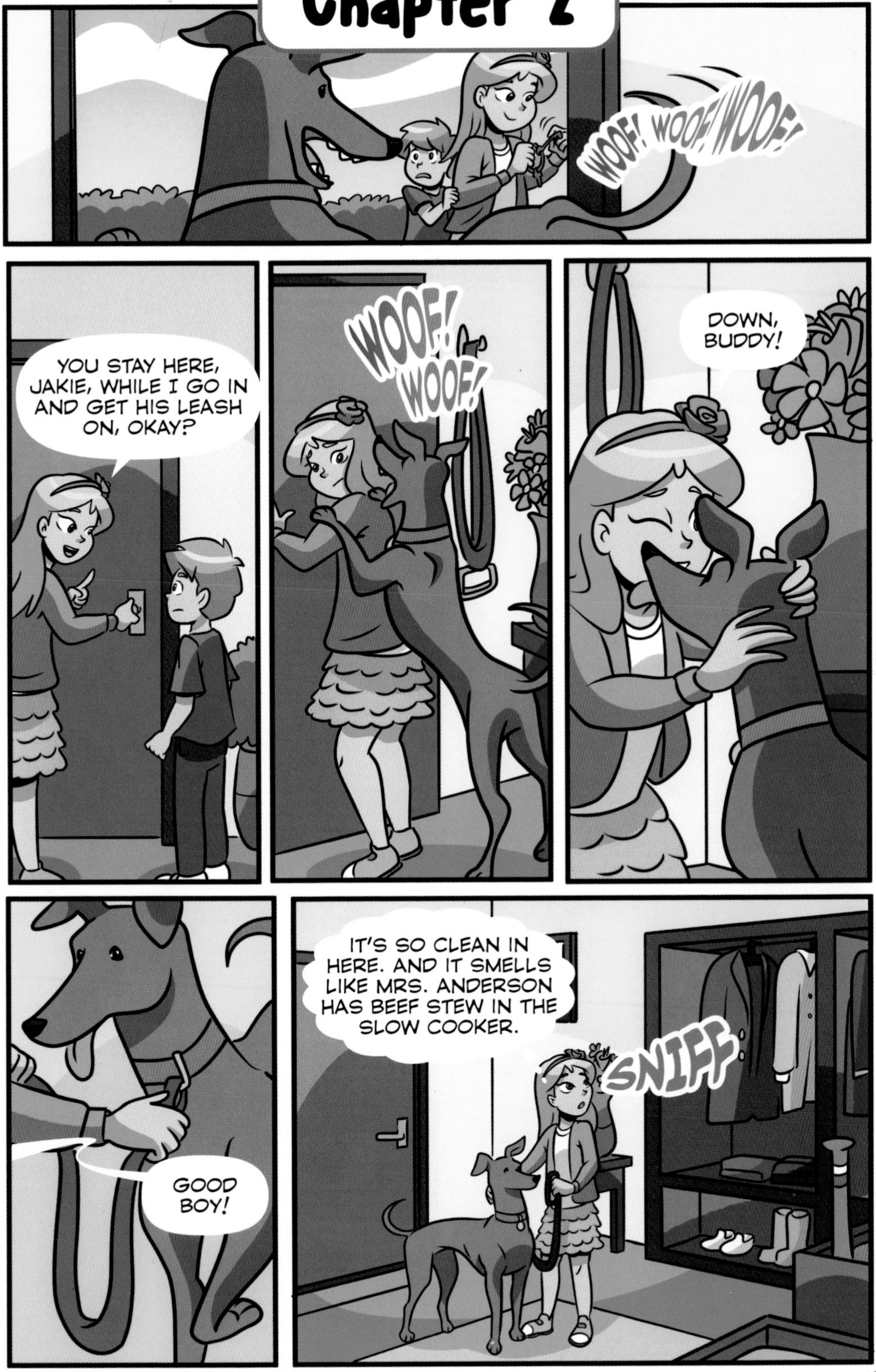
WOOF! WOOF! WOOF!
YOU STAY HERE, JAKIE, WHILE I GO IN AND GET HIS LEASH ON, OKAY?
WOOF! WOOF!
DOWN, BUDDY!
GOOD BOY!
IT'S SO CLEAN IN HERE. AND IT SMELLS LIKE MRS. ANDERSON HAS BEEF STEW IN THE SLOW COOKER.
SNIFF

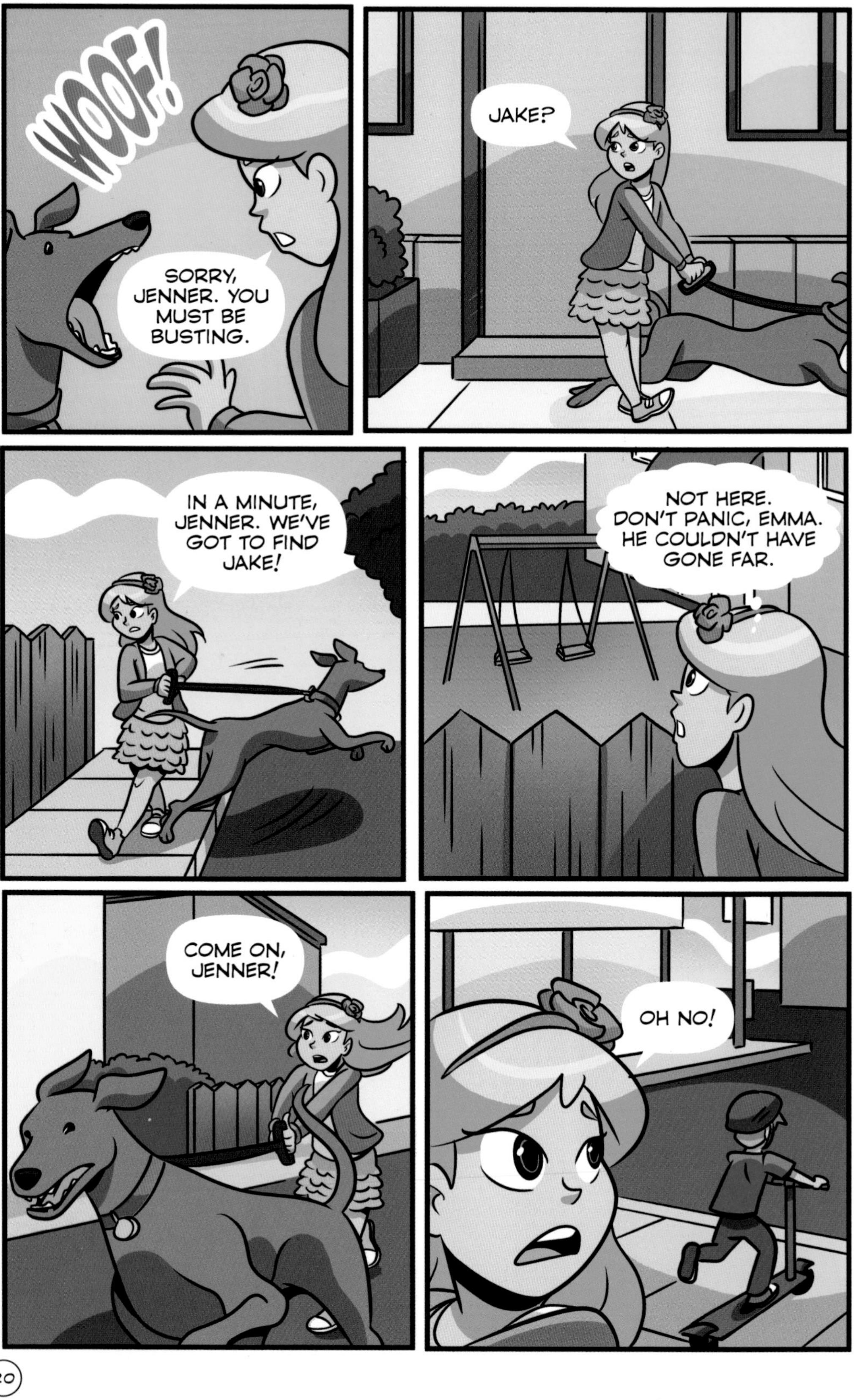
WOOF!
SORRY, JENNER. YOU MUST BE BUSTING.
JAKE?
IN A MINUTE, JENNER. WE'VE GOT TO FIND JAKE!
NOT HERE. DON'T PANIC, EMMA. HE COULDN'T HAVE GONE FAR.
COME ON, JENNER!
OH NO!

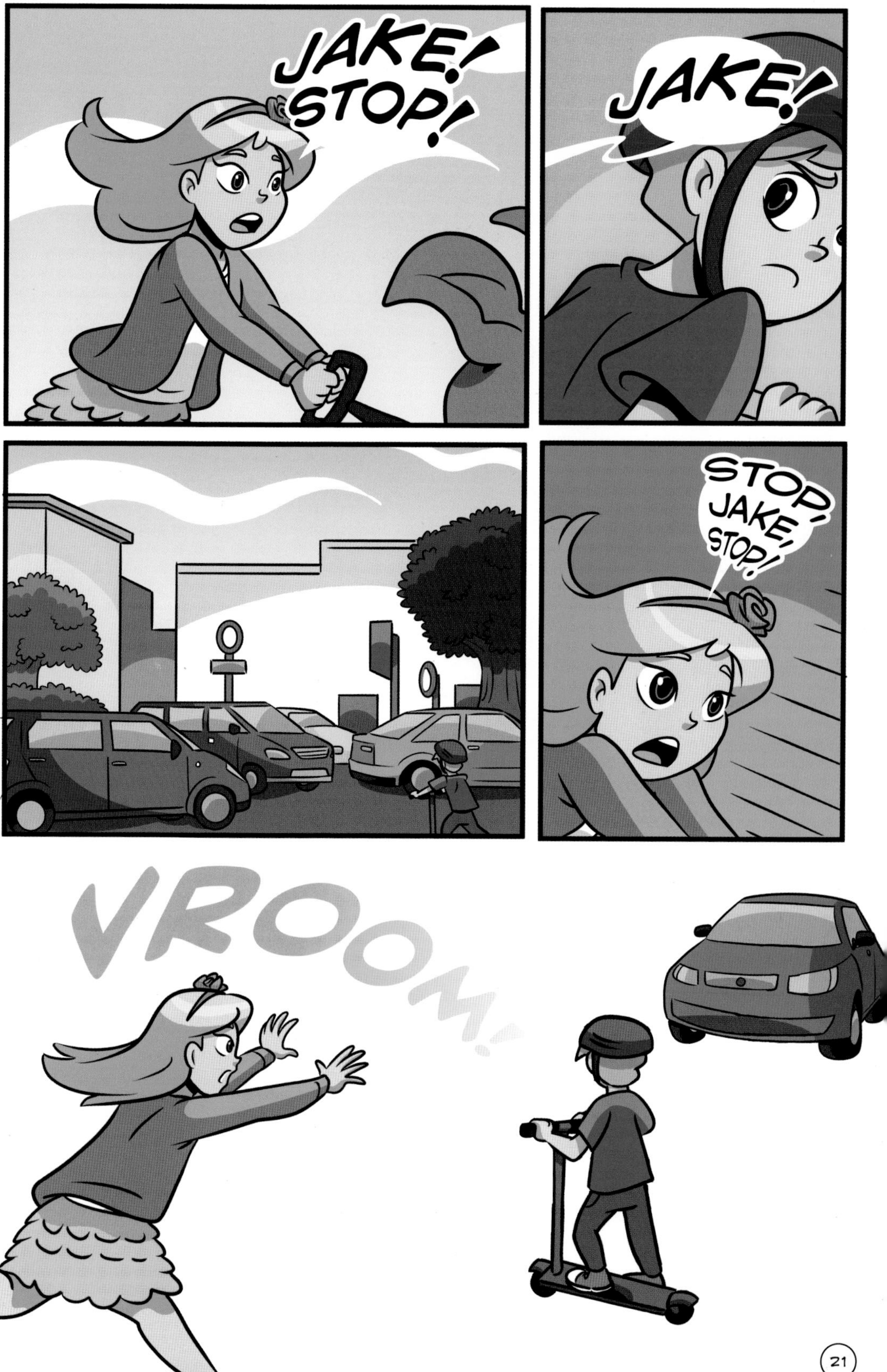
JAKE! STOP!
JAKE!
STOP, JAKE, STOP!
VROOM!

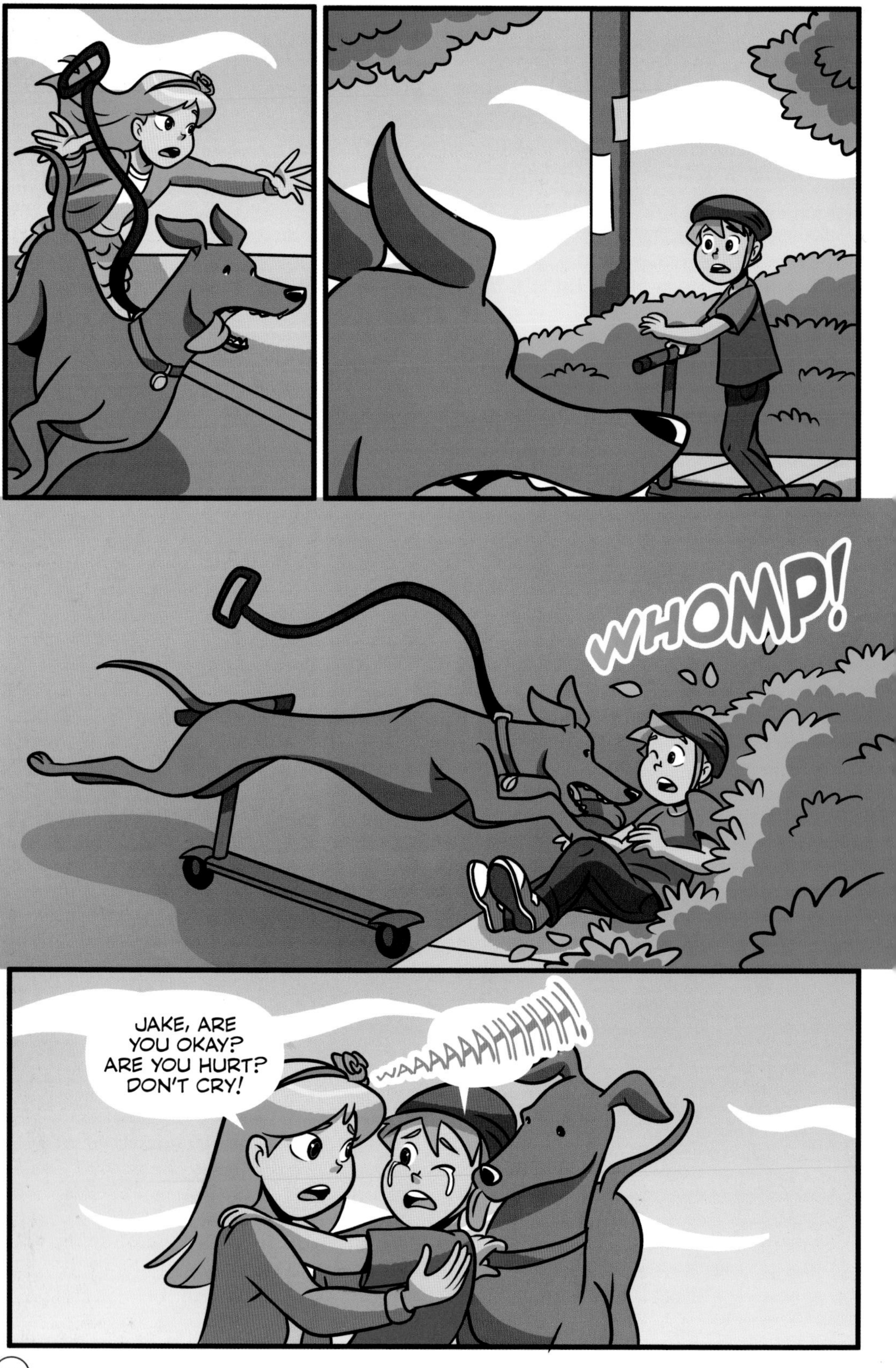
WHOMP!
JAKE, ARE YOU OKAY? ARE YOU HURT? DON'T CRY!
WAAAAAAHHHHH!

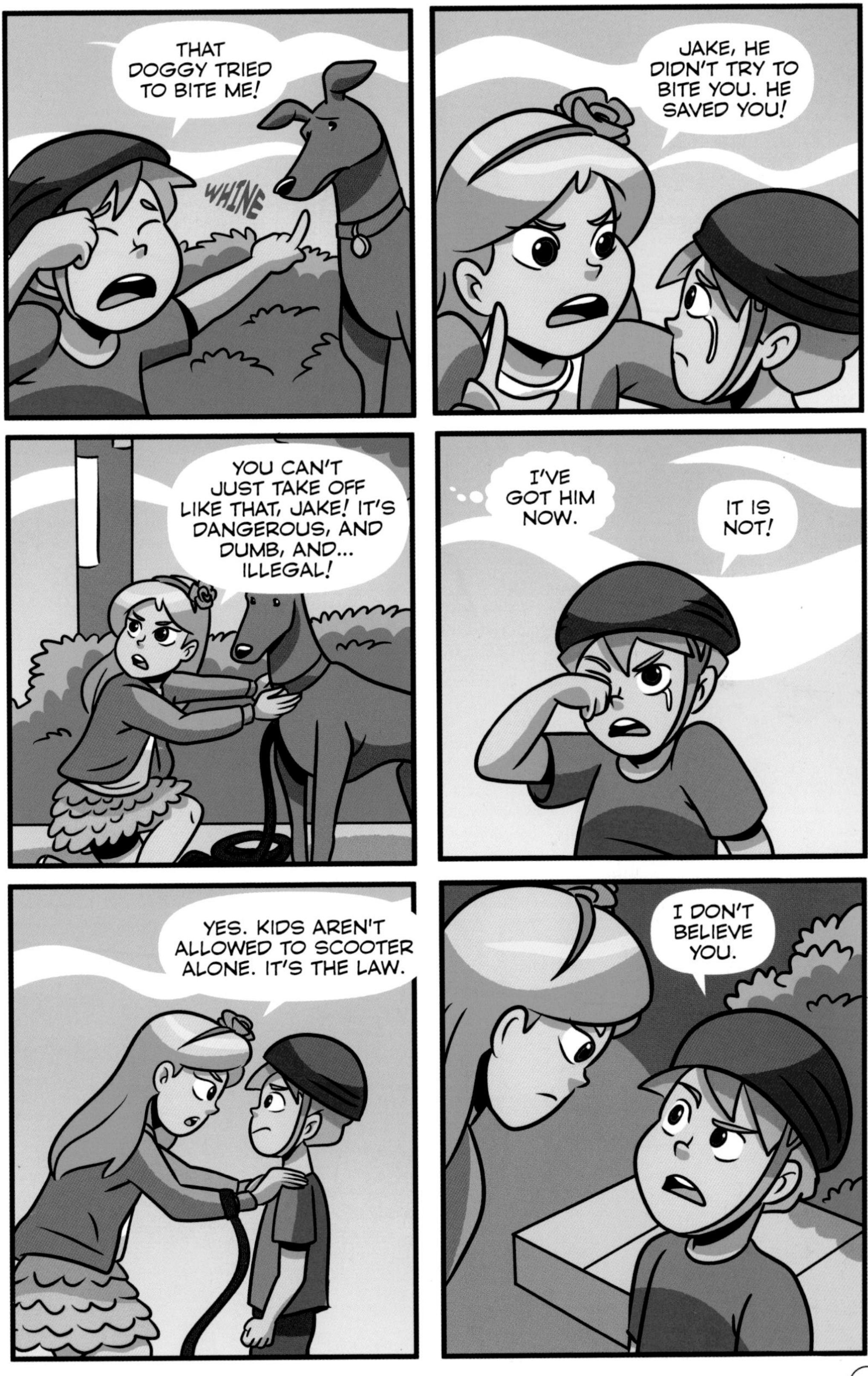
THAT DOGGY TRIED TO BITE ME!
WHINE
JAKE, HE DIDN'T TRY TO BITE YOU. HE SAVED YOU!
YOU CAN'T JUST TAKE OFF LIKE THAT, JAKE! IT'S DANGEROUS, AND DUMB, AND... ILLEGAL!
I'VE GOT HIM NOW.
IT IS NOT!
YES. KIDS AREN'T ALLOWED TO SCOOTER ALONE. IT'S THE LAW.
I DON'T BELIEVE YOU.

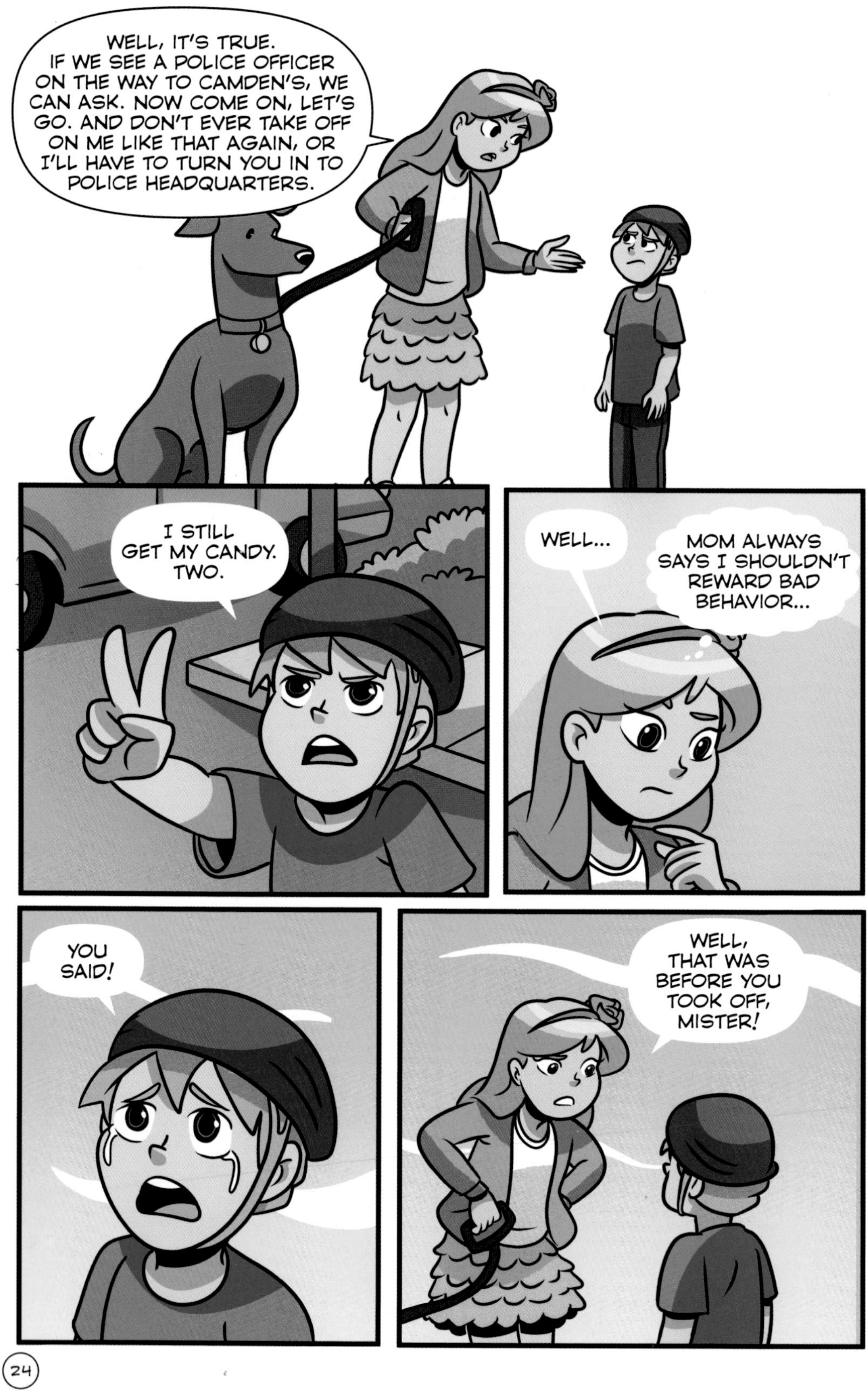
WELL, IT'S TRUE. IF WE SEE A POLICE OFFICER ON THE WAY TO CAMDEN'S, WE CAN ASK. NOW COME ON, LET'S GO. AND DON'T EVER TAKE OFF ON ME LIKE THAT AGAIN, OR I'LL HAVE TO TURN YOU IN TO POLICE HEADQUARTERS.
I STILL GET MY CANDY. TWO.
WELL...
MOM ALWAYS SAYS I SHOULDN'T REWARD BAD BEHAVIOR...
YOU SAID!
WELL, THAT WAS BEFORE YOU TOOK OFF, MISTER!

I HATE YOU!

CAN THIS DAY GET ANY WORSE?

GROSS!

IS THAT THE KID'S OR THE DOG'S?

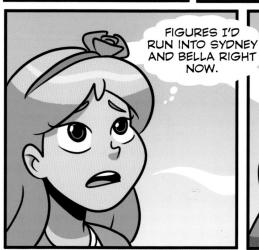

FIGURES I'D RUN INTO SYDNEY AND BELLA RIGHT NOW.

I DIDN'T KNOW YOU HAD A DOG.

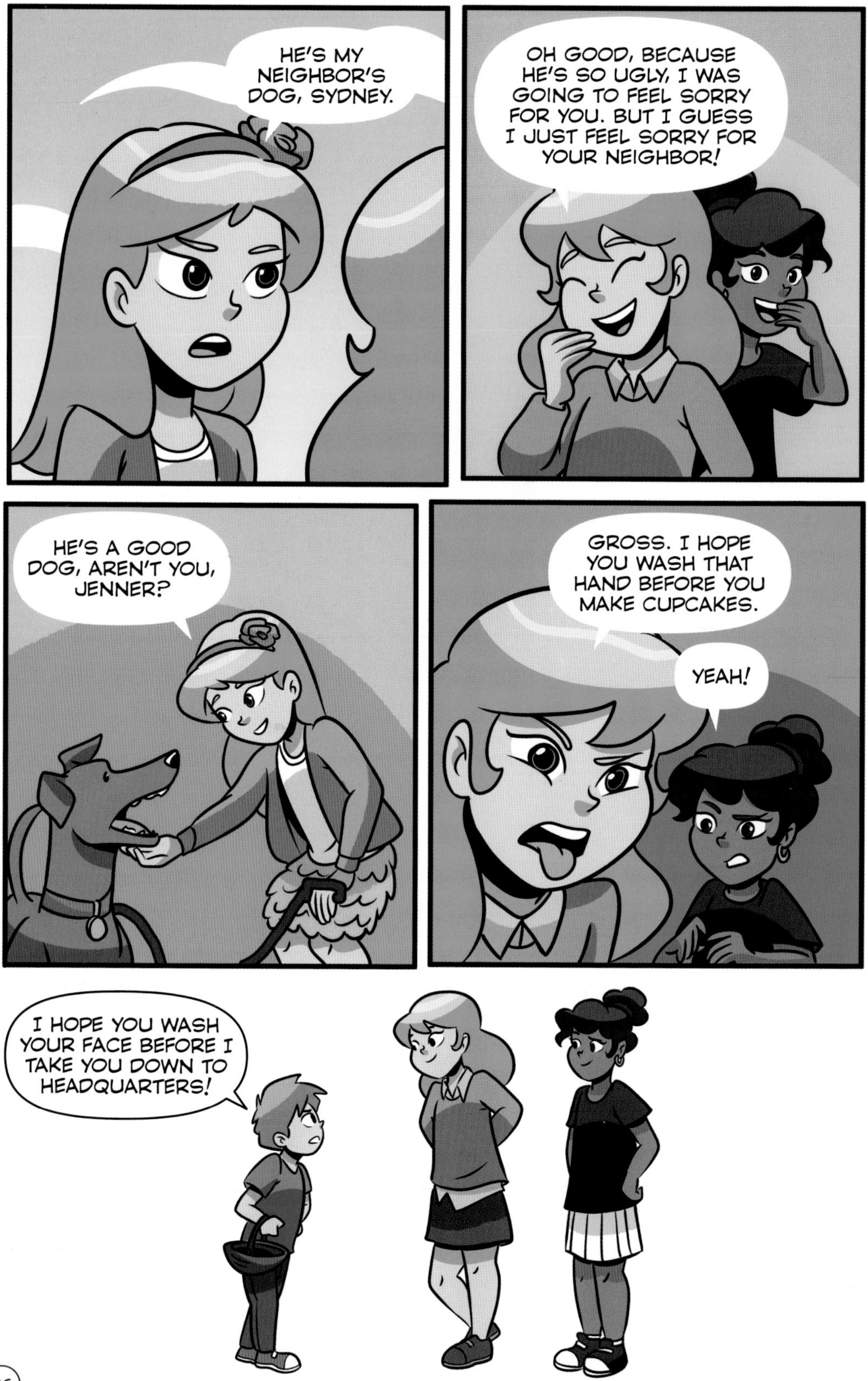
HE'S MY NEIGHBOR'S DOG, SYDNEY.
OH GOOD, BECAUSE HE'S SO UGLY, I WAS GOING TO FEEL SORRY FOR YOU. BUT I GUESS I JUST FEEL SORRY FOR YOUR NEIGHBOR!
HE'S A GOOD DOG, AREN'T YOU, JENNER?
GROSS. I HOPE YOU WASH THAT HAND BEFORE YOU MAKE CUPCAKES.
YEAH!
I HOPE YOU WASH YOUR FACE BEFORE I TAKE YOU DOWN TO HEADQUARTERS!

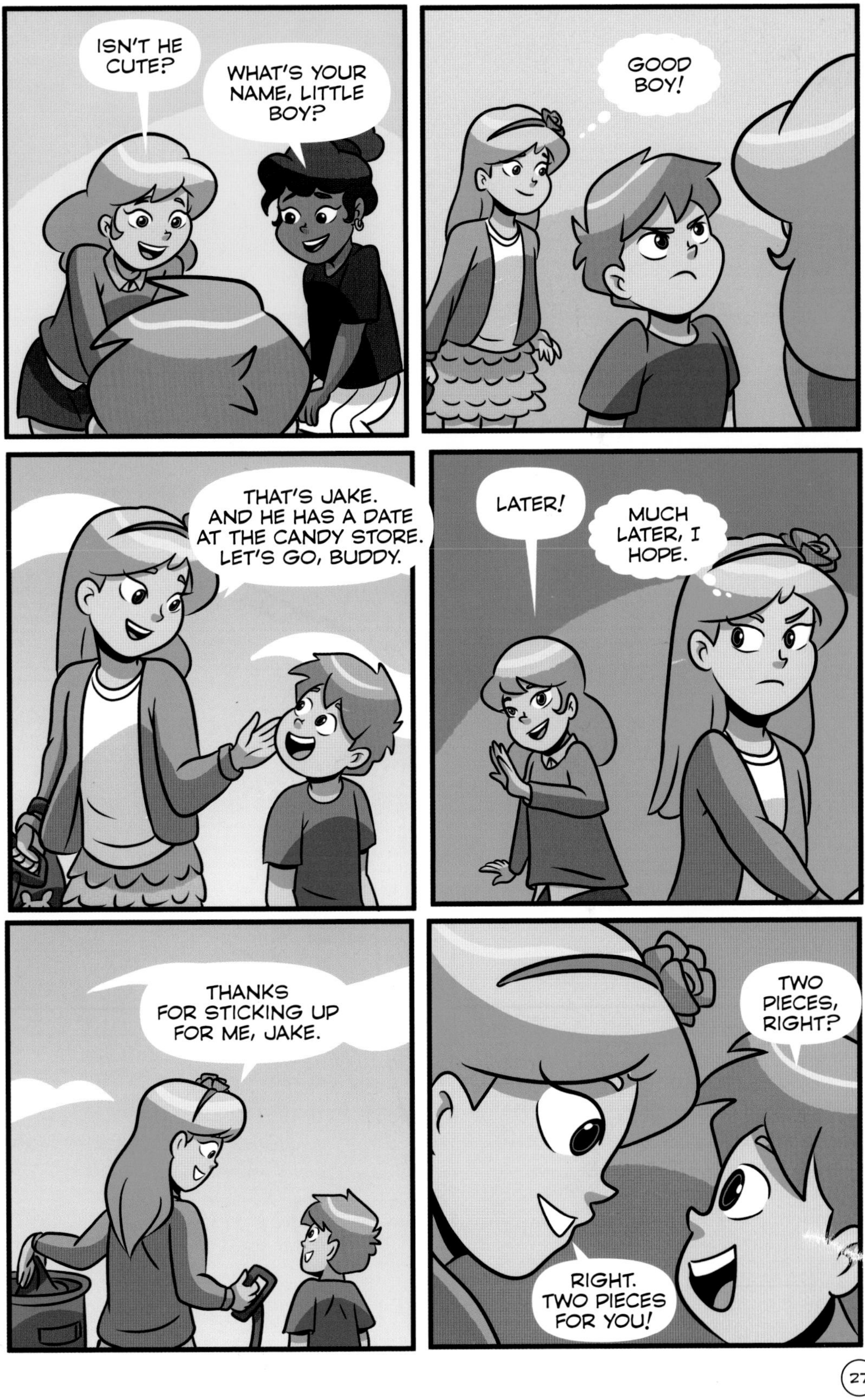
ISN'T HE CUTE?
WHAT'S YOUR NAME, LITTLE BOY?
GOOD BOY!
THAT'S JAKE. AND HE HAS A DATE AT THE CANDY STORE. LET'S GO, BUDDY.
LATER!
MUCH LATER, I HOPE.
THANKS FOR STICKING UP FOR ME, JAKE.
TWO PIECES, RIGHT?
RIGHT. TWO PIECES FOR YOU!

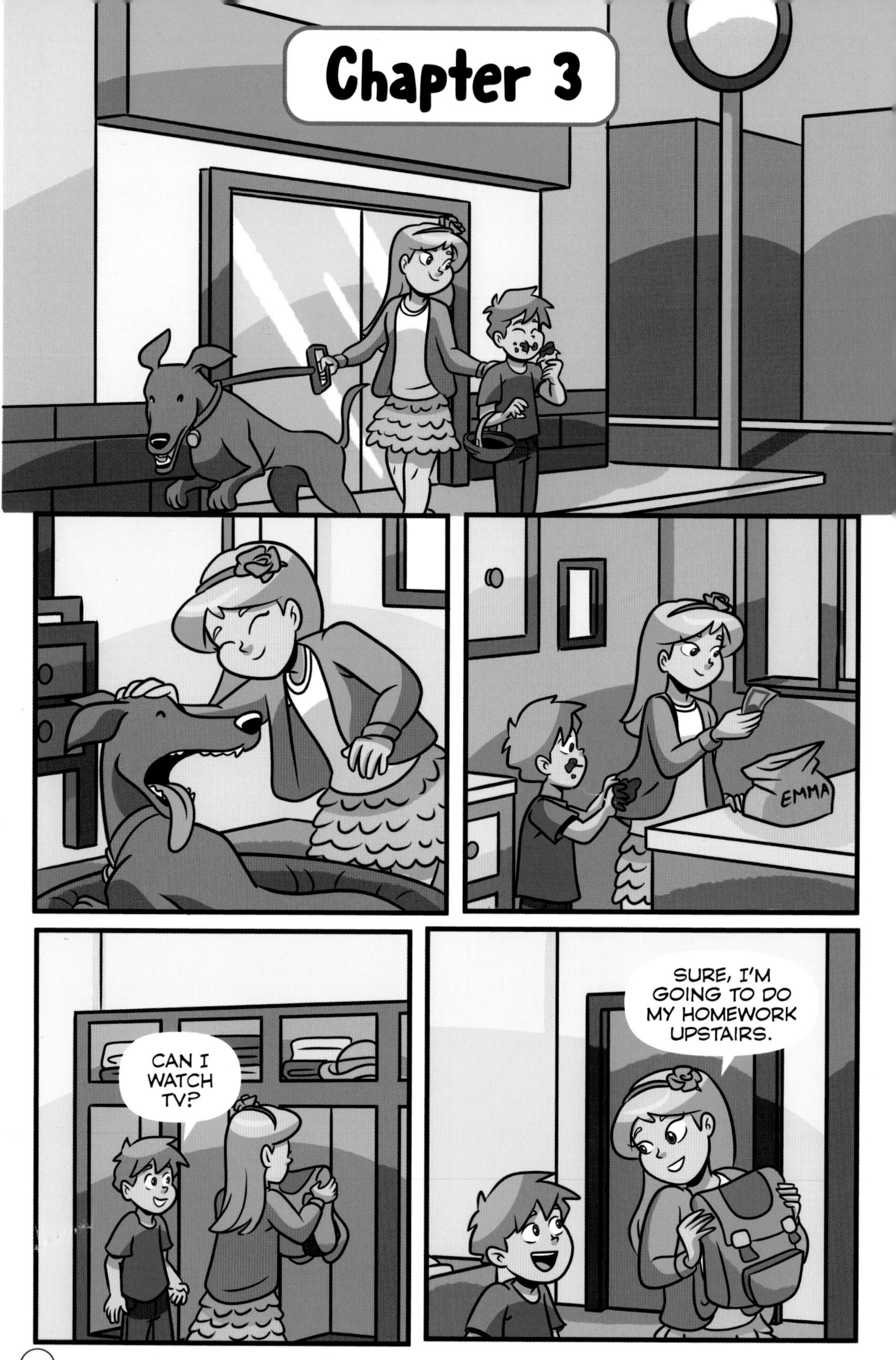
Chapter 3
EMMA
CAN I WATCH TV?
SURE, I'M GOING TO DO MY HOMEWORK UPSTAIRS.

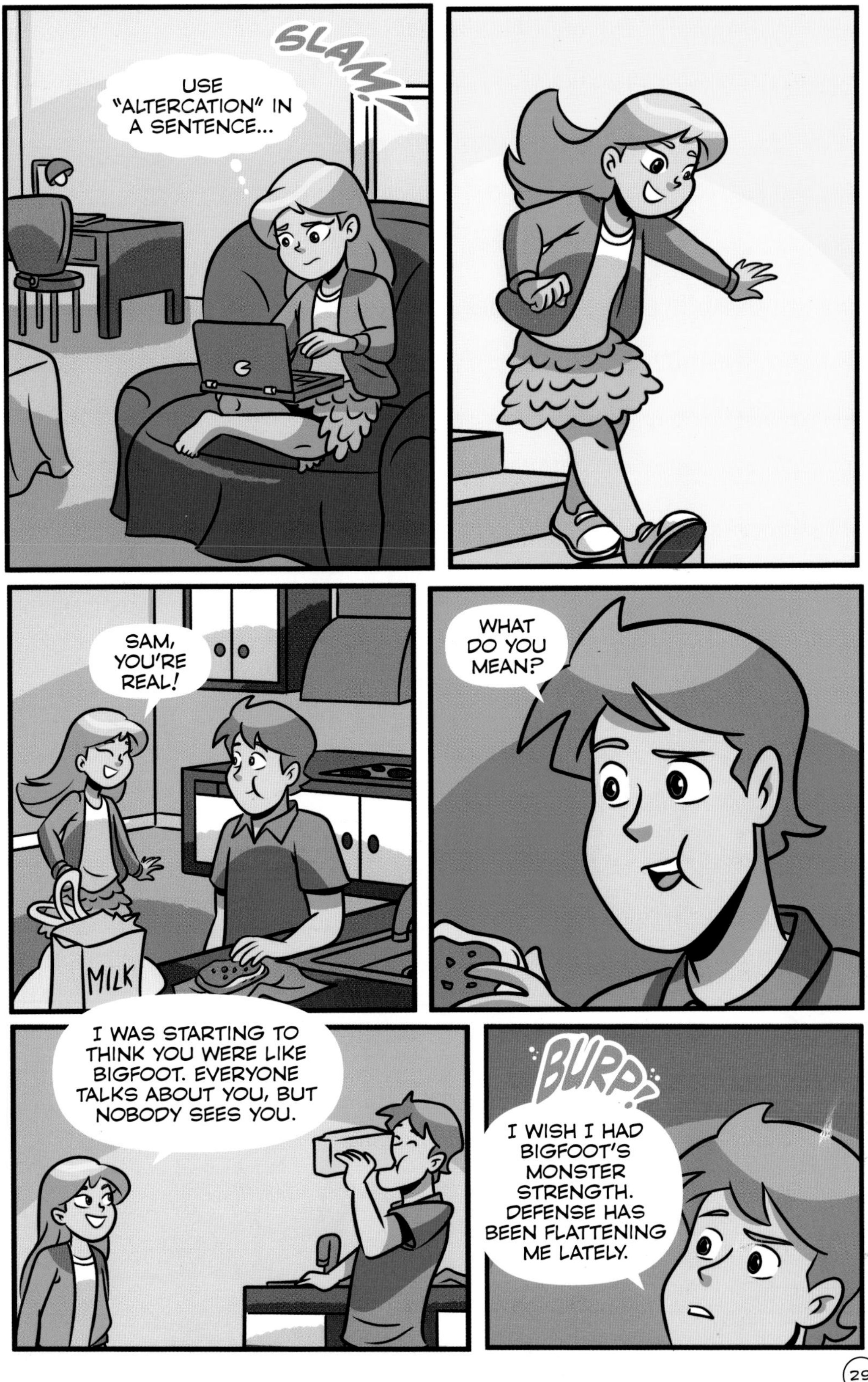
USE "ALTERCATION" IN A SENTENCE...
SLAM!
SAM, YOU'RE REAL!
MILK
WHAT DO YOU MEAN?
I WAS STARTING TO THINK YOU WERE LIKE BIGFOOT. EVERYONE TALKS ABOUT YOU, BUT NOBODY SEES YOU.
BURP!
I WISH I HAD BIGFOOT'S MONSTER STRENGTH. DEFENSE HAS BEEN FLATTENING ME LATELY.

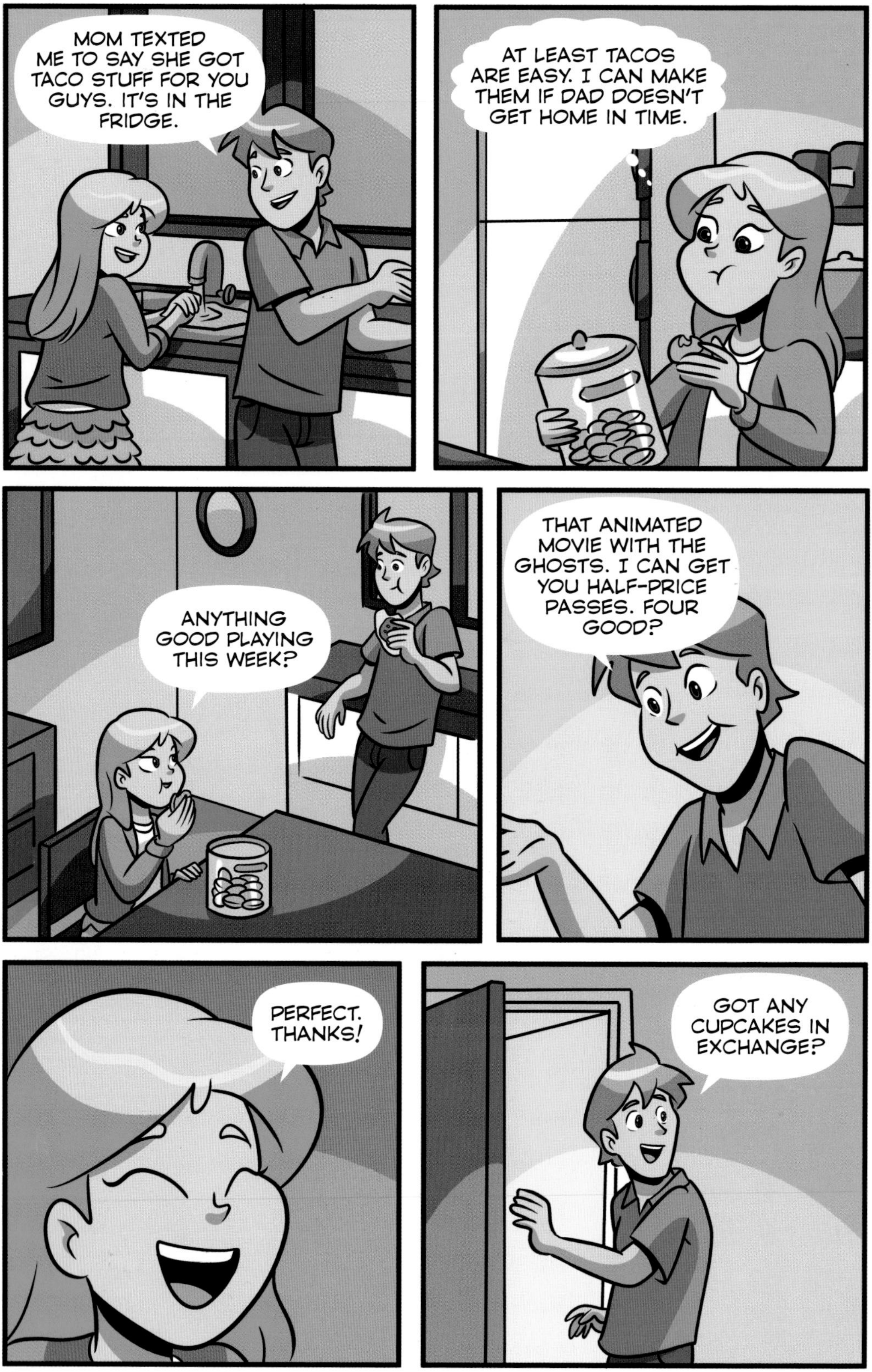
MOM TEXTED ME TO SAY SHE GOT TACO STUFF FOR YOU GUYS. IT'S IN THE FRIDGE.
AT LEAST TACOS ARE EASY. I CAN MAKE THEM IF DAD DOESN'T GET HOME IN TIME.
ANYTHING GOOD PLAYING THIS WEEK?
THAT ANIMATED MOVIE WITH THE GHOSTS. I CAN GET YOU HALF-PRICE PASSES. FOUR GOOD?
PERFECT. THANKS!
GOT ANY CUPCAKES IN EXCHANGE?

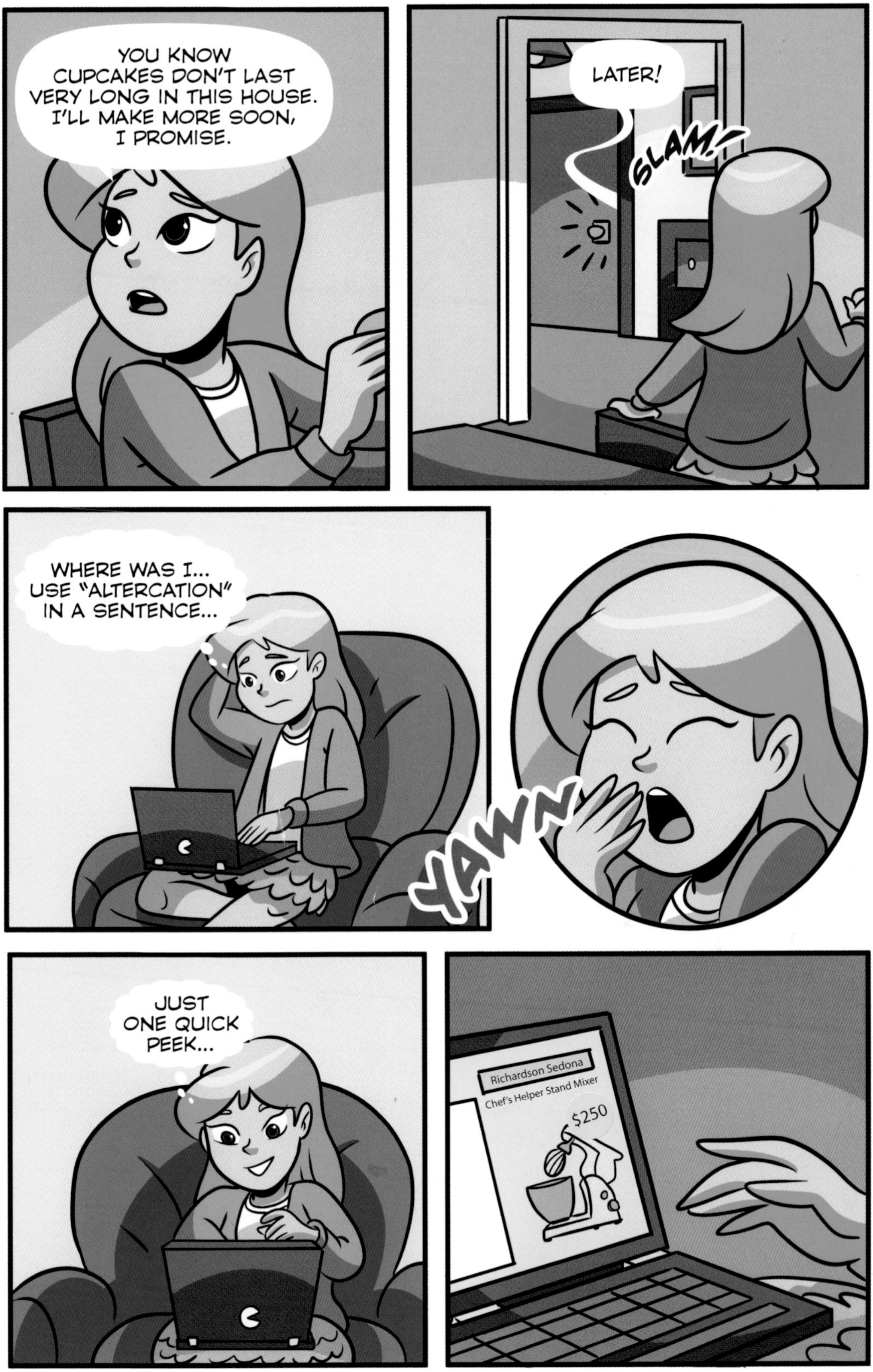

YOU KNOW CUPCAKES DON'T LAST VERY LONG IN THIS HOUSE. I'LL MAKE MORE SOON, I PROMISE.
LATER!
SLAM!
WHERE WAS I... USE "ALTERCATION" IN A SENTENCE...
YAWN
JUST ONE QUICK PEEK...
Richardson Sedona
Chef's Helper Stand Mixer
$250

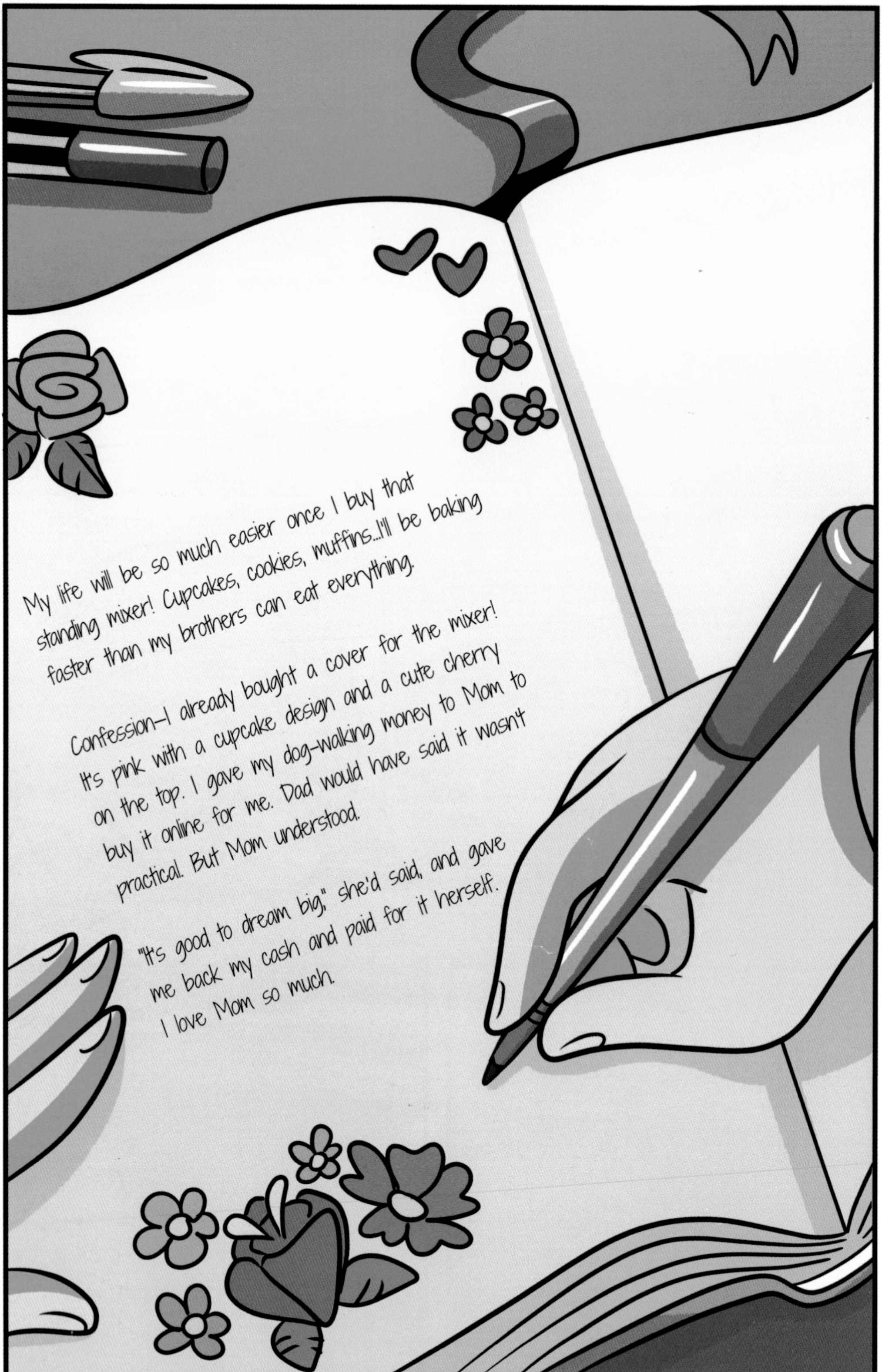
My life will be so much easier once I buy that standing mixer! Cupcakes, cookies, muffins...I'll be baking faster than my brothers can eat everything.
Confession—I already bought a cover for the mixer! It's pink with a cupcake design and a cute cherry on the top. I gave my dog-walking money to Mom to buy it online for me. Dad would have said it wasn't practical. But Mom understood.
"It's good to dream big," she'd said, and gave me back my cash and paid for it herself. I love Mom so much.

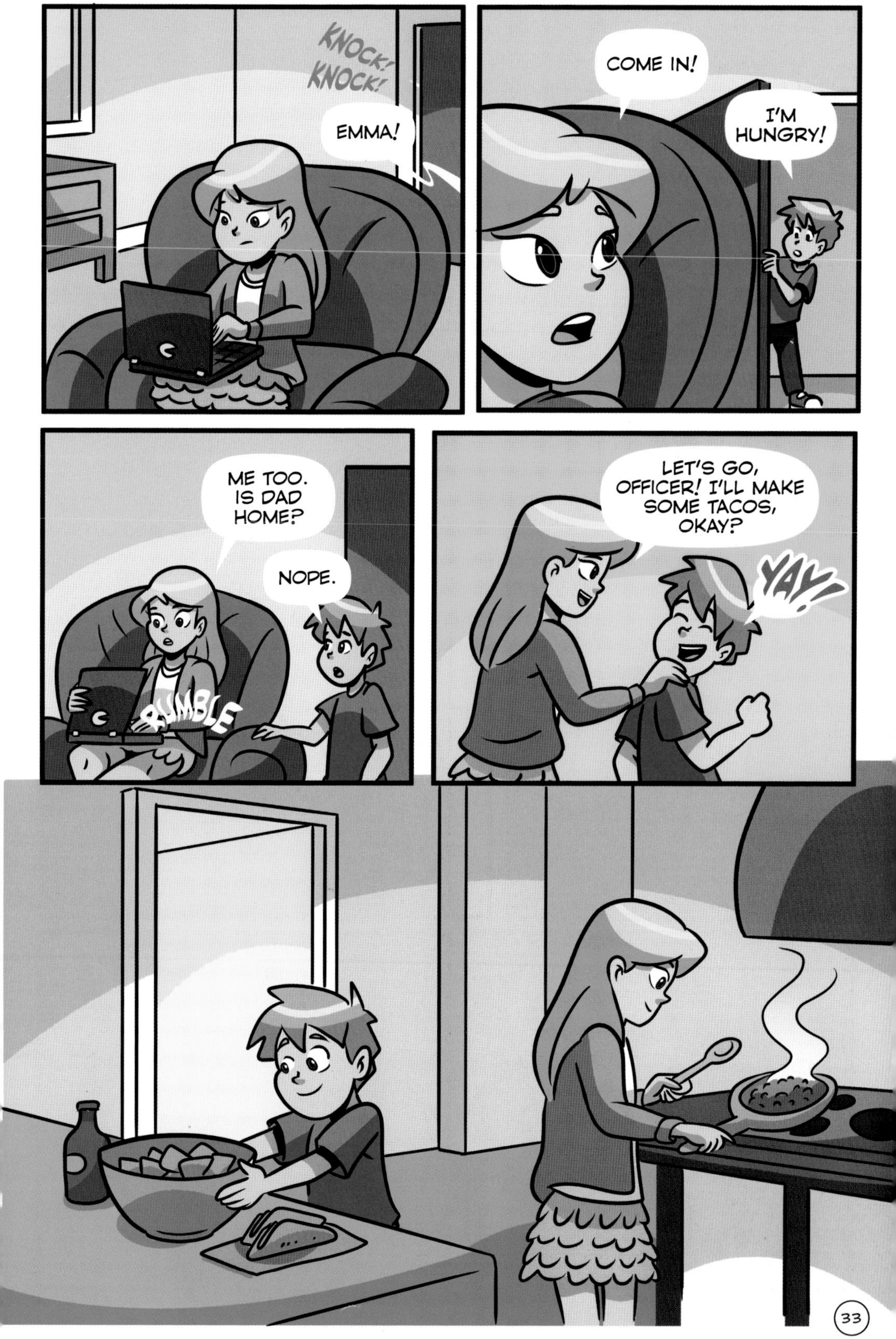
KNOCK! KNOCK!
EMMA!
COME IN!
I'M HUNGRY!
ME TOO. IS DAD HOME?
NOPE.
RUMBLE
LET'S GO, OFFICER! I'LL MAKE SOME TACOS, OKAY?
YAY!

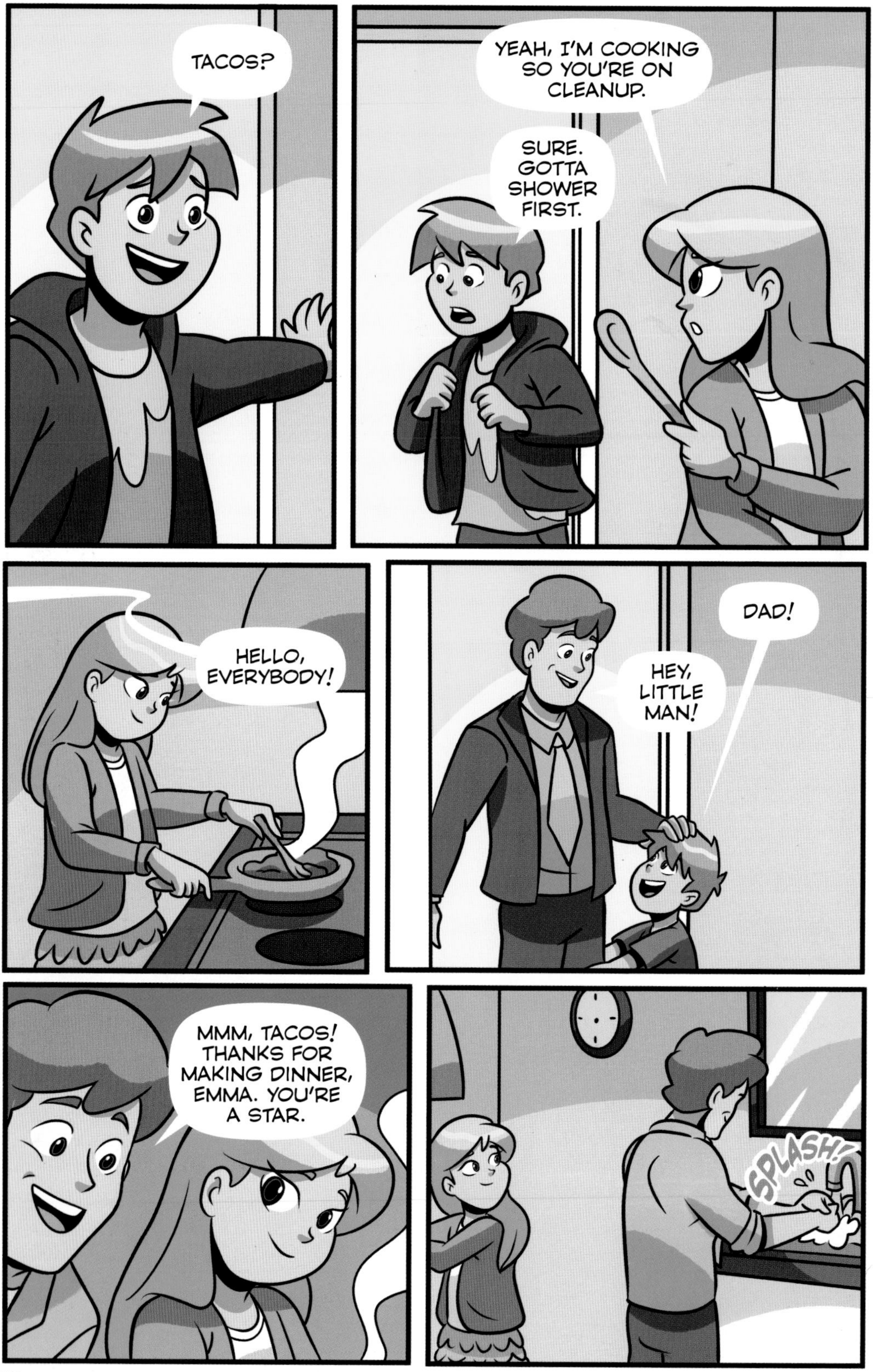
TACOS?
YEAH, I'M COOKING SO YOU'RE ON CLEANUP.
SURE. GOTTA SHOWER FIRST.
HELLO, EVERYBODY!
DAD!
HEY, LITTLE MAN!
MMM, TACOS! THANKS FOR MAKING DINNER, EMMA. YOU'RE A STAR.
SPLASH!

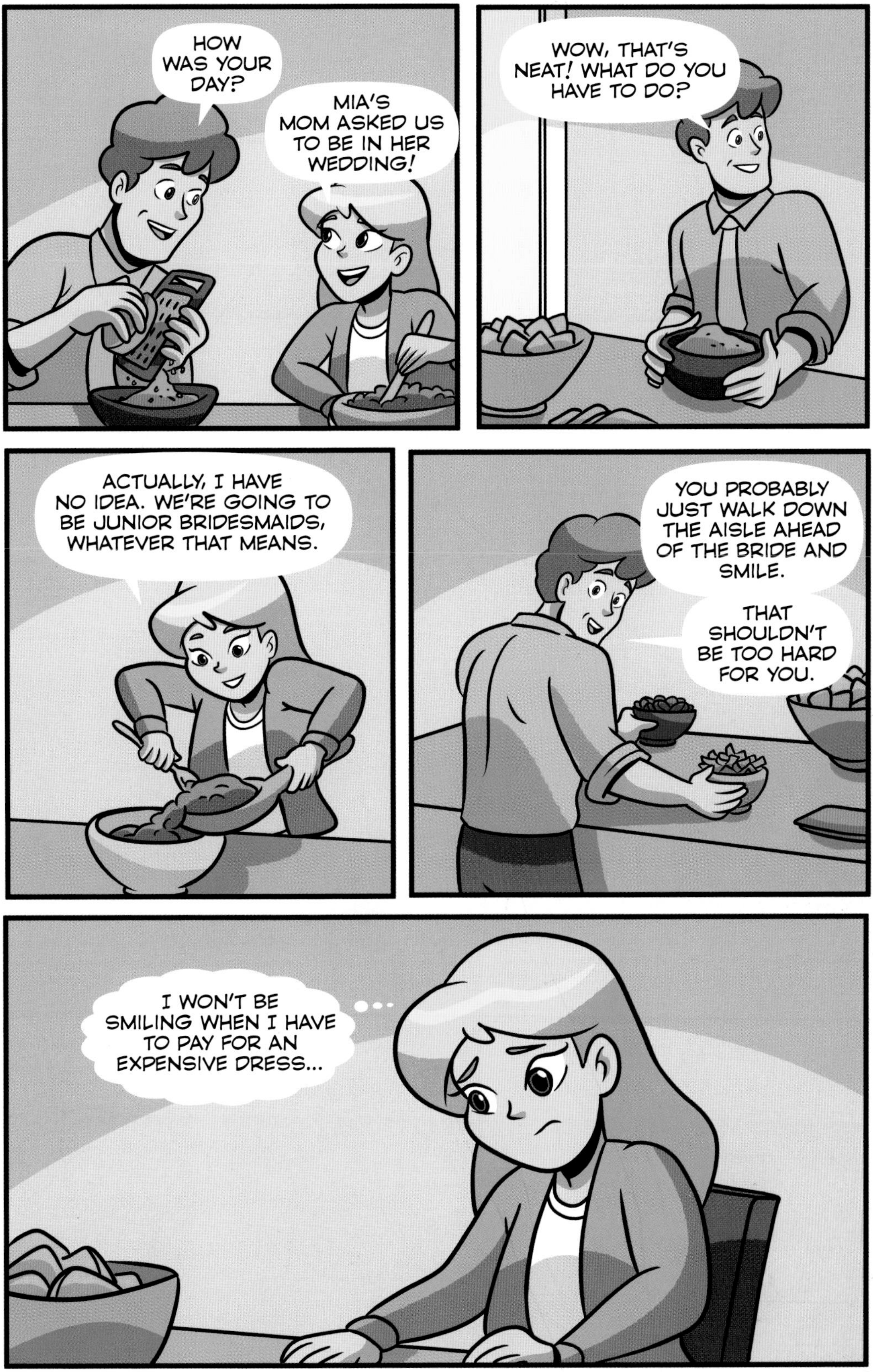
HOW WAS YOUR DAY?
MIA'S MOM ASKED US TO BE IN HER WEDDING!
WOW, THAT'S NEAT! WHAT DO YOU HAVE TO DO?
ACTUALLY, I HAVE NO IDEA. WE'RE GOING TO BE JUNIOR BRIDESMAIDS, WHATEVER THAT MEANS.
YOU PROBABLY JUST WALK DOWN THE AISLE AHEAD OF THE BRIDE AND SMILE.
THAT SHOULDN'T BE TOO HARD FOR YOU.
I WON'T BE SMILING WHEN I HAVE TO PAY FOR AN EXPENSIVE DRESS...

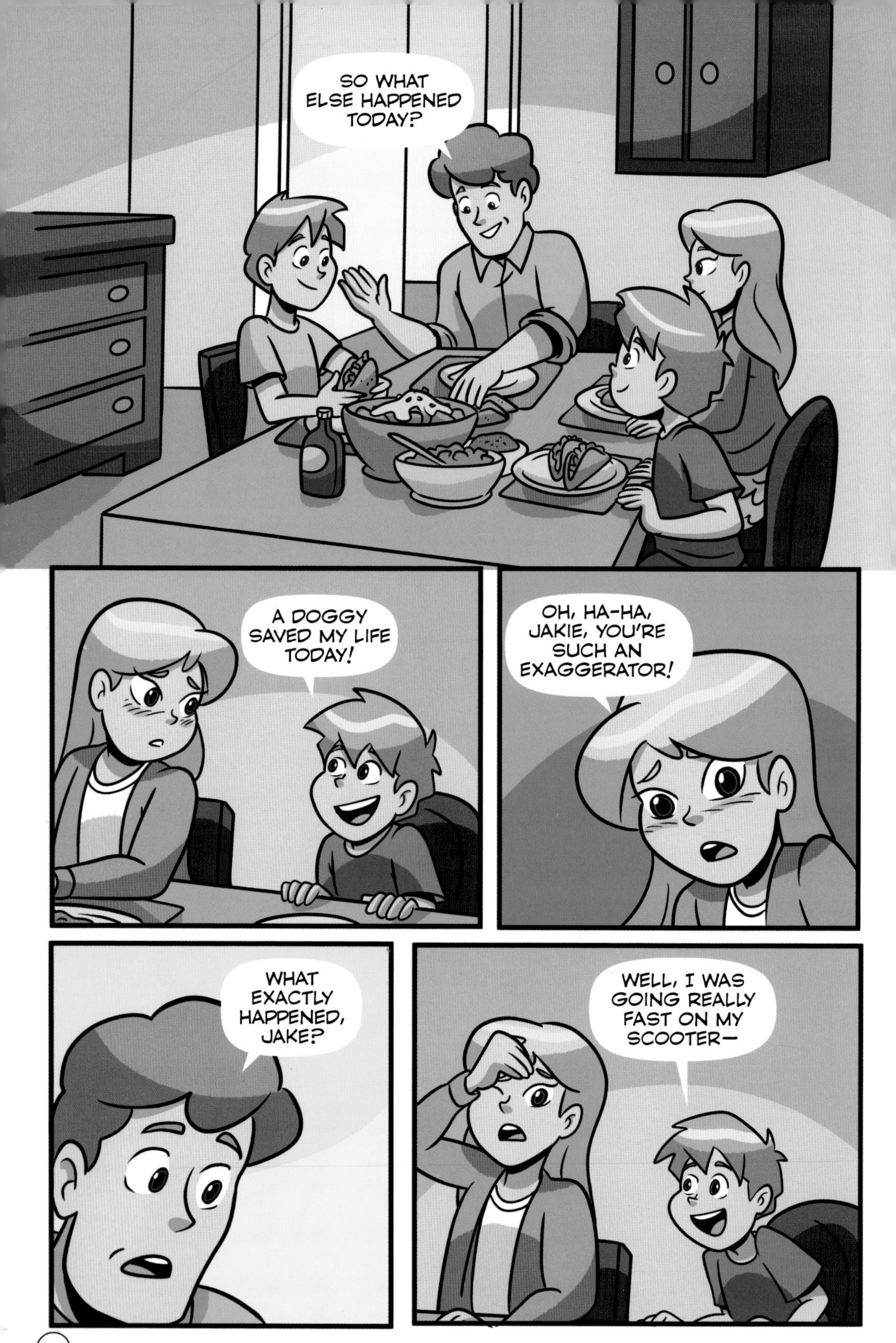
SO WHAT ELSE HAPPENED TODAY?
A DOGGY SAVED MY LIFE TODAY!
OH, HA-HA, JAKIE, YOU'RE SUCH AN EXAGGERATOR!
WHAT EXACTLY HAPPENED, JAKE?
WELL, I WAS GOING REALLY FAST ON MY SCOOTER—

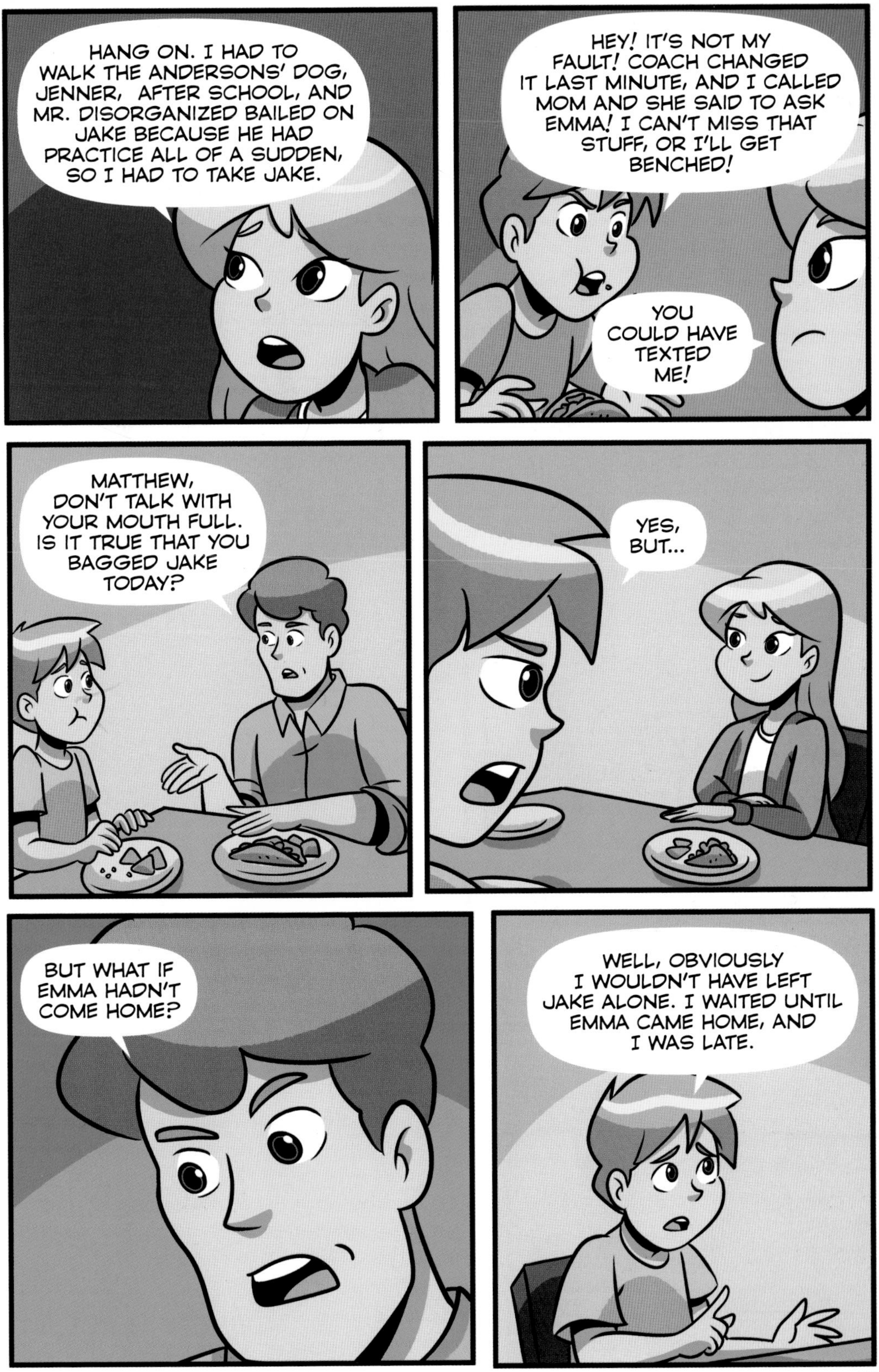
HANG ON. I HAD TO WALK THE ANDERSONS' DOG, JENNER, AFTER SCHOOL, AND MR. DISORGANIZED BAILED ON JAKE BECAUSE HE HAD PRACTICE ALL OF A SUDDEN, SO I HAD TO TAKE JAKE.
HEY! IT'S NOT MY FAULT! COACH CHANGED IT LAST MINUTE, AND I CALLED MOM AND SHE SAID TO ASK EMMA! I CAN'T MISS THAT STUFF, OR I'LL GET BENCHED!
YOU COULD HAVE TEXTED ME!
MATTHEW, DON'T TALK WITH YOUR MOUTH FULL. IS IT TRUE THAT YOU BAGGED JAKE TODAY?
YES, BUT...
BUT WHAT IF EMMA HADN'T COME HOME?
WELL, OBVIOUSLY I WOULDN'T HAVE LEFT JAKE ALONE. I WAITED UNTIL EMMA CAME HOME, AND I WAS LATE.

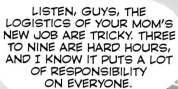

LISTEN, GUYS, THE LOGISTICS OF YOUR MOM'S NEW JOB ARE TRICKY. THREE TO NINE ARE HARD HOURS, AND I KNOW IT PUTS A LOT OF RESPONSIBILITY ON EVERYONE.

BUT WE'RE A FAMILY, AND FAMILIES CHIP IN AND HELP ONE ANOTHER OUT.

IF YOU CAN'T BABYSIT ON YOUR ASSIGNED DAY, THEN YOU HAVE TO LET THE OTHER PEOPLE KNOW AS SOON AS POSSIBLE. AND YOU OWE WHOMEVER TAKES OVER FOR YOU A DAY. EVERYONE UNDERSTAND?

CAN I GO TO BED?

RUN UP AND GET READY FOR YOUR SHOWER. I'LL BE THERE IN A MINUTE.

OKAY, YOU OWE ME A DAY. YOU HAVE FRIDAY.

NO WAY! I HAVE PLANS.

SO DO I, AND YOU OWE ME A DAY. I CAN STAY WITH HIM UNTIL FIVE, AND THEN HE'S ALL YOURS.

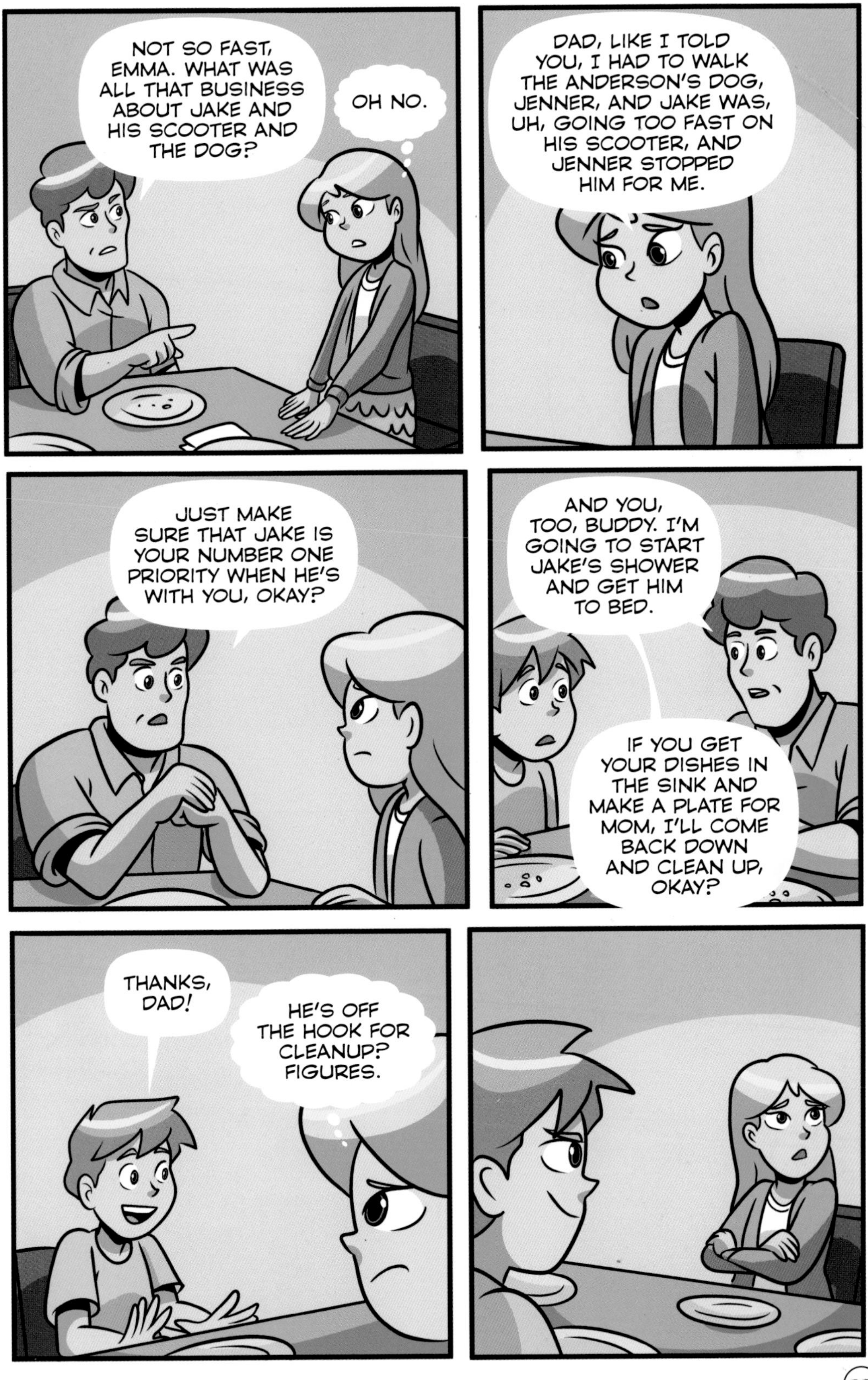
NOT SO FAST, EMMA. WHAT WAS ALL THAT BUSINESS ABOUT JAKE AND HIS SCOOTER AND THE DOG?
OH NO.
DAD, LIKE I TOLD YOU, I HAD TO WALK THE ANDERSON'S DOG, JENNER, AND JAKE WAS, UH, GOING TOO FAST ON HIS SCOOTER, AND JENNER STOPPED HIM FOR ME.
JUST MAKE SURE THAT JAKE IS YOUR NUMBER ONE PRIORITY WHEN HE'S WITH YOU, OKAY?
AND YOU, TOO, BUDDY. I'M GOING TO START JAKE'S SHOWER AND GET HIM TO BED.
IF YOU GET YOUR DISHES IN THE SINK AND MAKE A PLATE FOR MOM, I'LL COME BACK DOWN AND CLEAN UP, OKAY?
THANKS, DAD!
HE'S OFF THE HOOK FOR CLEANUP? FIGURES.

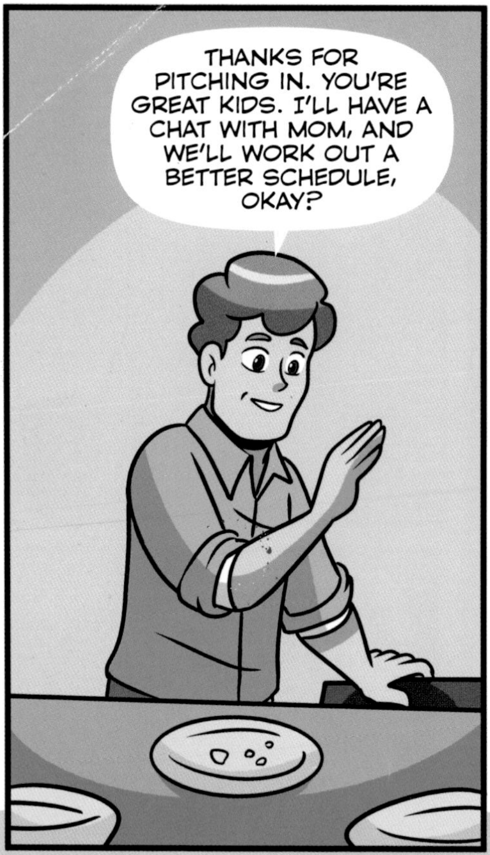
THANKS FOR PITCHING IN. YOU'RE GREAT KIDS. I'LL HAVE A CHAT WITH MOM, AND WE'LL WORK OUT A BETTER SCHEDULE, OKAY?

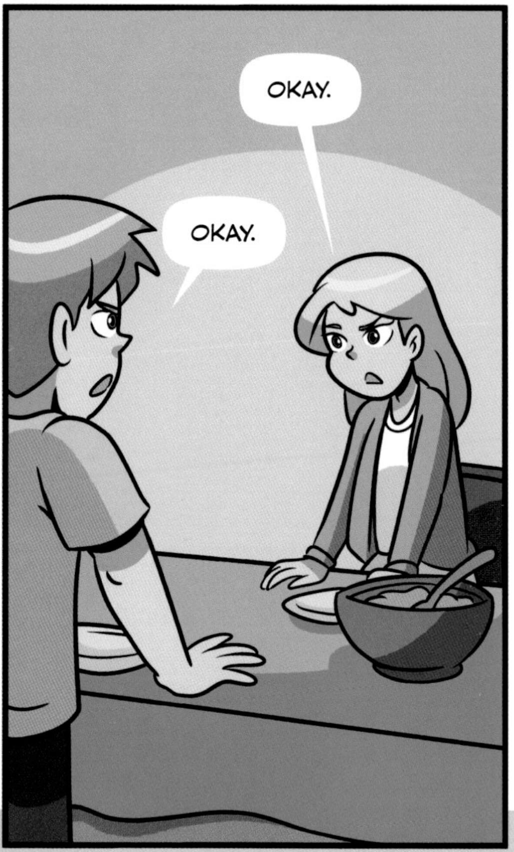
OKAY.
OKAY.

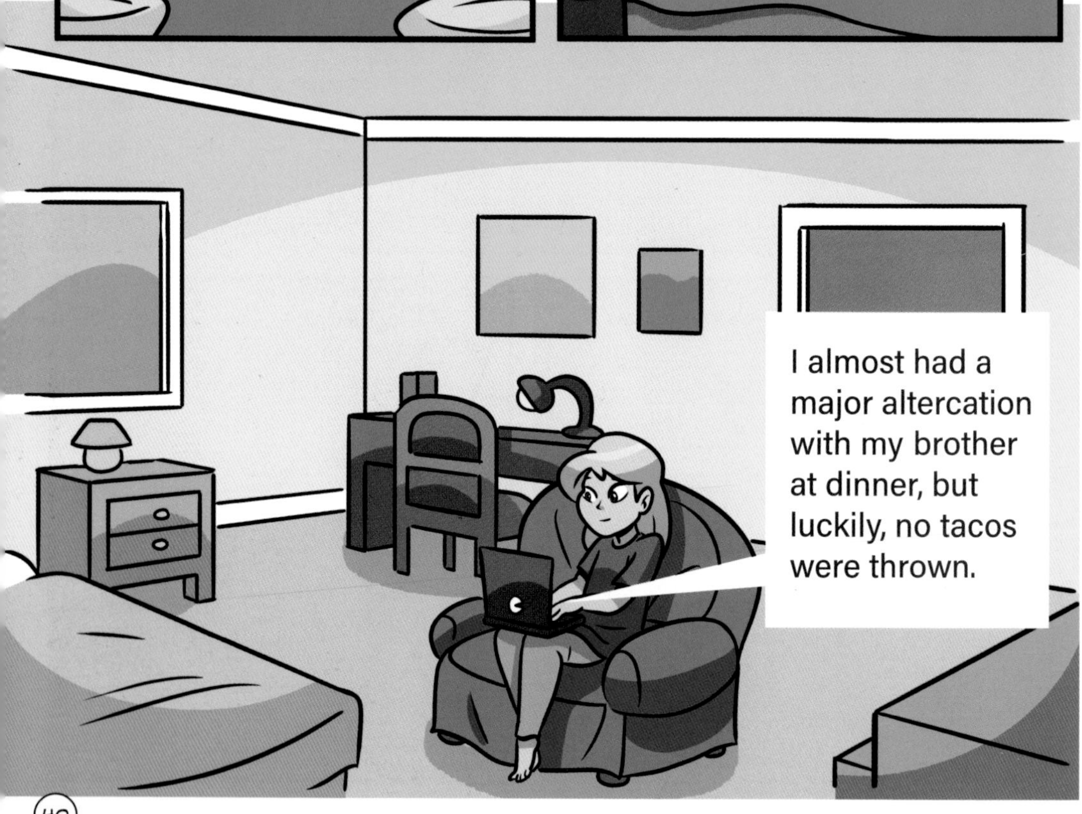
I almost had a major altercation with my brother at dinner, but luckily, no tacos were thrown.

Chapter 4

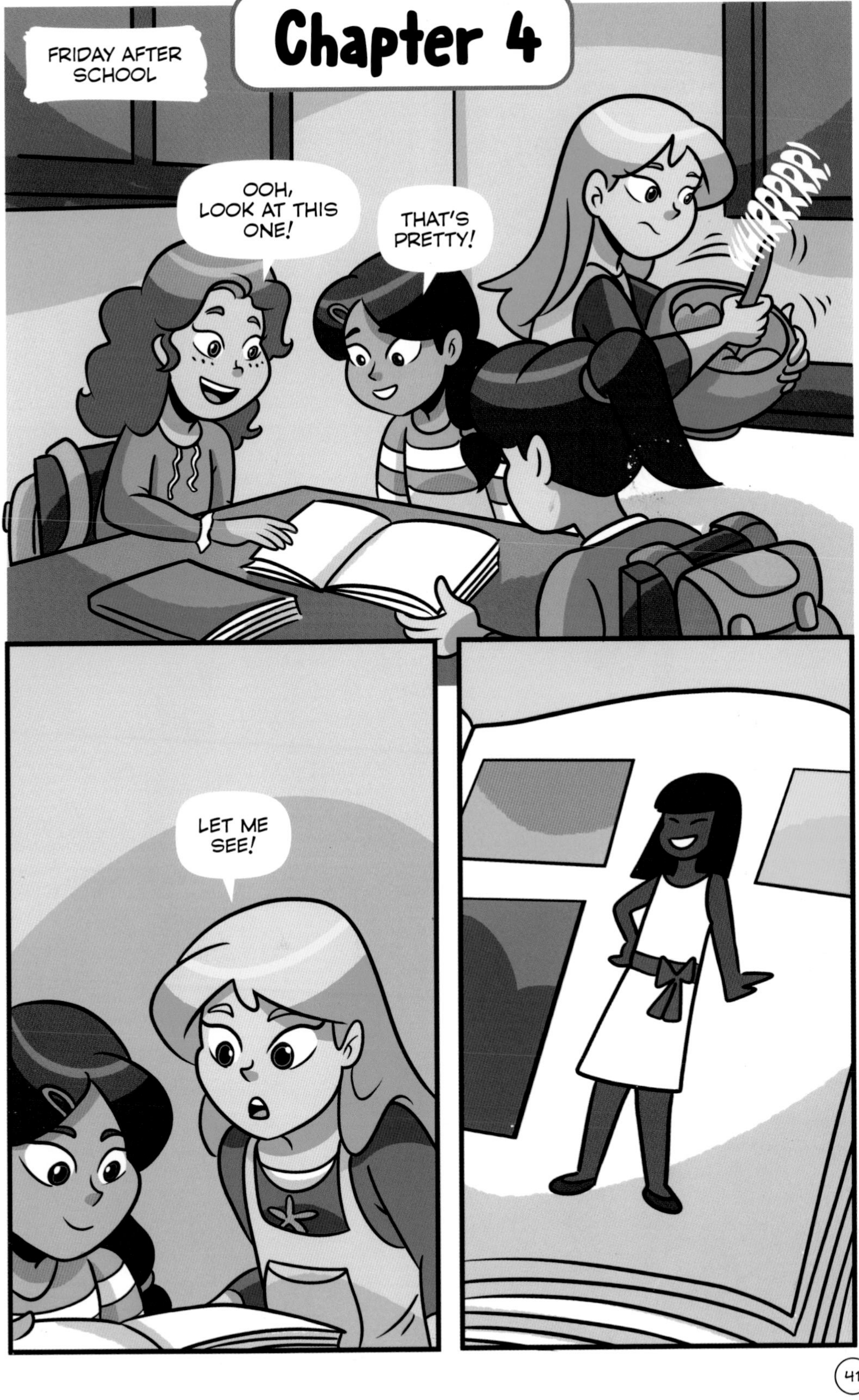
FRIDAY AFTER SCHOOL
OOH, LOOK AT THIS ONE!
THAT'S PRETTY!
WHIRRRRR!
LET ME SEE!

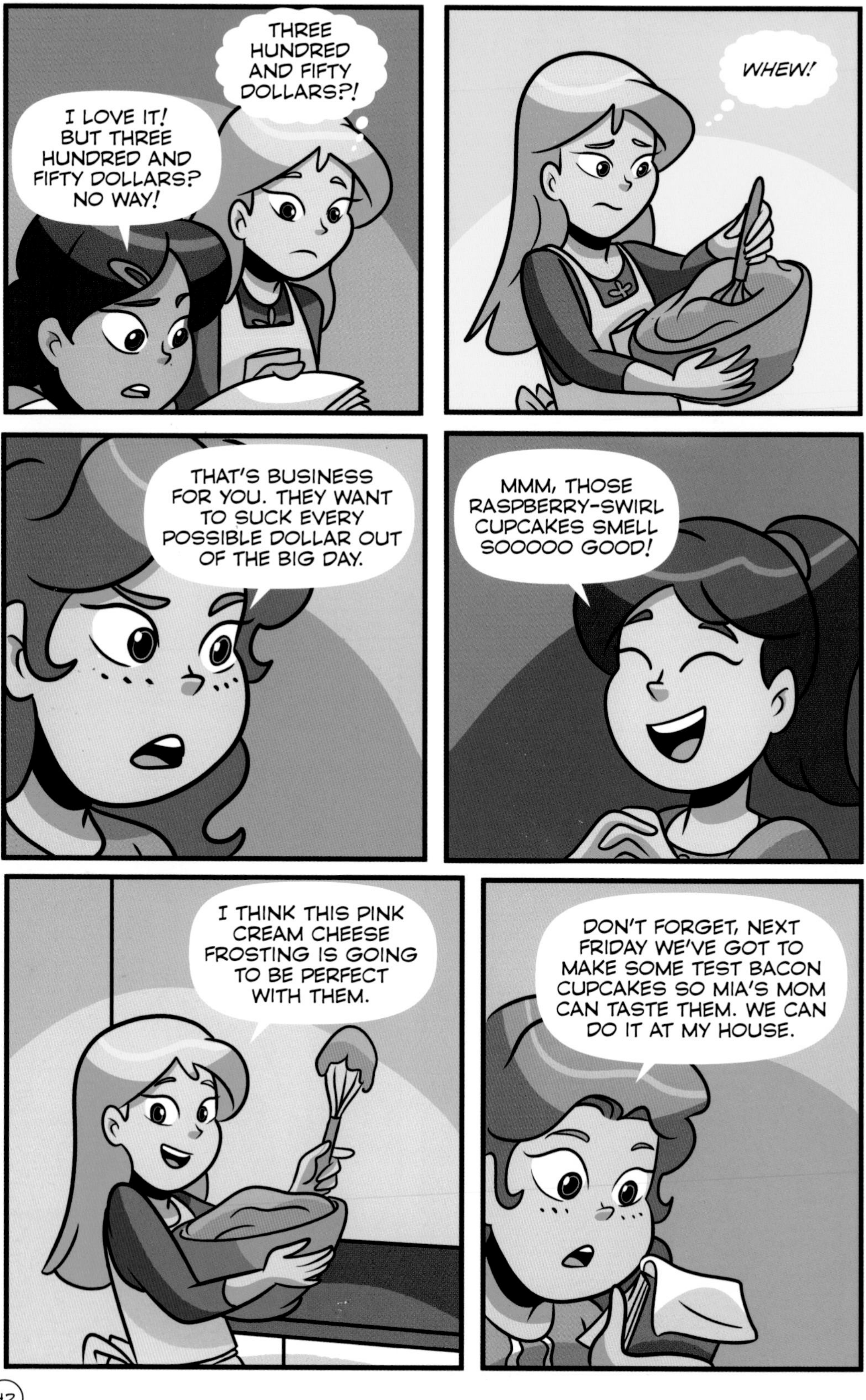
I LOVE IT! BUT THREE HUNDRED AND FIFTY DOLLARS? NO WAY!
THREE HUNDRED AND FIFTY DOLLARS?!
WHEW!
THAT'S BUSINESS FOR YOU. THEY WANT TO SUCK EVERY POSSIBLE DOLLAR OUT OF THE BIG DAY.
MMM, THOSE RASPBERRY-SWIRL CUPCAKES SMELL SOOOOO GOOD!
I THINK THIS PINK CREAM CHEESE FROSTING IS GOING TO BE PERFECT WITH THEM.
DON'T FORGET, NEXT FRIDAY WE'VE GOT TO MAKE SOME TEST BACON CUPCAKES SO MIA'S MOM CAN TASTE THEM. WE CAN DO IT AT MY HOUSE.

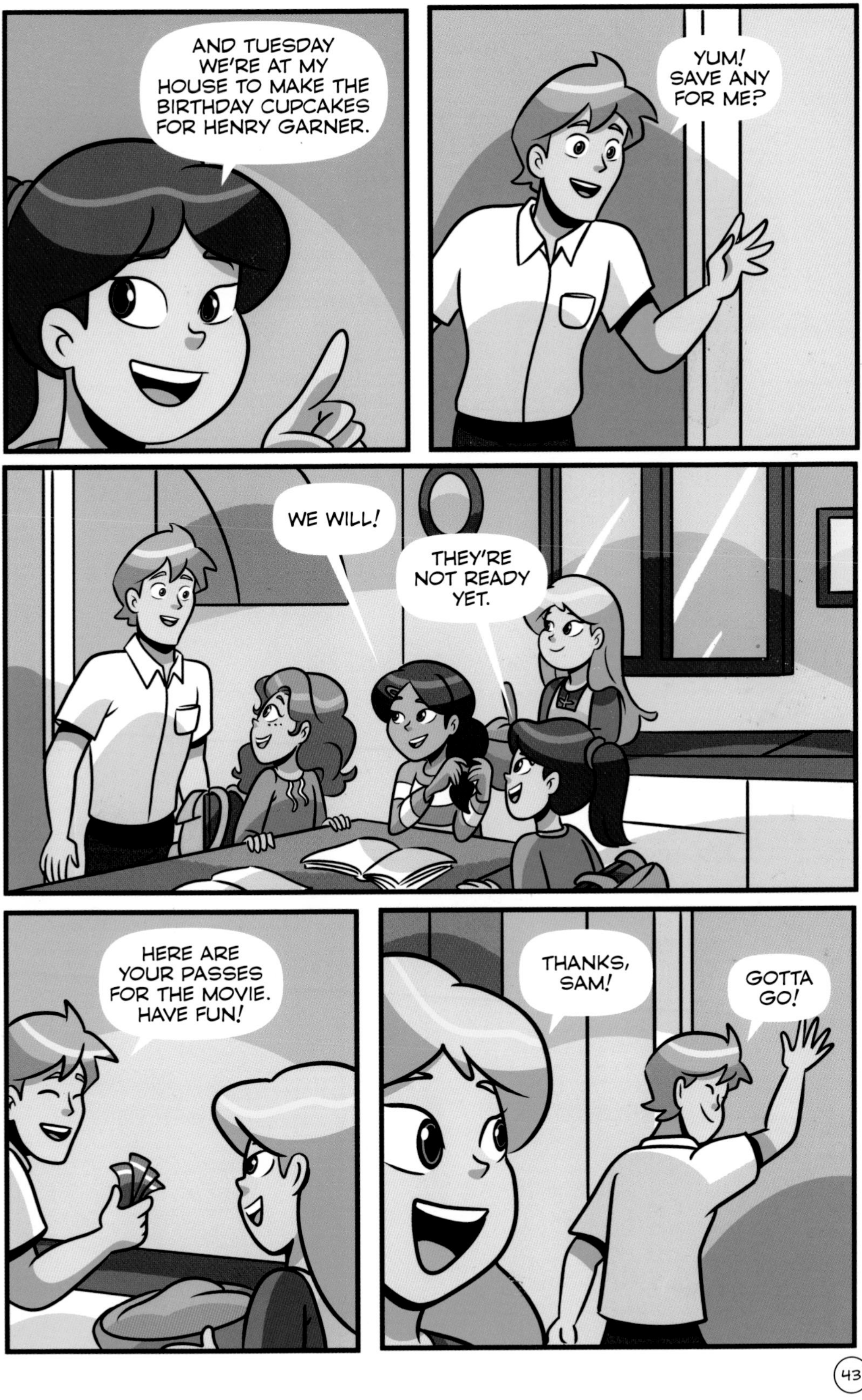
AND TUESDAY WE'RE AT MY HOUSE TO MAKE THE BIRTHDAY CUPCAKES FOR HENRY GARNER.
YUM! SAVE ANY FOR ME?
WE WILL!
THEY'RE NOT READY YET.
HERE ARE YOUR PASSES FOR THE MOVIE. HAVE FUN!
THANKS, SAM!
GOTTA GO!

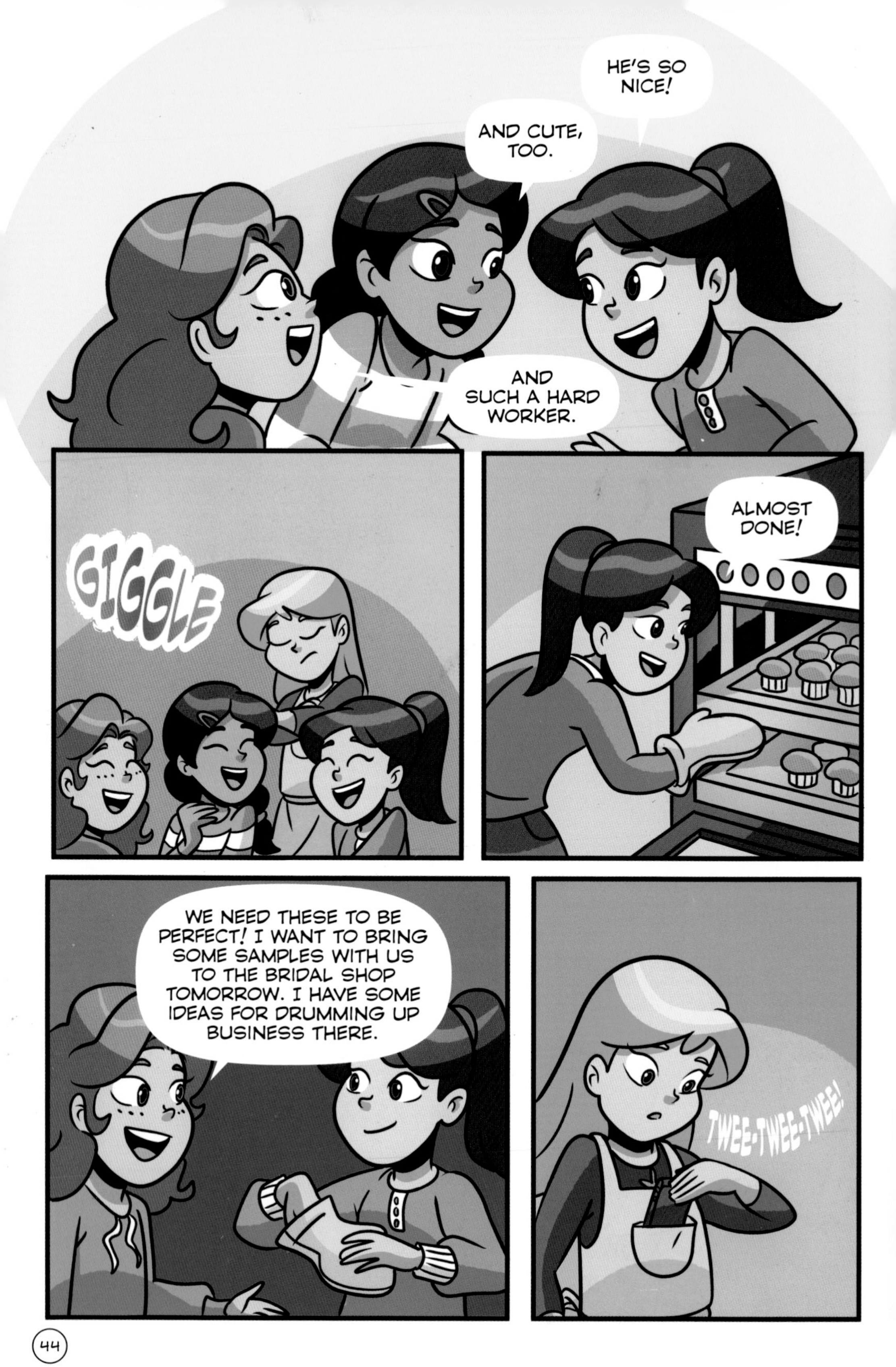
HE'S SO NICE!
AND CUTE, TOO.
AND SUCH A HARD WORKER.
GIGGLE
ALMOST DONE!
WE NEED THESE TO BE PERFECT! I WANT TO BRING SOME SAMPLES WITH US TO THE BRIDAL SHOP TOMORROW. I HAVE SOME IDEAS FOR DRUMMING UP BUSINESS THERE.
TWEE-TWEE-TWEE!

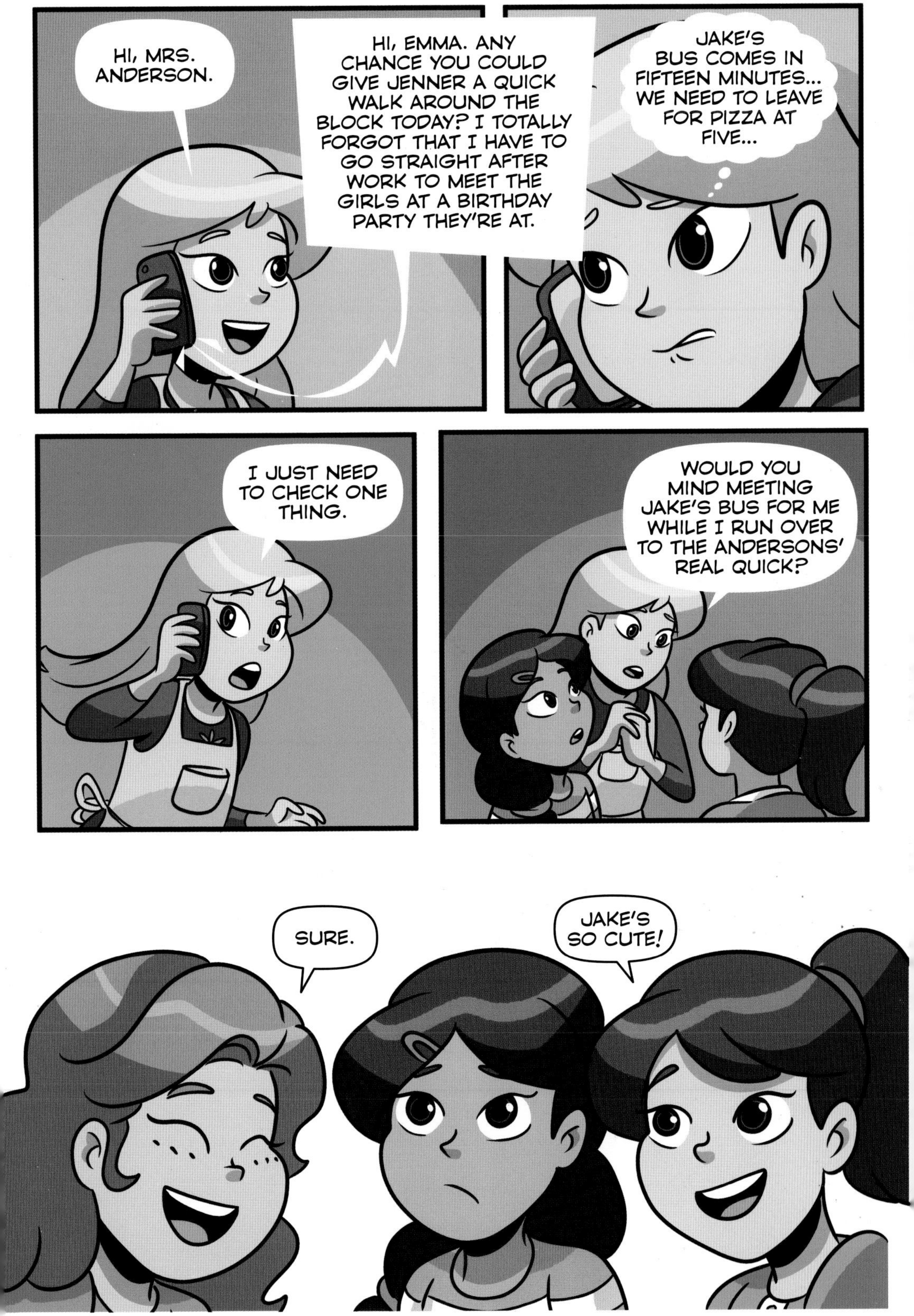
HI, MRS. ANDERSON.
HI, EMMA. ANY CHANCE YOU COULD GIVE JENNER A QUICK WALK AROUND THE BLOCK TODAY? I TOTALLY FORGOT THAT I HAVE TO GO STRAIGHT AFTER WORK TO MEET THE GIRLS AT A BIRTHDAY PARTY THEY'RE AT.
JAKE'S BUS COMES IN FIFTEEN MINUTES... WE NEED TO LEAVE FOR PIZZA AT FIVE...
I JUST NEED TO CHECK ONE THING.
WOULD YOU MIND MEETING JAKE'S BUS FOR ME WHILE I RUN OVER TO THE ANDERSONS' REAL QUICK?
SURE.
JAKE'S SO CUTE!

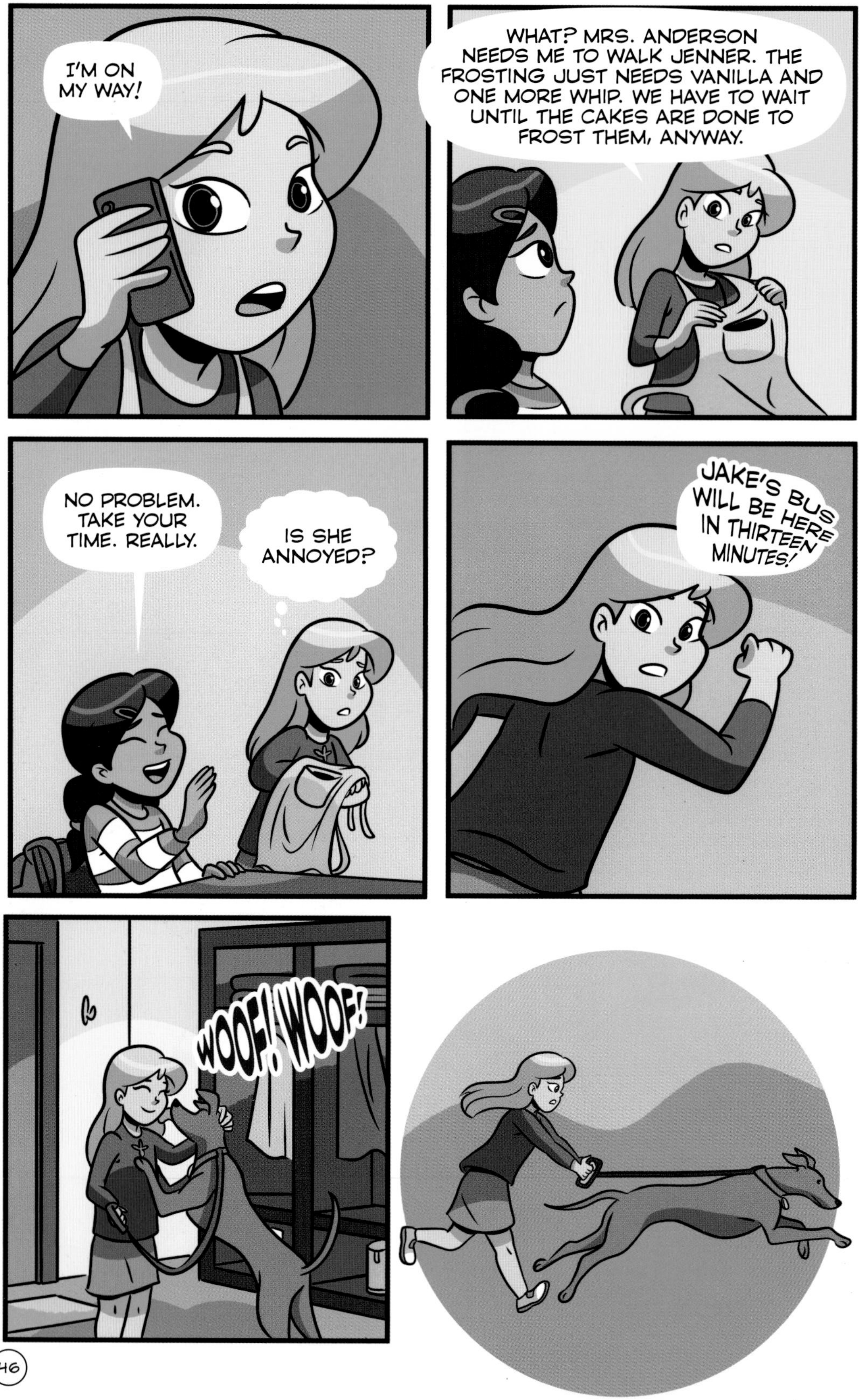
I'M ON MY WAY!
WHAT? MRS. ANDERSON NEEDS ME TO WALK JENNER. THE FROSTING JUST NEEDS VANILLA AND ONE MORE WHIP. WE HAVE TO WAIT UNTIL THE CAKES ARE DONE TO FROST THEM, ANYWAY.
NO PROBLEM. TAKE YOUR TIME. REALLY.
IS SHE ANNOYED?
JAKE'S BUS WILL BE HERE IN THIRTEEN MINUTES!
WOOF! WOOF!

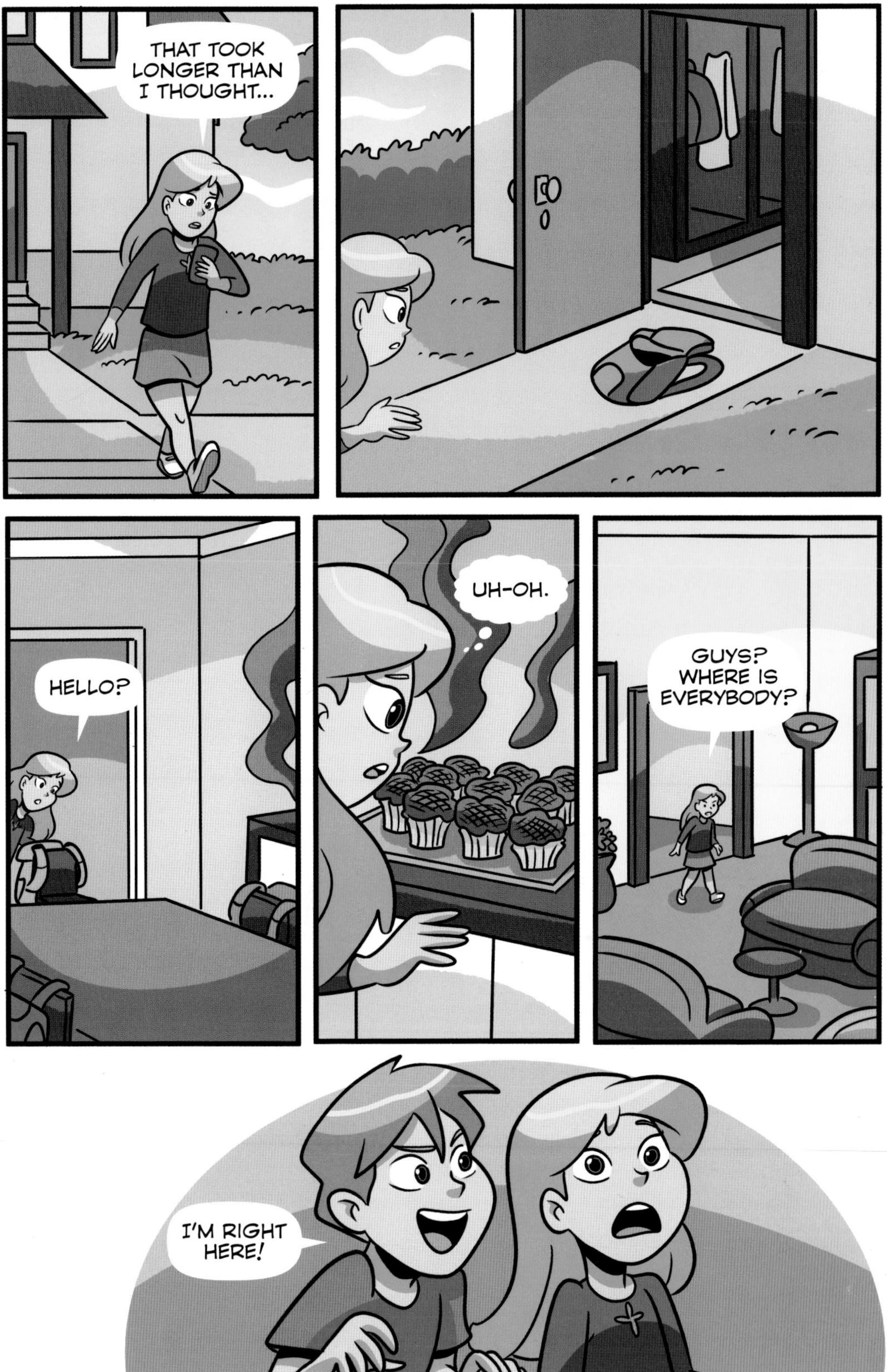
THAT TOOK LONGER THAN I THOUGHT...
HELLO?
UH-OH.
GUYS? WHERE IS EVERYBODY?
I'M RIGHT HERE!

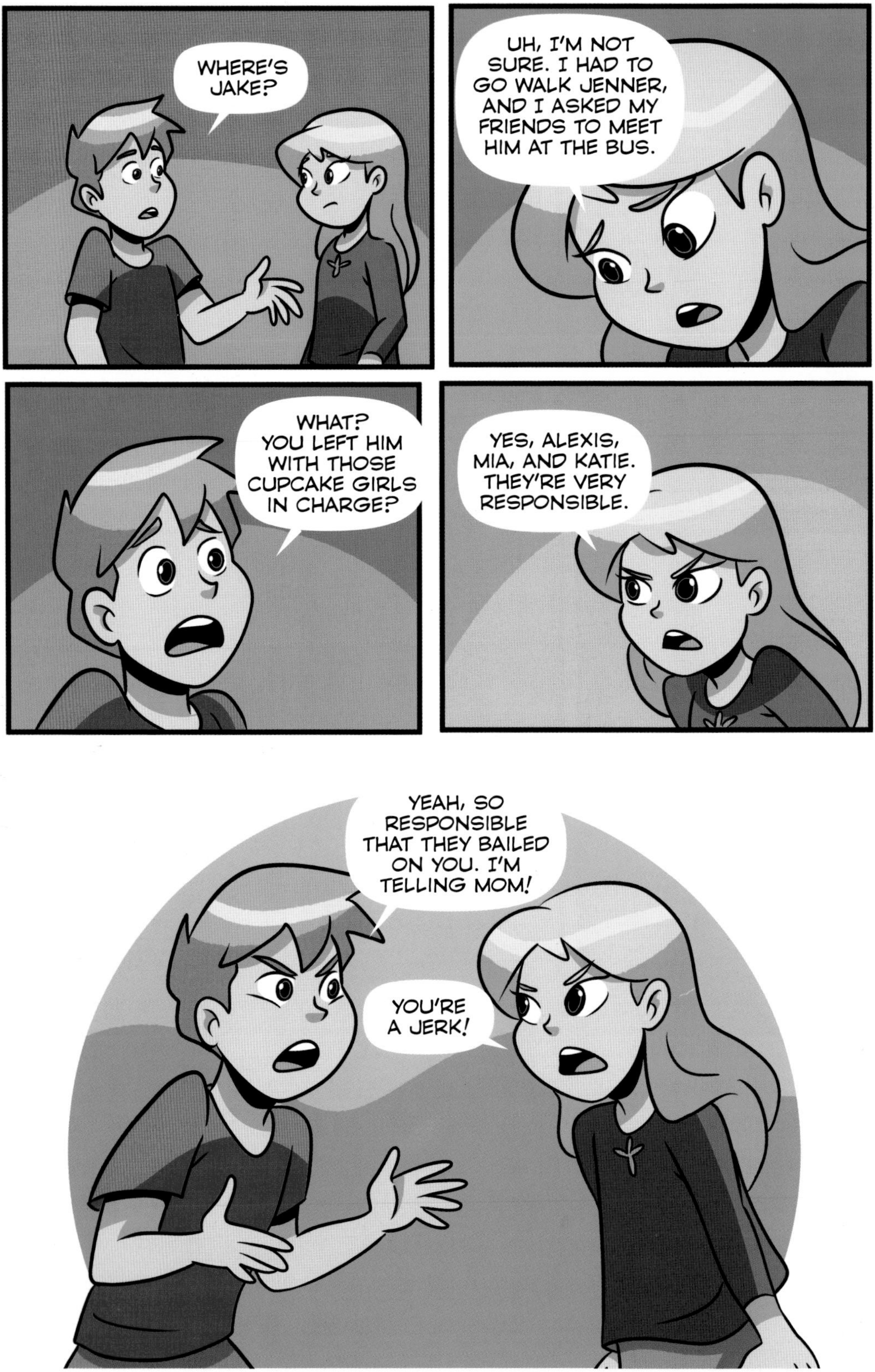
WHERE'S JAKE?
UH, I'M NOT SURE. I HAD TO GO WALK JENNER, AND I ASKED MY FRIENDS TO MEET HIM AT THE BUS.
WHAT? YOU LEFT HIM WITH THOSE CUPCAKE GIRLS IN CHARGE?
YES, ALEXIS, MIA, AND KATIE. THEY'RE VERY RESPONSIBLE.
YEAH, SO RESPONSIBLE THAT THEY BAILED ON YOU. I'M TELLING MOM!
YOU'RE A JERK!

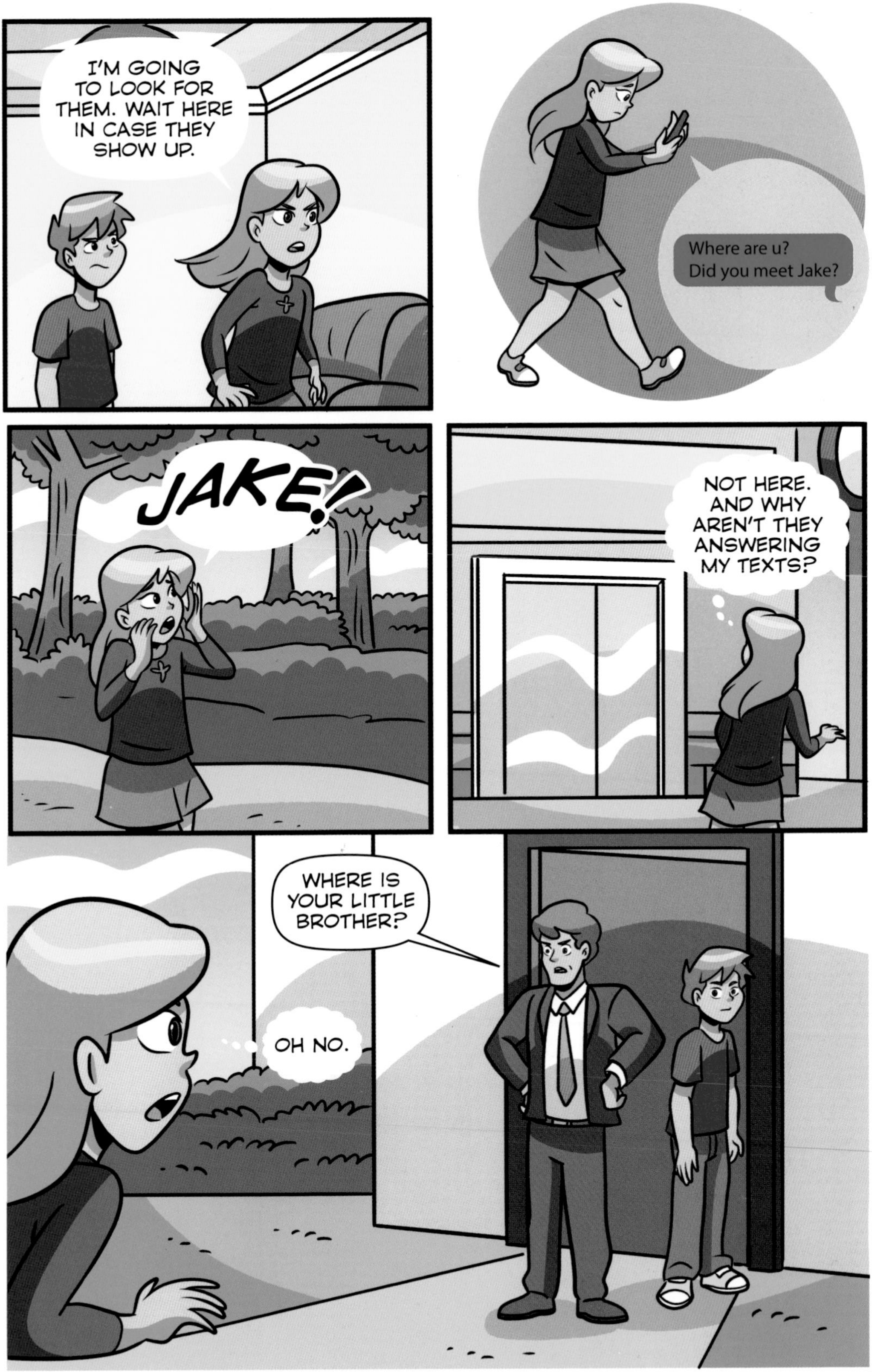
I'M GOING TO LOOK FOR THEM. WAIT HERE IN CASE THEY SHOW UP.
Where are u?
Did you meet Jake?
JAKE!
NOT HERE. AND WHY AREN'T THEY ANSWERING MY TEXTS?
WHERE IS YOUR LITTLE BROTHER?
OH NO.

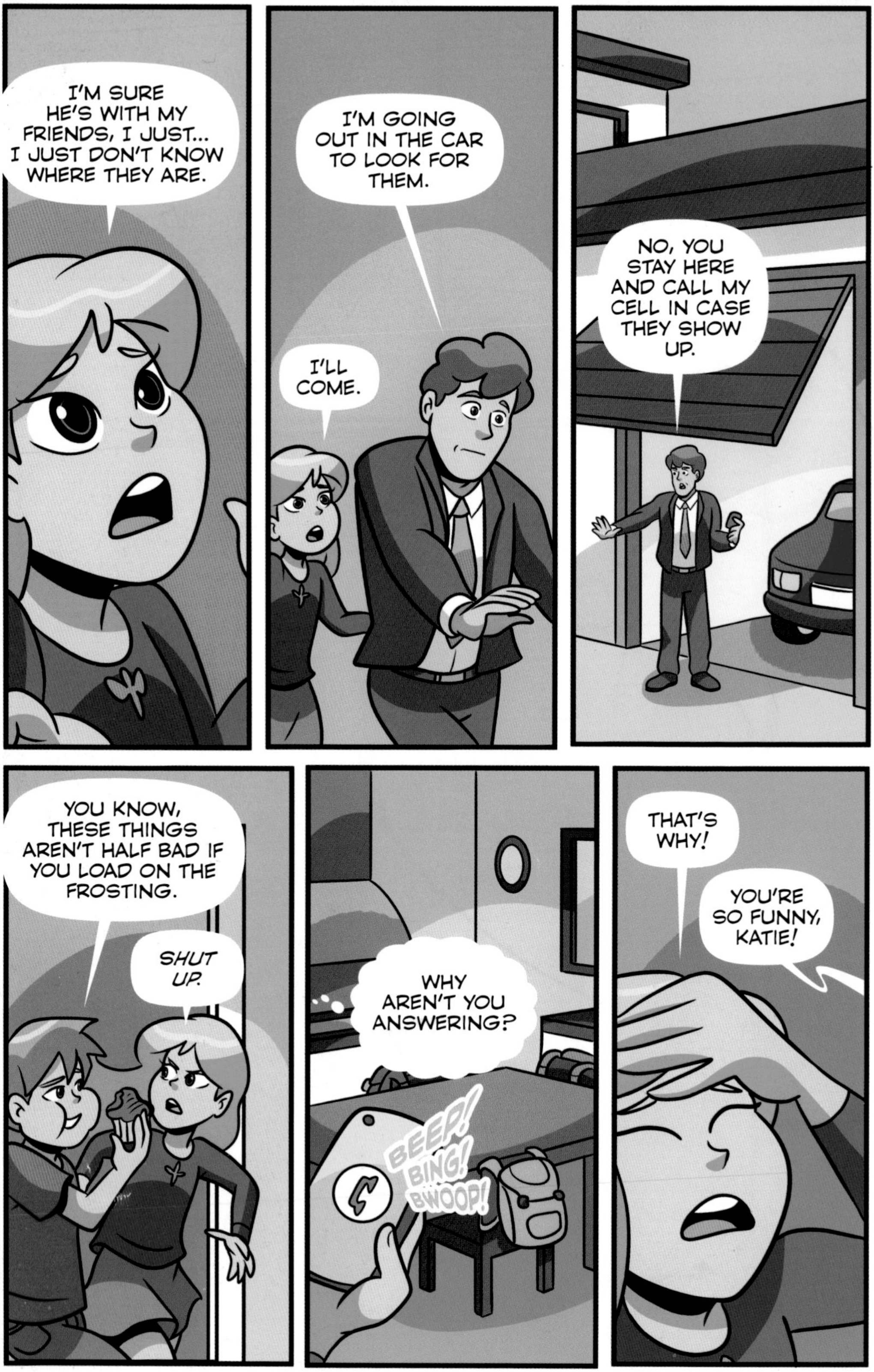
I'M SURE HE'S WITH MY FRIENDS, I JUST... I JUST DON'T KNOW WHERE THEY ARE.
I'M GOING OUT IN THE CAR TO LOOK FOR THEM.
I'LL COME.
NO, YOU STAY HERE AND CALL MY CELL IN CASE THEY SHOW UP.
YOU KNOW, THESE THINGS AREN'T HALF BAD IF YOU LOAD ON THE FROSTING.
SHUT UP.
WHY AREN'T YOU ANSWERING?
BEEP! BING! BWOOP!
THAT'S WHY!
YOU'RE SO FUNNY, KATIE!

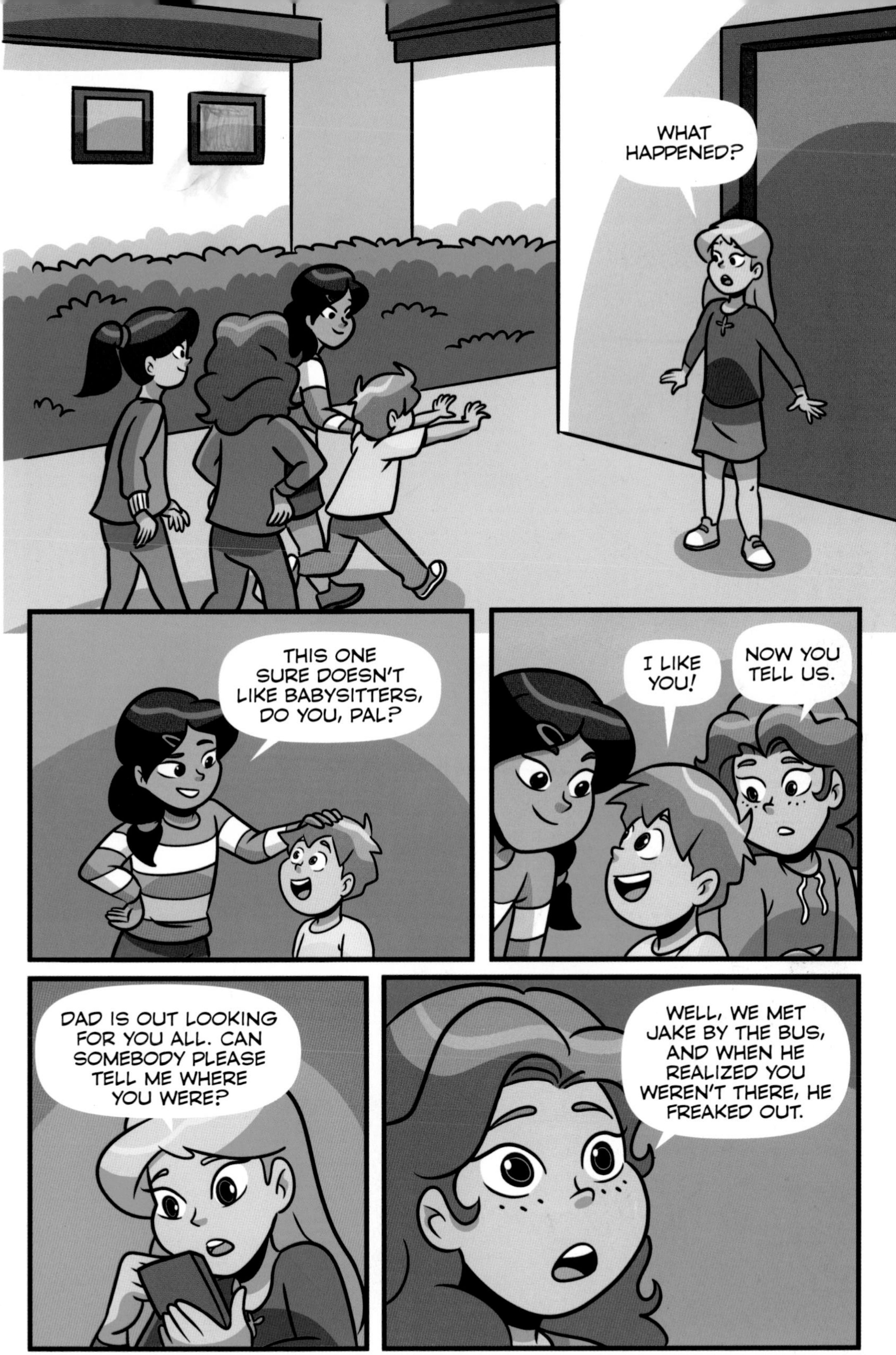
WHAT HAPPENED?
THIS ONE SURE DOESN'T LIKE BABYSITTERS, DO YOU, PAL?
I LIKE YOU!
NOW YOU TELL US.
DAD IS OUT LOOKING FOR YOU ALL. CAN SOMEBODY PLEASE TELL ME WHERE YOU WERE?
WELL, WE MET JAKE BY THE BUS, AND WHEN HE REALIZED YOU WEREN'T THERE, HE FREAKED OUT.

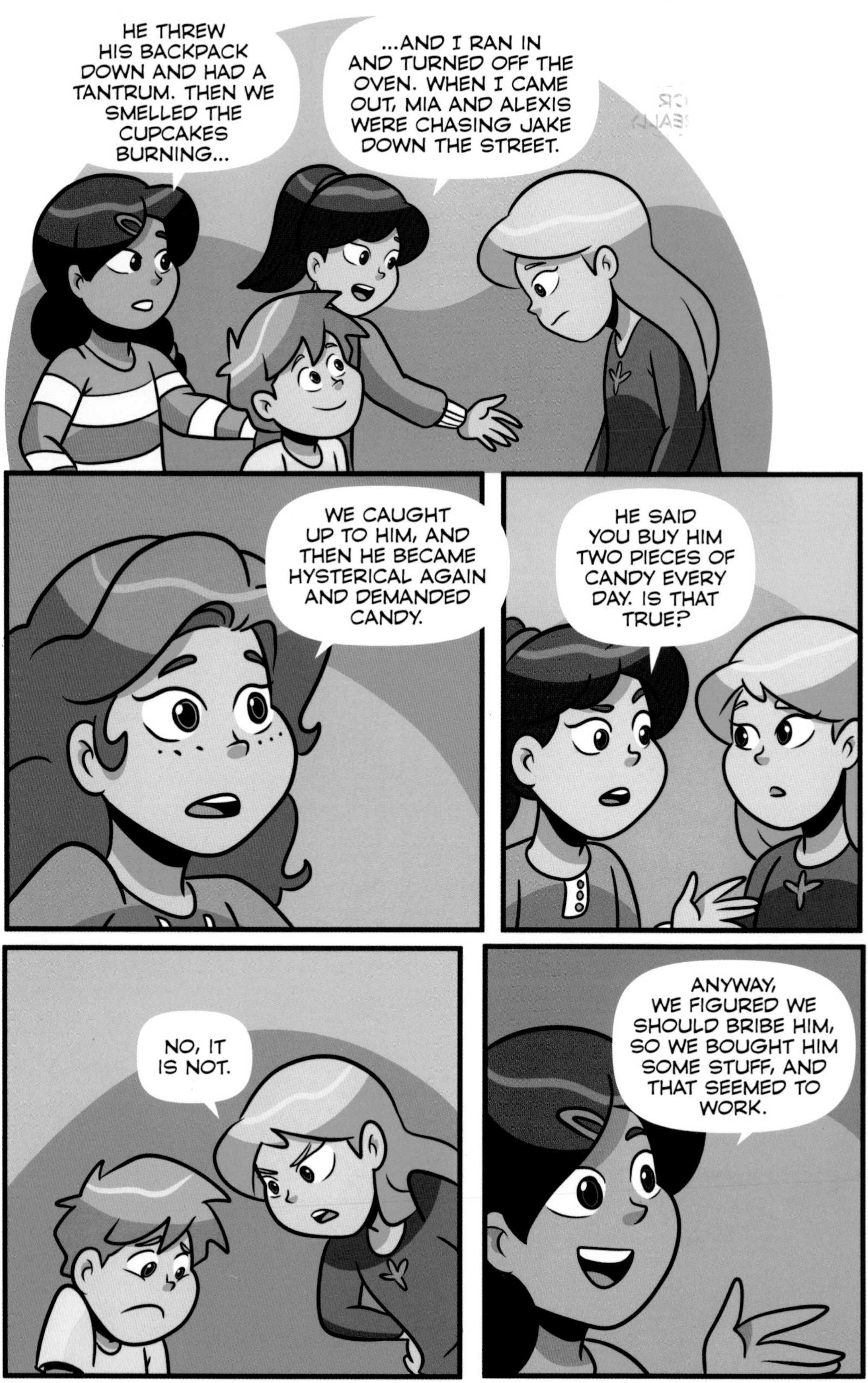
HE THREW HIS BACKPACK DOWN AND HAD A TANTRUM. THEN WE SMELLED THE CUPCAKES BURNING...
...AND I RAN IN AND TURNED OFF THE OVEN. WHEN I CAME OUT, MIA AND ALEXIS WERE CHASING JAKE DOWN THE STREET.
WE CAUGHT UP TO HIM, AND THEN HE BECAME HYSTERICAL AGAIN AND DEMANDED CANDY.
HE SAID YOU BUY HIM TWO PIECES OF CANDY EVERY DAY. IS THAT TRUE?
NO, IT IS NOT.
ANYWAY, WE FIGURED WE SHOULD BRIBE HIM, SO WE BOUGHT HIM SOME STUFF, AND THAT SEEMED TO WORK.

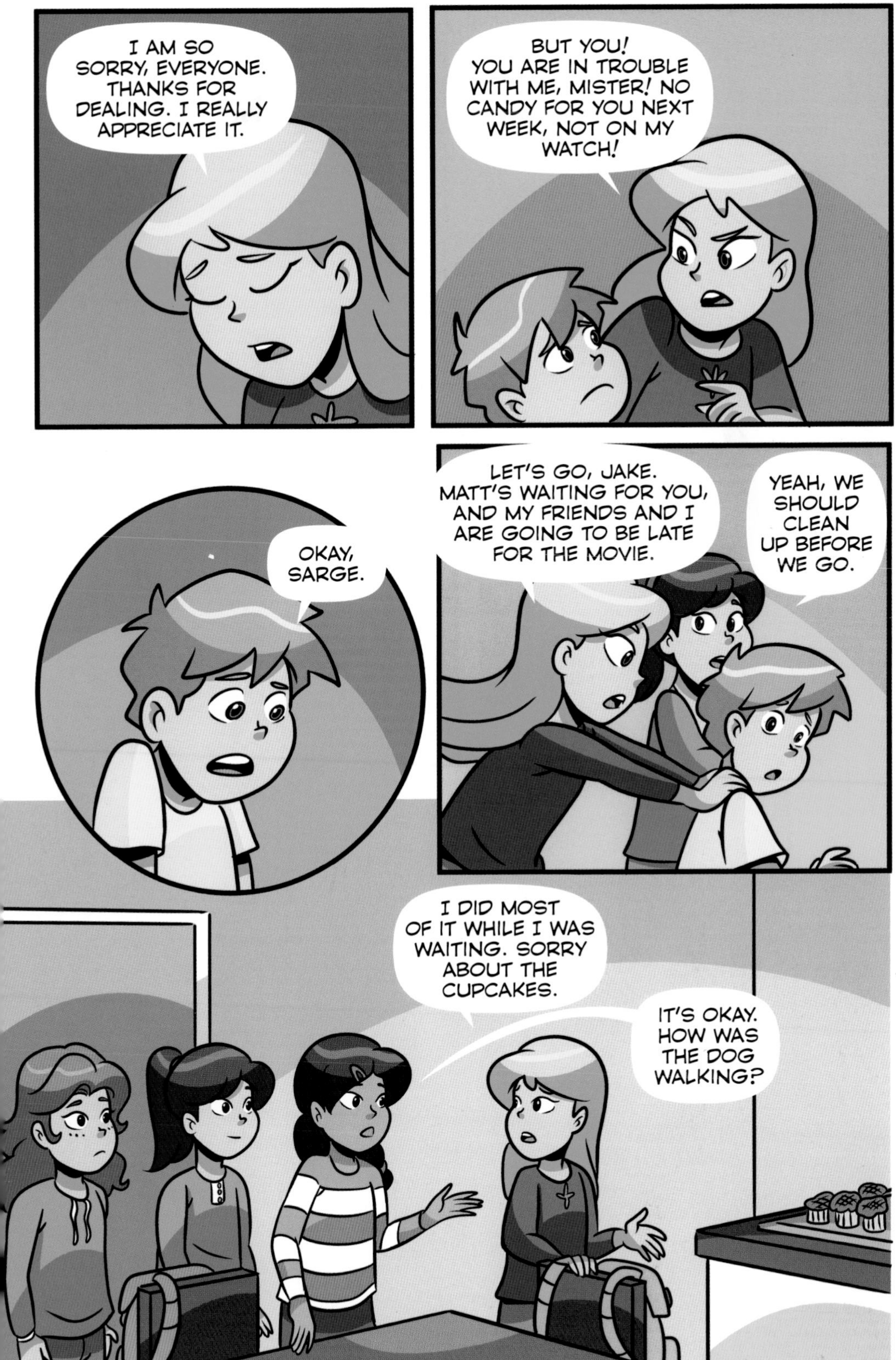
I AM SO SORRY, EVERYONE. THANKS FOR DEALING. I REALLY APPRECIATE IT.
BUT YOU! YOU ARE IN TROUBLE WITH ME, MISTER! NO CANDY FOR YOU NEXT WEEK, NOT ON MY WATCH!
OKAY, SARGE.
LET'S GO, JAKE. MATT'S WAITING FOR YOU, AND MY FRIENDS AND I ARE GOING TO BE LATE FOR THE MOVIE.
YEAH, WE SHOULD CLEAN UP BEFORE WE GO.
I DID MOST OF IT WHILE I WAS WAITING. SORRY ABOUT THE CUPCAKES.
IT'S OKAY. HOW WAS THE DOG WALKING?

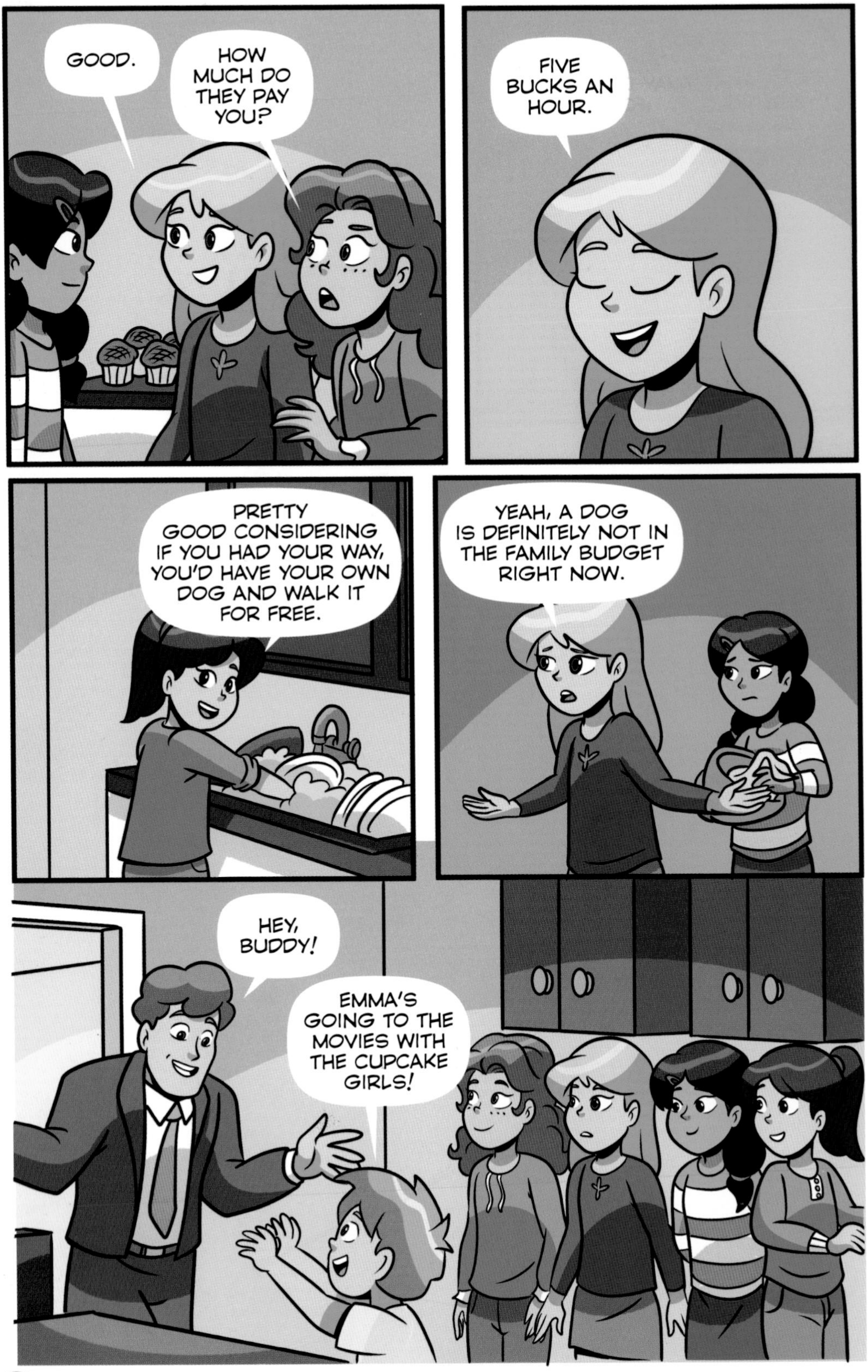
GOOD.
HOW MUCH DO THEY PAY YOU?
FIVE BUCKS AN HOUR.
PRETTY GOOD CONSIDERING IF YOU HAD YOUR WAY, YOU'D HAVE YOUR OWN DOG AND WALK IT FOR FREE.
YEAH, A DOG IS DEFINITELY NOT IN THE FAMILY BUDGET RIGHT NOW.
HEY, BUDDY!
EMMA'S GOING TO THE MOVIES WITH THE CUPCAKE GIRLS!

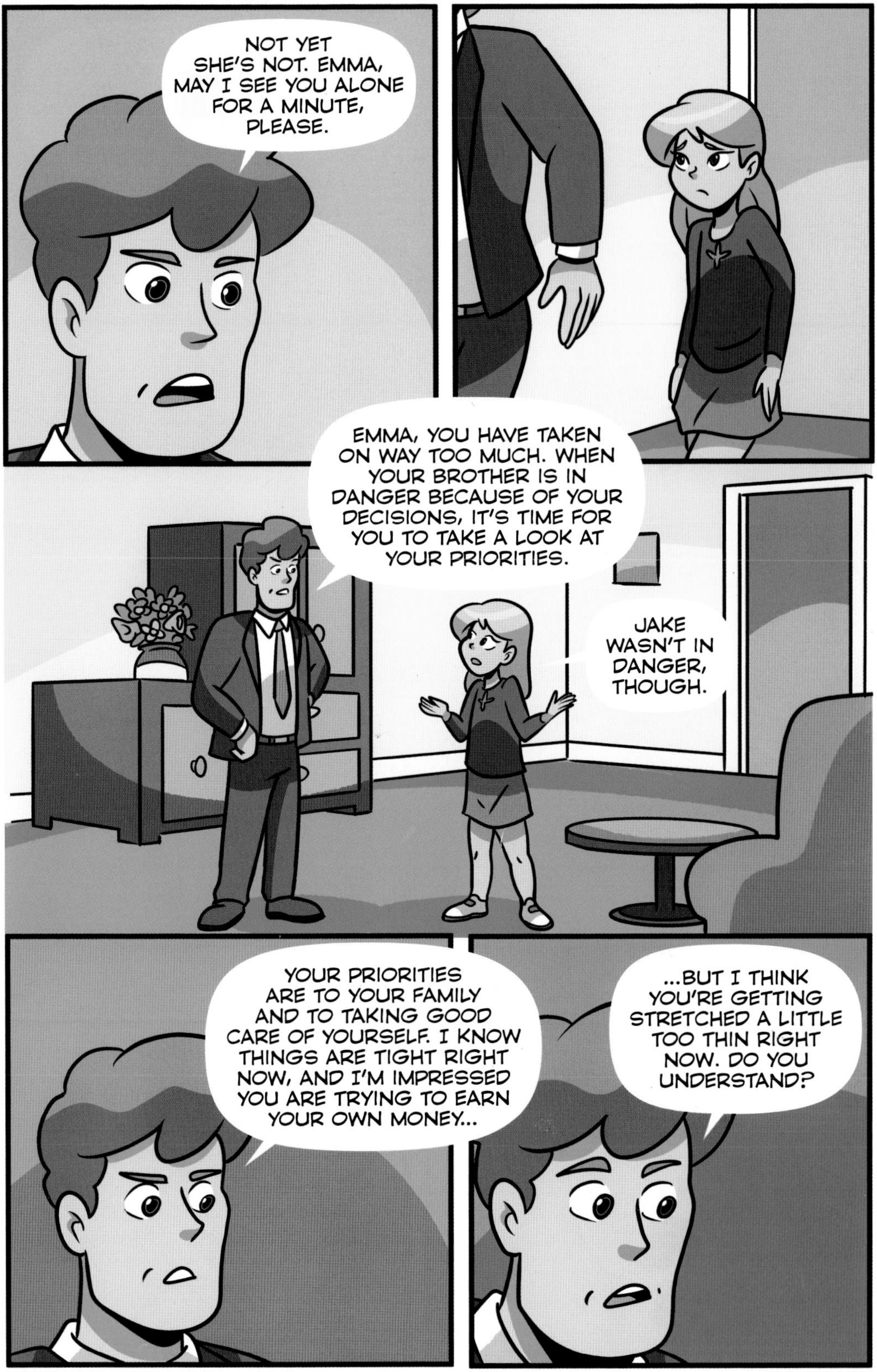
NOT YET SHE'S NOT. EMMA, MAY I SEE YOU ALONE FOR A MINUTE, PLEASE.
EMMA, YOU HAVE TAKEN ON WAY TOO MUCH. WHEN YOUR BROTHER IS IN DANGER BECAUSE OF YOUR DECISIONS, IT'S TIME FOR YOU TO TAKE A LOOK AT YOUR PRIORITIES.
JAKE WASN'T IN DANGER, THOUGH.
YOUR PRIORITIES ARE TO YOUR FAMILY AND TO TAKING GOOD CARE OF YOURSELF. I KNOW THINGS ARE TIGHT RIGHT NOW, AND I'M IMPRESSED YOU ARE TRYING TO EARN YOUR OWN MONEY...
...BUT I THINK YOU'RE GETTING STRETCHED A LITTLE TOO THIN RIGHT NOW. DO YOU UNDERSTAND?

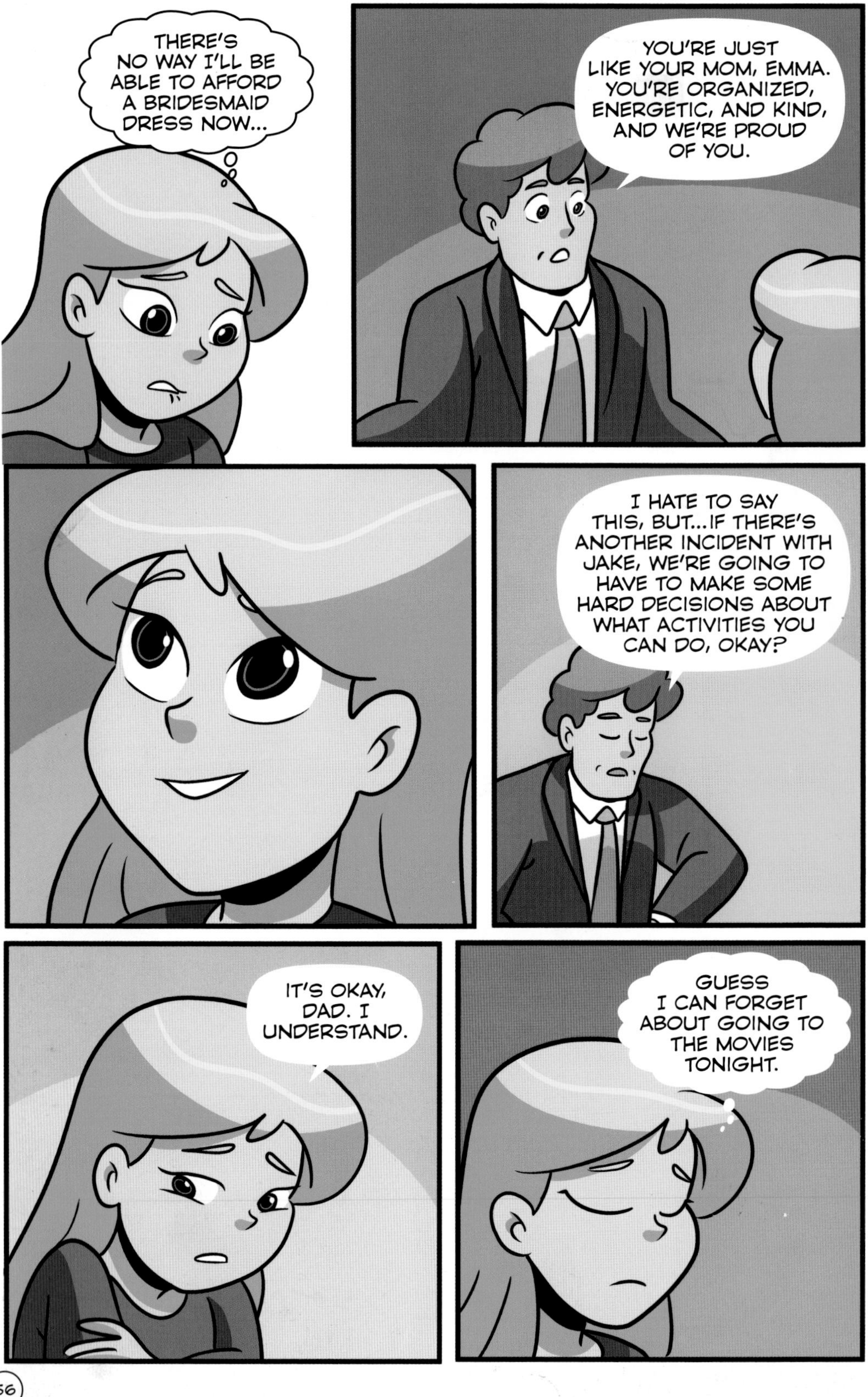
THERE'S NO WAY I'LL BE ABLE TO AFFORD A BRIDESMAID DRESS NOW...
YOU'RE JUST LIKE YOUR MOM, EMMA. YOU'RE ORGANIZED, ENERGETIC, AND KIND, AND WE'RE PROUD OF YOU.
I HATE TO SAY THIS, BUT...IF THERE'S ANOTHER INCIDENT WITH JAKE, WE'RE GOING TO HAVE TO MAKE SOME HARD DECISIONS ABOUT WHAT ACTIVITIES YOU CAN DO, OKAY?
IT'S OKAY, DAD. I UNDERSTAND.
GUESS I CAN FORGET ABOUT GOING TO THE MOVIES TONIGHT.

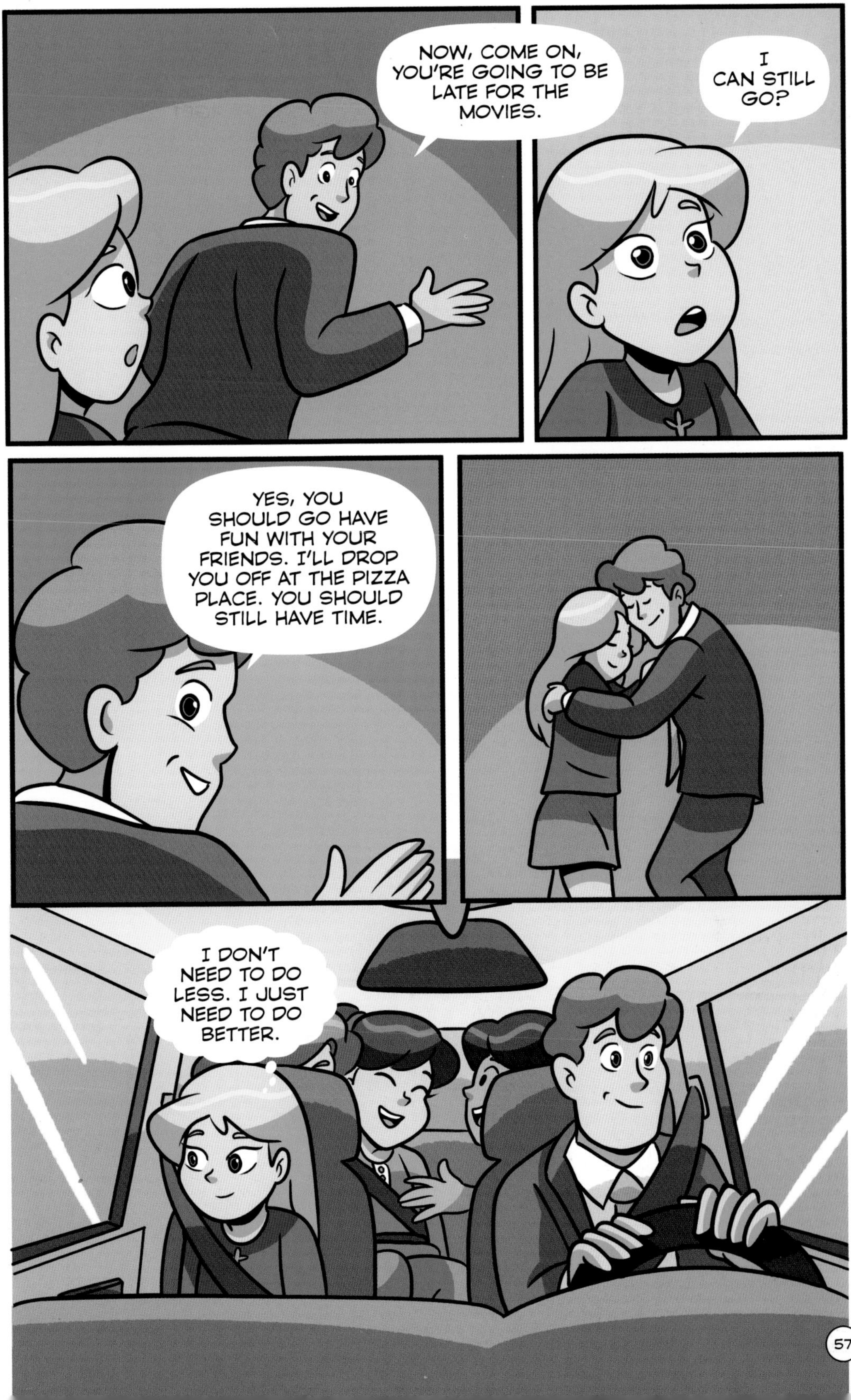
NOW, COME ON, YOU'RE GOING TO BE LATE FOR THE MOVIES.
I CAN STILL GO?
YES, YOU SHOULD GO HAVE FUN WITH YOUR FRIENDS. I'LL DROP YOU OFF AT THE PIZZA PLACE. YOU SHOULD STILL HAVE TIME.
I DON'T NEED TO DO LESS. I JUST NEED TO DO BETTER.

Chapter 5

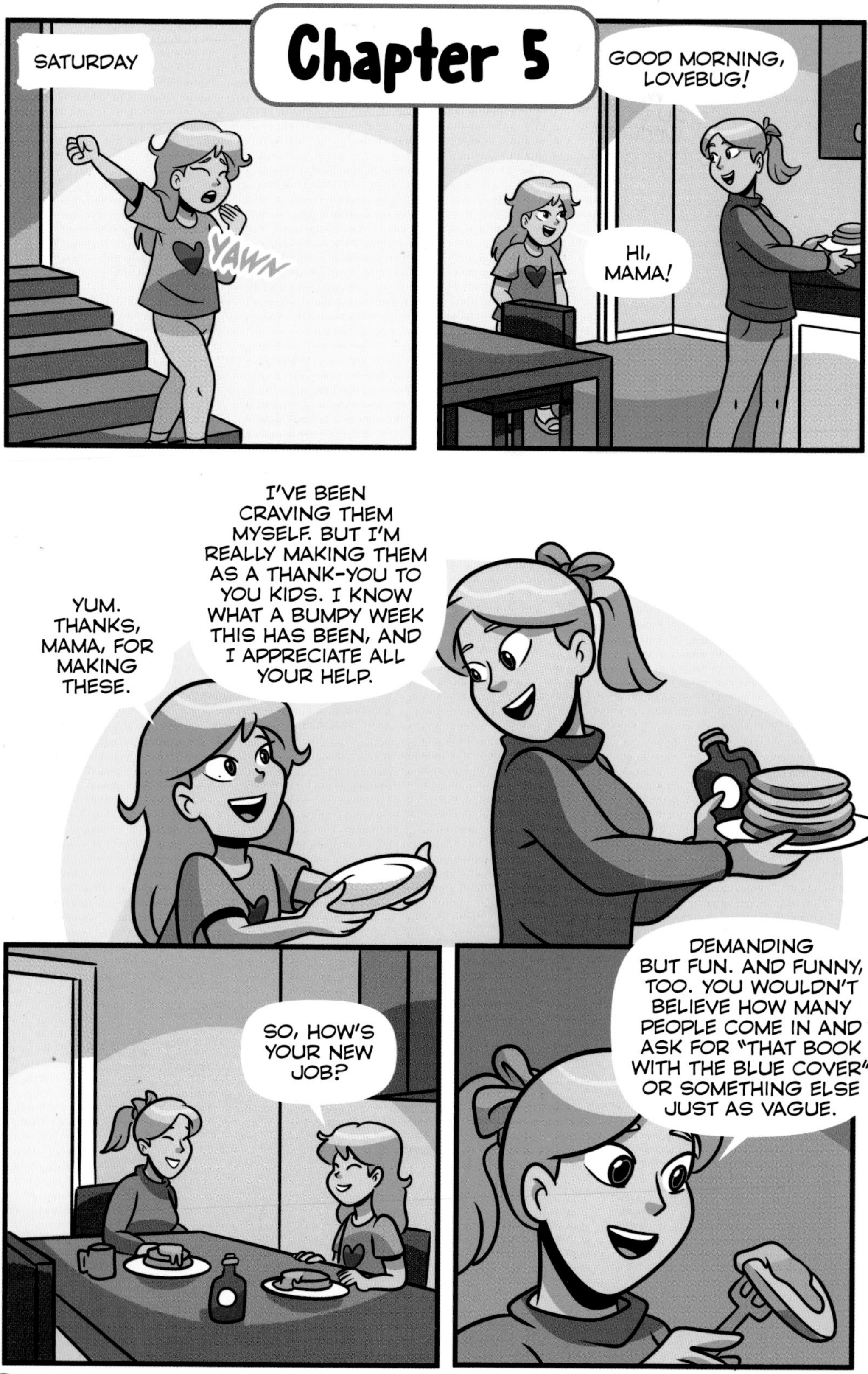

SATURDAY
YAWN
GOOD MORNING, LOVEBUG!
HI, MAMA!
YUM. THANKS, MAMA, FOR MAKING THESE.
I'VE BEEN CRAVING THEM MYSELF. BUT I'M REALLY MAKING THEM AS A THANK-YOU TO YOU KIDS. I KNOW WHAT A BUMPY WEEK THIS HAS BEEN, AND I APPRECIATE ALL YOUR HELP.
SO, HOW'S YOUR NEW JOB?
DEMANDING BUT FUN. AND FUNNY, TOO. YOU WOULDN'T BELIEVE HOW MANY PEOPLE COME IN AND ASK FOR "THAT BOOK WITH THE BLUE COVER" OR SOMETHING ELSE JUST AS VAGUE.

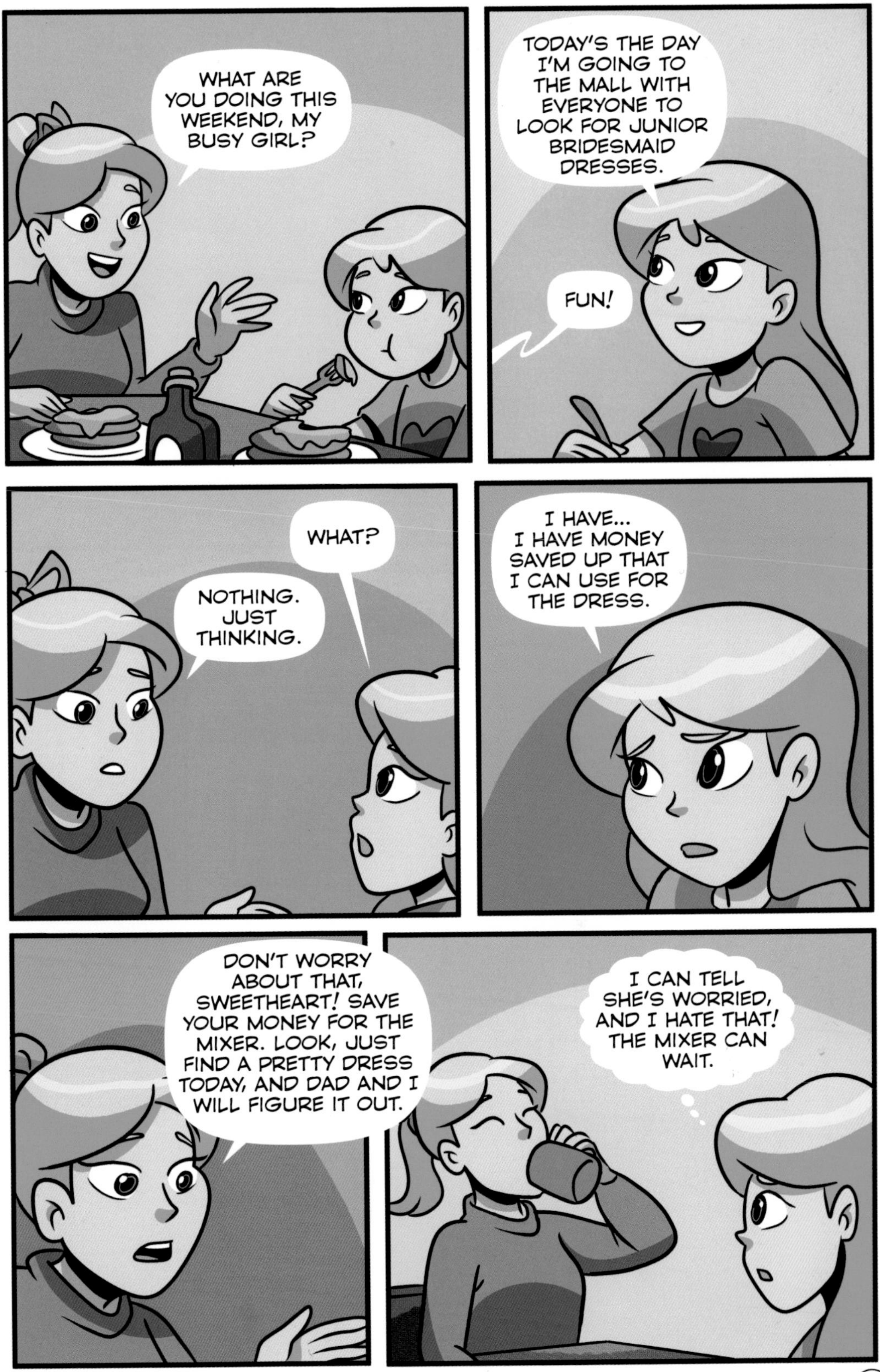
WHAT ARE YOU DOING THIS WEEKEND, MY BUSY GIRL?
TODAY'S THE DAY I'M GOING TO THE MALL WITH EVERYONE TO LOOK FOR JUNIOR BRIDESMAID DRESSES.
FUN!
WHAT?
NOTHING. JUST THINKING.
I HAVE... I HAVE MONEY SAVED UP THAT I CAN USE FOR THE DRESS.
DON'T WORRY ABOUT THAT, SWEETHEART! SAVE YOUR MONEY FOR THE MIXER. LOOK, JUST FIND A PRETTY DRESS TODAY, AND DAD AND I WILL FIGURE IT OUT.
I CAN TELL SHE'S WORRIED, AND I HATE THAT! THE MIXER CAN WAIT.

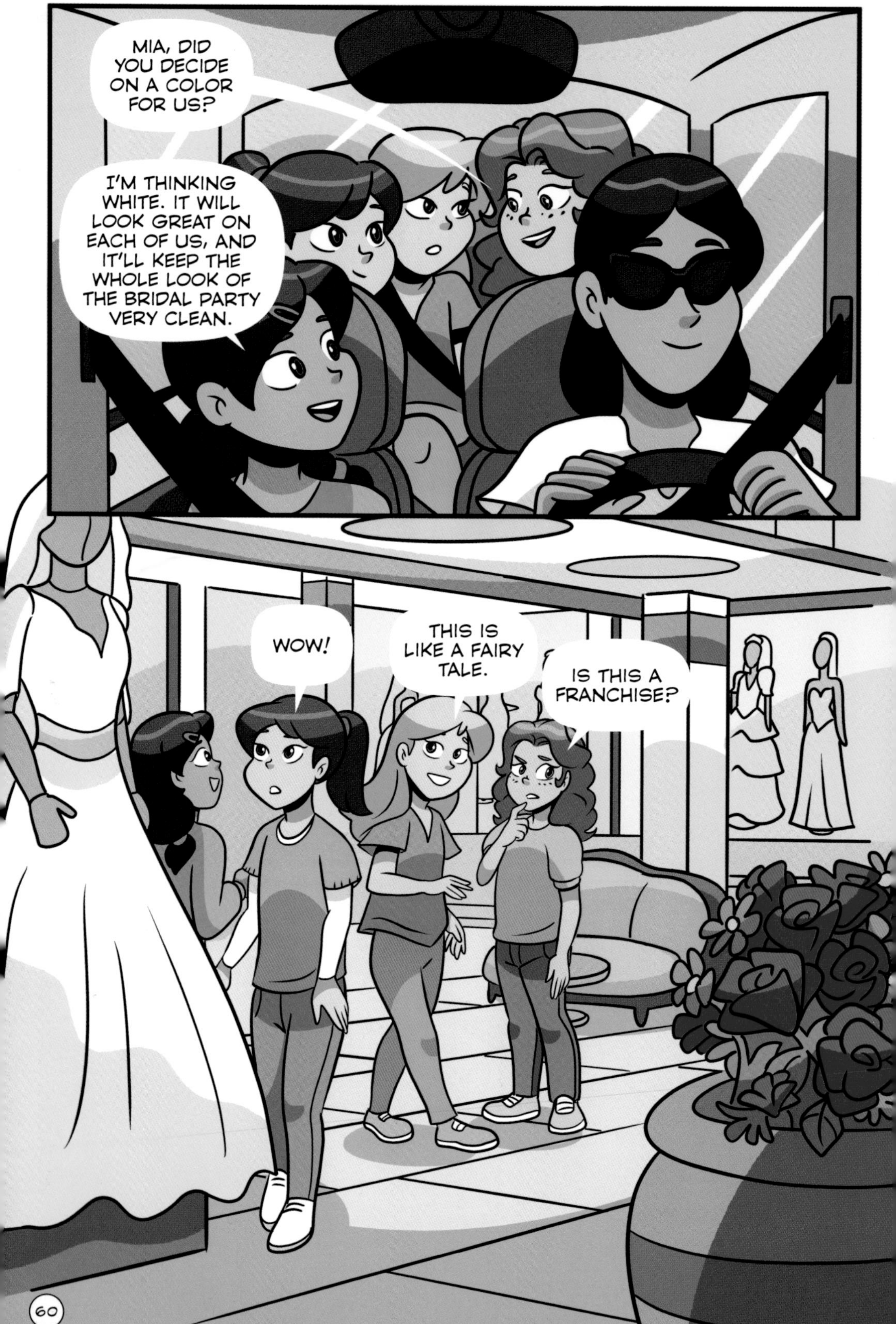
MIA, DID YOU DECIDE ON A COLOR FOR US?
I'M THINKING WHITE. IT WILL LOOK GREAT ON EACH OF US, AND IT'LL KEEP THE WHOLE LOOK OF THE BRIDAL PARTY VERY CLEAN.
WOW!
THIS IS LIKE A FAIRY TALE.
IS THIS A FRANCHISE?

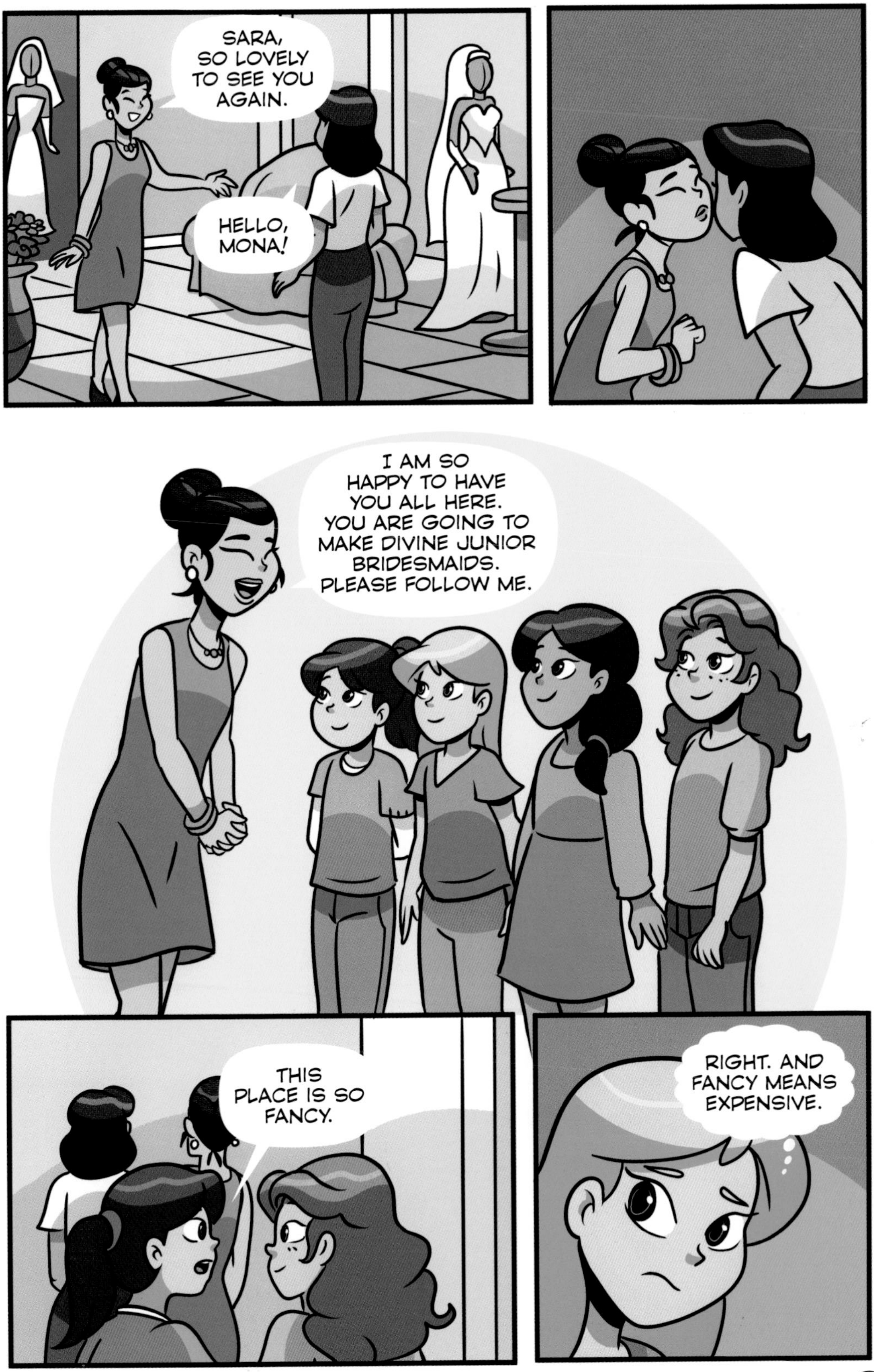
SARA, SO LOVELY TO SEE YOU AGAIN.
HELLO, MONA!
I AM SO HAPPY TO HAVE YOU ALL HERE. YOU ARE GOING TO MAKE DIVINE JUNIOR BRIDESMAIDS. PLEASE FOLLOW ME.
THIS PLACE IS SO FANCY.
RIGHT. AND FANCY MEANS EXPENSIVE.

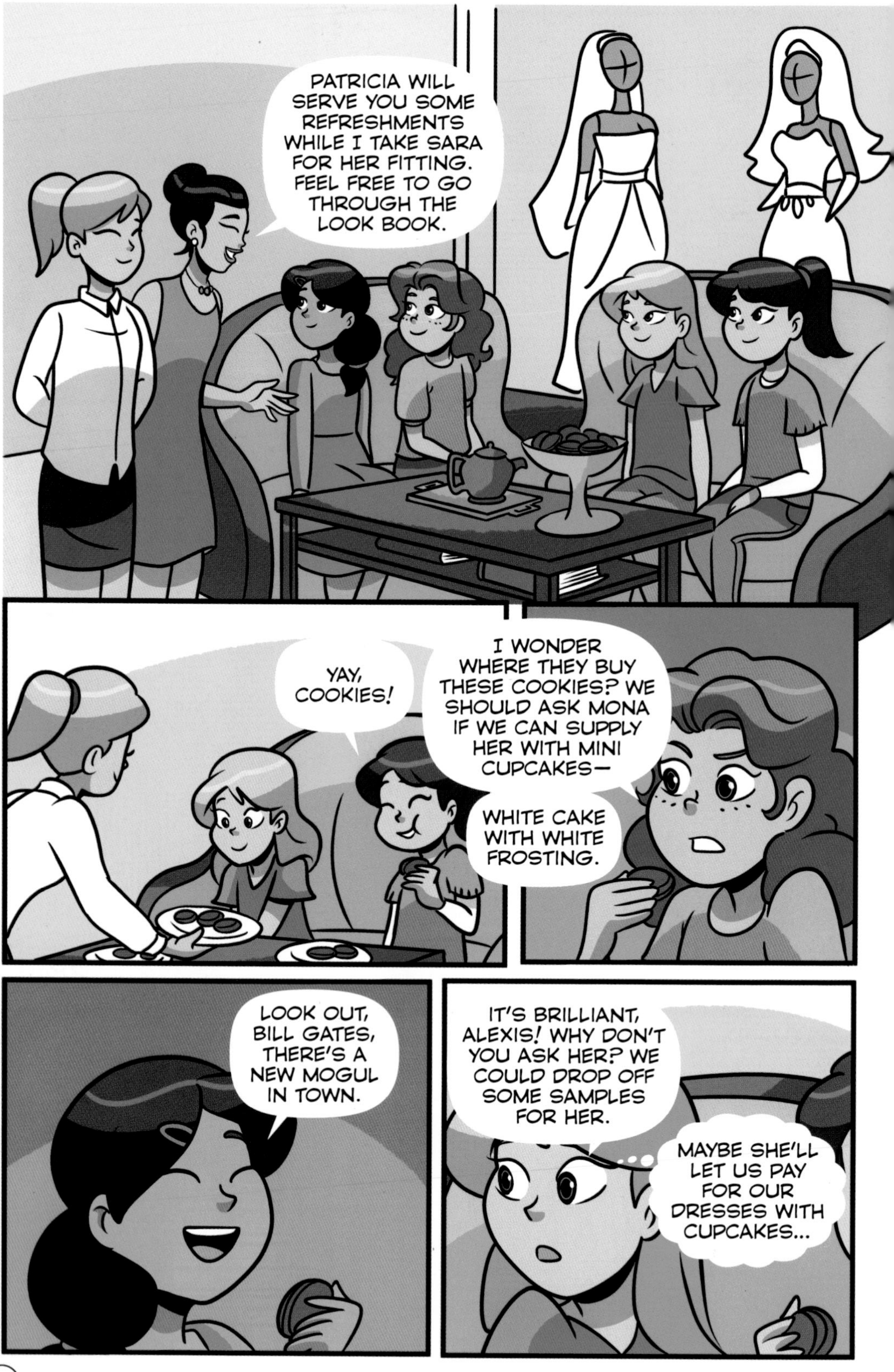
PATRICIA WILL SERVE YOU SOME REFRESHMENTS WHILE I TAKE SARA FOR HER FITTING. FEEL FREE TO GO THROUGH THE LOOK BOOK.
YAY, COOKIES!
I WONDER WHERE THEY BUY THESE COOKIES? WE SHOULD ASK MONA IF WE CAN SUPPLY HER WITH MINI CUPCAKES—
WHITE CAKE WITH WHITE FROSTING.
LOOK OUT, BILL GATES, THERE'S A NEW MOGUL IN TOWN.
IT'S BRILLIANT, ALEXIS! WHY DON'T YOU ASK HER? WE COULD DROP OFF SOME SAMPLES FOR HER.
MAYBE SHE'LL LET US PAY FOR OUR DRESSES WITH CUPCAKES...

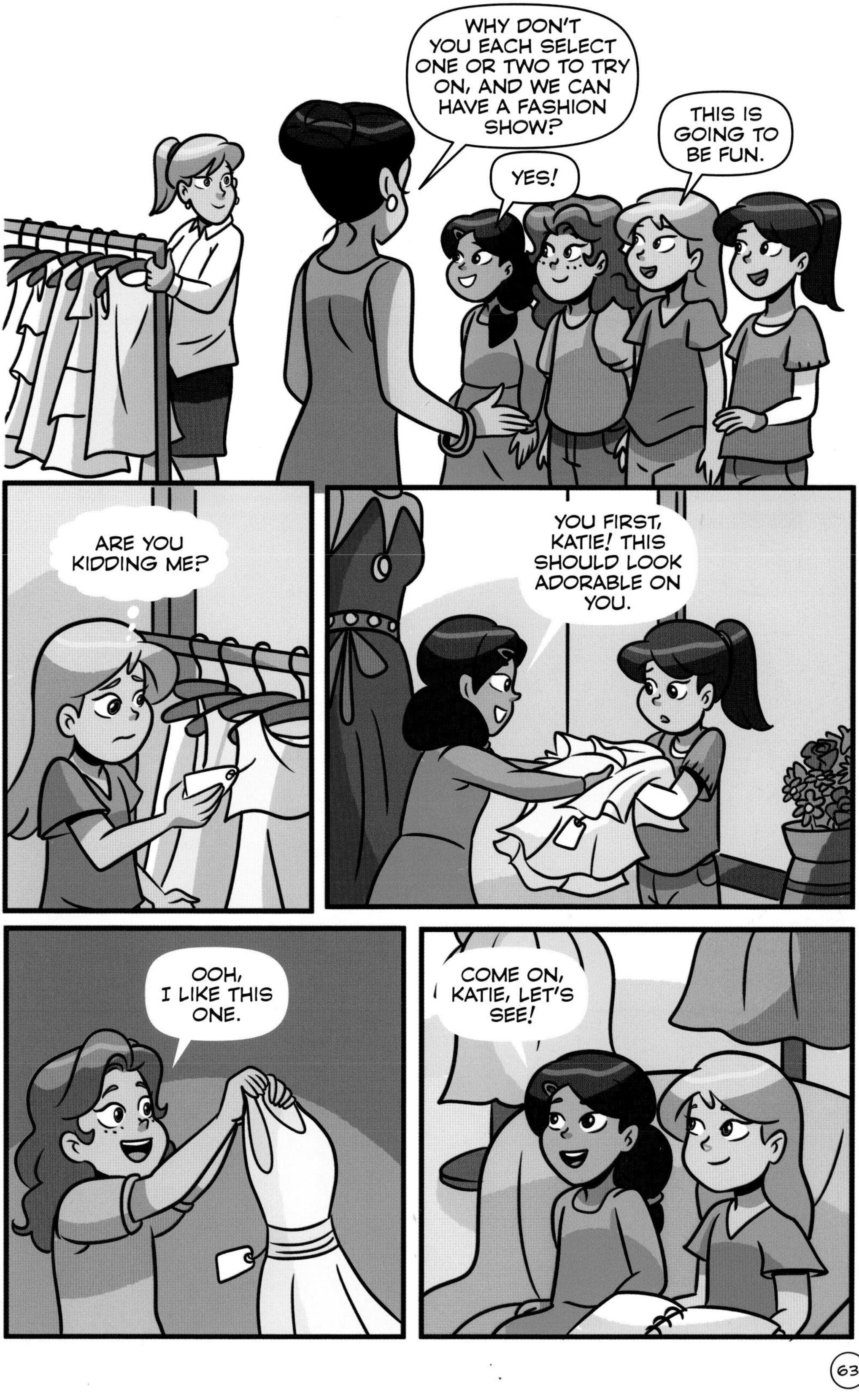
WHY DON'T YOU EACH SELECT ONE OR TWO TO TRY ON, AND WE CAN HAVE A FASHION SHOW?
YES!
THIS IS GOING TO BE FUN.
ARE YOU KIDDING ME?
YOU FIRST, KATIE! THIS SHOULD LOOK ADORABLE ON YOU.
OOH, I LIKE THIS ONE.
COME ON, KATIE, LET'S SEE!

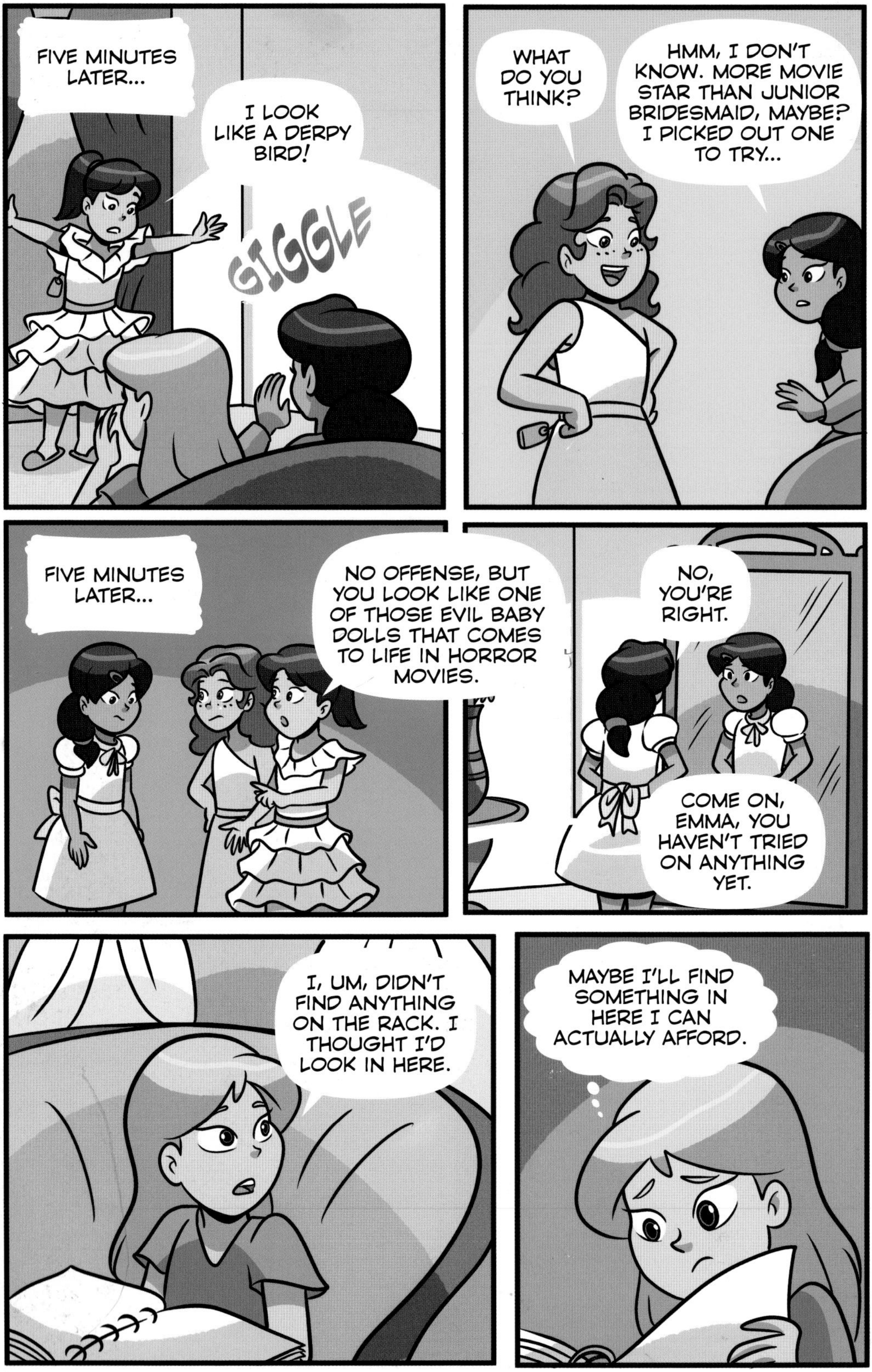
FIVE MINUTES LATER...
I LOOK LIKE A DERPY BIRD!
GIGGLE
WHAT DO YOU THINK?
HMM, I DON'T KNOW. MORE MOVIE STAR THAN JUNIOR BRIDESMAID, MAYBE? I PICKED OUT ONE TO TRY...
FIVE MINUTES LATER...
NO OFFENSE, BUT YOU LOOK LIKE ONE OF THOSE EVIL BABY DOLLS THAT COMES TO LIFE IN HORROR MOVIES.
NO, YOU'RE RIGHT.
COME ON, EMMA, YOU HAVEN'T TRIED ON ANYTHING YET.
I, UM, DIDN'T FIND ANYTHING ON THE RACK. I THOUGHT I'D LOOK IN HERE.
MAYBE I'LL FIND SOMETHING IN HERE I CAN ACTUALLY AFFORD.

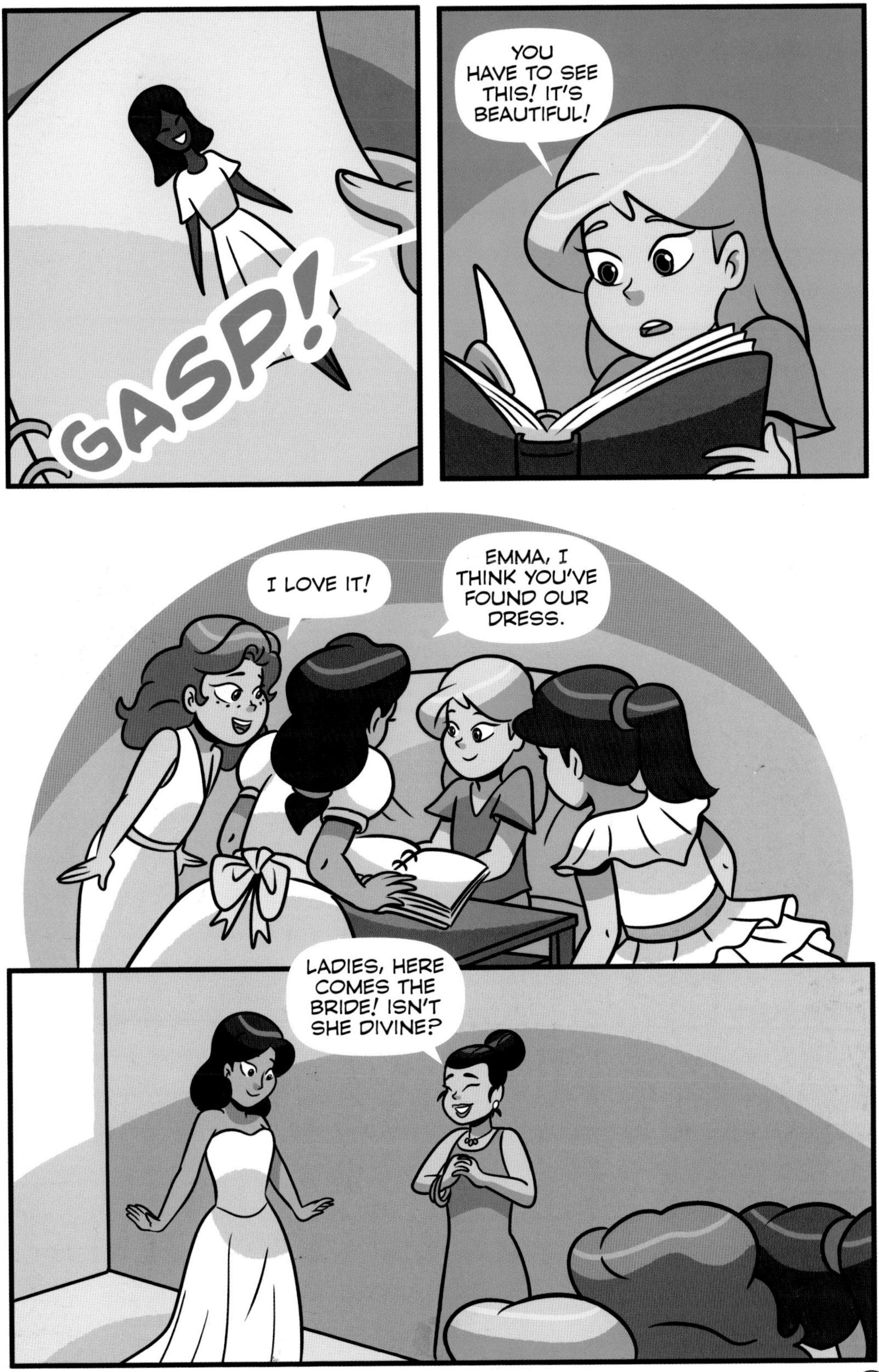
GASP!
YOU HAVE TO SEE THIS! IT'S BEAUTIFUL!
I LOVE IT!
EMMA, I THINK YOU'VE FOUND OUR DRESS.
LADIES, HERE COMES THE BRIDE! ISN'T SHE DIVINE?

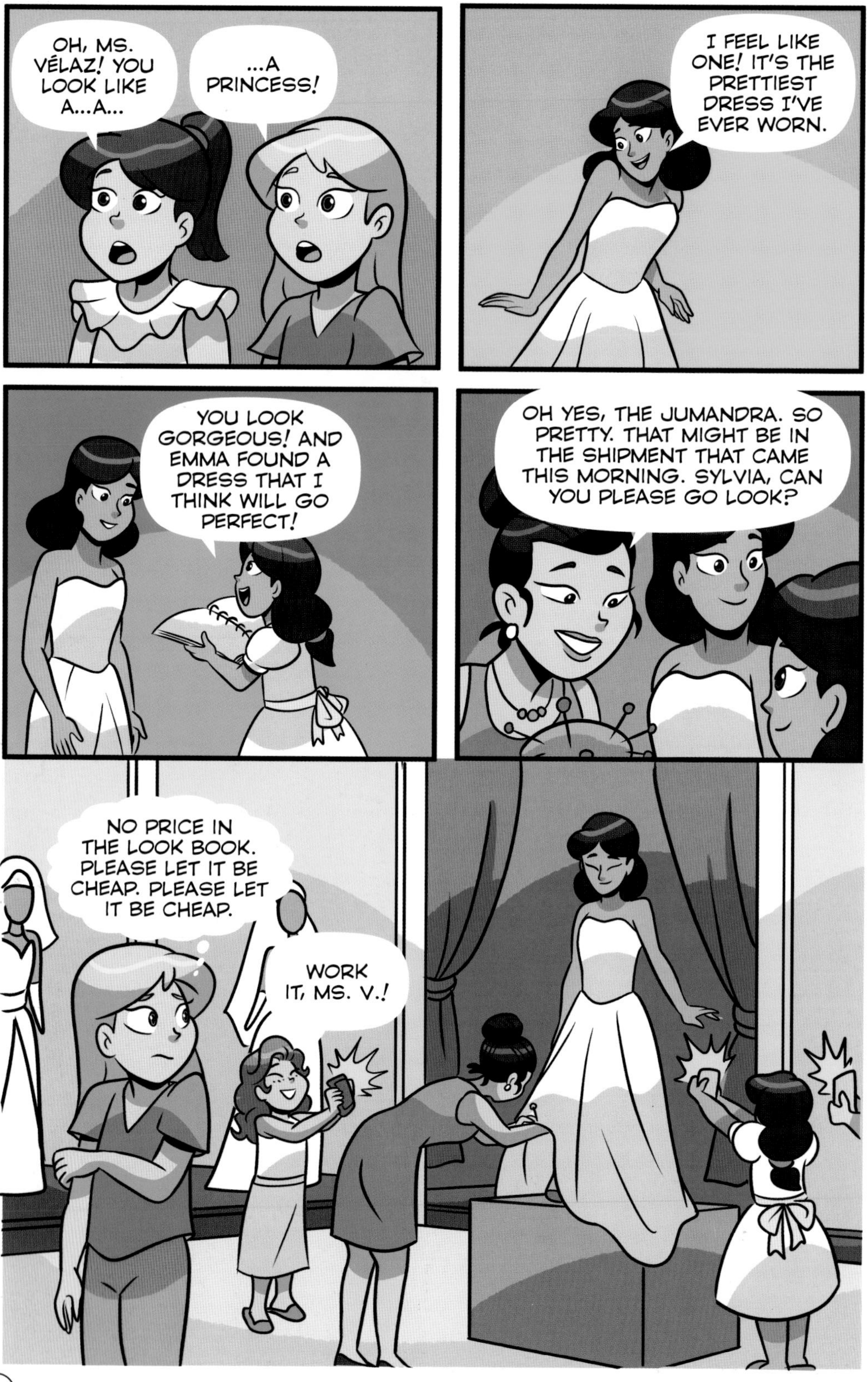
OH, MS. VÉLAZ! YOU LOOK LIKE A...A...
...A PRINCESS!
I FEEL LIKE ONE! IT'S THE PRETTIEST DRESS I'VE EVER WORN.
YOU LOOK GORGEOUS! AND EMMA FOUND A DRESS THAT I THINK WILL GO PERFECT!
OH YES, THE JUMANDRA. SO PRETTY. THAT MIGHT BE IN THE SHIPMENT THAT CAME THIS MORNING. SYLVIA, CAN YOU PLEASE GO LOOK?
NO PRICE IN THE LOOK BOOK. PLEASE LET IT BE CHEAP. PLEASE LET IT BE CHEAP.
WORK IT, MS. V.!

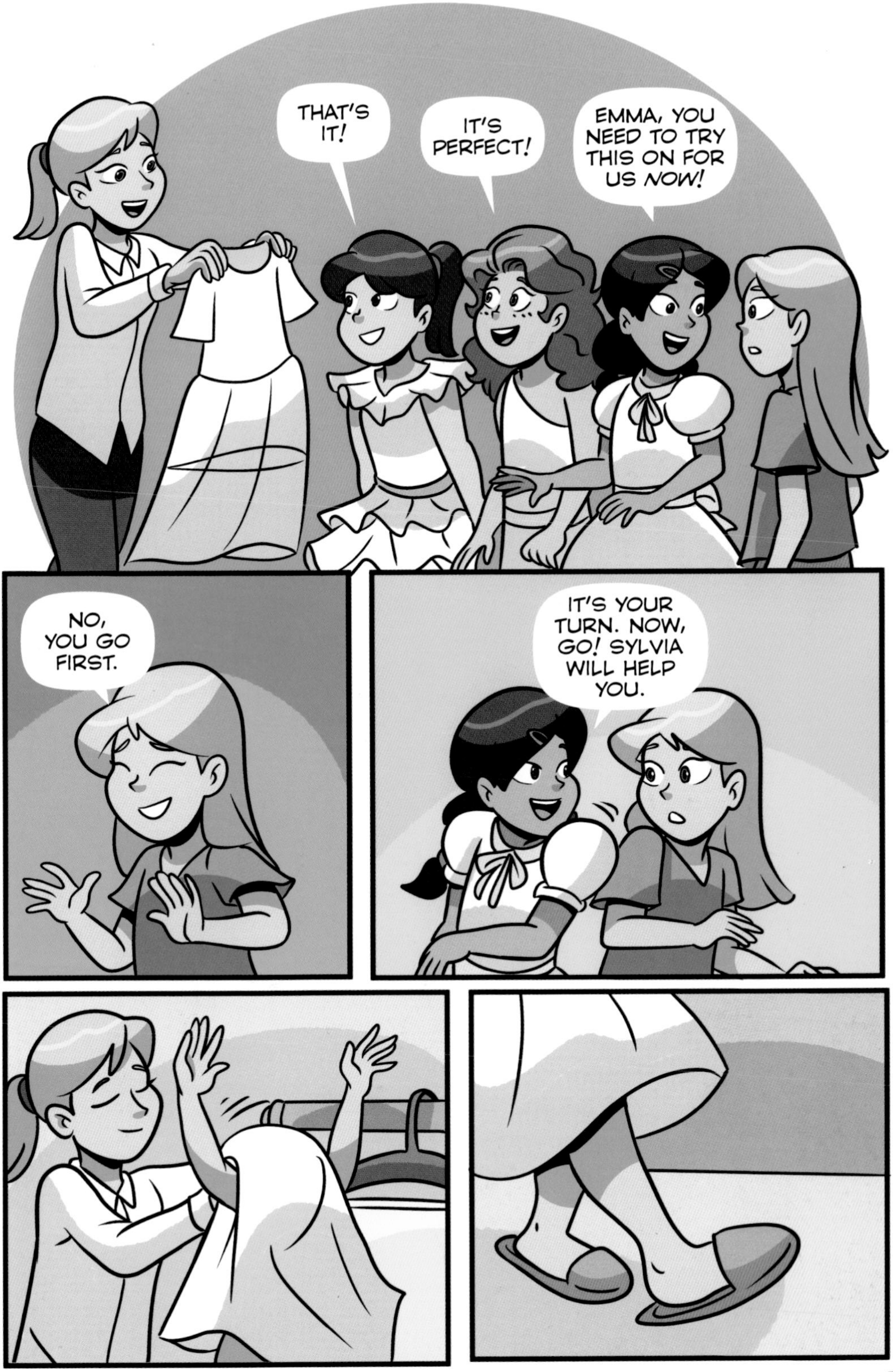
THAT'S IT!
IT'S PERFECT!
EMMA, YOU NEED TO TRY THIS ON FOR US NOW!
NO, YOU GO FIRST.
IT'S YOUR TURN. NOW, GO! SYLVIA WILL HELP YOU.

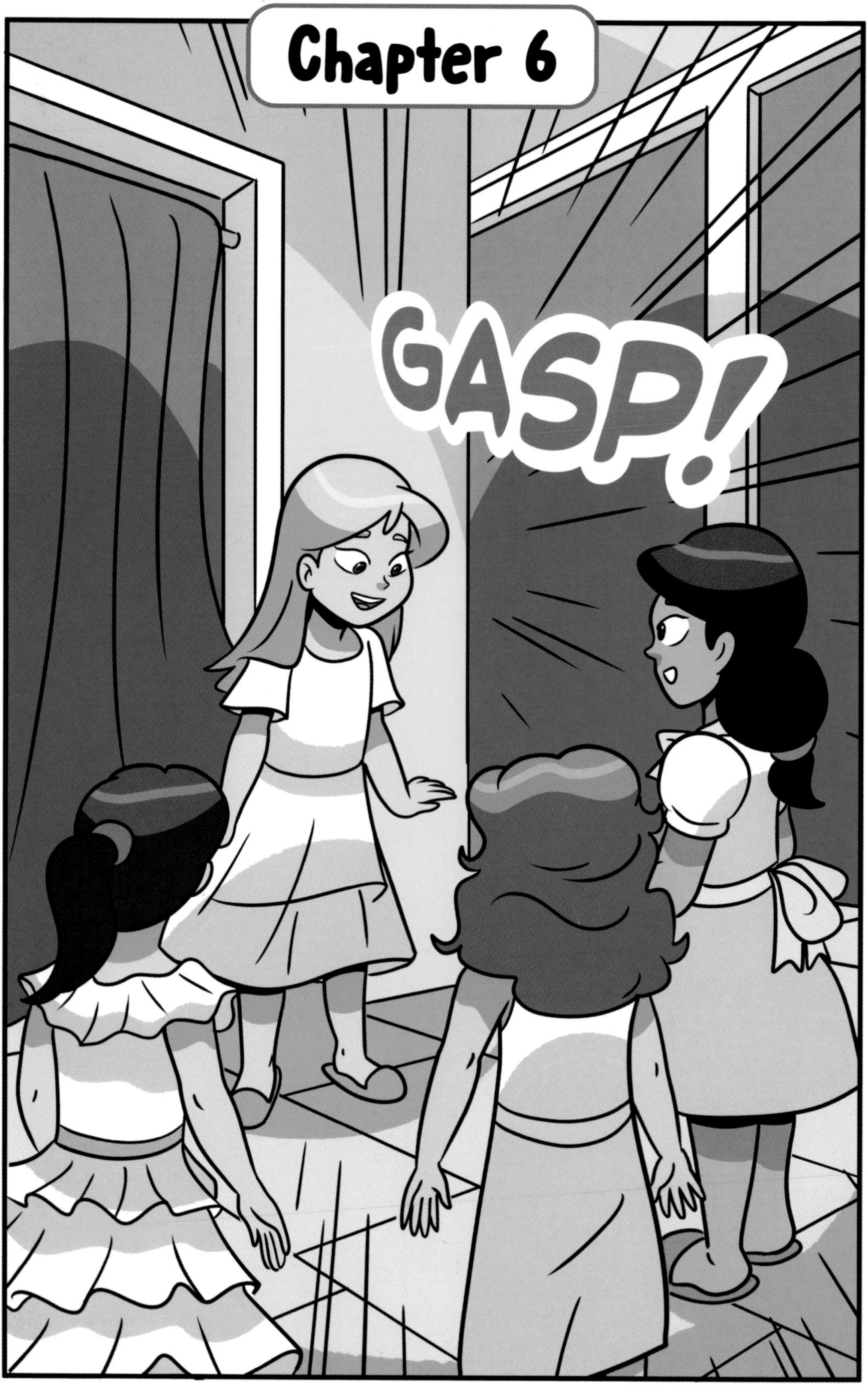
Chapter 6
GASP!

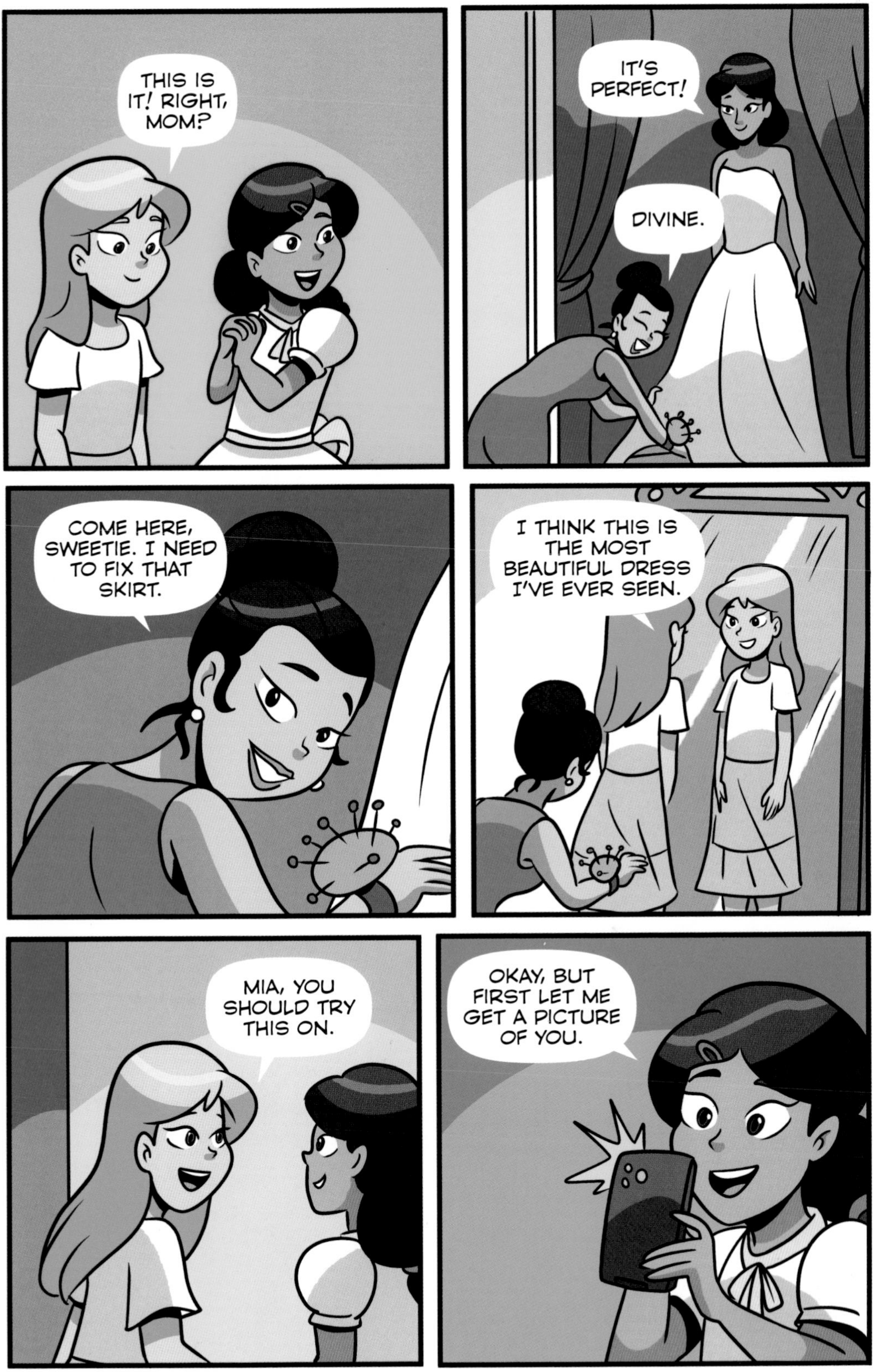
THIS IS IT! RIGHT, MOM?
IT'S PERFECT!
DIVINE.
COME HERE, SWEETIE. I NEED TO FIX THAT SKIRT.
I THINK THIS IS THE MOST BEAUTIFUL DRESS I'VE EVER SEEN.
MIA, YOU SHOULD TRY THIS ON.
OKAY, BUT FIRST LET ME GET A PICTURE OF YOU.

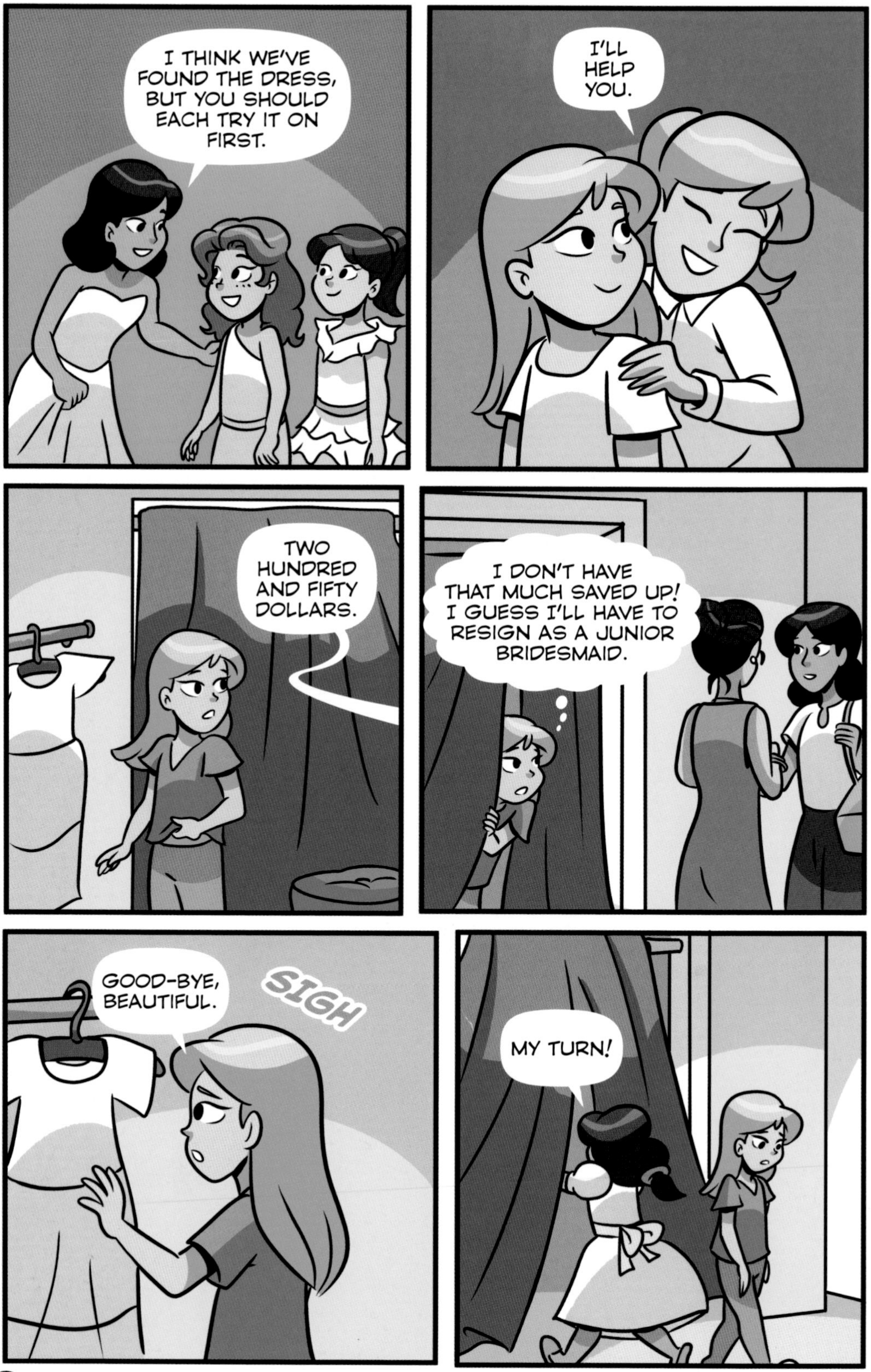
I THINK WE'VE FOUND THE DRESS, BUT YOU SHOULD EACH TRY IT ON FIRST.
I'LL HELP YOU.
TWO HUNDRED AND FIFTY DOLLARS.
I DON'T HAVE THAT MUCH SAVED UP! I GUESS I'LL HAVE TO RESIGN AS A JUNIOR BRIDESMAID.
GOOD-BYE, BEAUTIFUL.
SIGH
MY TURN!

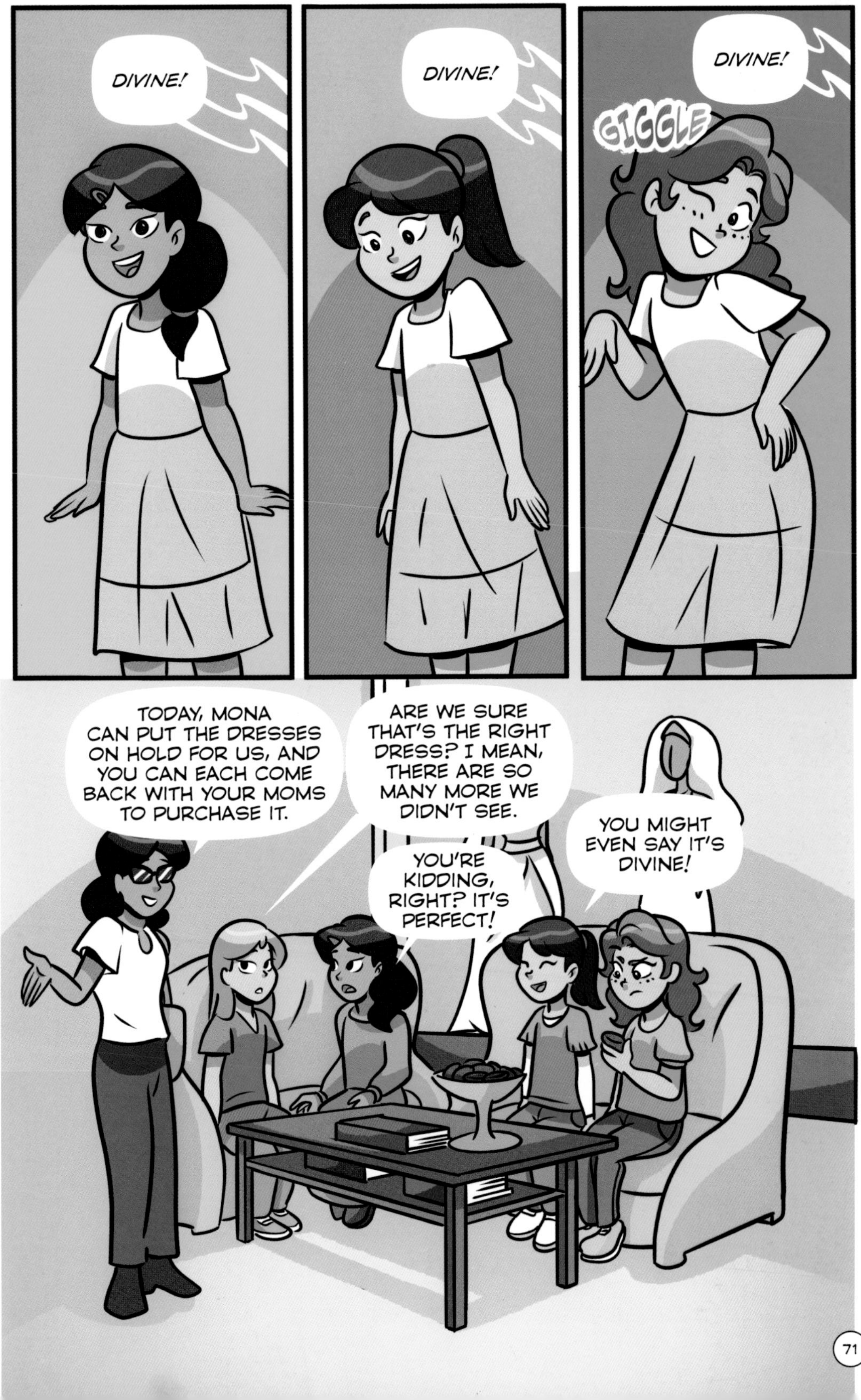
DIVINE!
DIVINE!
DIVINE!
GIGGLE
TODAY, MONA CAN PUT THE DRESSES ON HOLD FOR US, AND YOU CAN EACH COME BACK WITH YOUR MOMS TO PURCHASE IT.
ARE WE SURE THAT'S THE RIGHT DRESS? I MEAN, THERE ARE SO MANY MORE WE DIDN'T SEE.
YOU'RE KIDDING, RIGHT? IT'S PERFECT!
YOU MIGHT EVEN SAY IT'S DIVINE!

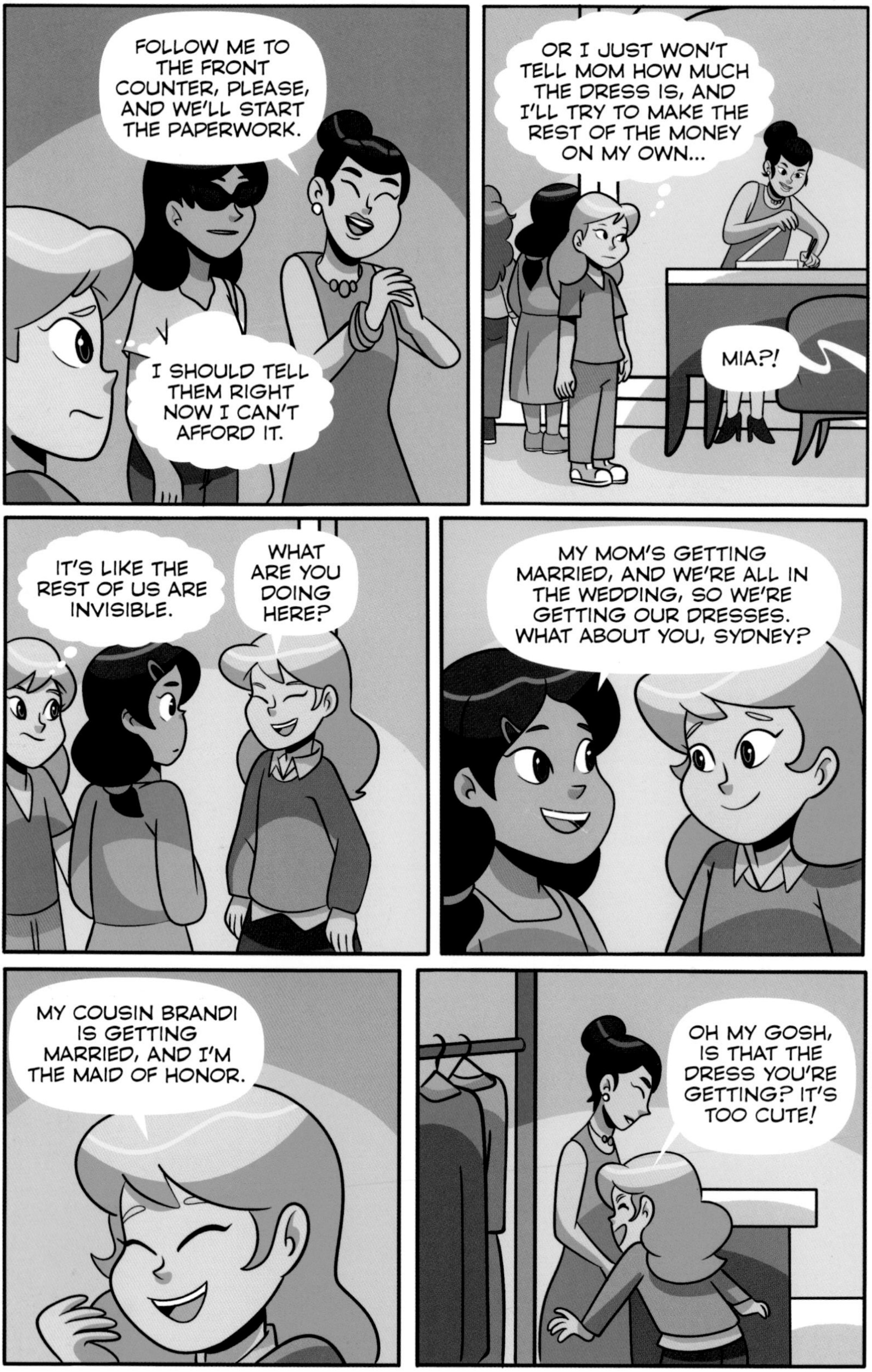
FOLLOW ME TO THE FRONT COUNTER, PLEASE, AND WE'LL START THE PAPERWORK.
I SHOULD TELL THEM RIGHT NOW I CAN'T AFFORD IT.
OR I JUST WON'T TELL MOM HOW MUCH THE DRESS IS, AND I'LL TRY TO MAKE THE REST OF THE MONEY ON MY OWN...
MIA?!
IT'S LIKE THE REST OF US ARE INVISIBLE.
WHAT ARE YOU DOING HERE?
MY MOM'S GETTING MARRIED, AND WE'RE ALL IN THE WEDDING, SO WE'RE GETTING OUR DRESSES. WHAT ABOUT YOU, SYDNEY?
MY COUSIN BRANDI IS GETTING MARRIED, AND I'M THE MAID OF HONOR.
OH MY GOSH, IS THAT THE DRESS YOU'RE GETTING? IT'S TOO CUTE!

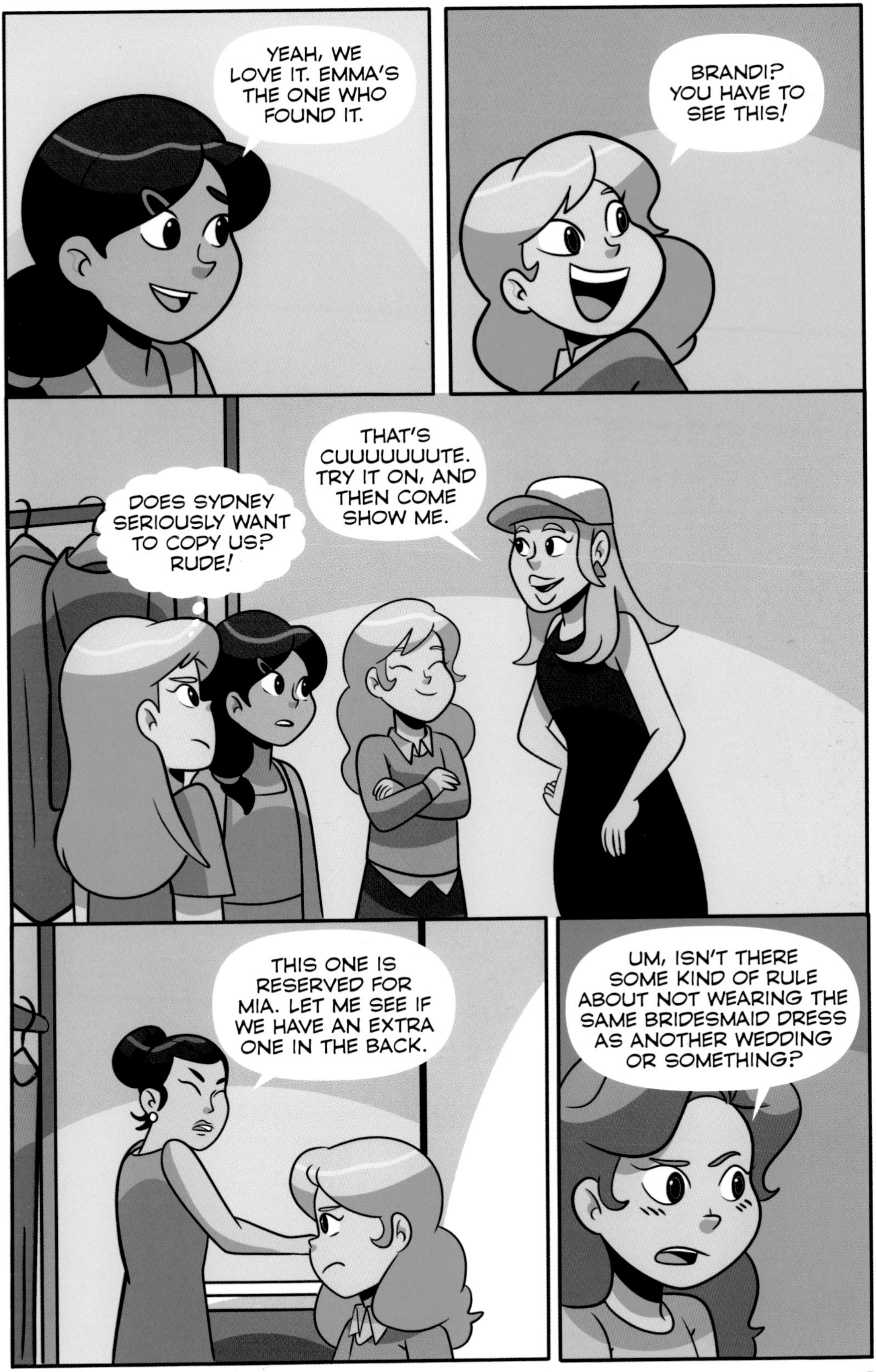
YEAH, WE LOVE IT. EMMA'S THE ONE WHO FOUND IT.
BRANDI? YOU HAVE TO SEE THIS!
DOES SYDNEY SERIOUSLY WANT TO COPY US? RUDE!
THAT'S CUUUUUUUTE. TRY IT ON, AND THEN COME SHOW ME.
THIS ONE IS RESERVED FOR MIA. LET ME SEE IF WE HAVE AN EXTRA ONE IN THE BACK.
UM, ISN'T THERE SOME KIND OF RULE ABOUT NOT WEARING THE SAME BRIDESMAID DRESS AS ANOTHER WEDDING OR SOMETHING?

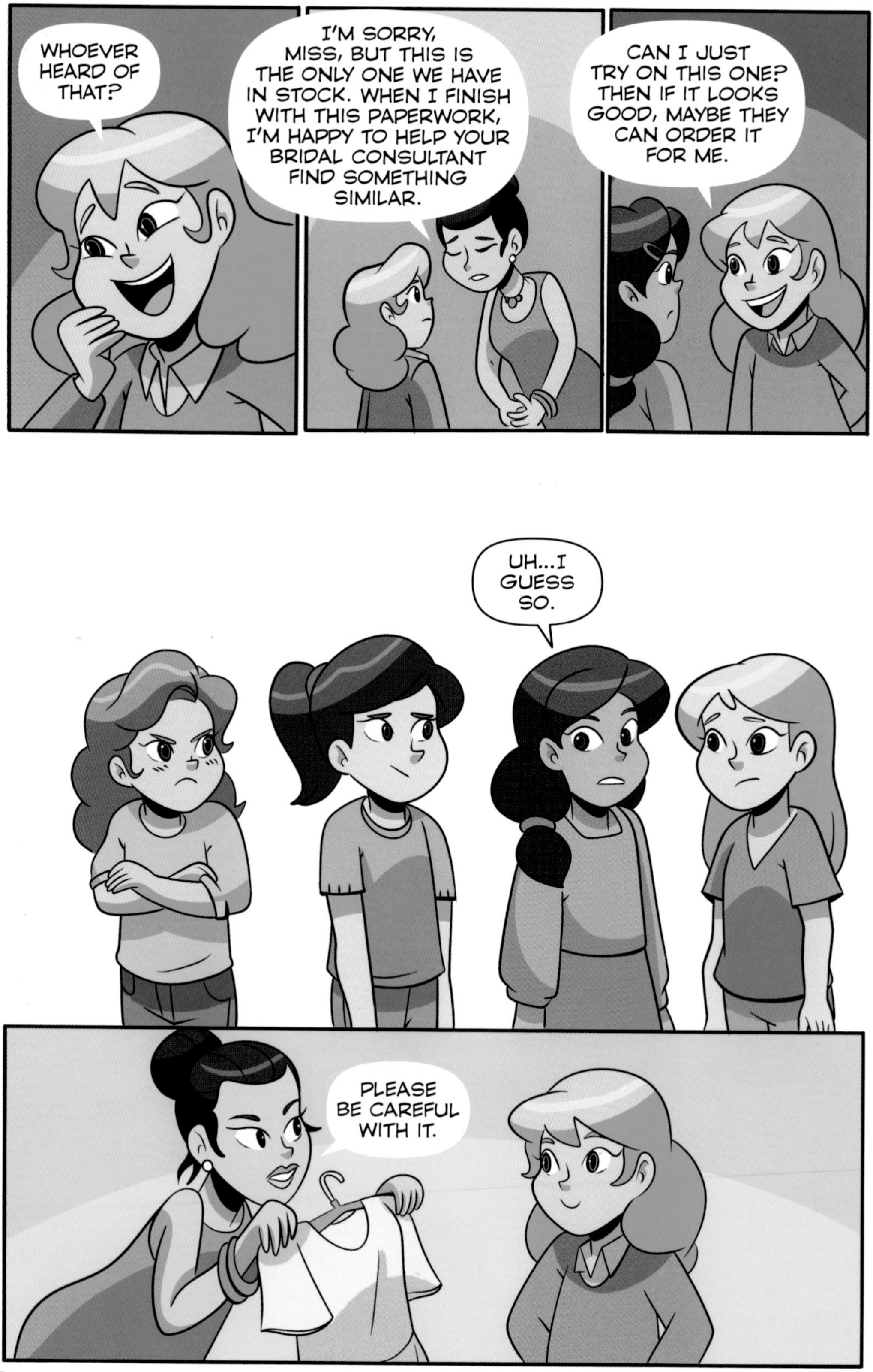
WHOEVER HEARD OF THAT?
I'M SORRY, MISS, BUT THIS IS THE ONLY ONE WE HAVE IN STOCK. WHEN I FINISH WITH THIS PAPERWORK, I'M HAPPY TO HELP YOUR BRIDAL CONSULTANT FIND SOMETHING SIMILAR.
CAN I JUST TRY ON THIS ONE? THEN IF IT LOOKS GOOD, MAYBE THEY CAN ORDER IT FOR ME.
UH...I GUESS SO.
PLEASE BE CAREFUL WITH IT.

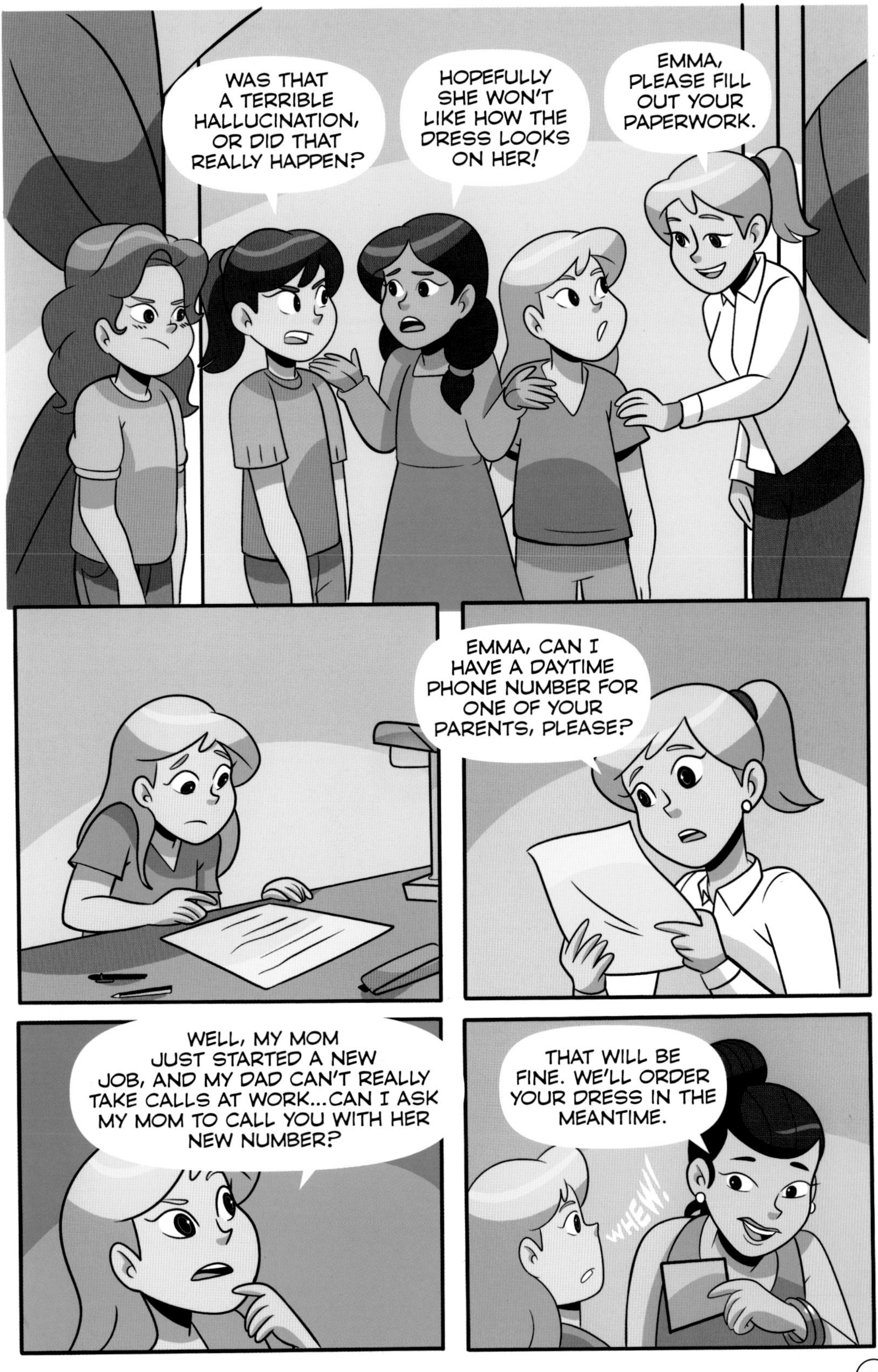
WAS THAT A TERRIBLE HALLUCINATION, OR DID THAT REALLY HAPPEN?
HOPEFULLY SHE WON'T LIKE HOW THE DRESS LOOKS ON HER!
EMMA, PLEASE FILL OUT YOUR PAPERWORK.
EMMA, CAN I HAVE A DAYTIME PHONE NUMBER FOR ONE OF YOUR PARENTS, PLEASE?
WELL, MY MOM JUST STARTED A NEW JOB, AND MY DAD CAN'T REALLY TAKE CALLS AT WORK...CAN I ASK MY MOM TO CALL YOU WITH HER NEW NUMBER?
THAT WILL BE FINE. WE'LL ORDER YOUR DRESS IN THE MEANTIME.
WHEW!

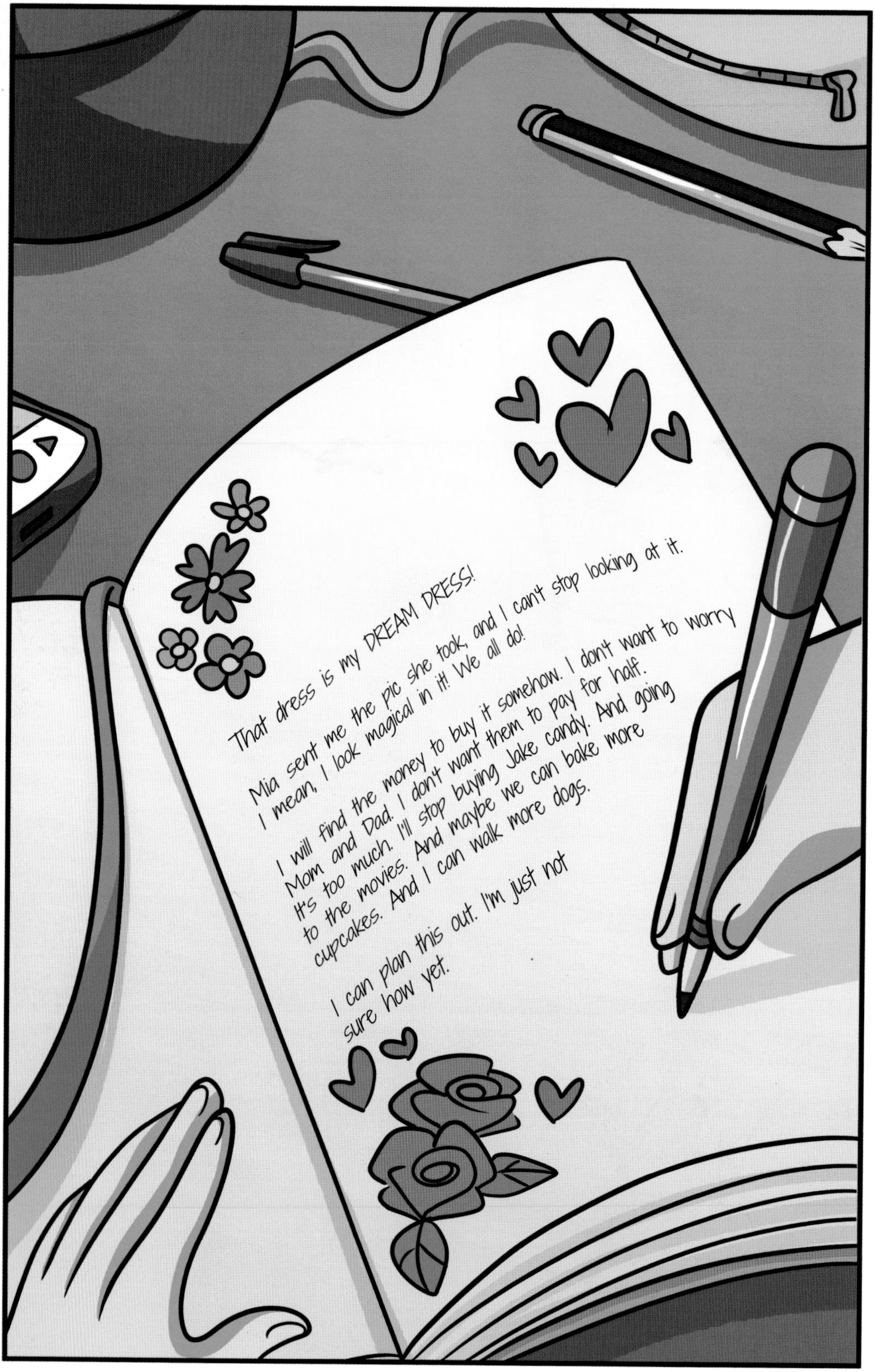
That dress is my DREAM DRESS!
Mia sent me the pic she took, and I can't stop looking at it. I mean, I look magical in it! We all do!
I will find the money to buy it somehow. I don't want to worry Mom and Dad. I don't want them to pay for half. It's too much. I'll stop buying Jake candy. And going to the movies. And maybe we can bake more cupcakes. And I can walk more dogs.
I can plan this out. I'm just not sure how yet.

Chapter 7

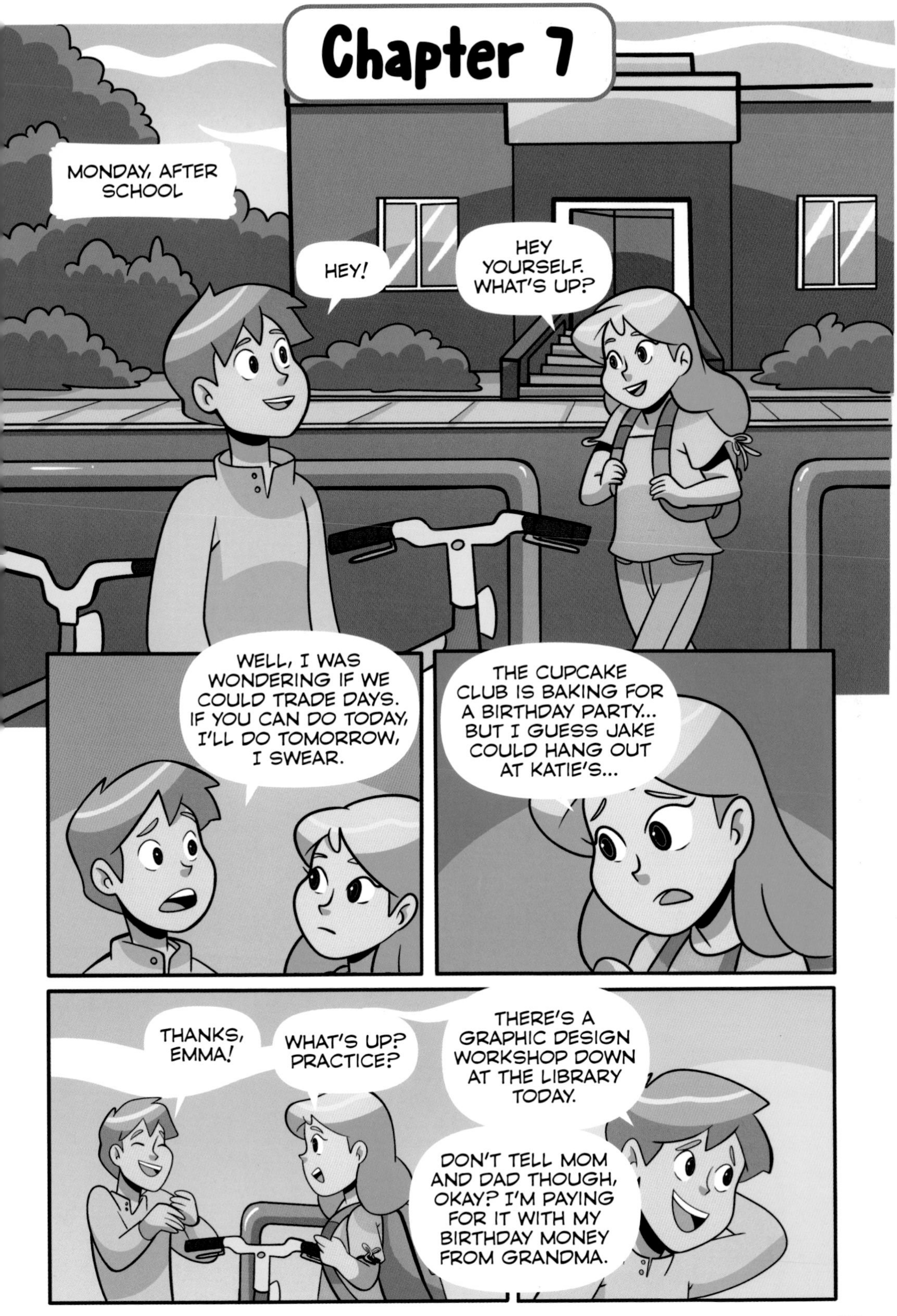
MONDAY, AFTER SCHOOL
HEY!
HEY YOURSELF. WHAT'S UP?
WELL, I WAS WONDERING IF WE COULD TRADE DAYS. IF YOU CAN DO TODAY, I'LL DO TOMORROW, I SWEAR.
THE CUPCAKE CLUB IS BAKING FOR A BIRTHDAY PARTY... BUT I GUESS JAKE COULD HANG OUT AT KATIE'S...
THANKS, EMMA!
WHAT'S UP? PRACTICE?
THERE'S A GRAPHIC DESIGN WORKSHOP DOWN AT THE LIBRARY TODAY.
DON'T TELL MOM AND DAD THOUGH, OKAY? I'M PAYING FOR IT WITH MY BIRTHDAY MONEY FROM GRANDMA.

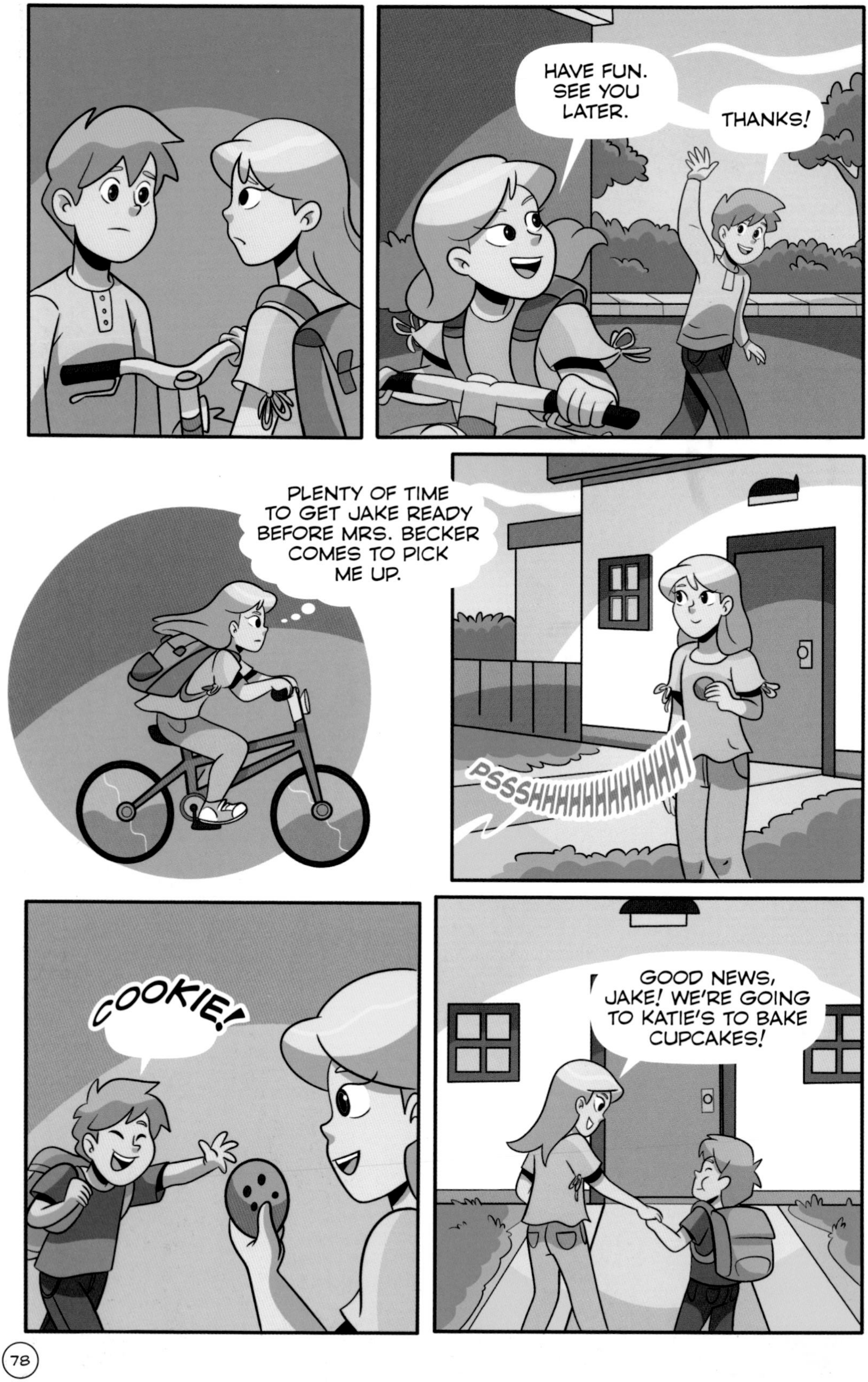
HAVE FUN. SEE YOU LATER.
THANKS!
PLENTY OF TIME TO GET JAKE READY BEFORE MRS. BECKER COMES TO PICK ME UP.
PSSSHHHHHHHHHHHHT
COOKIE!
GOOD NEWS, JAKE! WE'RE GOING TO KATIE'S TO BAKE CUPCAKES!

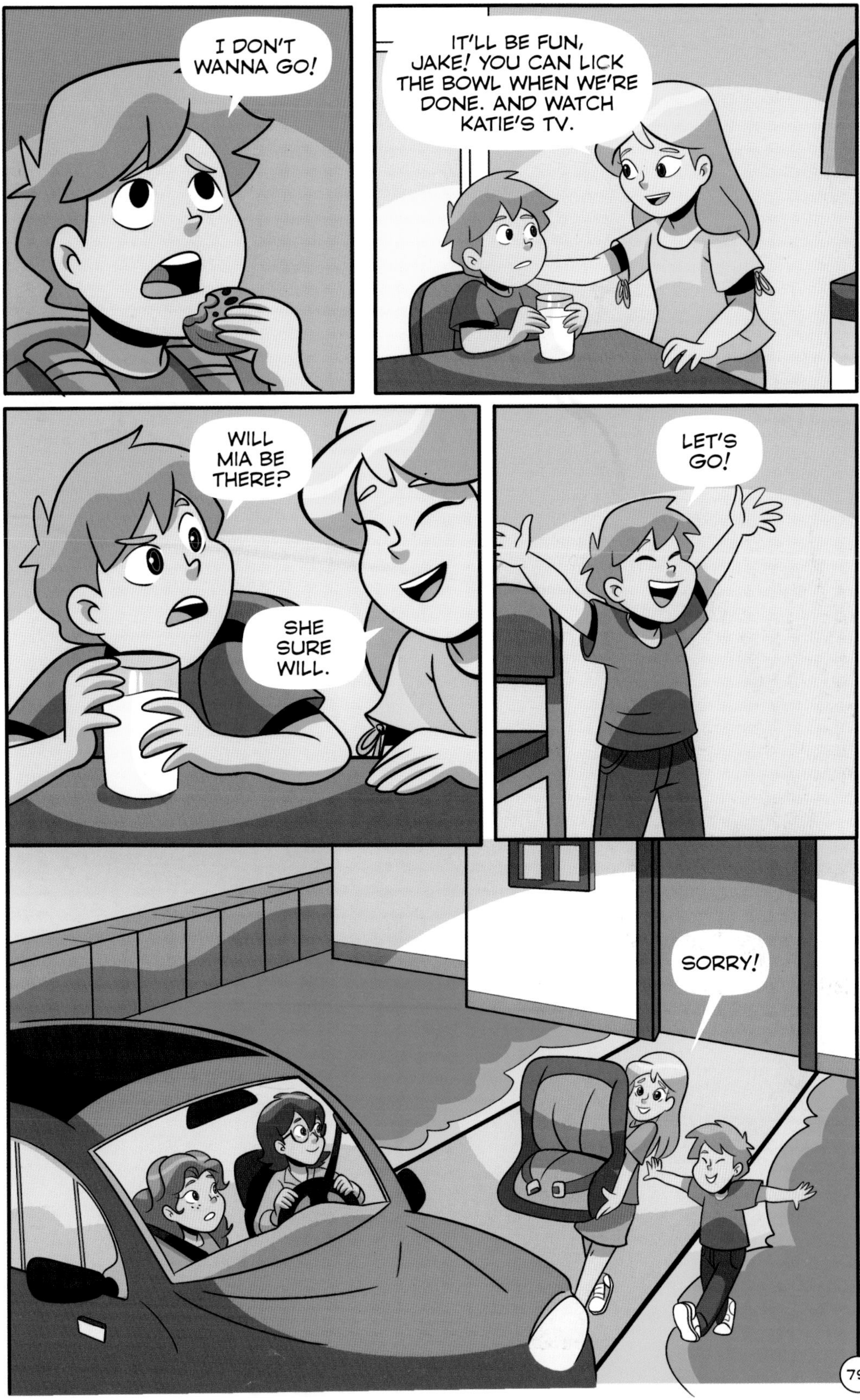
I DON'T WANNA GO!
IT'LL BE FUN, JAKE! YOU CAN LICK THE BOWL WHEN WE'RE DONE. AND WATCH KATIE'S TV.
WILL MIA BE THERE?
SHE SURE WILL.
LET'S GO!
SORRY!

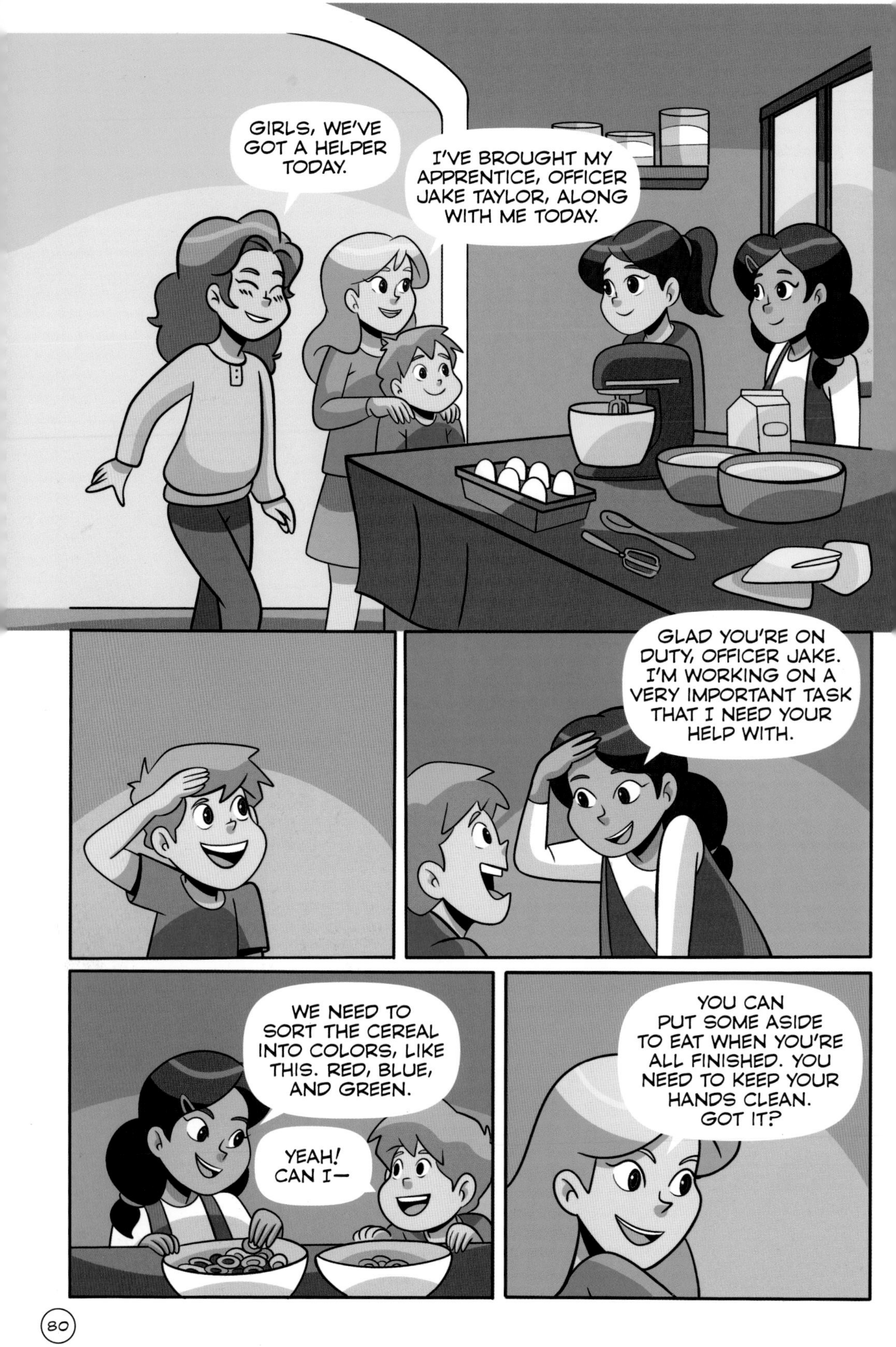
GIRLS, WE'VE GOT A HELPER TODAY.
I'VE BROUGHT MY APPRENTICE, OFFICER JAKE TAYLOR, ALONG WITH ME TODAY.
GLAD YOU'RE ON DUTY, OFFICER JAKE. I'M WORKING ON A VERY IMPORTANT TASK THAT I NEED YOUR HELP WITH.
WE NEED TO SORT THE CEREAL INTO COLORS, LIKE THIS. RED, BLUE, AND GREEN.
YEAH! CAN I—
YOU CAN PUT SOME ASIDE TO EAT WHEN YOU'RE ALL FINISHED. YOU NEED TO KEEP YOUR HANDS CLEAN. GOT IT?

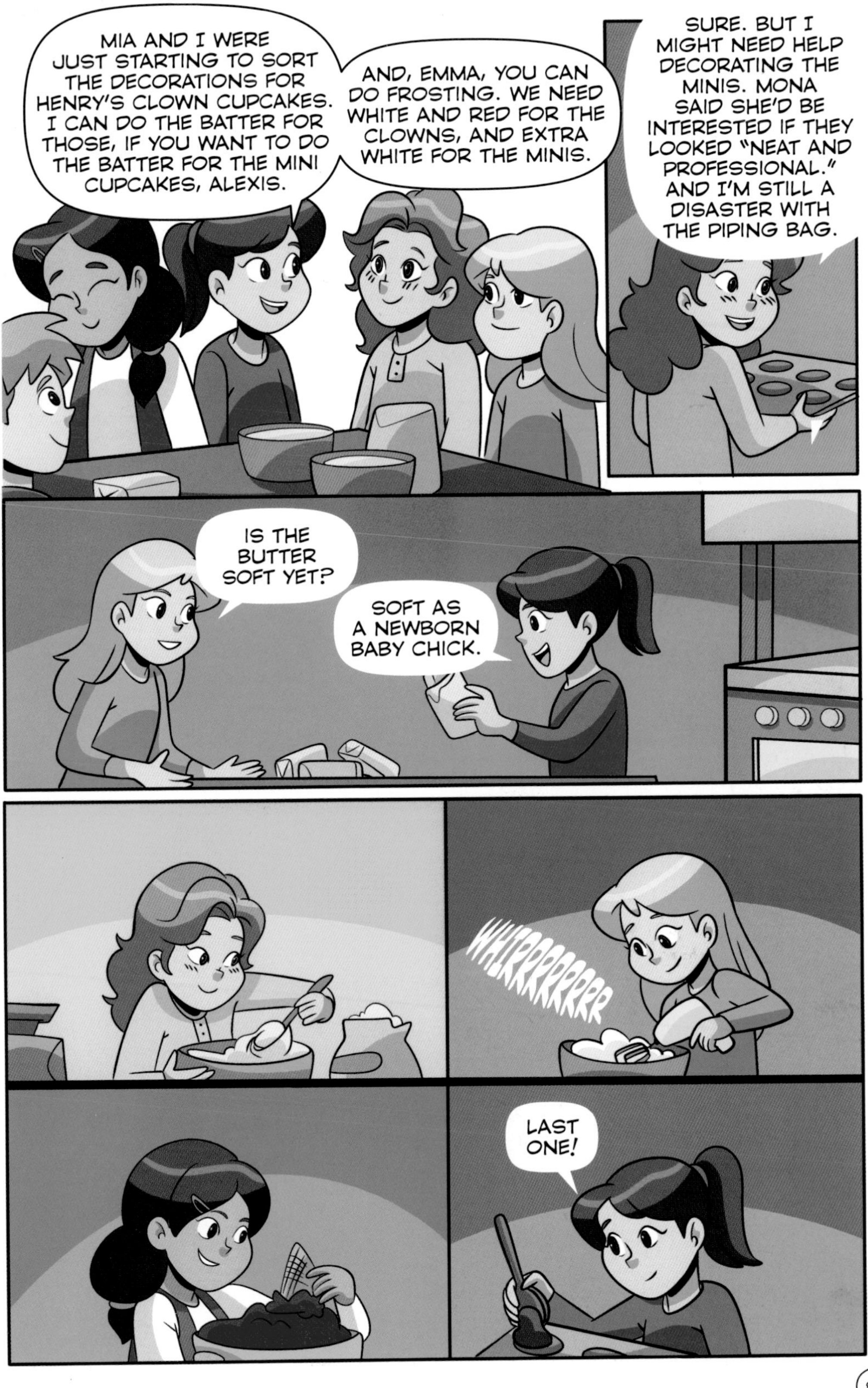
MIA AND I WERE JUST STARTING TO SORT THE DECORATIONS FOR HENRY'S CLOWN CUPCAKES. I CAN DO THE BATTER FOR THOSE, IF YOU WANT TO DO THE BATTER FOR THE MINI CUPCAKES, ALEXIS.
AND, EMMA, YOU CAN DO FROSTING. WE NEED WHITE AND RED FOR THE CLOWNS, AND EXTRA WHITE FOR THE MINIS.
SURE. BUT I MIGHT NEED HELP DECORATING THE MINIS. MONA SAID SHE'D BE INTERESTED IF THEY LOOKED "NEAT AND PROFESSIONAL." AND I'M STILL A DISASTER WITH THE PIPING BAG.
IS THE BUTTER SOFT YET?
SOFT AS A NEWBORN BABY CHICK.
WHIRRRRRRRR
LAST ONE!

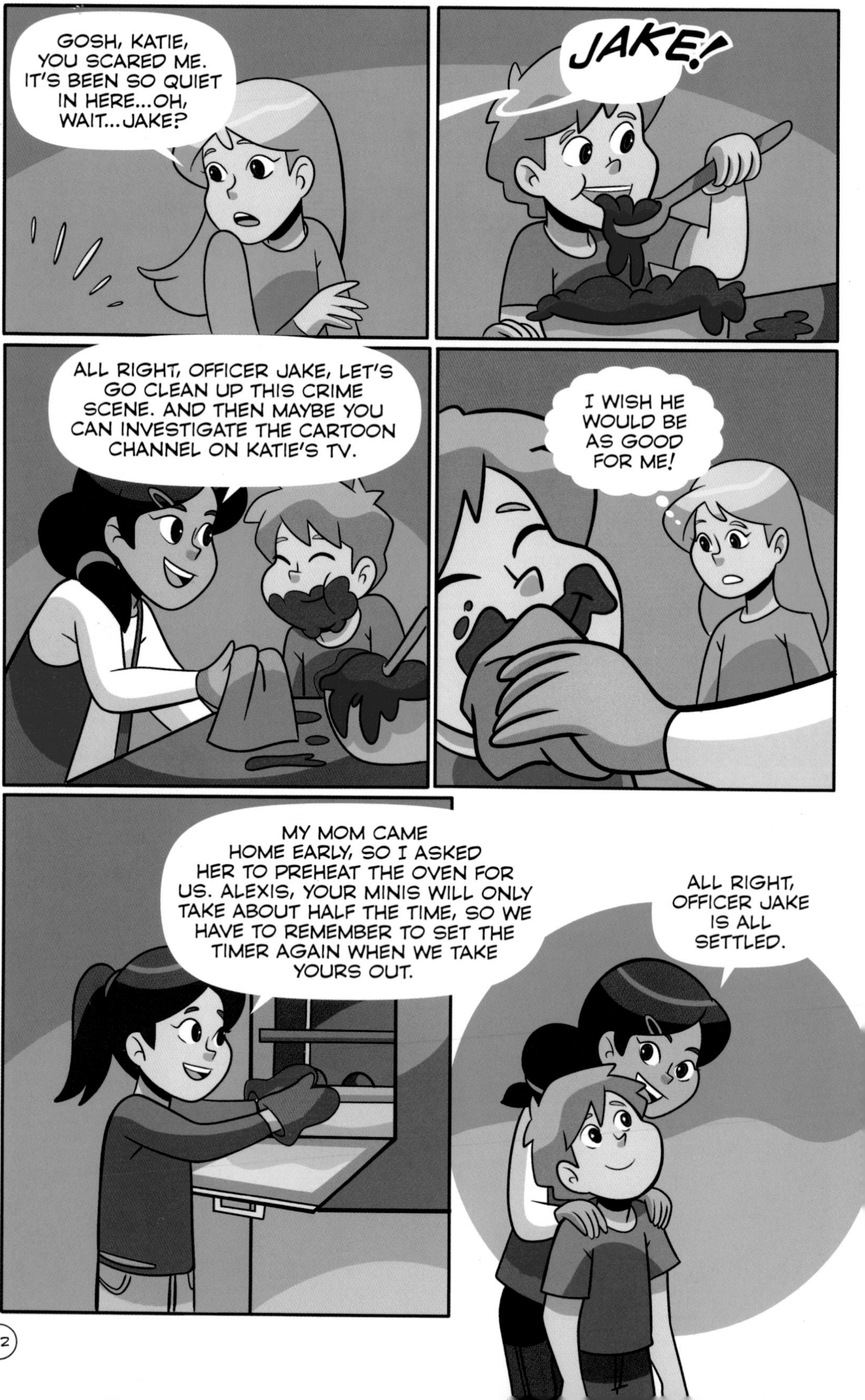
GOSH, KATIE, YOU SCARED ME. IT'S BEEN SO QUIET IN HERE...OH, WAIT...JAKE?
JAKE!
ALL RIGHT, OFFICER JAKE, LET'S GO CLEAN UP THIS CRIME SCENE. AND THEN MAYBE YOU CAN INVESTIGATE THE CARTOON CHANNEL ON KATIE'S TV.
I WISH HE WOULD BE AS GOOD FOR ME!
MY MOM CAME HOME EARLY, SO I ASKED HER TO PREHEAT THE OVEN FOR US. ALEXIS, YOUR MINIS WILL ONLY TAKE ABOUT HALF THE TIME, SO WE HAVE TO REMEMBER TO SET THE TIMER AGAIN WHEN WE TAKE YOURS OUT.
ALL RIGHT, OFFICER JAKE IS ALL SETTLED.

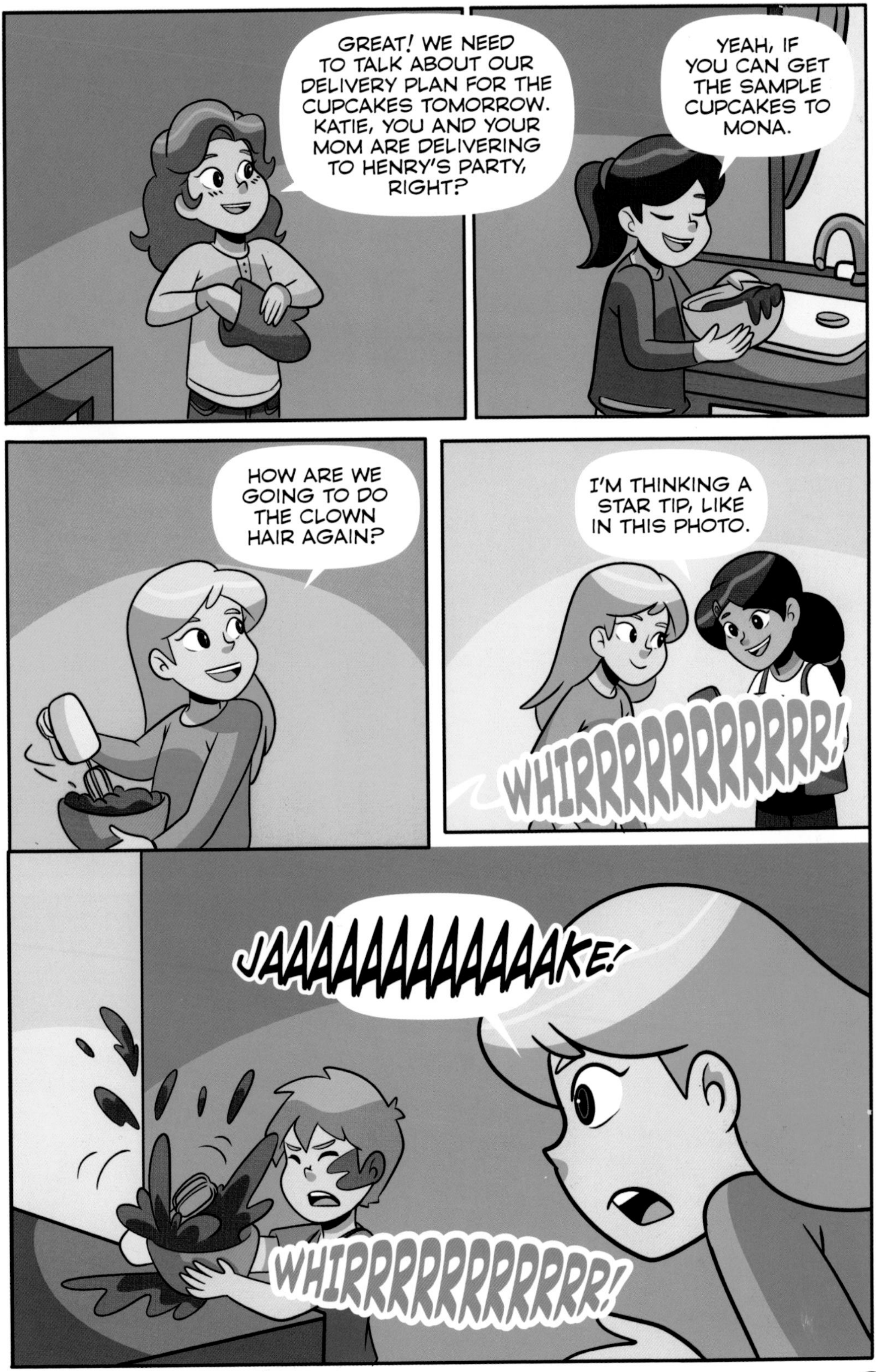
GREAT! WE NEED TO TALK ABOUT OUR DELIVERY PLAN FOR THE CUPCAKES TOMORROW. KATIE, YOU AND YOUR MOM ARE DELIVERING TO HENRY'S PARTY, RIGHT?
YEAH, IF YOU CAN GET THE SAMPLE CUPCAKES TO MONA.
HOW ARE WE GOING TO DO THE CLOWN HAIR AGAIN?
I'M THINKING A STAR TIP, LIKE IN THIS PHOTO.
WHIRRRRRRRRRRR!
JAAAAAAAAAAAAKE!
WHIRRRRRRRRRRRR!

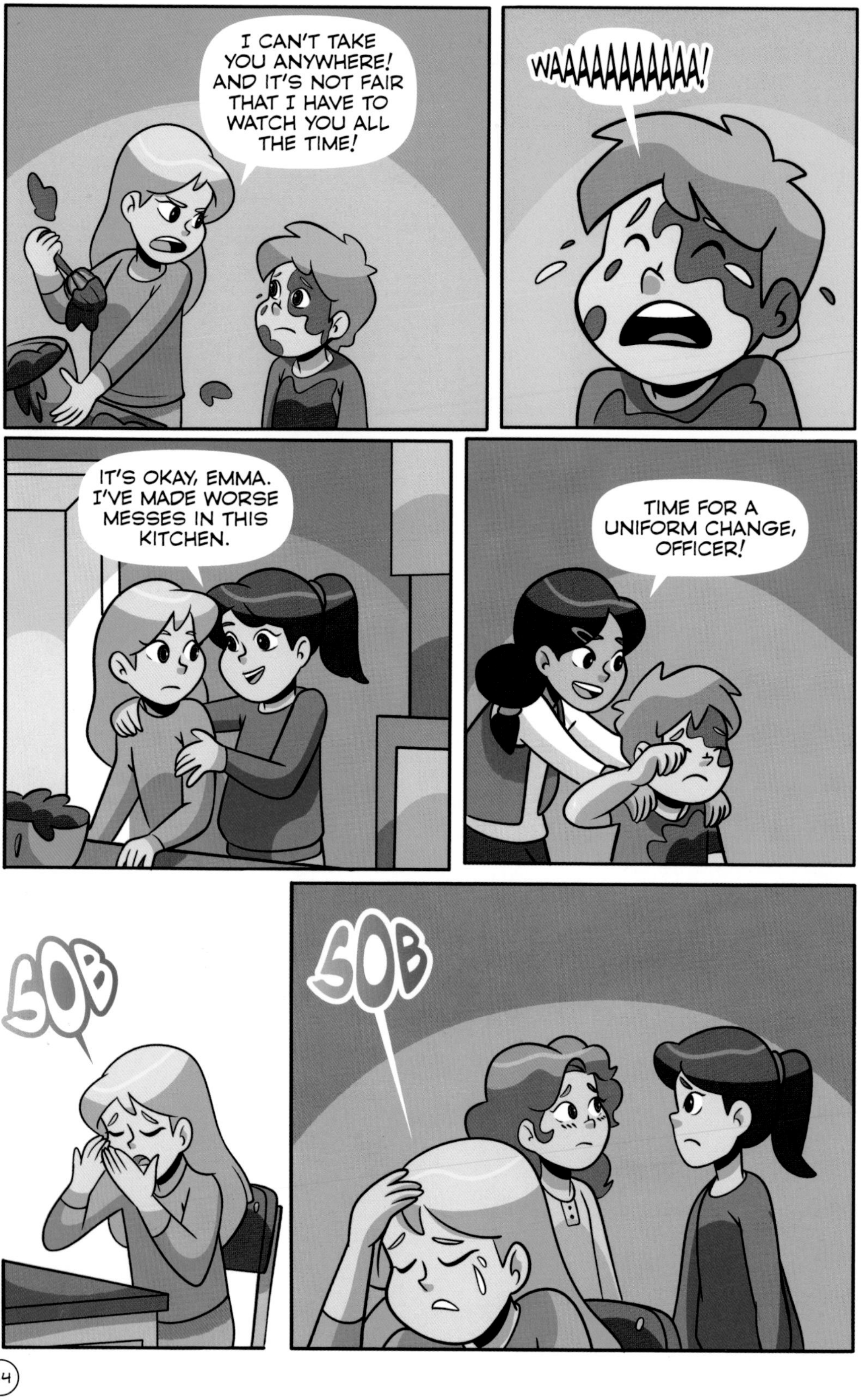
I CAN'T TAKE YOU ANYWHERE! AND IT'S NOT FAIR THAT I HAVE TO WATCH YOU ALL THE TIME!
WAAAAAAAAAAA!
IT'S OKAY, EMMA. I'VE MADE WORSE MESSES IN THIS KITCHEN.
TIME FOR A UNIFORM CHANGE, OFFICER!
SOB
SOB

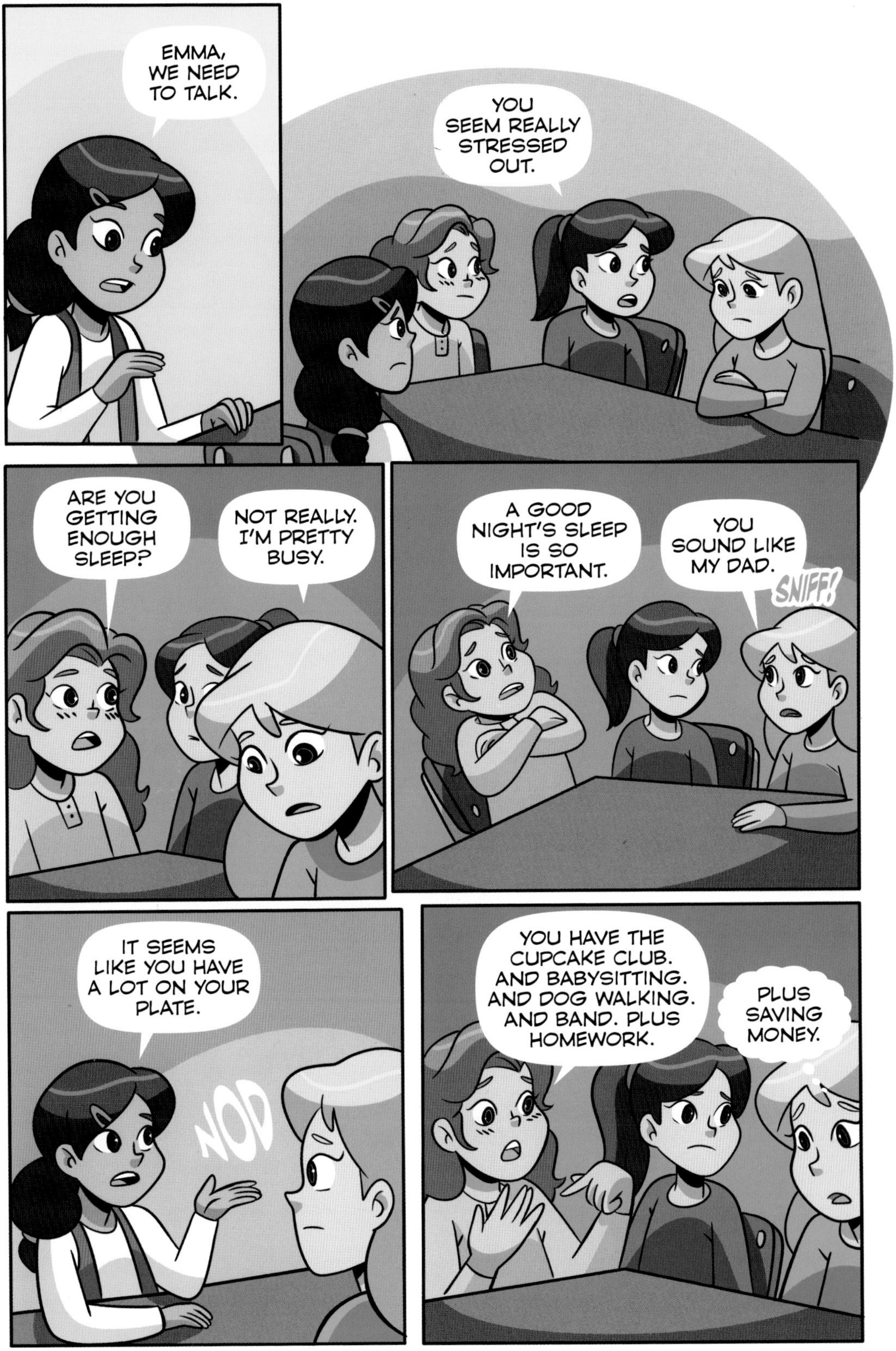
EMMA, WE NEED TO TALK.
YOU SEEM REALLY STRESSED OUT.
ARE YOU GETTING ENOUGH SLEEP?
NOT REALLY. I'M PRETTY BUSY.
A GOOD NIGHT'S SLEEP IS SO IMPORTANT.
YOU SOUND LIKE MY DAD.
SNIFF!
IT SEEMS LIKE YOU HAVE A LOT ON YOUR PLATE.
NOD
YOU HAVE THE CUPCAKE CLUB. AND BABYSITTING. AND DOG WALKING. AND BAND. PLUS HOMEWORK.
PLUS SAVING MONEY.

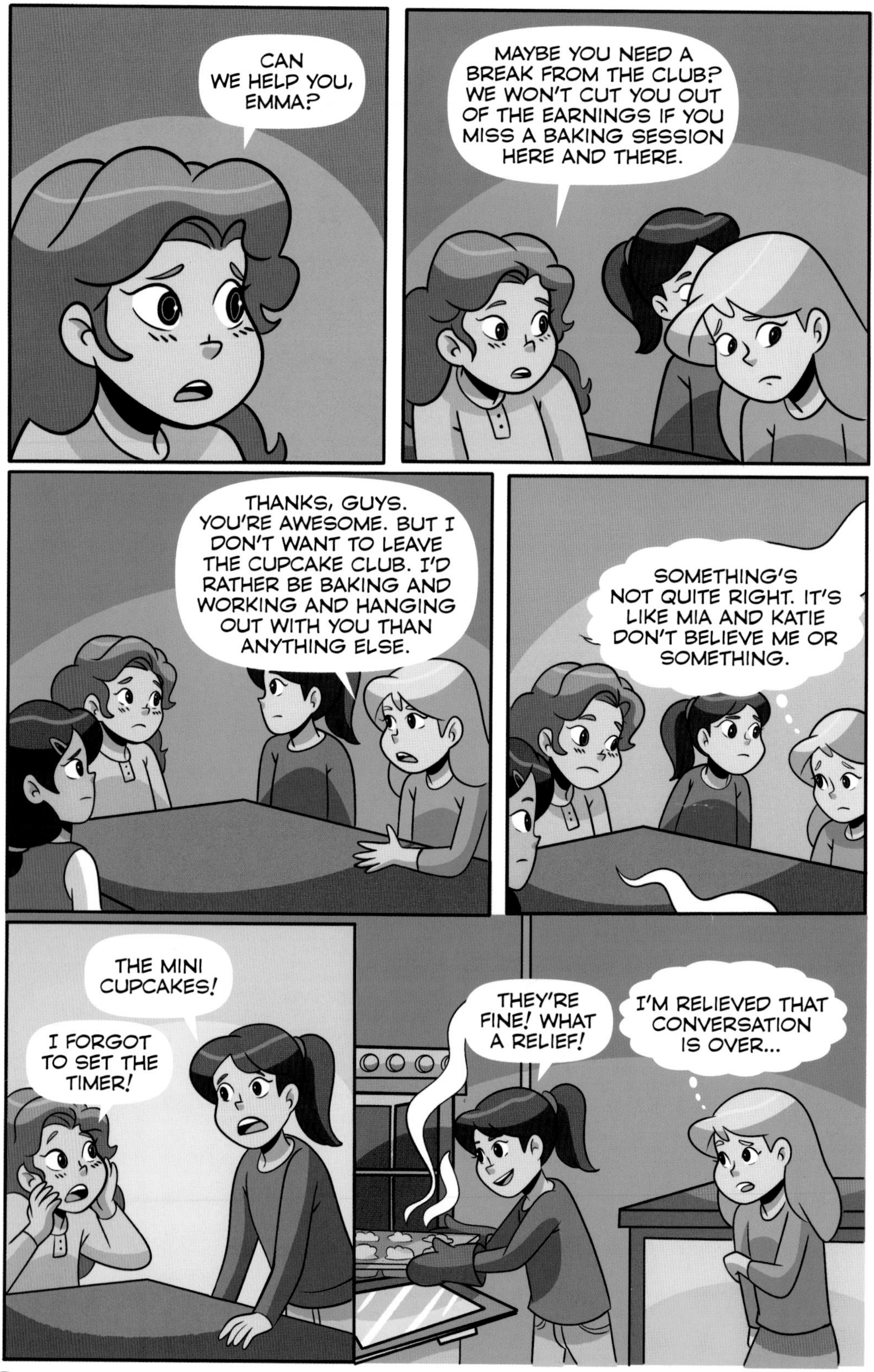
CAN WE HELP YOU, EMMA?
MAYBE YOU NEED A BREAK FROM THE CLUB? WE WON'T CUT YOU OUT OF THE EARNINGS IF YOU MISS A BAKING SESSION HERE AND THERE.
THANKS, GUYS. YOU'RE AWESOME. BUT I DON'T WANT TO LEAVE THE CUPCAKE CLUB. I'D RATHER BE BAKING AND WORKING AND HANGING OUT WITH YOU THAN ANYTHING ELSE.
SOMETHING'S NOT QUITE RIGHT. IT'S LIKE MIA AND KATIE DON'T BELIEVE ME OR SOMETHING.
THE MINI CUPCAKES!
I FORGOT TO SET THE TIMER!
THEY'RE FINE! WHAT A RELIEF!
I'M RELIEVED THAT CONVERSATION IS OVER...

Chapter 8

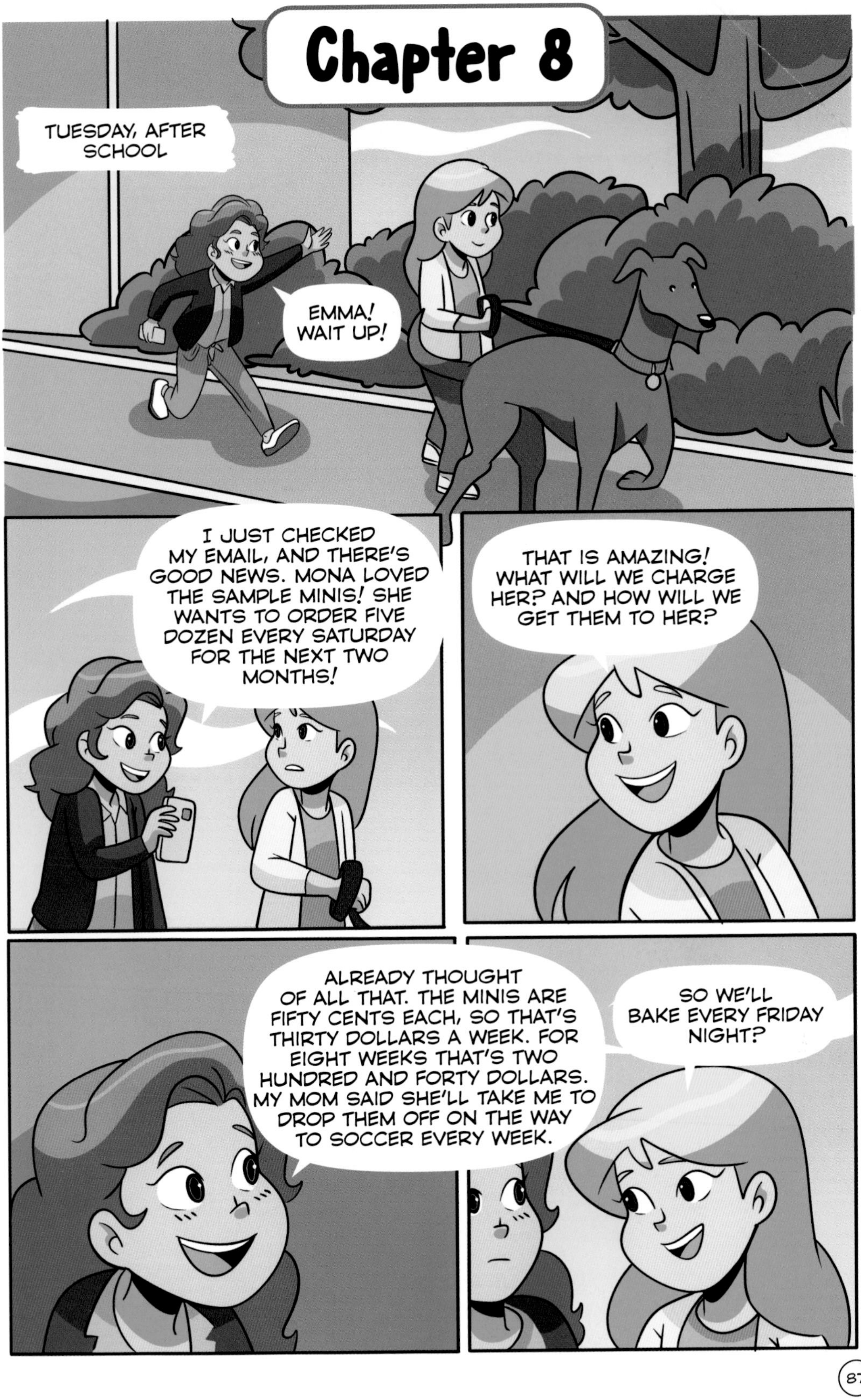
TUESDAY, AFTER SCHOOL
EMMA! WAIT UP!
I JUST CHECKED MY EMAIL, AND THERE'S GOOD NEWS. MONA LOVED THE SAMPLE MINIS! SHE WANTS TO ORDER FIVE DOZEN EVERY SATURDAY FOR THE NEXT TWO MONTHS!
THAT IS AMAZING! WHAT WILL WE CHARGE HER? AND HOW WILL WE GET THEM TO HER?
ALREADY THOUGHT OF ALL THAT. THE MINIS ARE FIFTY CENTS EACH, SO THAT'S THIRTY DOLLARS A WEEK. FOR EIGHT WEEKS THAT'S TWO HUNDRED AND FORTY DOLLARS. MY MOM SAID SHE'LL TAKE ME TO DROP THEM OFF ON THE WAY TO SOCCER EVERY WEEK.
SO WE'LL BAKE EVERY FRIDAY NIGHT?

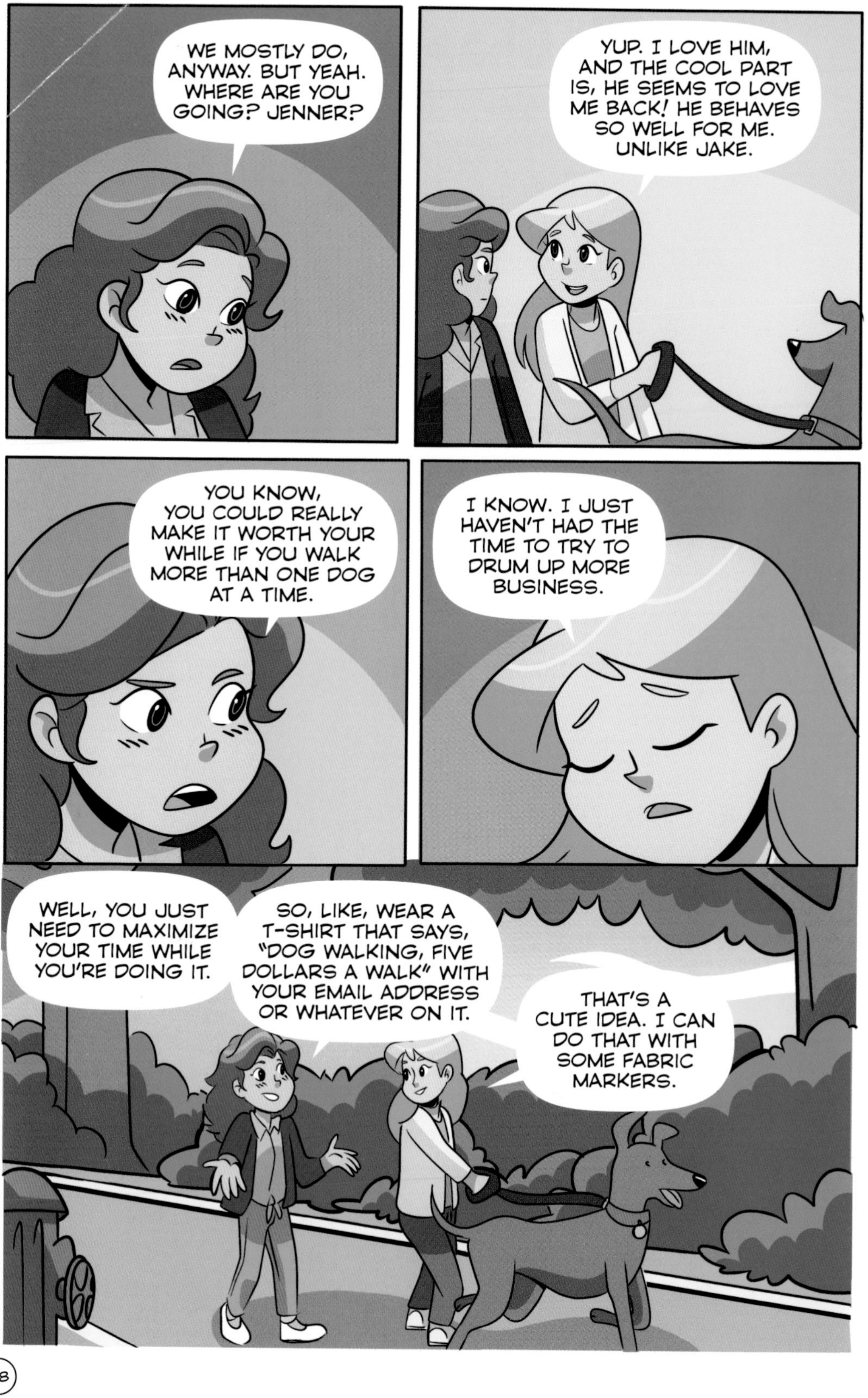
WE MOSTLY DO, ANYWAY. BUT YEAH. WHERE ARE YOU GOING? JENNER?
YUP. I LOVE HIM, AND THE COOL PART IS, HE SEEMS TO LOVE ME BACK! HE BEHAVES SO WELL FOR ME. UNLIKE JAKE.
YOU KNOW, YOU COULD REALLY MAKE IT WORTH YOUR WHILE IF YOU WALK MORE THAN ONE DOG AT A TIME.
I KNOW. I JUST HAVEN'T HAD THE TIME TO TRY TO DRUM UP MORE BUSINESS.
WELL, YOU JUST NEED TO MAXIMIZE YOUR TIME WHILE YOU'RE DOING IT.
SO, LIKE, WEAR A T-SHIRT THAT SAYS, "DOG WALKING, FIVE DOLLARS A WALK" WITH YOUR EMAIL ADDRESS OR WHATEVER ON IT.
THAT'S A CUTE IDEA. I CAN DO THAT WITH SOME FABRIC MARKERS.

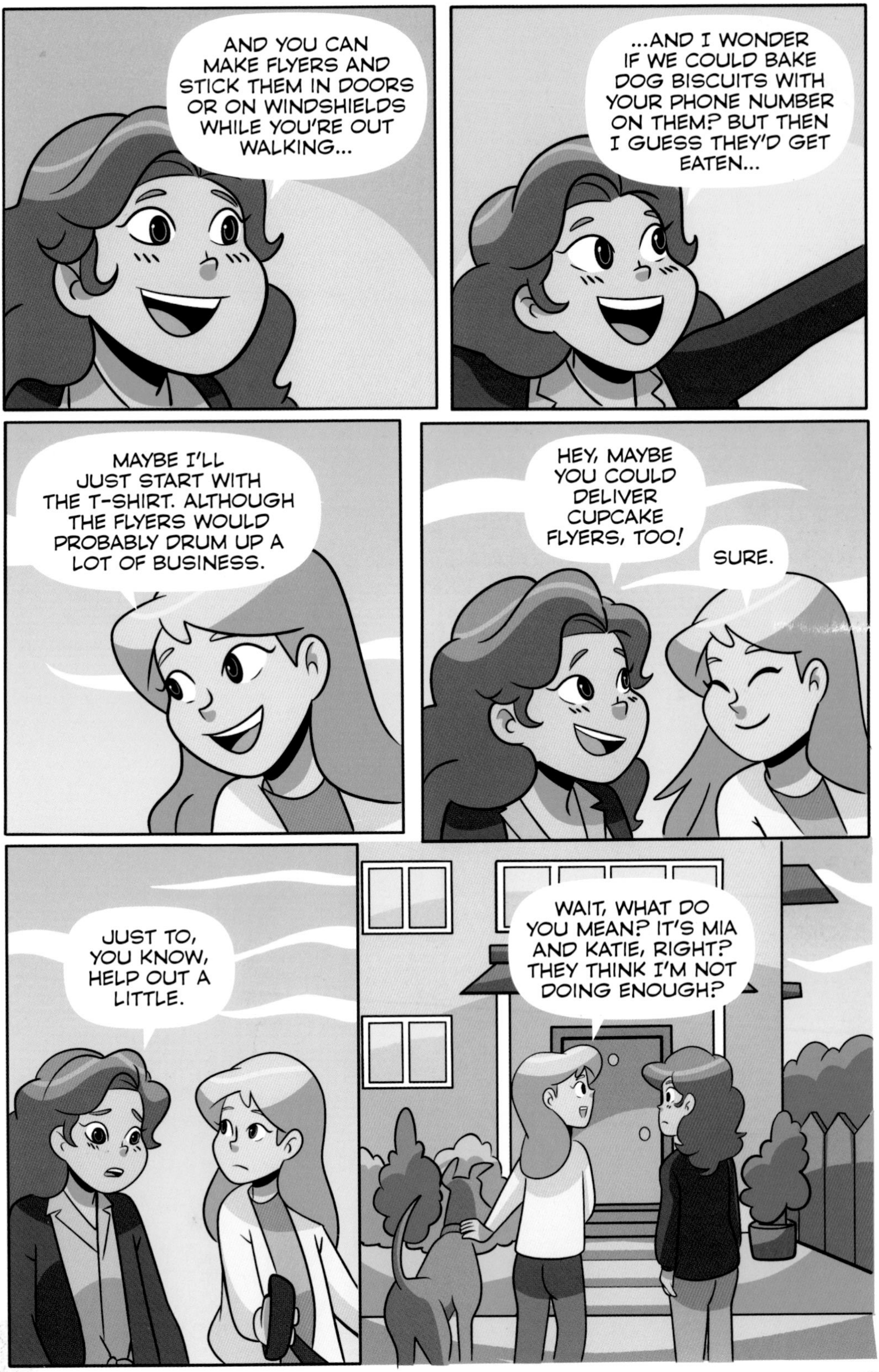
AND YOU CAN MAKE FLYERS AND STICK THEM IN DOORS OR ON WINDSHIELDS WHILE YOU'RE OUT WALKING...
...AND I WONDER IF WE COULD BAKE DOG BISCUITS WITH YOUR PHONE NUMBER ON THEM? BUT THEN I GUESS THEY'D GET EATEN...
MAYBE I'LL JUST START WITH THE T-SHIRT. ALTHOUGH THE FLYERS WOULD PROBABLY DRUM UP A LOT OF BUSINESS.
HEY, MAYBE YOU COULD DELIVER CUPCAKE FLYERS, TOO!
SURE.
JUST TO, YOU KNOW, HELP OUT A LITTLE.
WAIT, WHAT DO YOU MEAN? IT'S MIA AND KATIE, RIGHT? THEY THINK I'M NOT DOING ENOUGH?

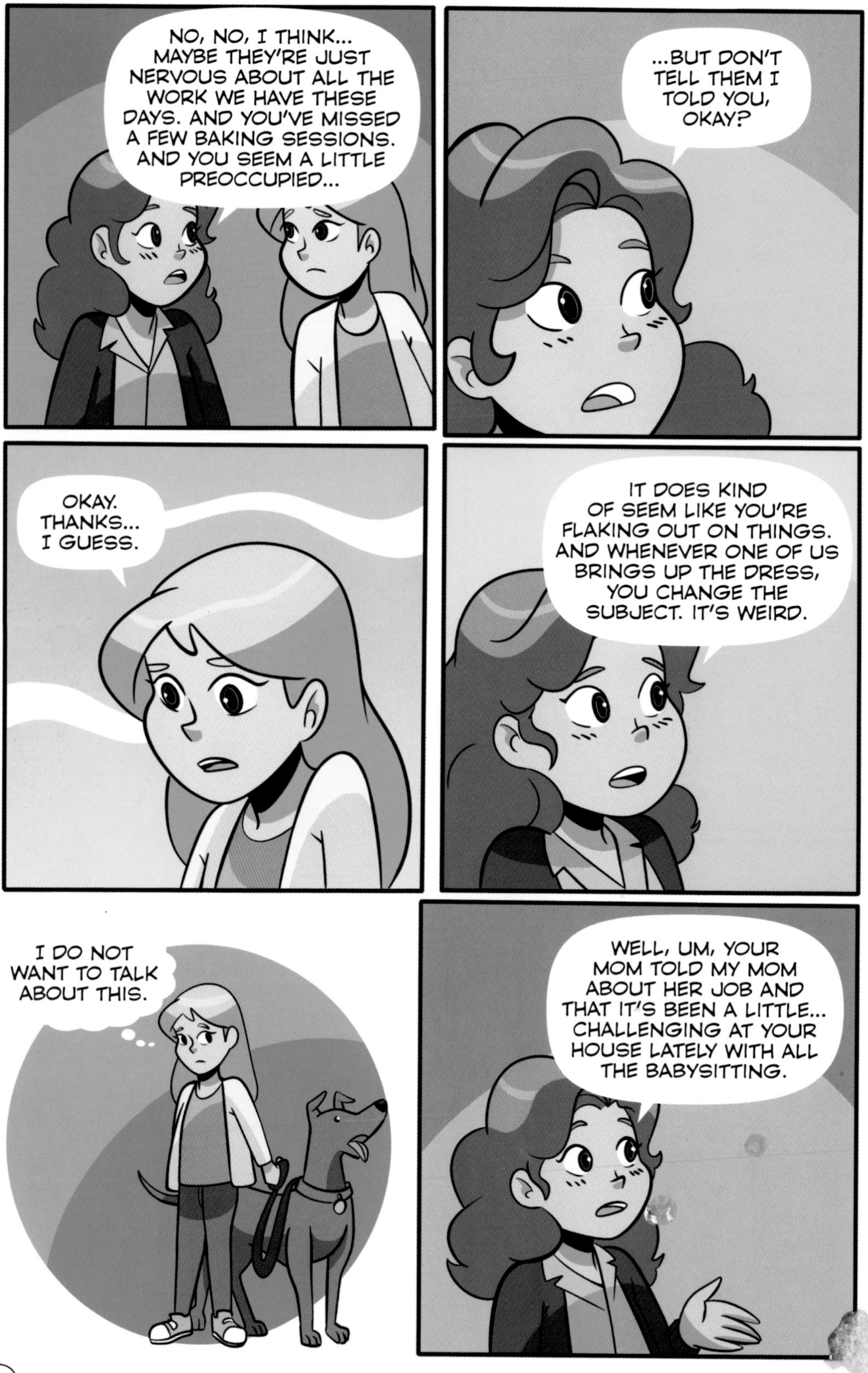
NO, NO, I THINK... MAYBE THEY'RE JUST NERVOUS ABOUT ALL THE WORK WE HAVE THESE DAYS. AND YOU'VE MISSED A FEW BAKING SESSIONS. AND YOU SEEM A LITTLE PREOCCUPIED...
...BUT DON'T TELL THEM I TOLD YOU, OKAY?
OKAY. THANKS... I GUESS.
IT DOES KIND OF SEEM LIKE YOU'RE FLAKING OUT ON THINGS. AND WHENEVER ONE OF US BRINGS UP THE DRESS, YOU CHANGE THE SUBJECT. IT'S WEIRD.
I DO NOT WANT TO TALK ABOUT THIS.
WELL, UM, YOUR MOM TOLD MY MOM ABOUT HER JOB AND THAT IT'S BEEN A LITTLE... CHALLENGING AT YOUR HOUSE LATELY WITH ALL THE BABYSITTING.

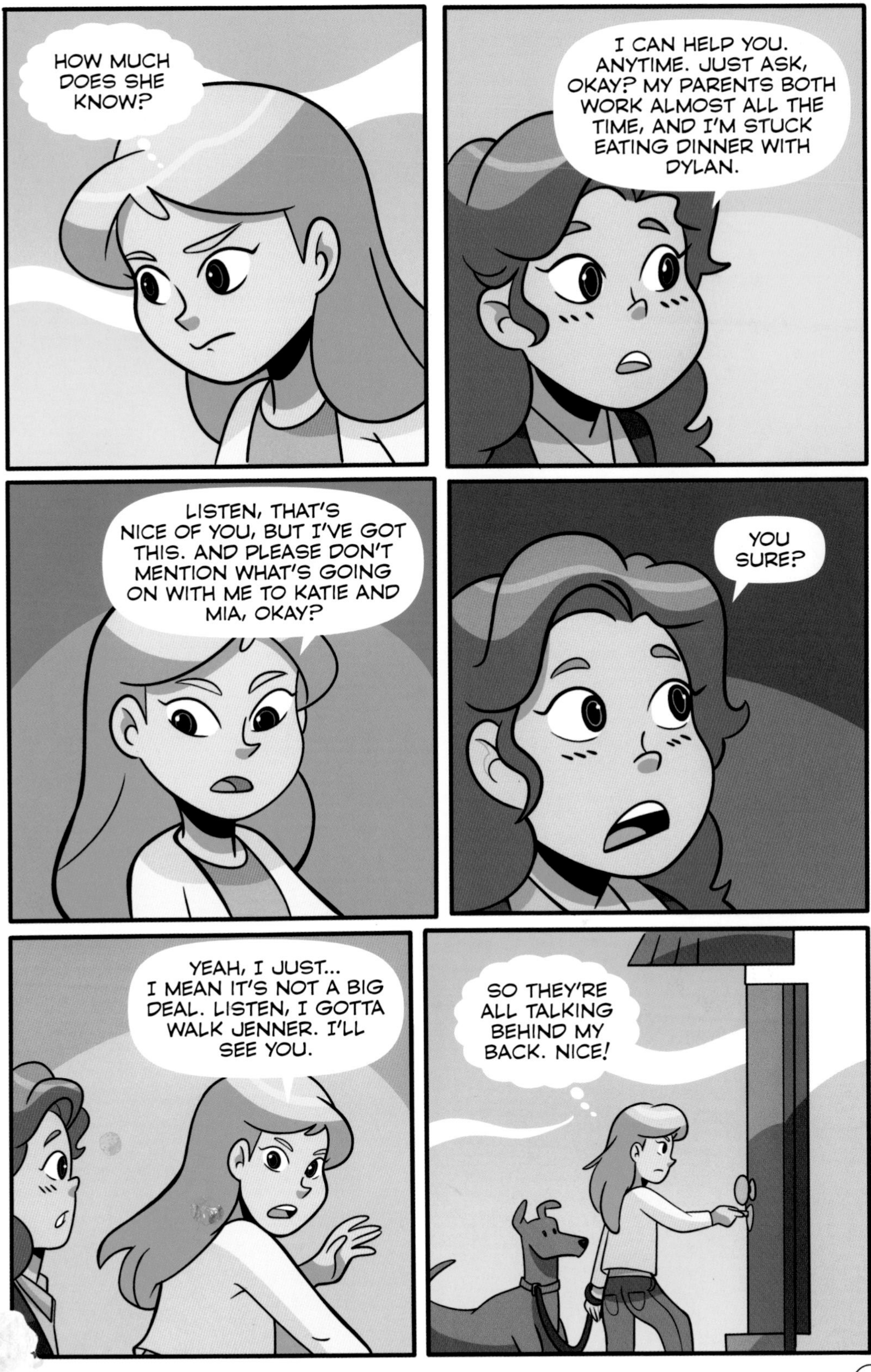
HOW MUCH DOES SHE KNOW?
I CAN HELP YOU. ANYTIME. JUST ASK, OKAY? MY PARENTS BOTH WORK ALMOST ALL THE TIME, AND I'M STUCK EATING DINNER WITH DYLAN.
LISTEN, THAT'S NICE OF YOU, BUT I'VE GOT THIS. AND PLEASE DON'T MENTION WHAT'S GOING ON WITH ME TO KATIE AND MIA, OKAY?
YOU SURE?
YEAH, I JUST... I MEAN IT'S NOT A BIG DEAL. LISTEN, I GOTTA WALK JENNER. I'LL SEE YOU.
SO THEY'RE ALL TALKING BEHIND MY BACK. NICE!

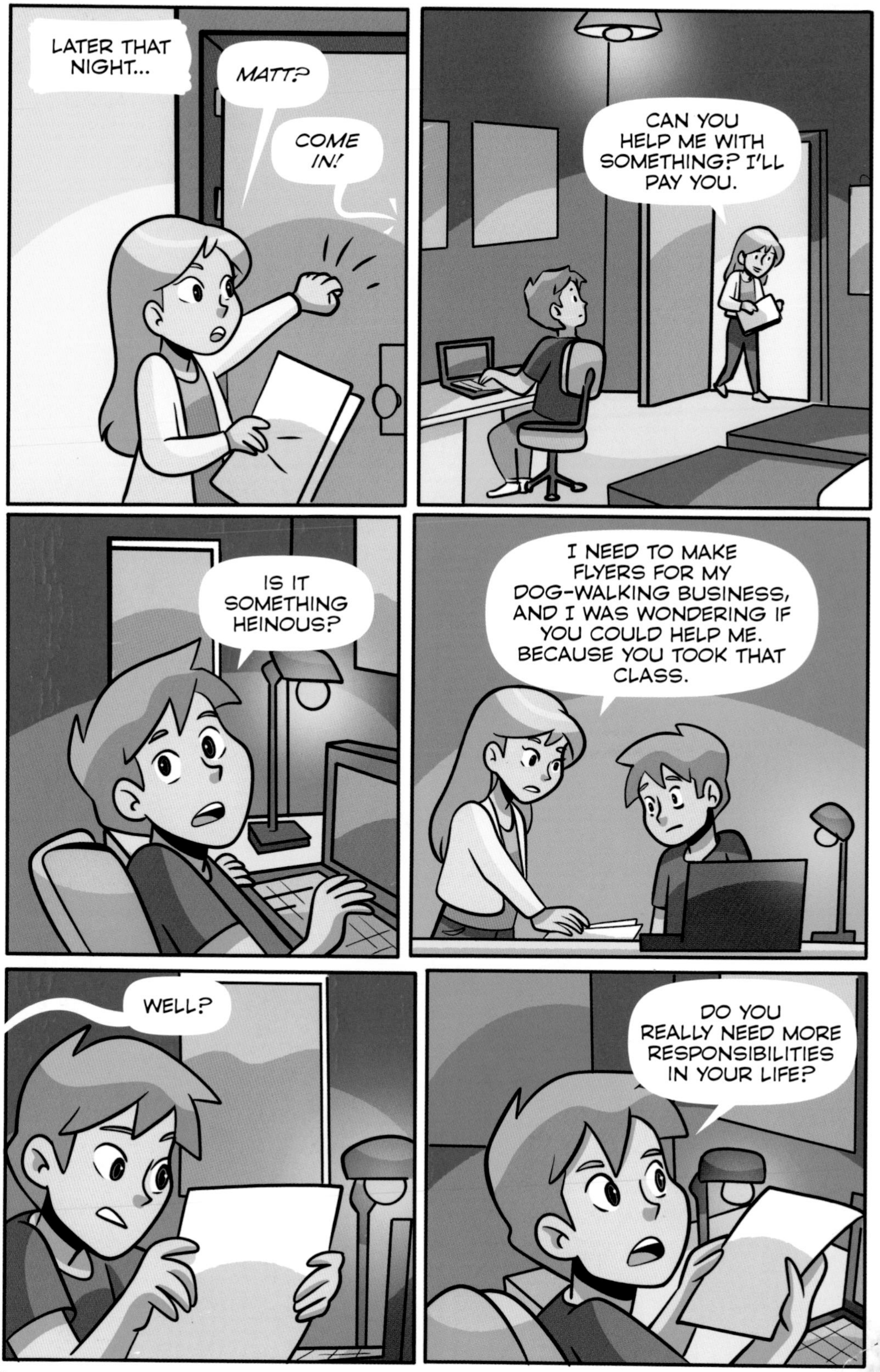
LATER THAT NIGHT...
MATT?
COME IN!
CAN YOU HELP ME WITH SOMETHING? I'LL PAY YOU.
IS IT SOMETHING HEINOUS?
I NEED TO MAKE FLYERS FOR MY DOG-WALKING BUSINESS, AND I WAS WONDERING IF YOU COULD HELP ME. BECAUSE YOU TOOK THAT CLASS.
WELL?
DO YOU REALLY NEED MORE RESPONSIBILITIES IN YOUR LIFE?

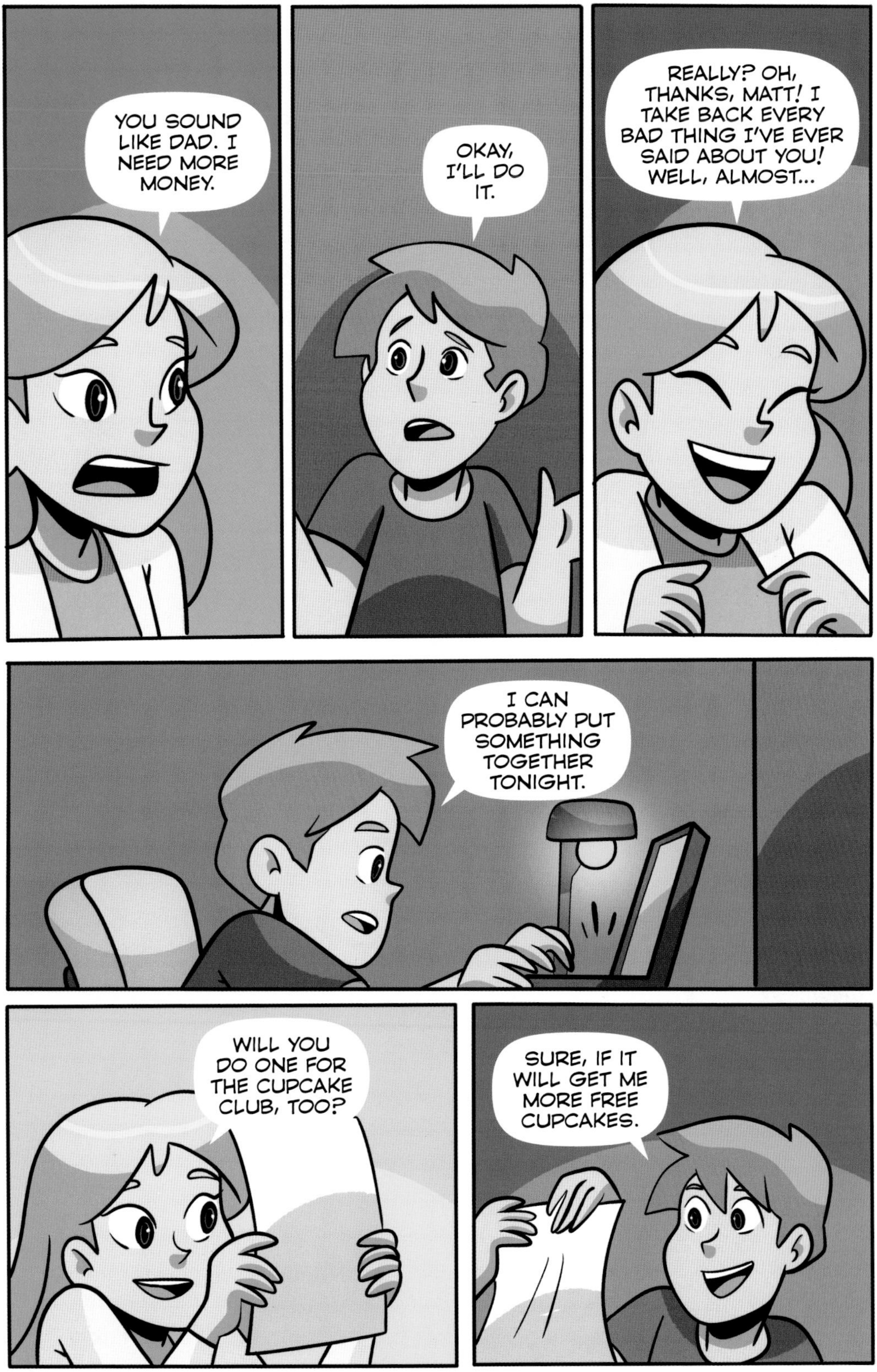
YOU SOUND LIKE DAD. I NEED MORE MONEY.
OKAY, I'LL DO IT.
REALLY? OH, THANKS, MATT! I TAKE BACK EVERY BAD THING I'VE EVER SAID ABOUT YOU! WELL, ALMOST...
I CAN PROBABLY PUT SOMETHING TOGETHER TONIGHT.
WILL YOU DO ONE FOR THE CUPCAKE CLUB, TOO?
SURE, IF IT WILL GET ME MORE FREE CUPCAKES.

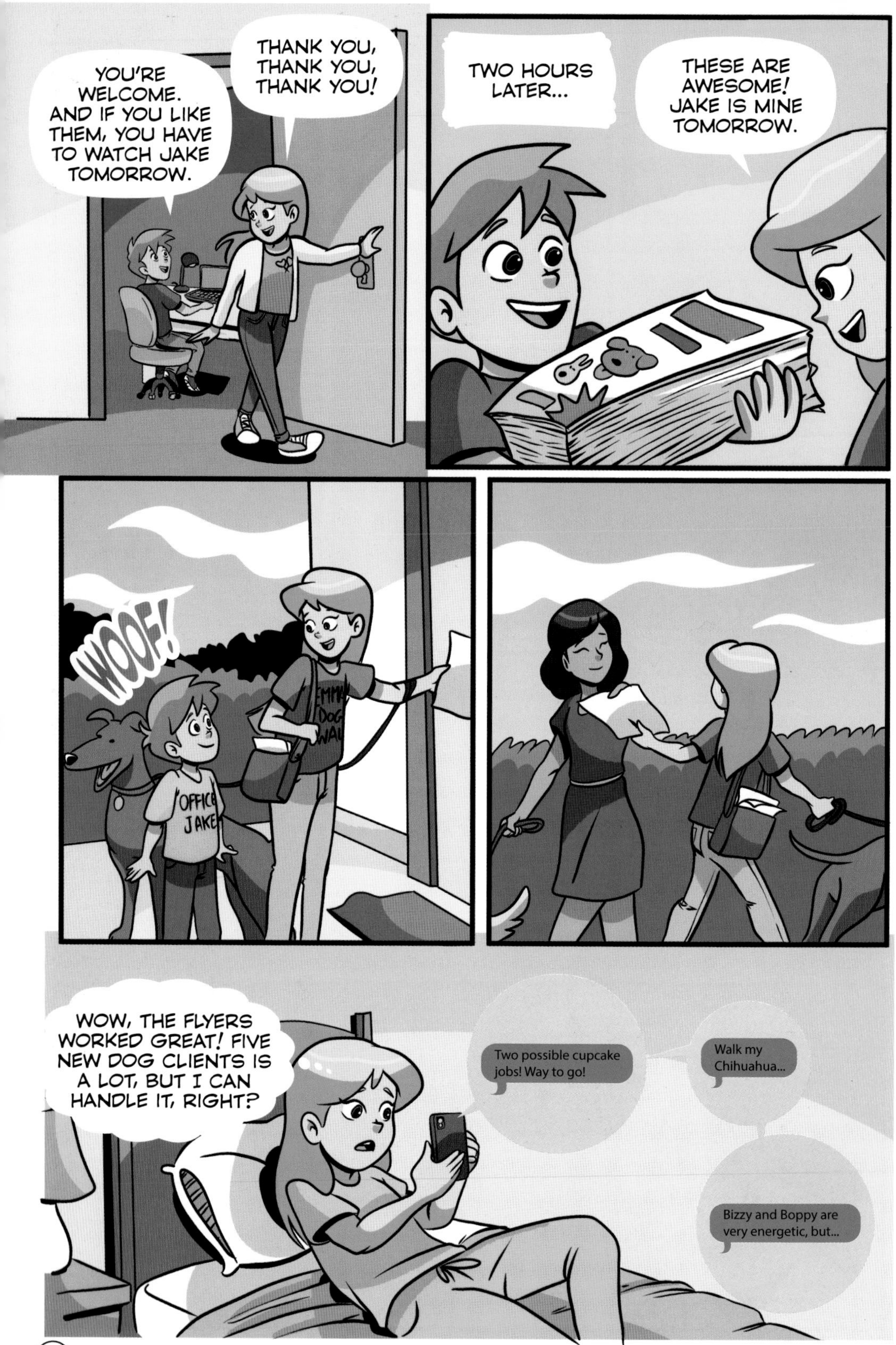
YOU'RE WELCOME. AND IF YOU LIKE THEM, YOU HAVE TO WATCH JAKE TOMORROW.
THANK YOU, THANK YOU, THANK YOU!
TWO HOURS LATER...
THESE ARE AWESOME! JAKE IS MINE TOMORROW.
WOOF!
EMMA'S DOG WAL
OFFIC JAKE
WOW, THE FLYERS WORKED GREAT! FIVE NEW DOG CLIENTS IS A LOT, BUT I CAN HANDLE IT, RIGHT?
Two possible cupcake jobs! Way to go!
Walk my Chihuahua...
Bizzy and Boppy are very energetic, but...

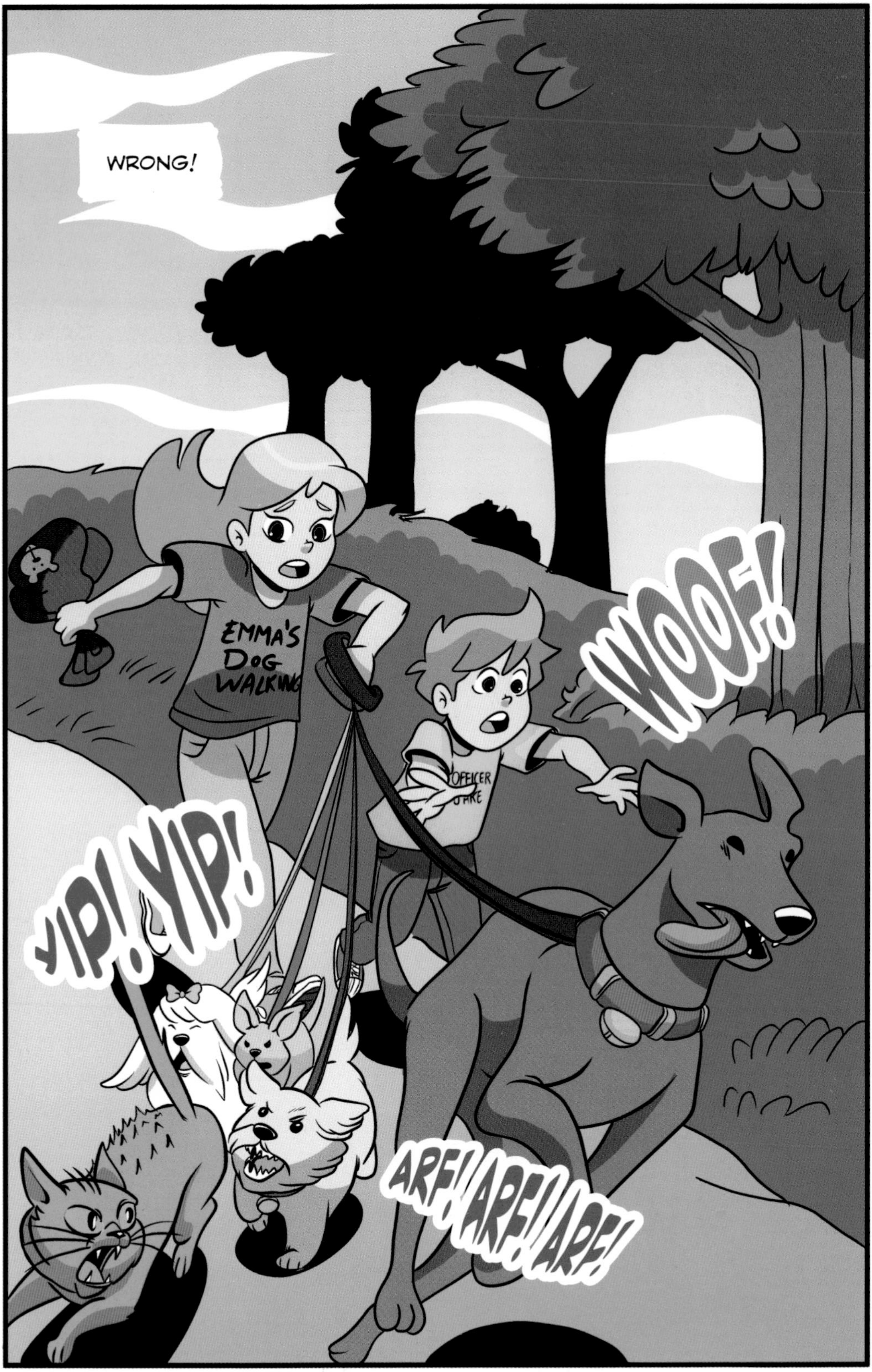
WRONG!
EMMA'S DOG WALKING
WOOF!
OFFICER JAKE
YIP! YIP!
ARF! ARF! ARF!

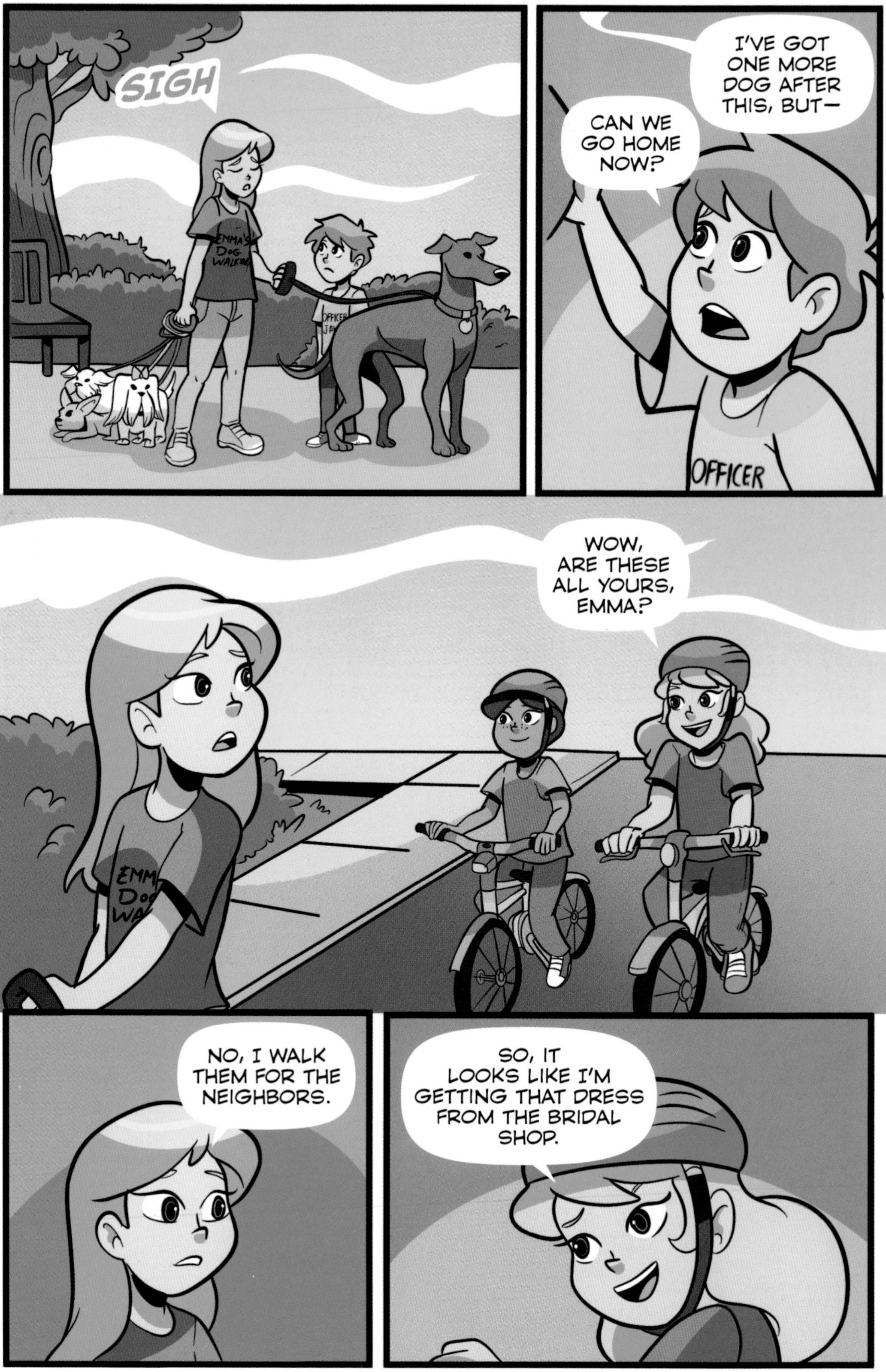
SIGH
EMMA'S DOG WALKING
OFFICER JAY
I'VE GOT ONE MORE DOG AFTER THIS, BUT—
CAN WE GO HOME NOW?
OFFICER
WOW, ARE THESE ALL YOURS, EMMA?
NO, I WALK THEM FOR THE NEIGHBORS.
SO, IT LOOKS LIKE I'M GETTING THAT DRESS FROM THE BRIDAL SHOP.

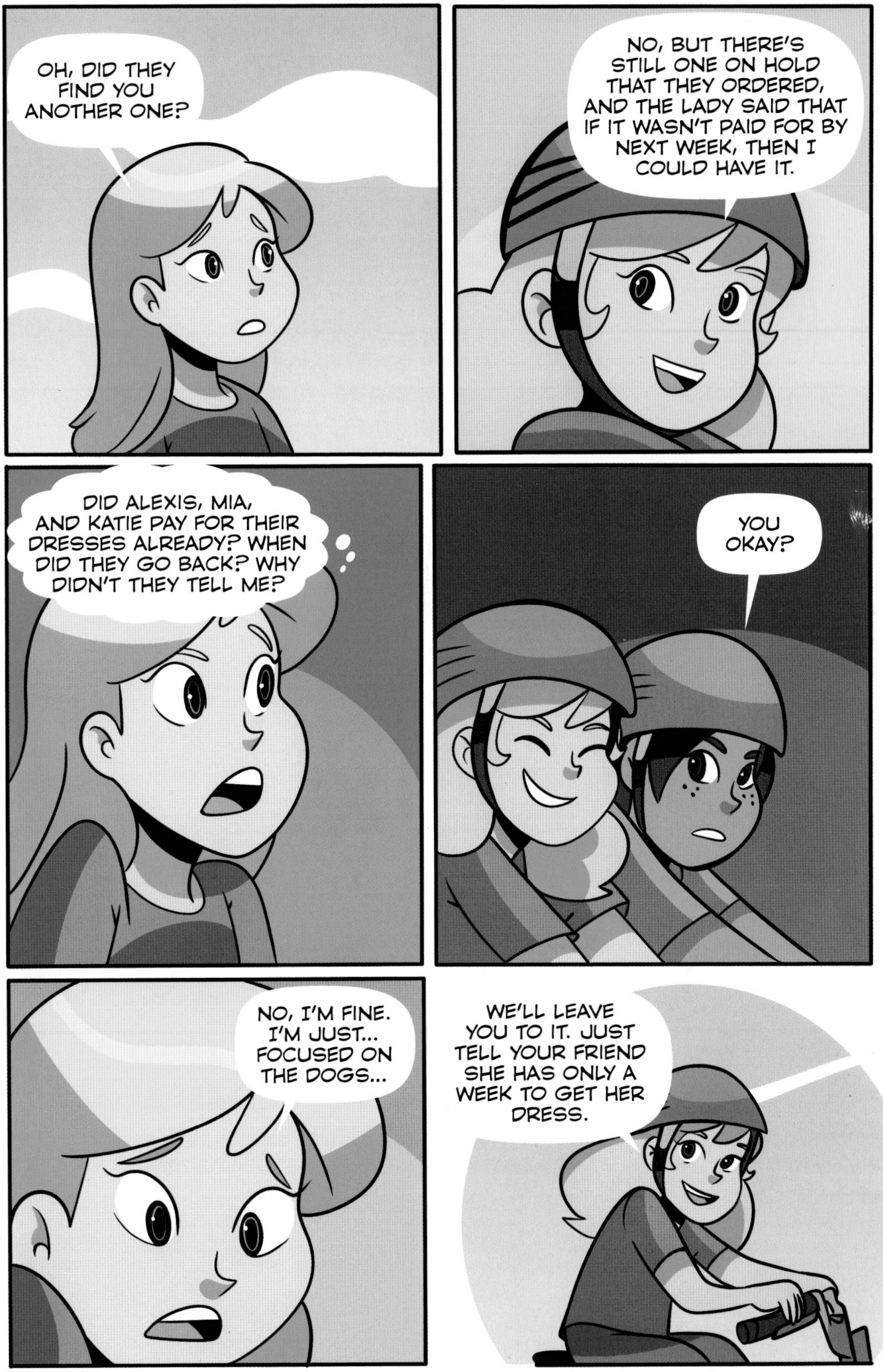
OH, DID THEY FIND YOU ANOTHER ONE?
NO, BUT THERE'S STILL ONE ON HOLD THAT THEY ORDERED, AND THE LADY SAID THAT IF IT WASN'T PAID FOR BY NEXT WEEK, THEN I COULD HAVE IT.
DID ALEXIS, MIA, AND KATIE PAY FOR THEIR DRESSES ALREADY? WHEN DID THEY GO BACK? WHY DIDN'T THEY TELL ME?
YOU OKAY?
NO, I'M FINE. I'M JUST... FOCUSED ON THE DOGS...
WE'LL LEAVE YOU TO IT. JUST TELL YOUR FRIEND SHE HAS ONLY A WEEK TO GET HER DRESS.

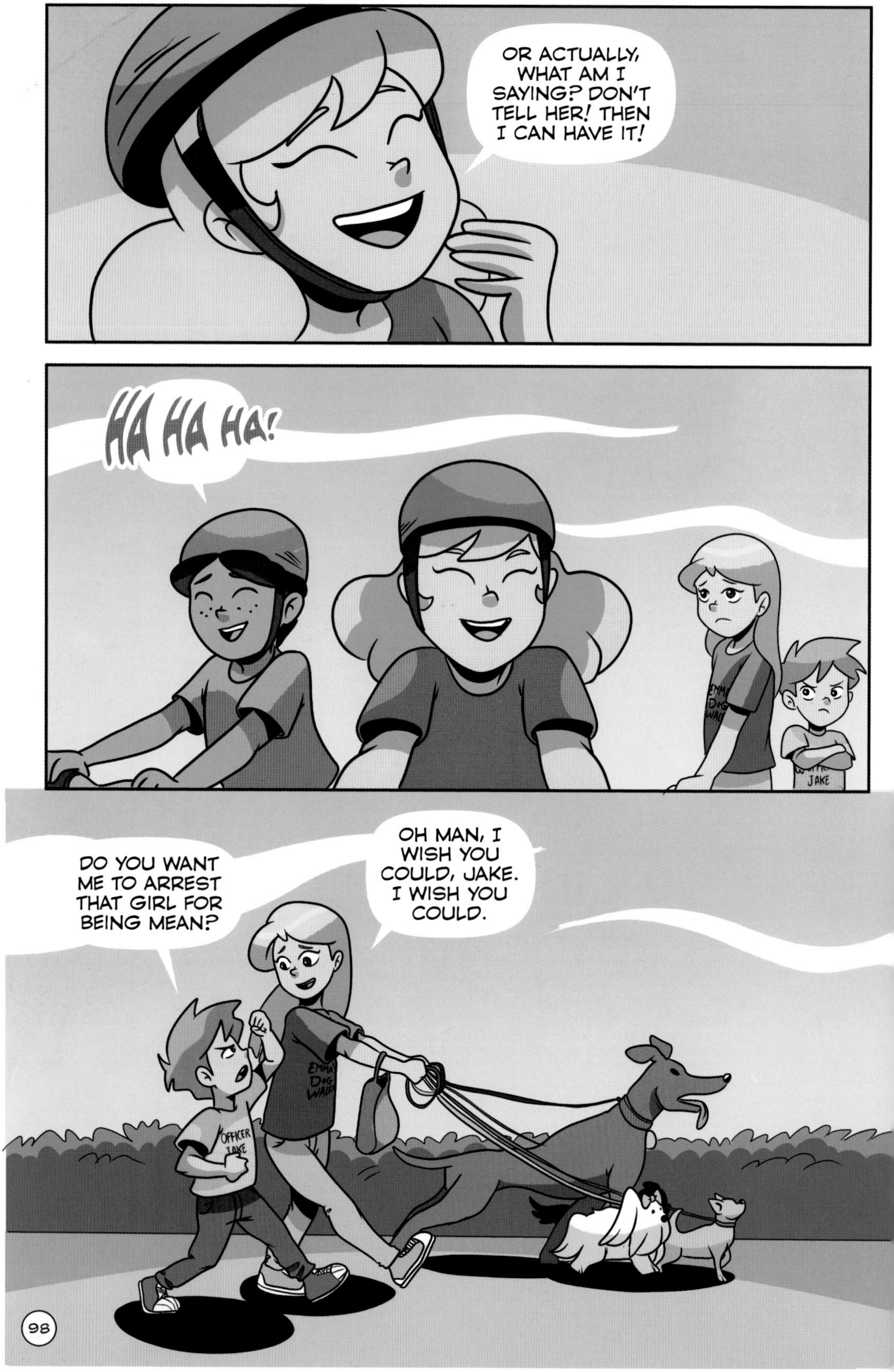
OR ACTUALLY, WHAT AM I SAYING? DON'T TELL HER! THEN I CAN HAVE IT!
HA HA HA!
EMMA'S DOG WALK
JAKE
DO YOU WANT ME TO ARREST THAT GIRL FOR BEING MEAN?
OH MAN, I WISH YOU COULD, JAKE. I WISH YOU COULD.
EMMA'S DOG WALK
OFFICER JAKE

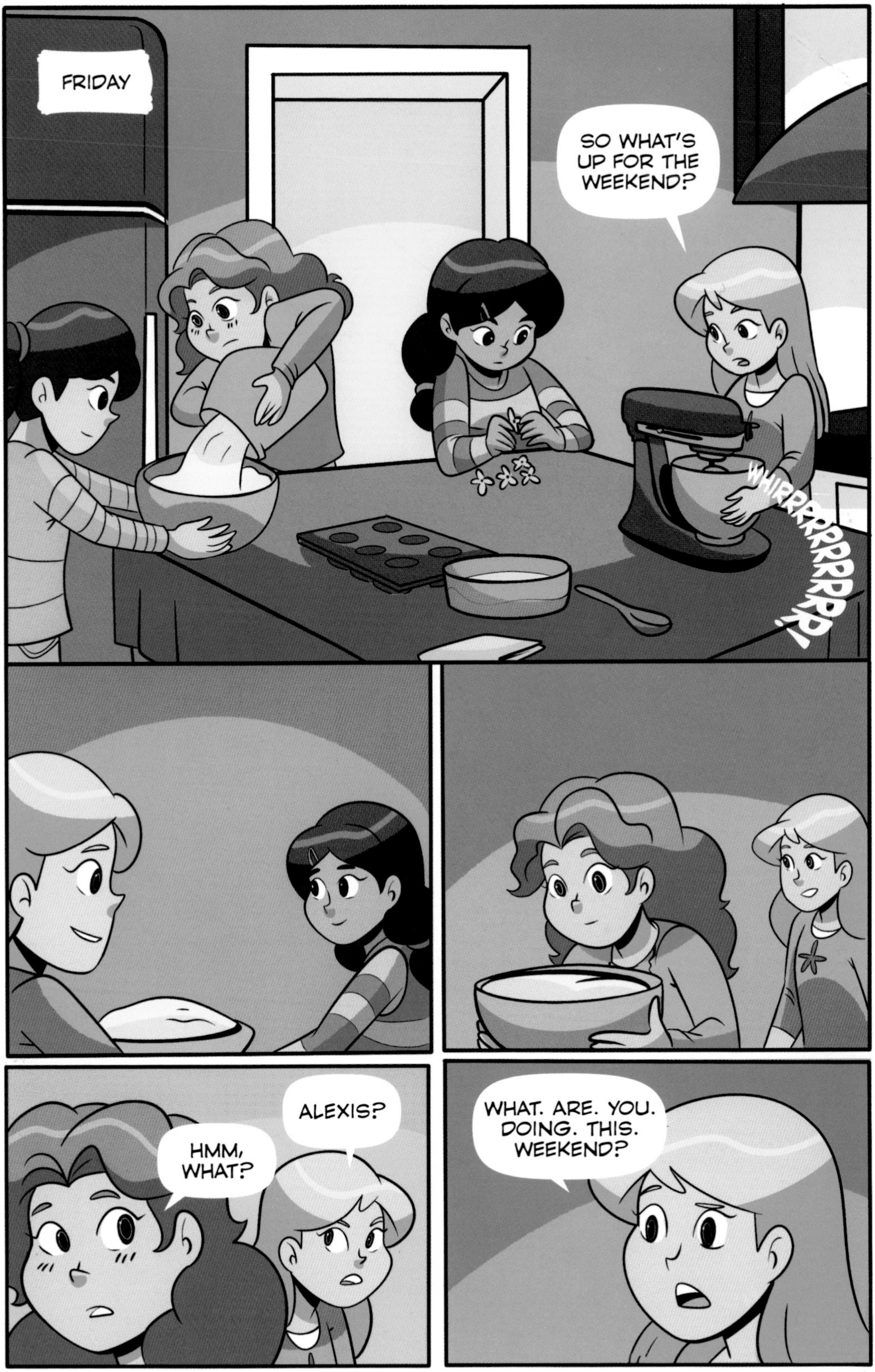
FRIDAY
SO WHAT'S UP FOR THE WEEKEND?
WHIRRRRRRRRRR!
ALEXIS?
HMM, WHAT?
WHAT. ARE. YOU. DOING. THIS. WEEKEND?

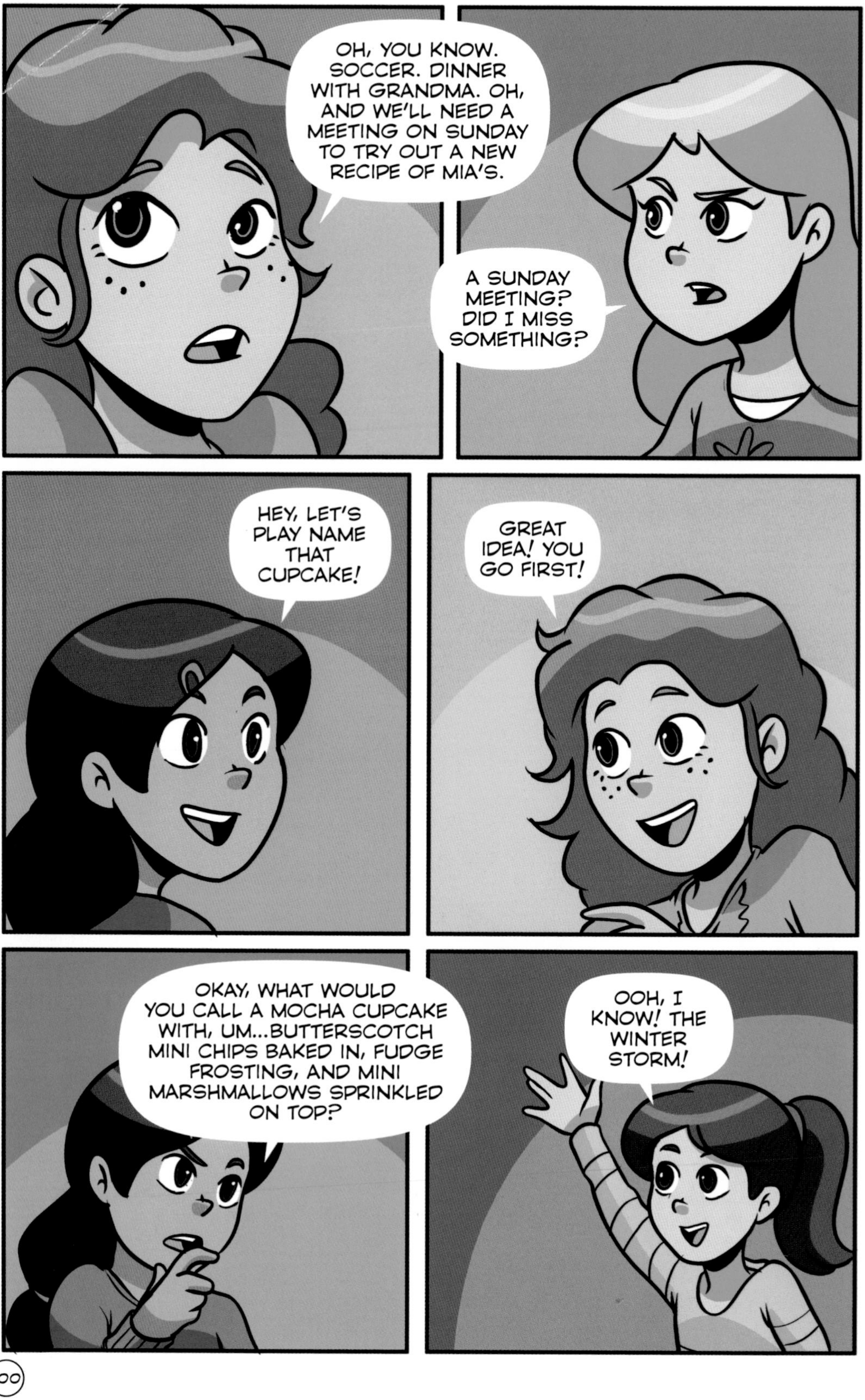
OH, YOU KNOW. SOCCER. DINNER WITH GRANDMA. OH, AND WE'LL NEED A MEETING ON SUNDAY TO TRY OUT A NEW RECIPE OF MIA'S.
A SUNDAY MEETING? DID I MISS SOMETHING?
HEY, LET'S PLAY NAME THAT CUPCAKE!
GREAT IDEA! YOU GO FIRST!
OKAY, WHAT WOULD YOU CALL A MOCHA CUPCAKE WITH, UM...BUTTERSCOTCH MINI CHIPS BAKED IN, FUDGE FROSTING, AND MINI MARSHMALLOWS SPRINKLED ON TOP?
OOH, I KNOW! THE WINTER STORM!

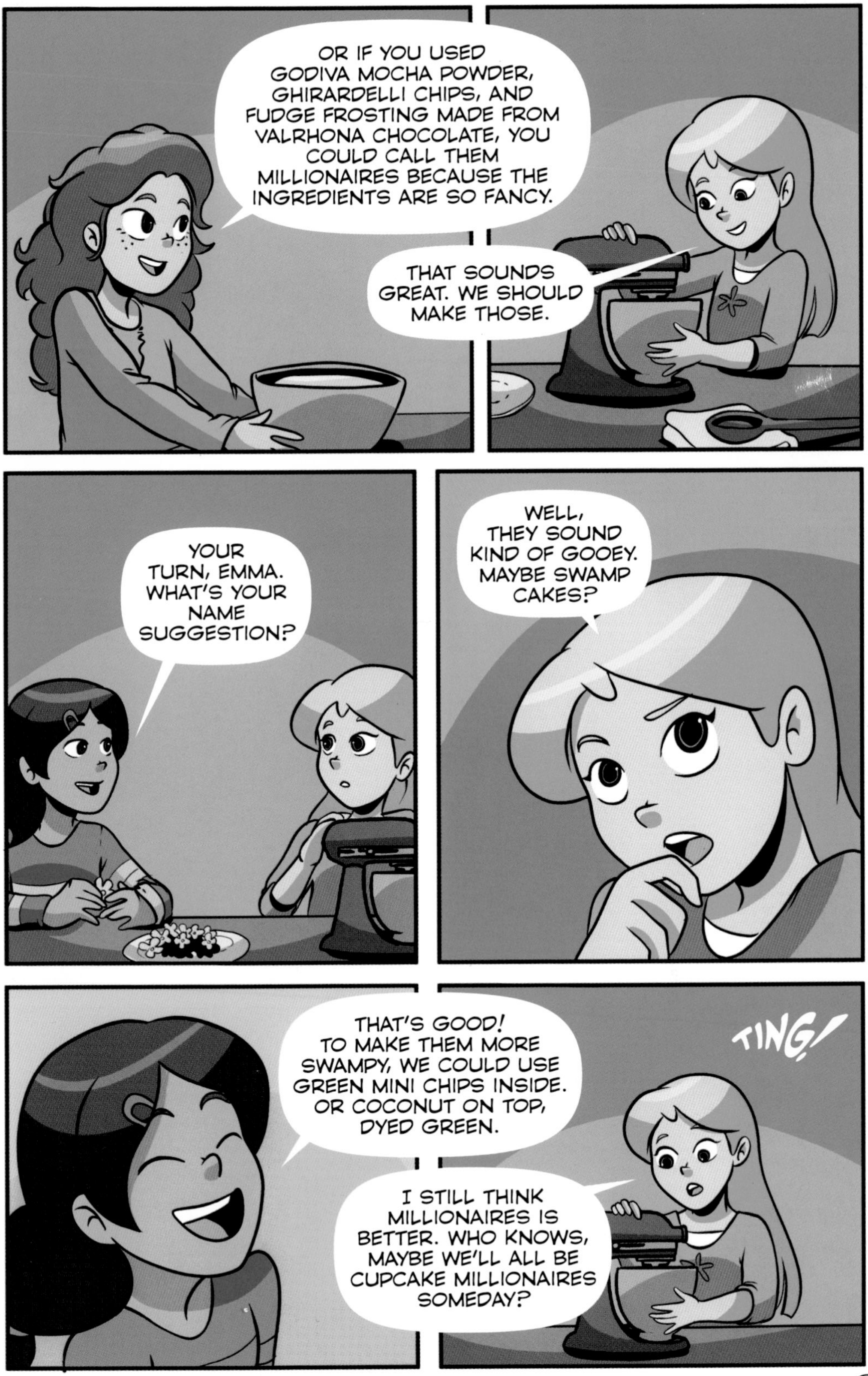
OR IF YOU USED GODIVA MOCHA POWDER, GHIRARDELLI CHIPS, AND FUDGE FROSTING MADE FROM VALRHONA CHOCOLATE, YOU COULD CALL THEM MILLIONAIRES BECAUSE THE INGREDIENTS ARE SO FANCY.
THAT SOUNDS GREAT. WE SHOULD MAKE THOSE.
YOUR TURN, EMMA. WHAT'S YOUR NAME SUGGESTION?
WELL, THEY SOUND KIND OF GOOEY. MAYBE SWAMP CAKES?
THAT'S GOOD! TO MAKE THEM MORE SWAMPY, WE COULD USE GREEN MINI CHIPS INSIDE. OR COCONUT ON TOP, DYED GREEN.
TING!
I STILL THINK MILLIONAIRES IS BETTER. WHO KNOWS, MAYBE WE'LL ALL BE CUPCAKE MILLIONAIRES SOMEDAY?

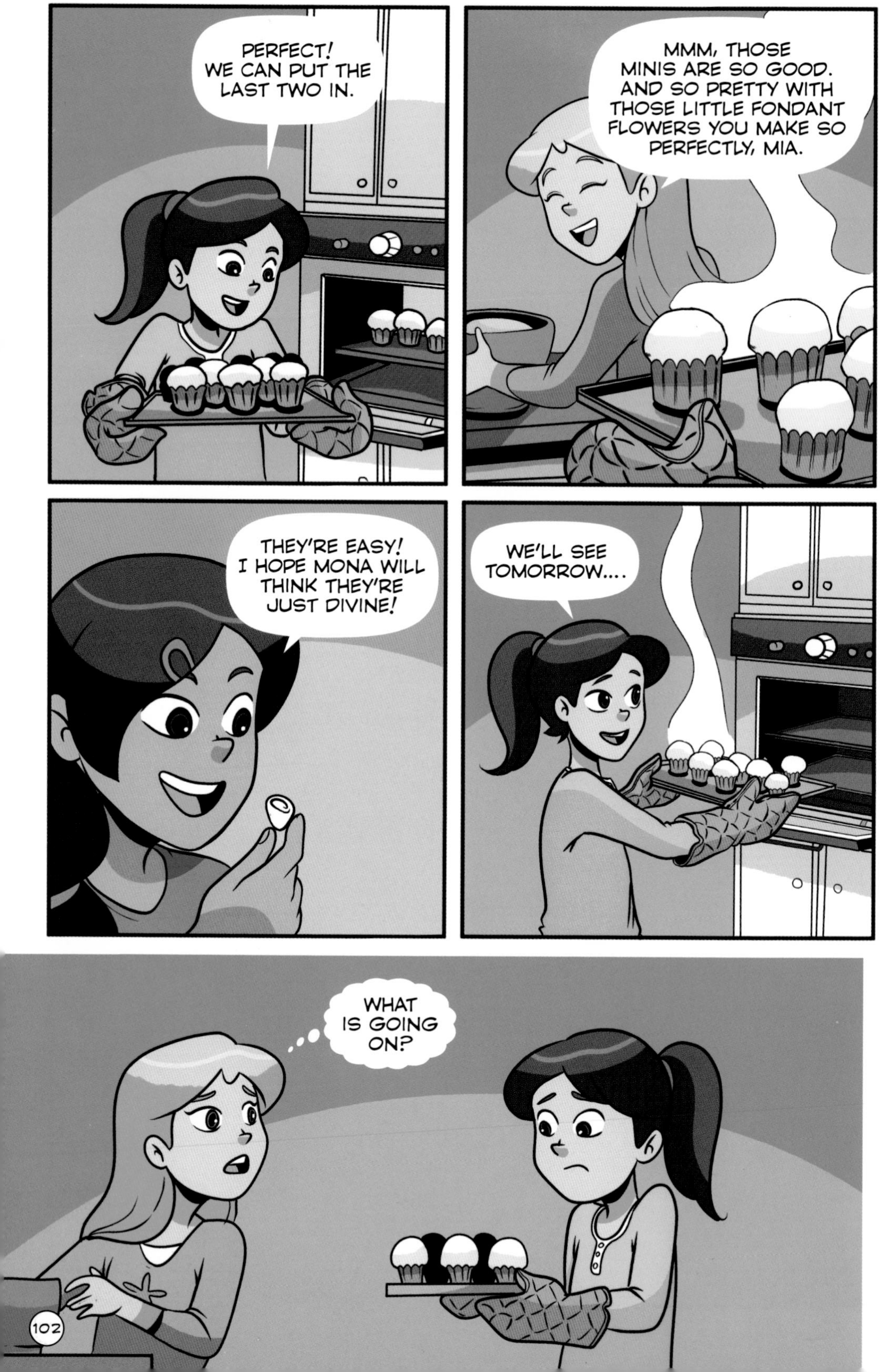
PERFECT! WE CAN PUT THE LAST TWO IN.
MMM, THOSE MINIS ARE SO GOOD. AND SO PRETTY WITH THOSE LITTLE FONDANT FLOWERS YOU MAKE SO PERFECTLY, MIA.
THEY'RE EASY! I HOPE MONA WILL THINK THEY'RE JUST DIVINE!
WE'LL SEE TOMORROW....
WHAT IS GOING ON?

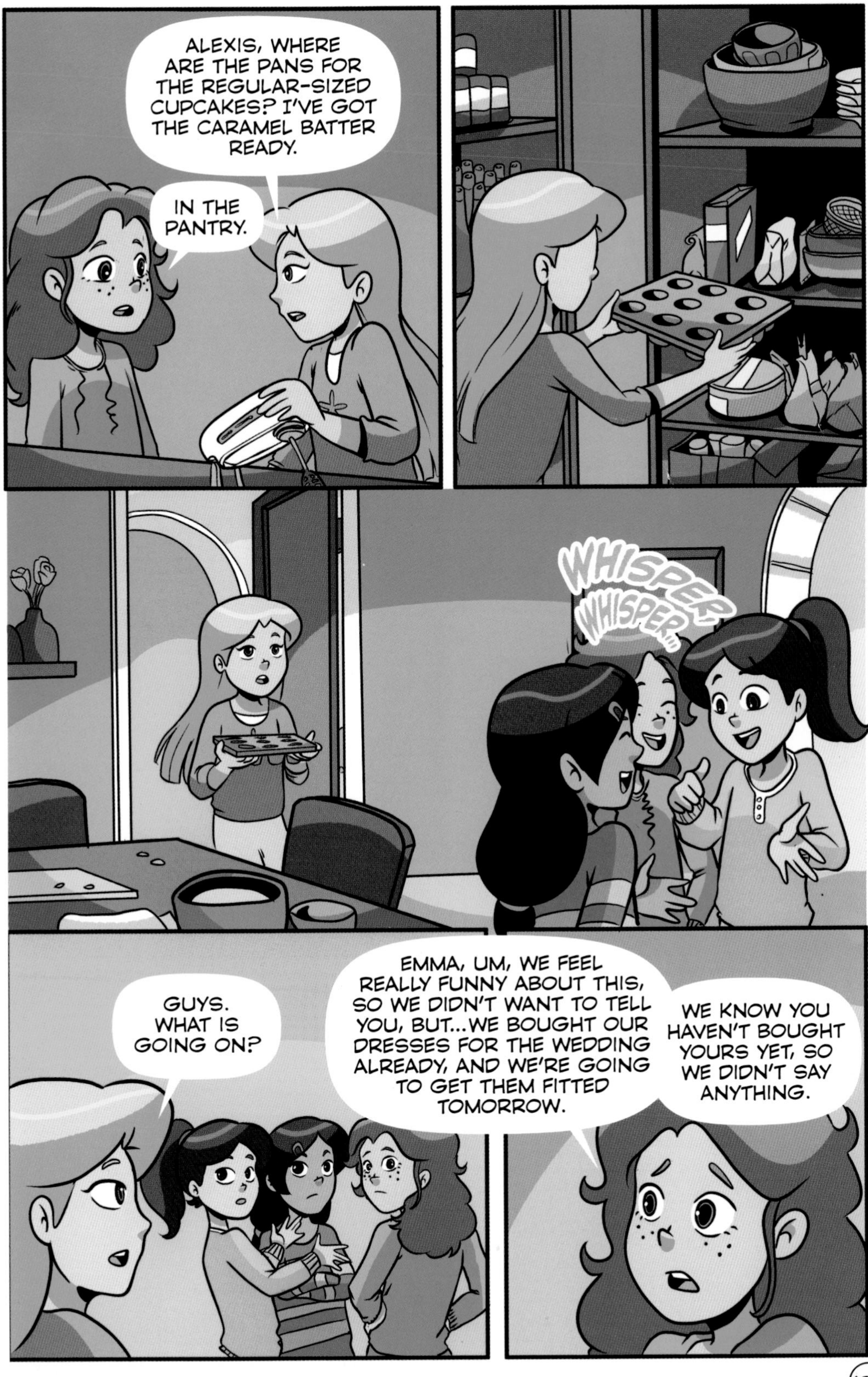
ALEXIS, WHERE ARE THE PANS FOR THE REGULAR-SIZED CUPCAKES? I'VE GOT THE CARAMEL BATTER READY.
IN THE PANTRY.
WHISPER. WHISPER...
GUYS. WHAT IS GOING ON?
EMMA, UM, WE FEEL REALLY FUNNY ABOUT THIS, SO WE DIDN'T WANT TO TELL YOU, BUT...WE BOUGHT OUR DRESSES FOR THE WEDDING ALREADY, AND WE'RE GOING TO GET THEM FITTED TOMORROW.
WE KNOW YOU HAVEN'T BOUGHT YOURS YET, SO WE DIDN'T SAY ANYTHING.

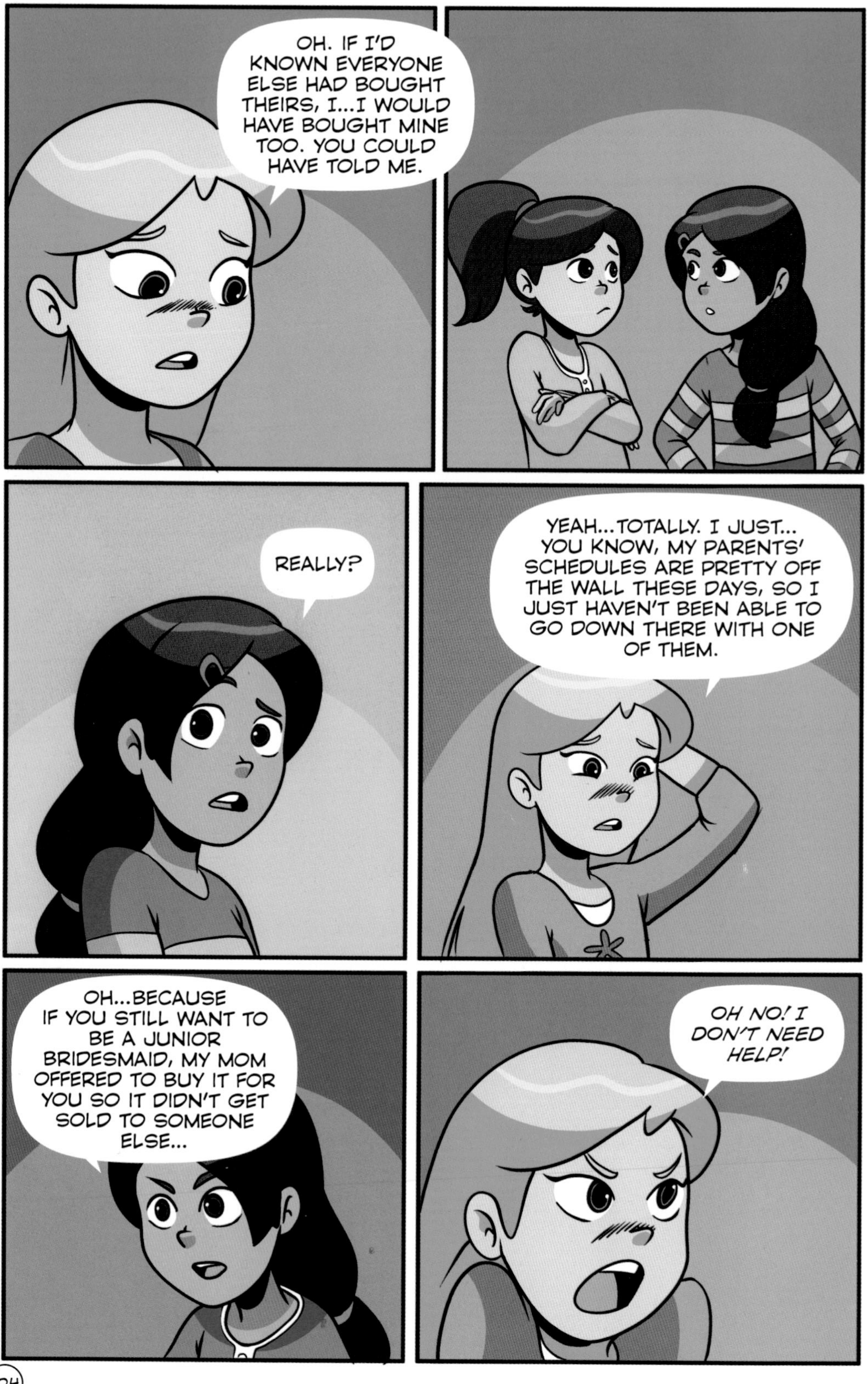
OH. IF I'D KNOWN EVERYONE ELSE HAD BOUGHT THEIRS, I...I WOULD HAVE BOUGHT MINE TOO. YOU COULD HAVE TOLD ME.
REALLY?
YEAH...TOTALLY. I JUST... YOU KNOW, MY PARENTS' SCHEDULES ARE PRETTY OFF THE WALL THESE DAYS, SO I JUST HAVEN'T BEEN ABLE TO GO DOWN THERE WITH ONE OF THEM.
OH...BECAUSE IF YOU STILL WANT TO BE A JUNIOR BRIDESMAID, MY MOM OFFERED TO BUY IT FOR YOU SO IT DIDN'T GET SOLD TO SOMEONE ELSE...
OH NO! I DON'T NEED HELP!

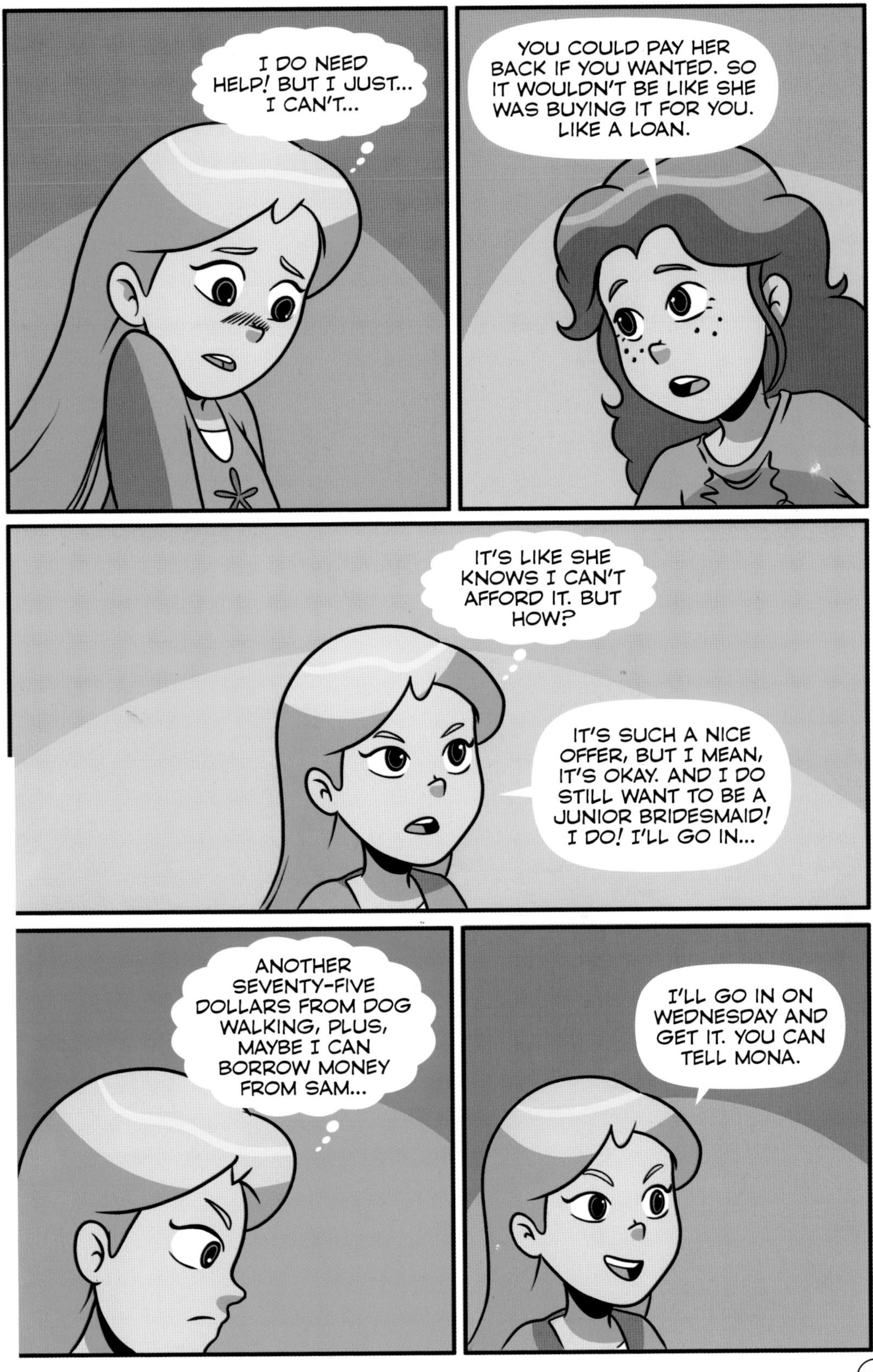
I DO NEED HELP! BUT I JUST... I CAN'T...
YOU COULD PAY HER BACK IF YOU WANTED. SO IT WOULDN'T BE LIKE SHE WAS BUYING IT FOR YOU. LIKE A LOAN.
IT'S LIKE SHE KNOWS I CAN'T AFFORD IT. BUT HOW?
IT'S SUCH A NICE OFFER, BUT I MEAN, IT'S OKAY. AND I DO STILL WANT TO BE A JUNIOR BRIDESMAID! I DO! I'LL GO IN...
ANOTHER SEVENTY-FIVE DOLLARS FROM DOG WALKING, PLUS, MAYBE I CAN BORROW MONEY FROM SAM...
I'LL GO IN ON WEDNESDAY AND GET IT. YOU CAN TELL MONA.

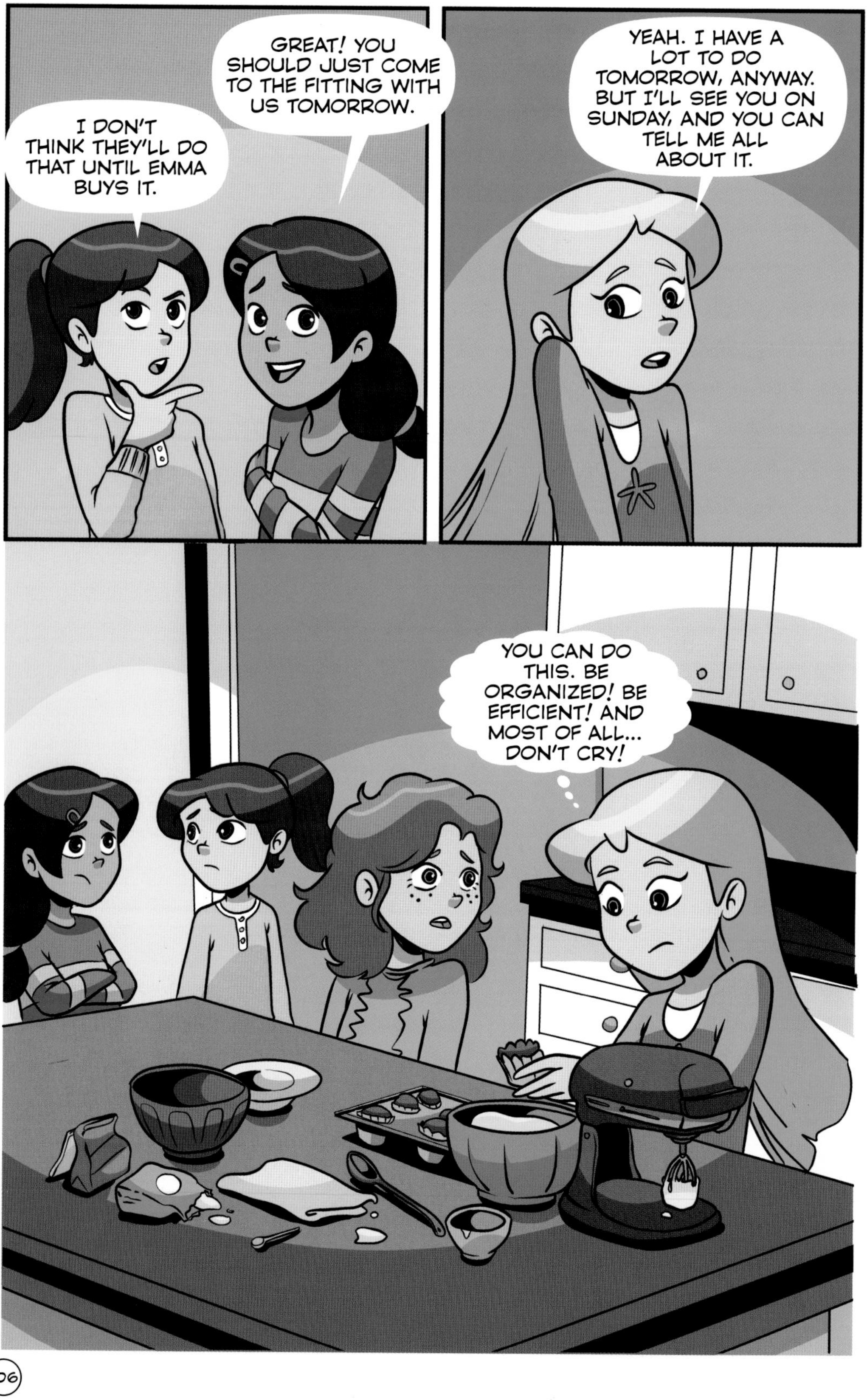
I DON'T THINK THEY'LL DO THAT UNTIL EMMA BUYS IT.
GREAT! YOU SHOULD JUST COME TO THE FITTING WITH US TOMORROW.
YEAH. I HAVE A LOT TO DO TOMORROW, ANYWAY. BUT I'LL SEE YOU ON SUNDAY, AND YOU CAN TELL ME ALL ABOUT IT.
YOU CAN DO THIS. BE ORGANIZED! BE EFFICIENT! AND MOST OF ALL... DON'T CRY!

Chapter 9

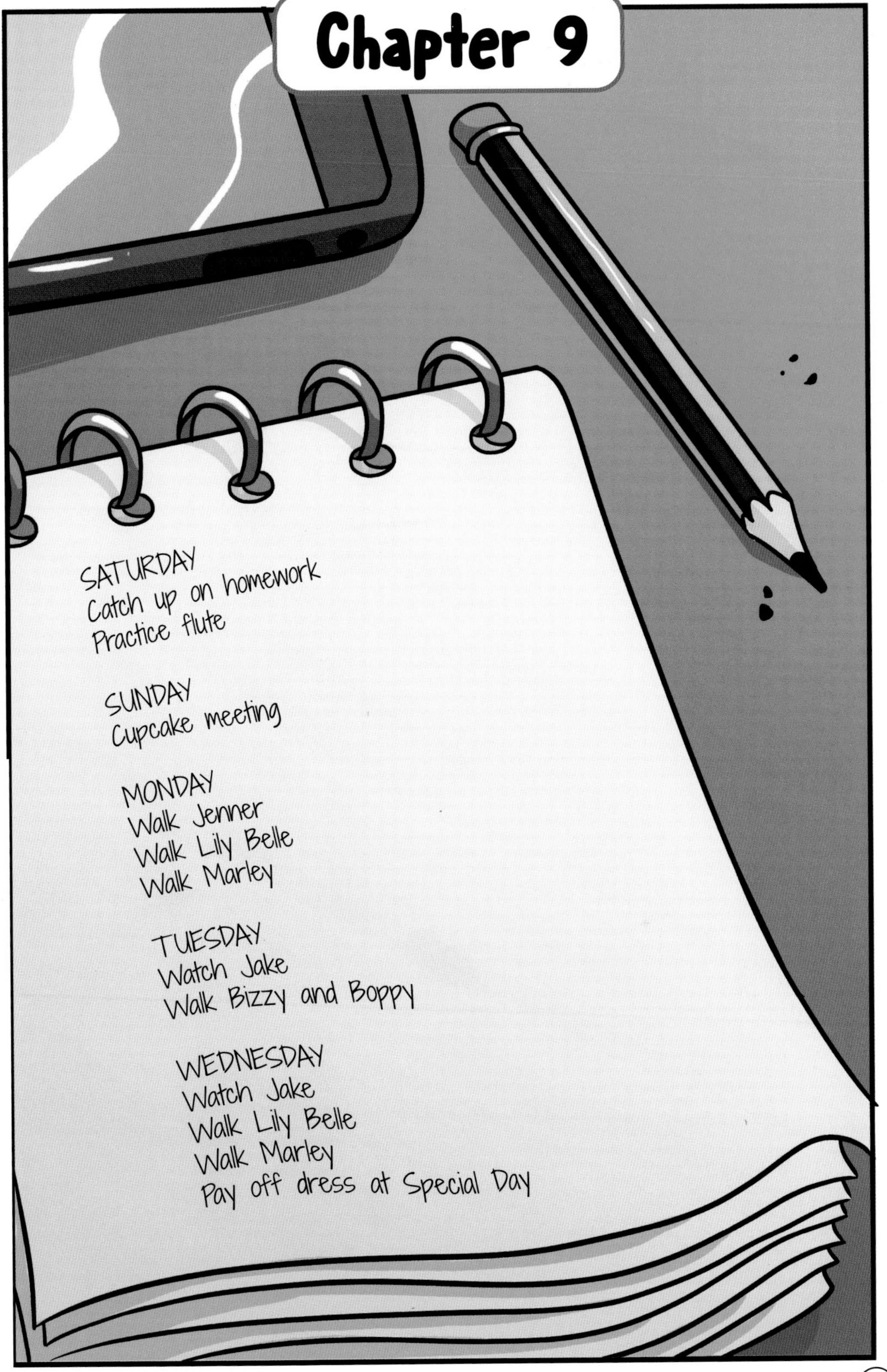
SATURDAY
Catch up on homework
Practice flute
SUNDAY
Cupcake meeting
MONDAY
Walk Jenner
Walk Lily Belle
Walk Marley
TUESDAY
Watch Jake
Walk Bizzy and Boppy
WEDNESDAY
Watch Jake
Walk Lily Belle
Walk Marley
Pay off dress at Special Day

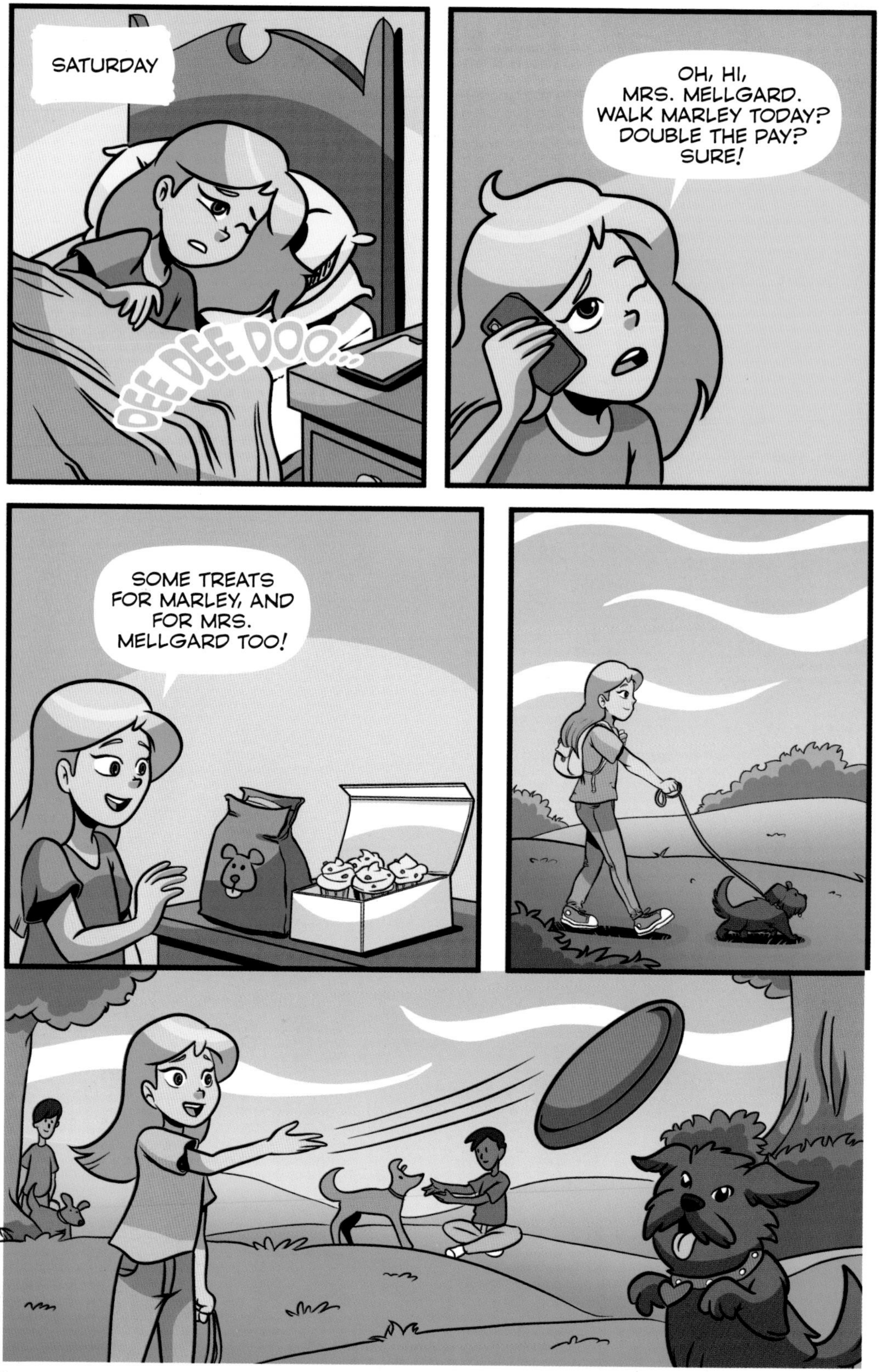
SATURDAY
DEE DEE DOO...
OH, HI, MRS. MELLGARD. WALK MARLEY TODAY? DOUBLE THE PAY? SURE!
SOME TREATS FOR MARLEY, AND FOR MRS. MELLGARD TOO!

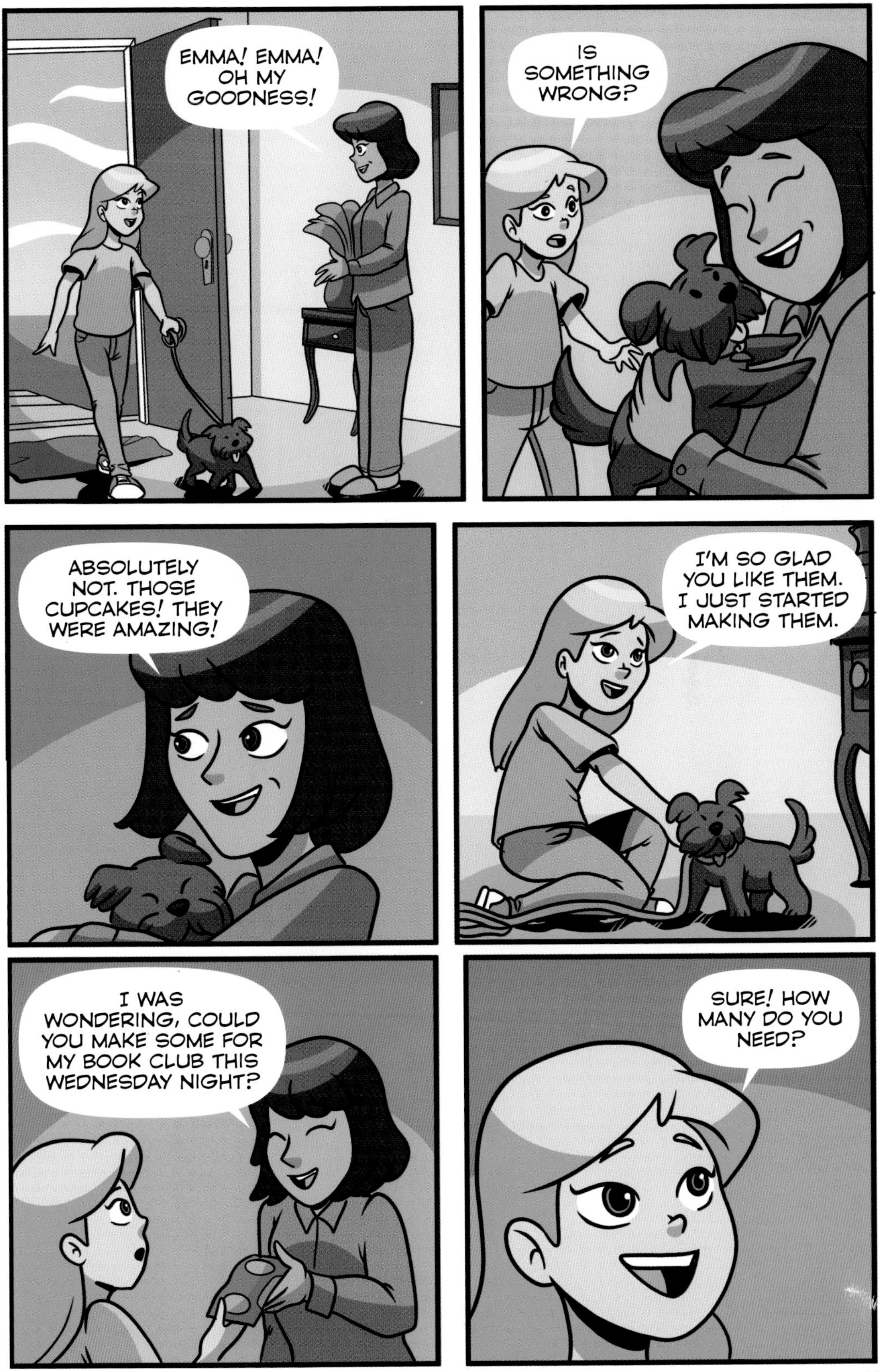
EMMA! EMMA! OH MY GOODNESS!
IS SOMETHING WRONG?
ABSOLUTELY NOT. THOSE CUPCAKES! THEY WERE AMAZING!
I'M SO GLAD YOU LIKE THEM. I JUST STARTED MAKING THEM.
I WAS WONDERING, COULD YOU MAKE SOME FOR MY BOOK CLUB THIS WEDNESDAY NIGHT?
SURE! HOW MANY DO YOU NEED?

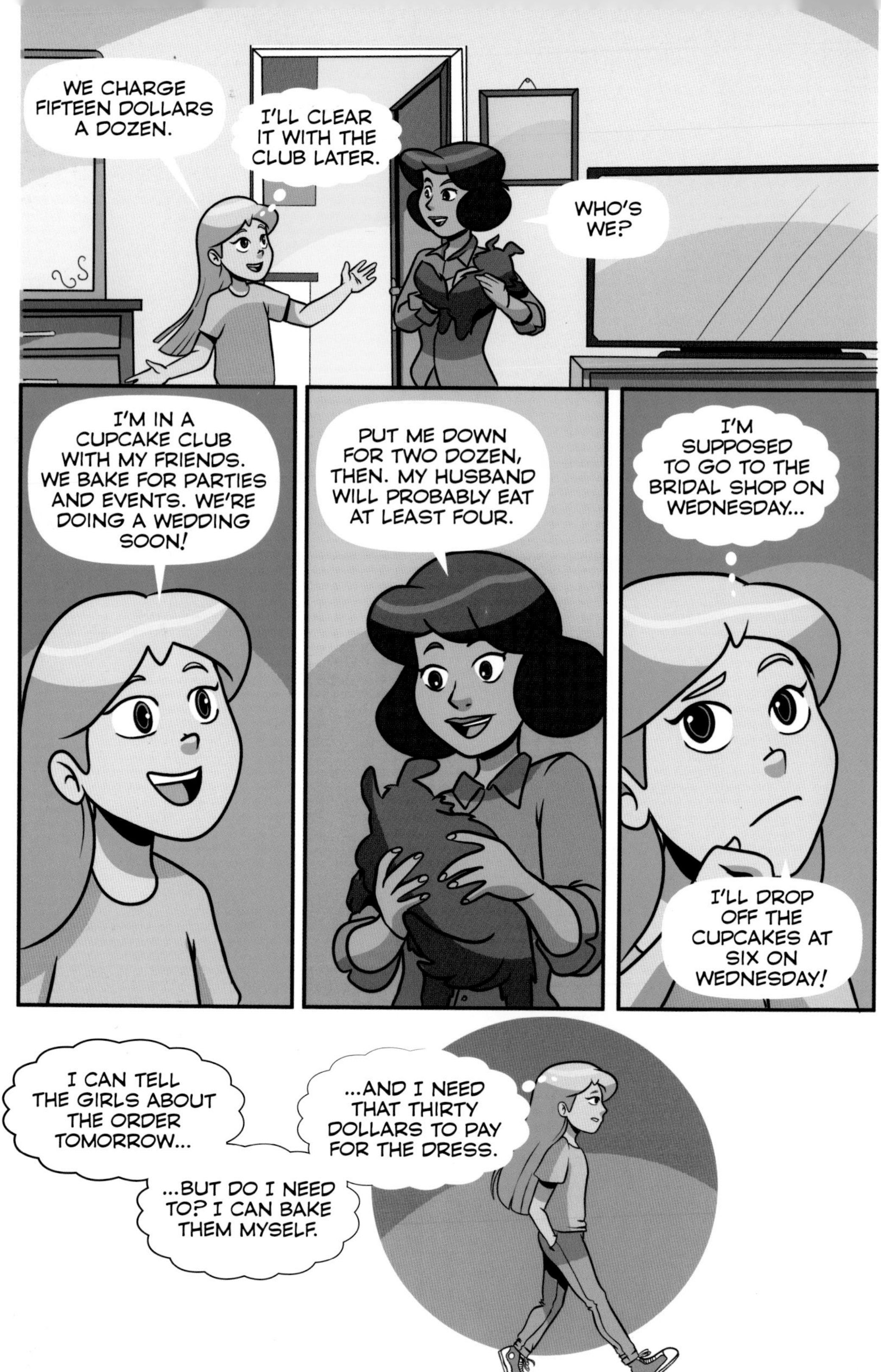
WE CHARGE FIFTEEN DOLLARS A DOZEN.
I'LL CLEAR IT WITH THE CLUB LATER.
WHO'S WE?
I'M IN A CUPCAKE CLUB WITH MY FRIENDS. WE BAKE FOR PARTIES AND EVENTS. WE'RE DOING A WEDDING SOON!
PUT ME DOWN FOR TWO DOZEN, THEN. MY HUSBAND WILL PROBABLY EAT AT LEAST FOUR.
I'M SUPPOSED TO GO TO THE BRIDAL SHOP ON WEDNESDAY...
I'LL DROP OFF THE CUPCAKES AT SIX ON WEDNESDAY!
I CAN TELL THE GIRLS ABOUT THE ORDER TOMORROW...
...AND I NEED THAT THIRTY DOLLARS TO PAY FOR THE DRESS.
...BUT DO I NEED TO? I CAN BAKE THEM MYSELF.

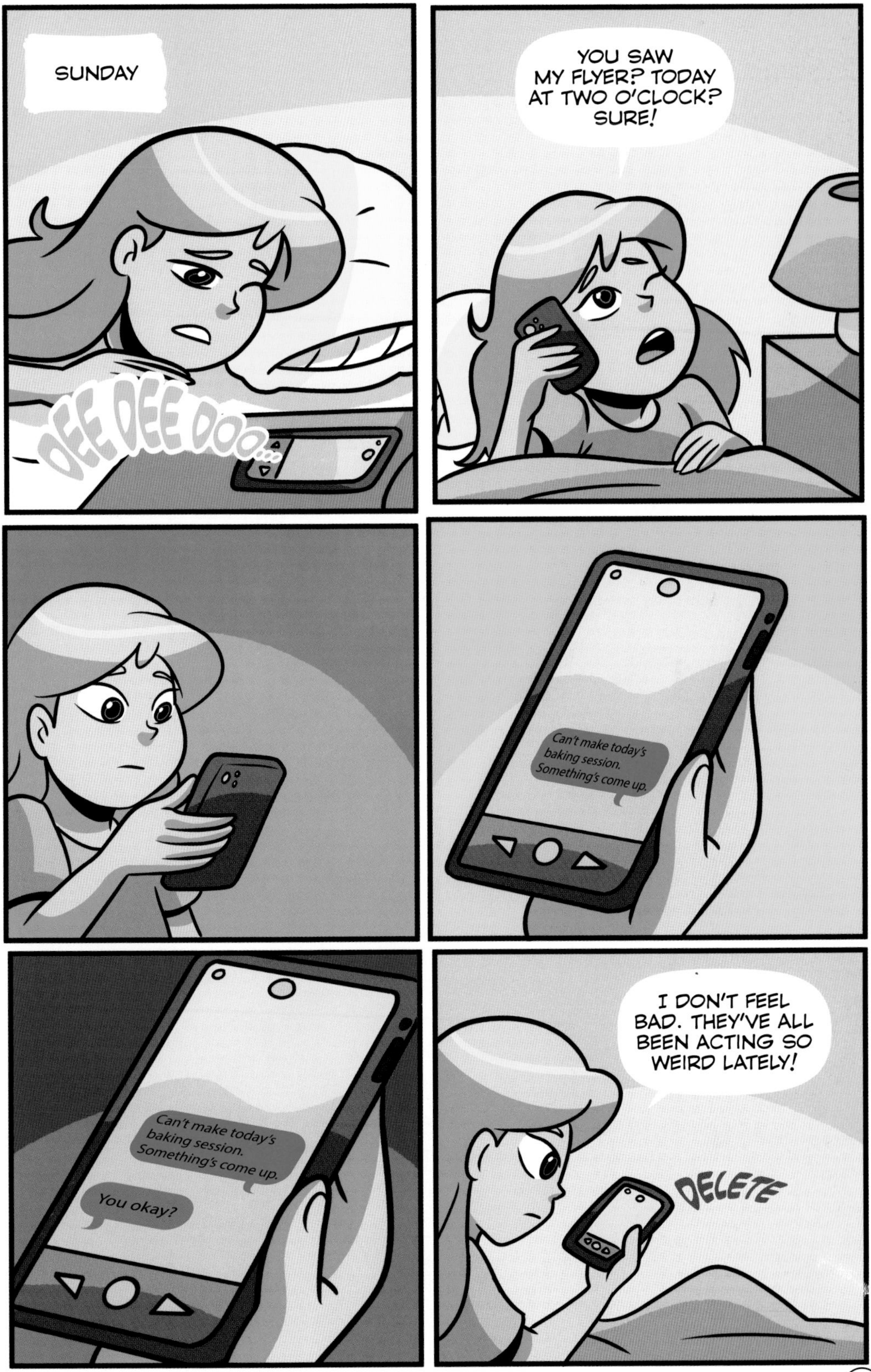
SUNDAY
DEE DEE DOO...
YOU SAW MY FLYER? TODAY AT TWO O'CLOCK? SURE!
Can't make today's baking session. Something's come up.
Can't make today's baking session. Something's come up.
You okay?
I DON'T FEEL BAD. THEY'VE ALL BEEN ACTING SO WEIRD LATELY!
DELETE

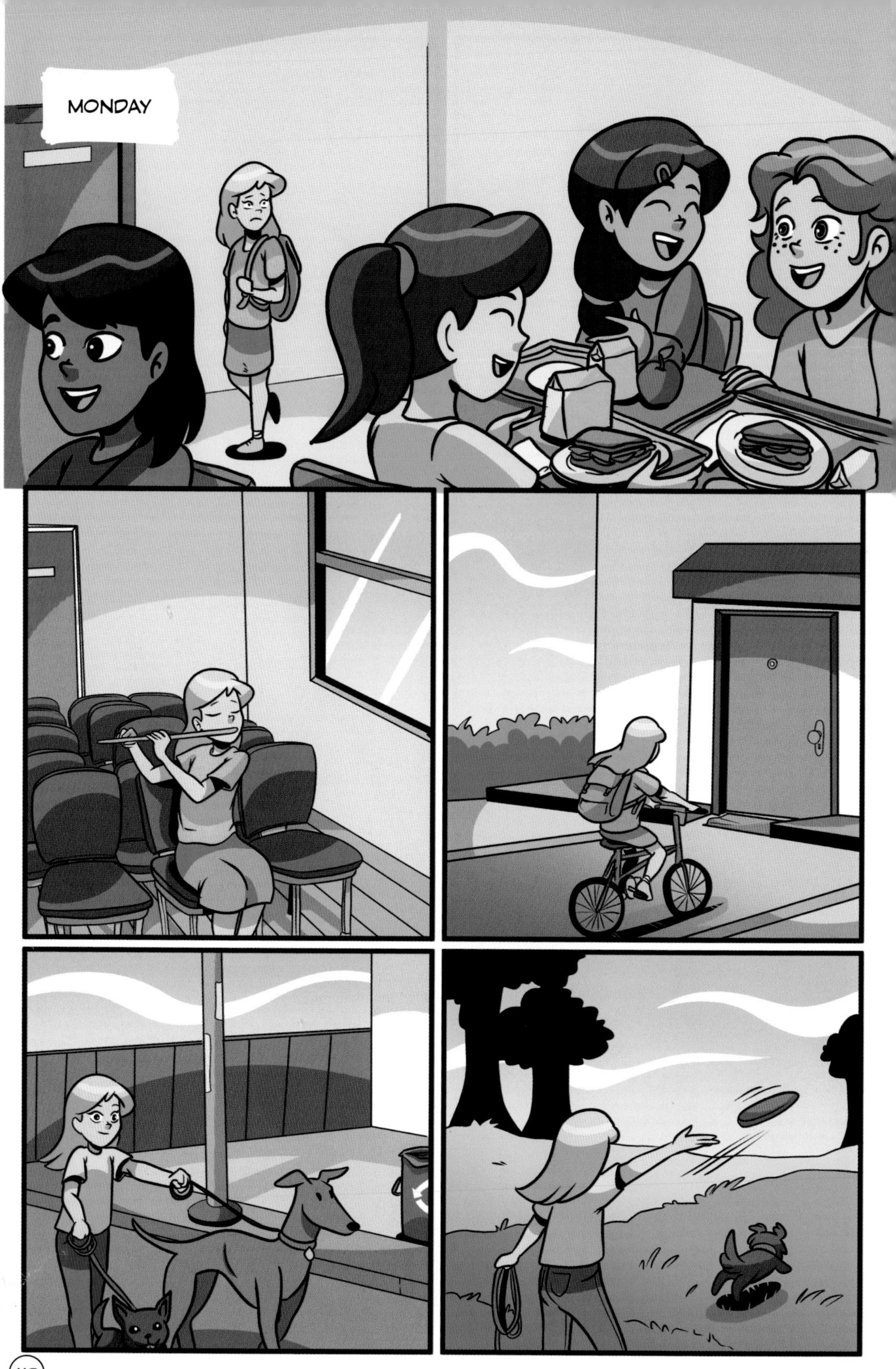
MONDAY

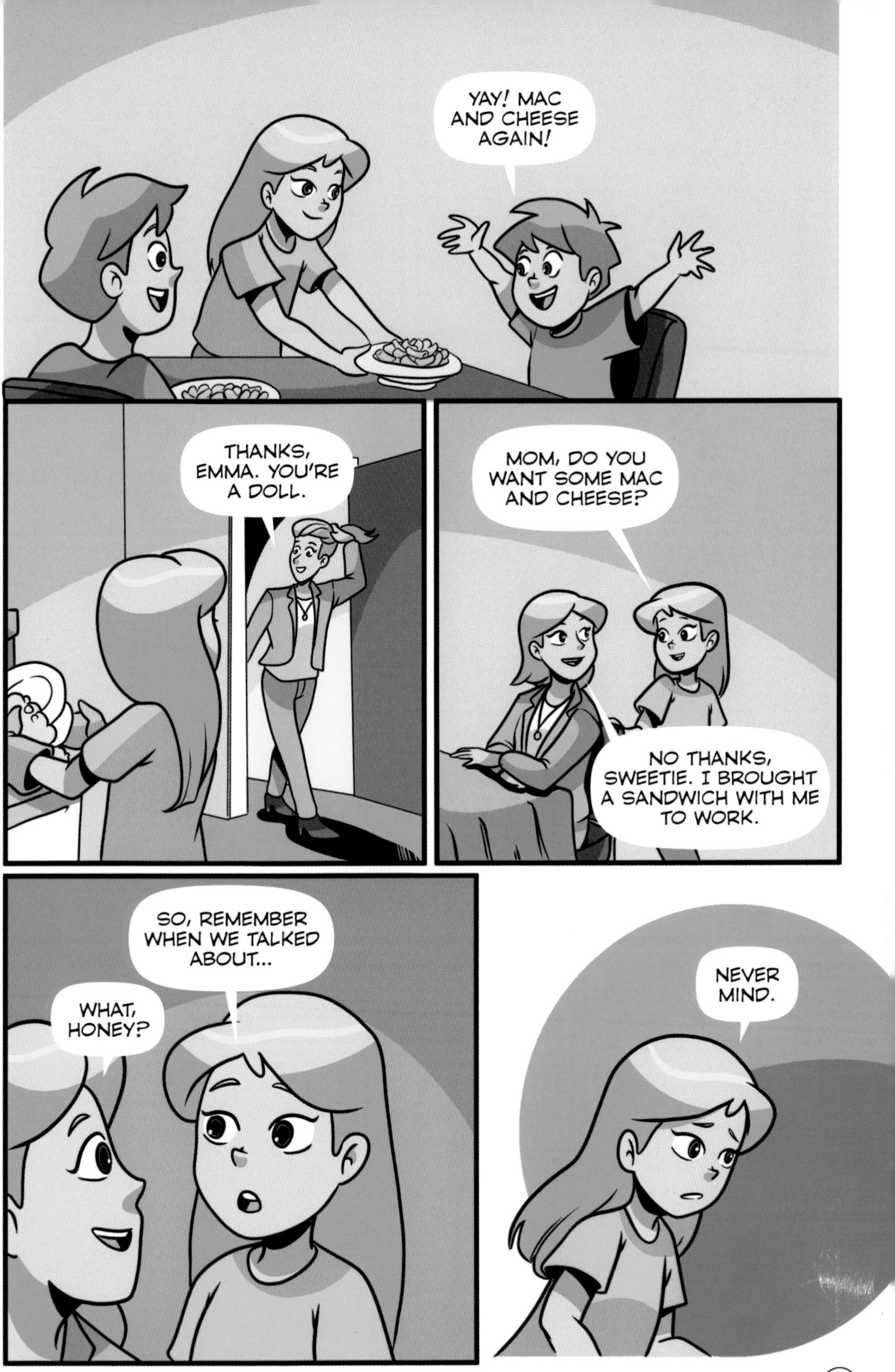
YAY! MAC AND CHEESE AGAIN!
THANKS, EMMA. YOU'RE A DOLL.
MOM, DO YOU WANT SOME MAC AND CHEESE?
NO THANKS, SWEETIE. I BROUGHT A SANDWICH WITH ME TO WORK.
SO, REMEMBER WHEN WE TALKED ABOUT...
WHAT, HONEY?
NEVER MIND.

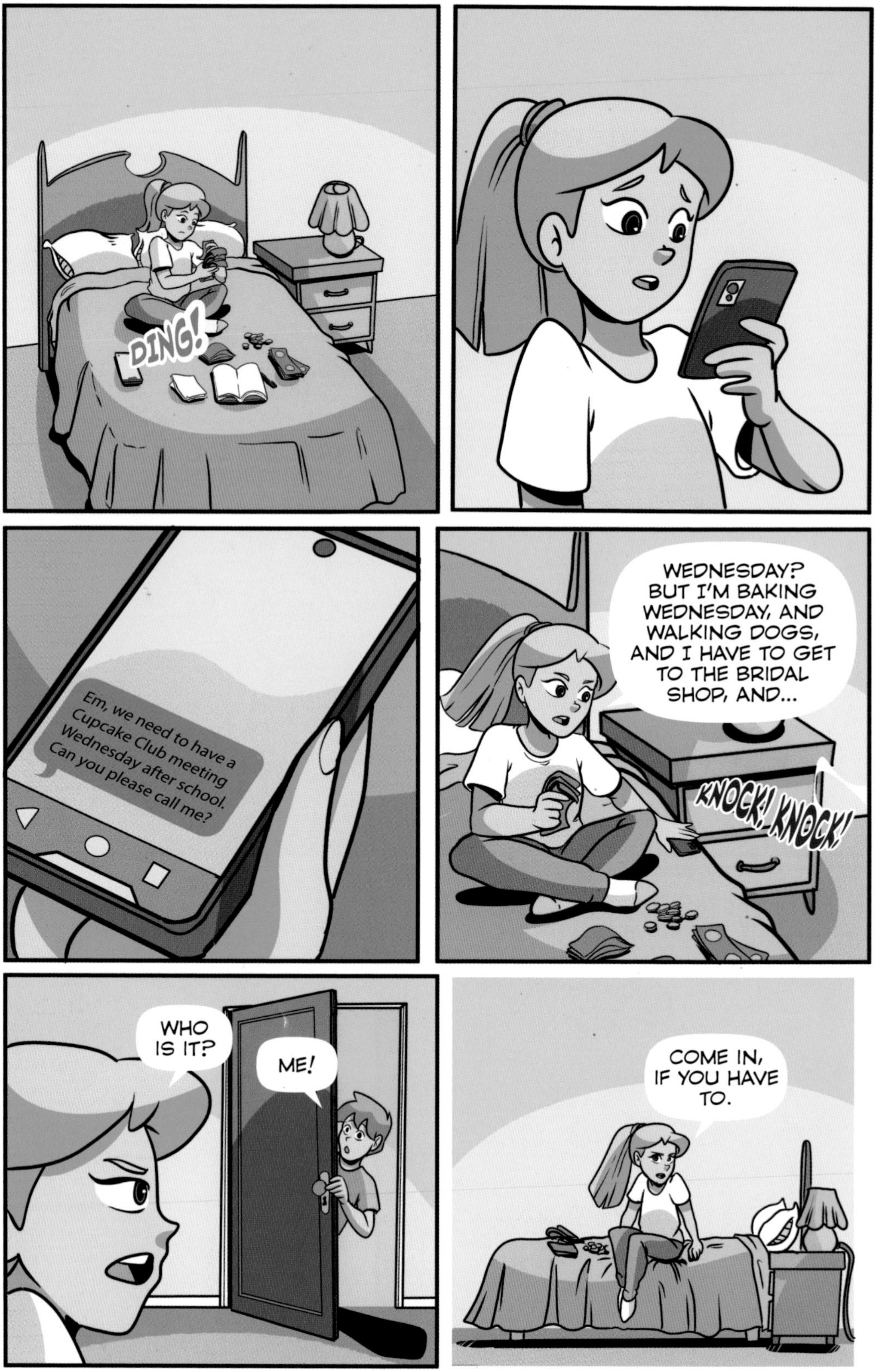
DING!
Em, we need to have a Cupcake Club meeting Wednesday after school. Can you please call me?
WEDNESDAY? BUT I'M BAKING WEDNESDAY, AND WALKING DOGS, AND I HAVE TO GET TO THE BRIDAL SHOP, AND...
KNOCK! KNOCK!
WHO IS IT?
ME!
COME IN, IF YOU HAVE TO.

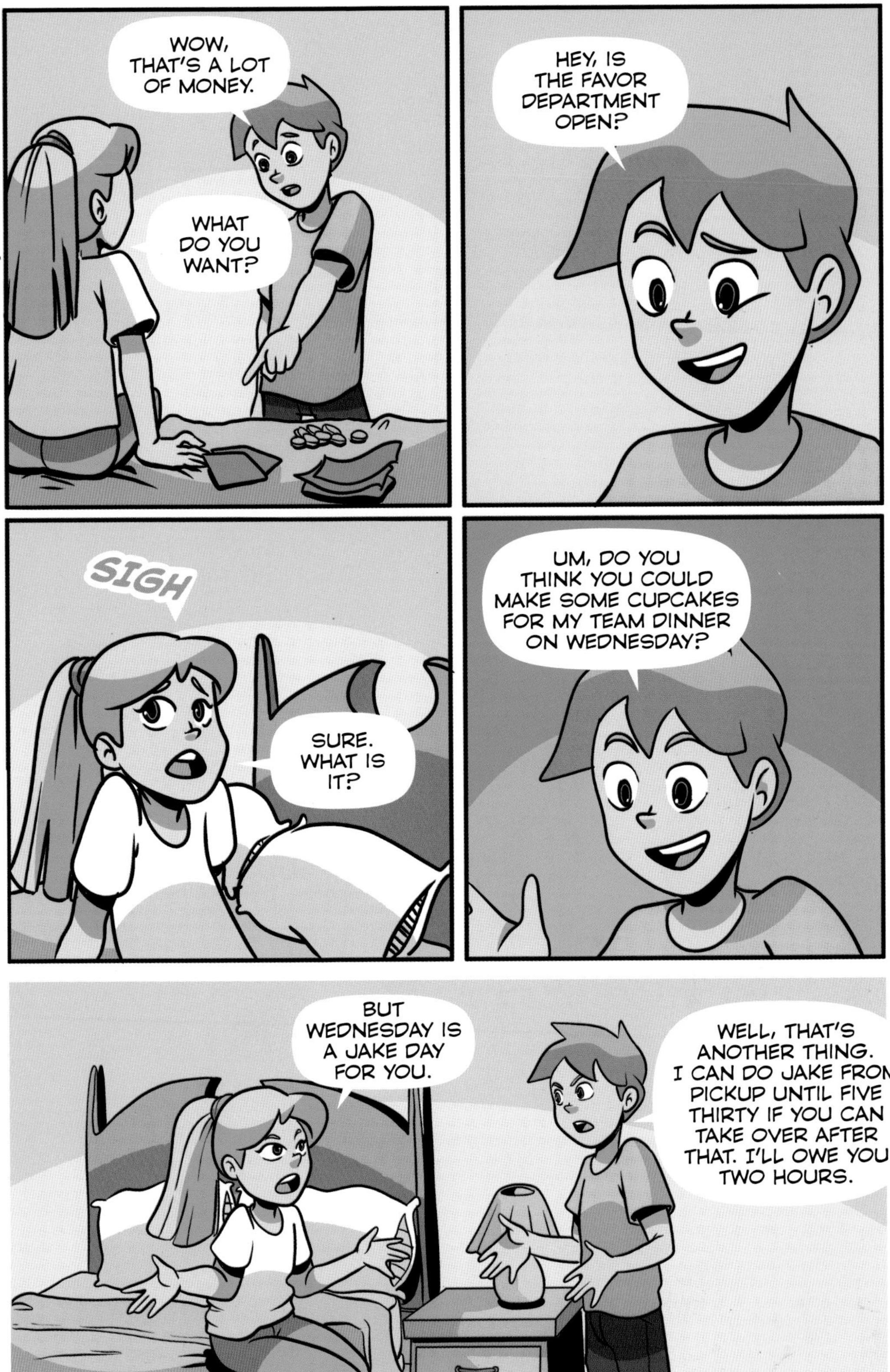
WOW, THAT'S A LOT OF MONEY.
WHAT DO YOU WANT?
HEY, IS THE FAVOR DEPARTMENT OPEN?
SIGH
SURE. WHAT IS IT?
UM, DO YOU THINK YOU COULD MAKE SOME CUPCAKES FOR MY TEAM DINNER ON WEDNESDAY?
BUT WEDNESDAY IS A JAKE DAY FOR YOU.
WELL, THAT'S ANOTHER THING. I CAN DO JAKE FROM PICKUP UNTIL FIVE THIRTY IF YOU CAN TAKE OVER AFTER THAT. I'LL OWE YOU TWO HOURS.

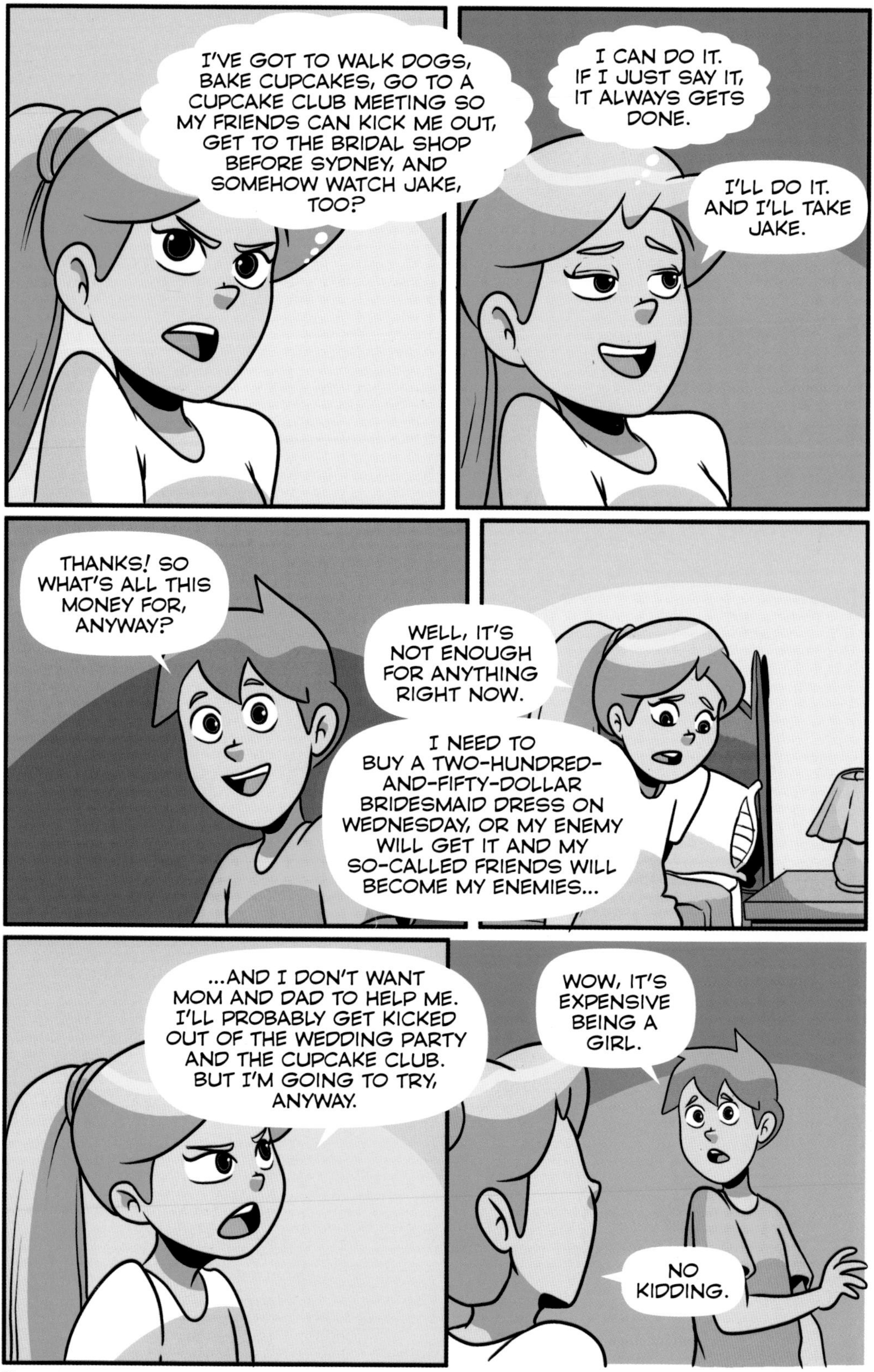
I'VE GOT TO WALK DOGS, BAKE CUPCAKES, GO TO A CUPCAKE CLUB MEETING SO MY FRIENDS CAN KICK ME OUT, GET TO THE BRIDAL SHOP BEFORE SYDNEY, AND SOMEHOW WATCH JAKE, TOO?
I CAN DO IT. IF I JUST SAY IT, IT ALWAYS GETS DONE.
I'LL DO IT. AND I'LL TAKE JAKE.
THANKS! SO WHAT'S ALL THIS MONEY FOR, ANYWAY?
WELL, IT'S NOT ENOUGH FOR ANYTHING RIGHT NOW.
I NEED TO BUY A TWO-HUNDRED-AND-FIFTY-DOLLAR BRIDESMAID DRESS ON WEDNESDAY, OR MY ENEMY WILL GET IT AND MY SO-CALLED FRIENDS WILL BECOME MY ENEMIES...
...AND I DON'T WANT MOM AND DAD TO HELP ME. I'LL PROBABLY GET KICKED OUT OF THE WEDDING PARTY AND THE CUPCAKE CLUB. BUT I'M GOING TO TRY, ANYWAY.
WOW, IT'S EXPENSIVE BEING A GIRL.
NO KIDDING.

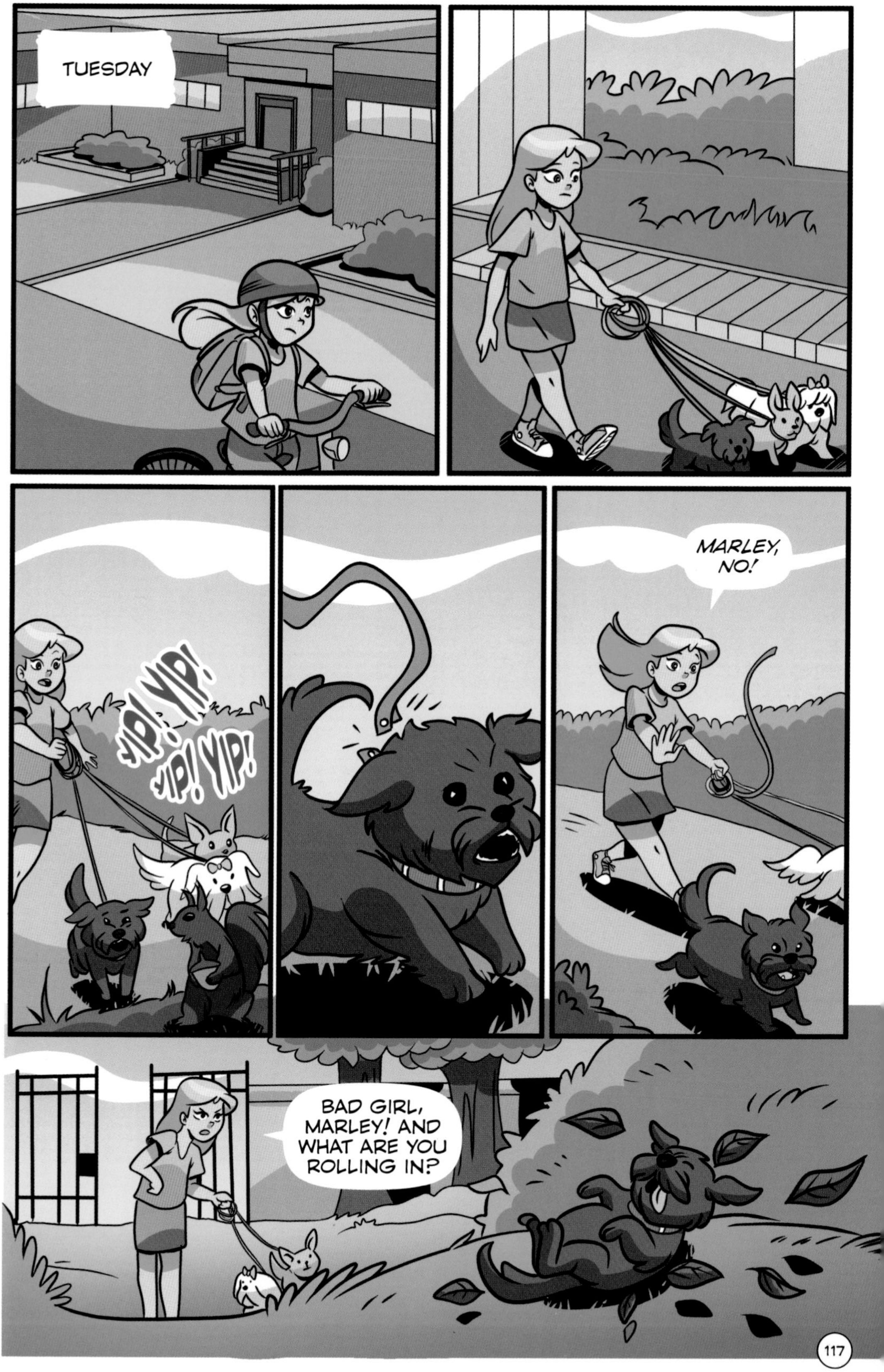
TUESDAY
YIP! YIP!
YIP! YIP!
MARLEY, NO!
BAD GIRL, MARLEY! AND WHAT ARE YOU ROLLING IN?

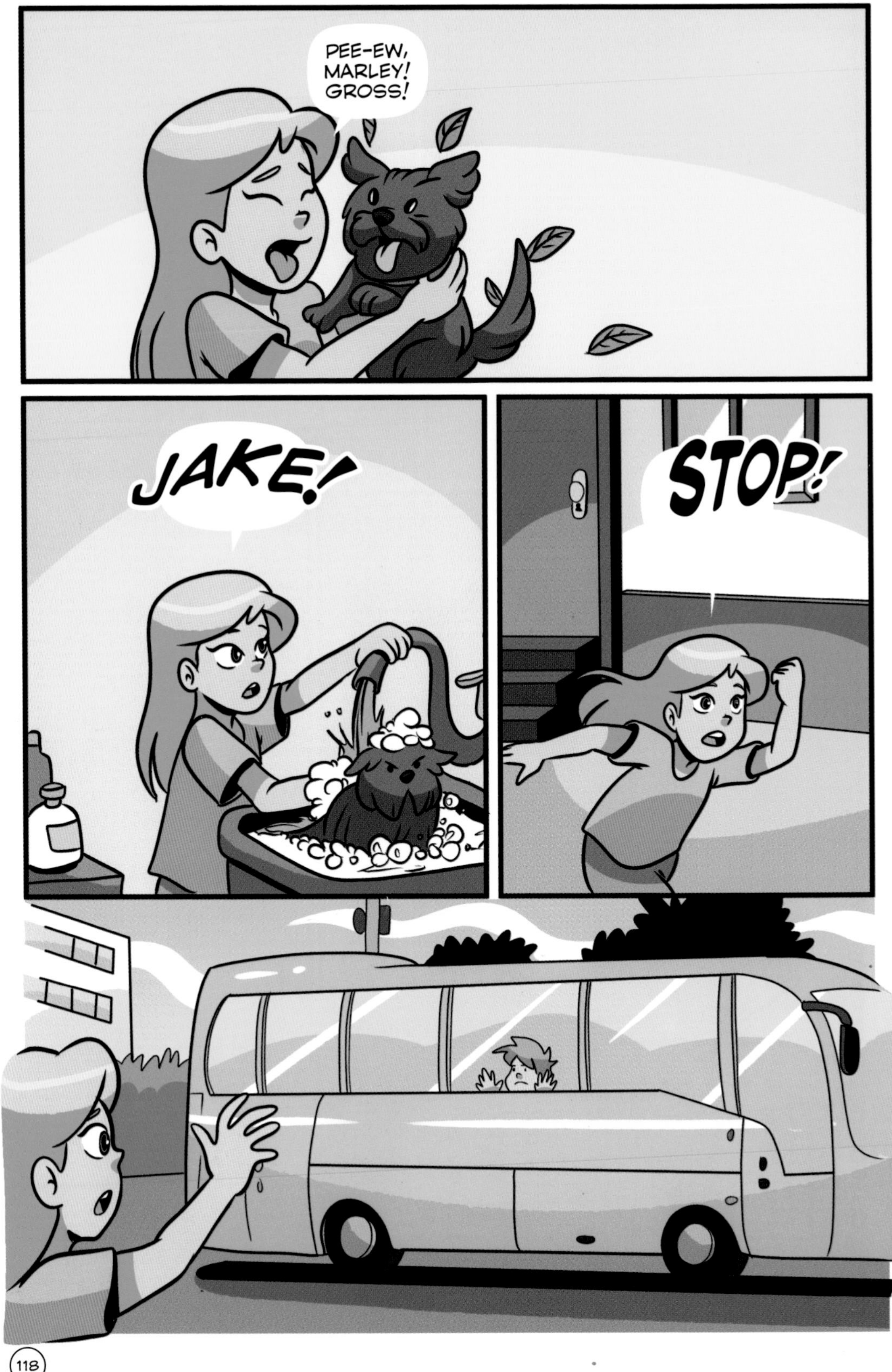
PEE-EW, MARLEY! GROSS!
JAKE!
STOP!

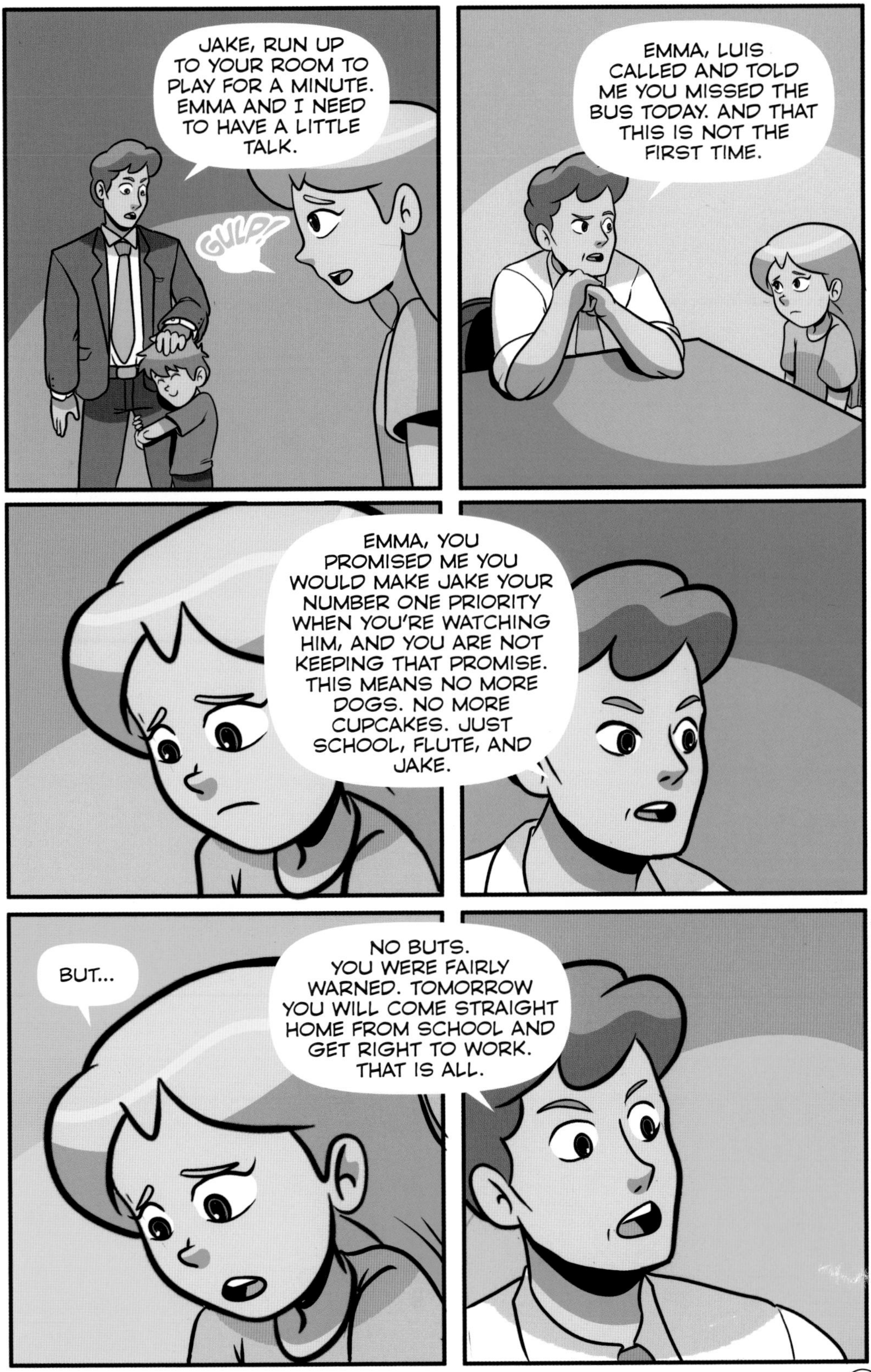
JAKE, RUN UP TO YOUR ROOM TO PLAY FOR A MINUTE. EMMA AND I NEED TO HAVE A LITTLE TALK.
GULP!
EMMA, LUIS CALLED AND TOLD ME YOU MISSED THE BUS TODAY. AND THAT THIS IS NOT THE FIRST TIME.
EMMA, YOU PROMISED ME YOU WOULD MAKE JAKE YOUR NUMBER ONE PRIORITY WHEN YOU'RE WATCHING HIM, AND YOU ARE NOT KEEPING THAT PROMISE. THIS MEANS NO MORE DOGS. NO MORE CUPCAKES. JUST SCHOOL, FLUTE, AND JAKE.
BUT...
NO BUTS. YOU WERE FAIRLY WARNED. TOMORROW YOU WILL COME STRAIGHT HOME FROM SCHOOL AND GET RIGHT TO WORK. THAT IS ALL.

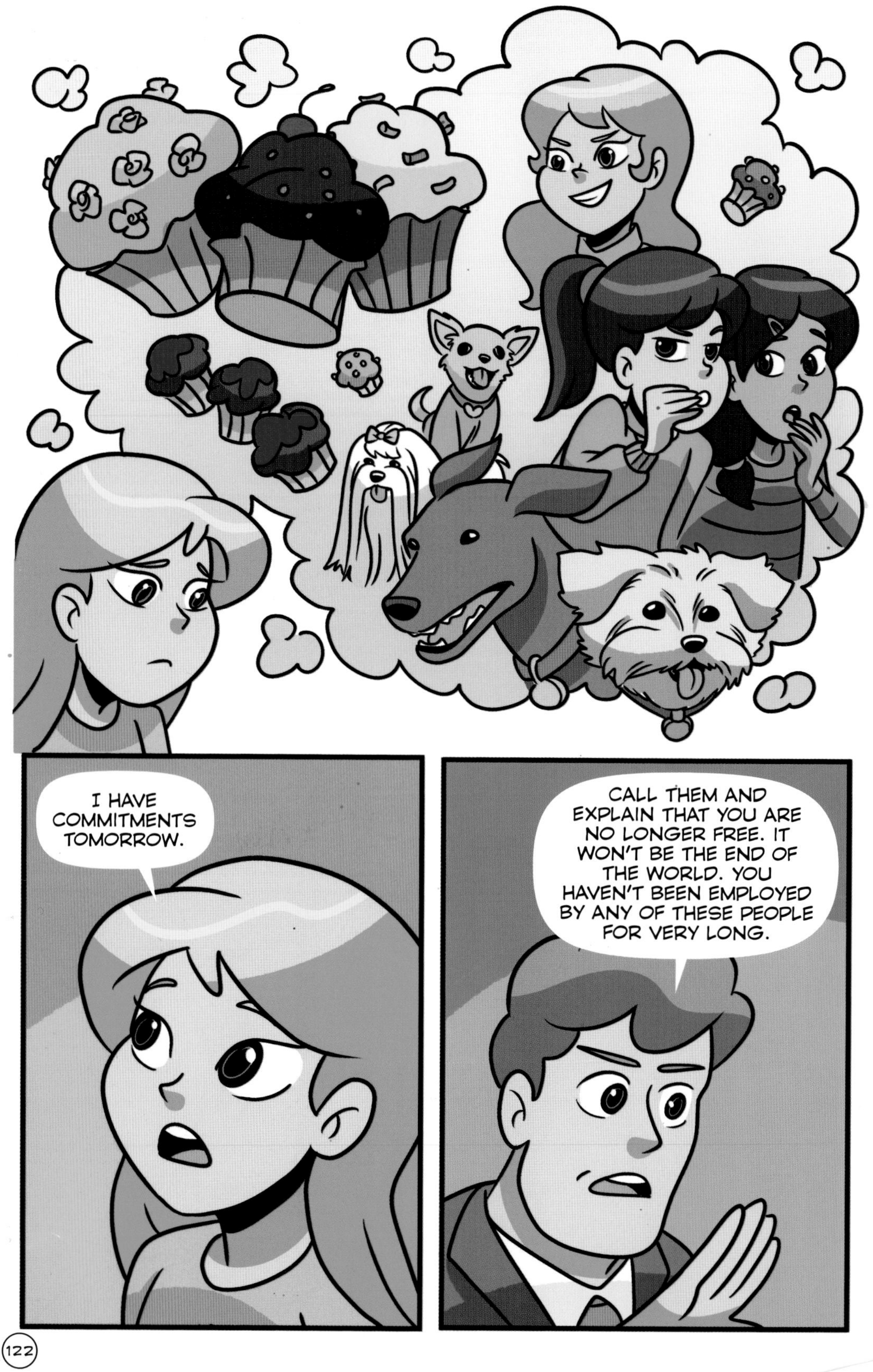
I HAVE COMMITMENTS TOMORROW.
CALL THEM AND EXPLAIN THAT YOU ARE NO LONGER FREE. IT WON'T BE THE END OF THE WORLD. YOU HAVEN'T BEEN EMPLOYED BY ANY OF THESE PEOPLE FOR VERY LONG.

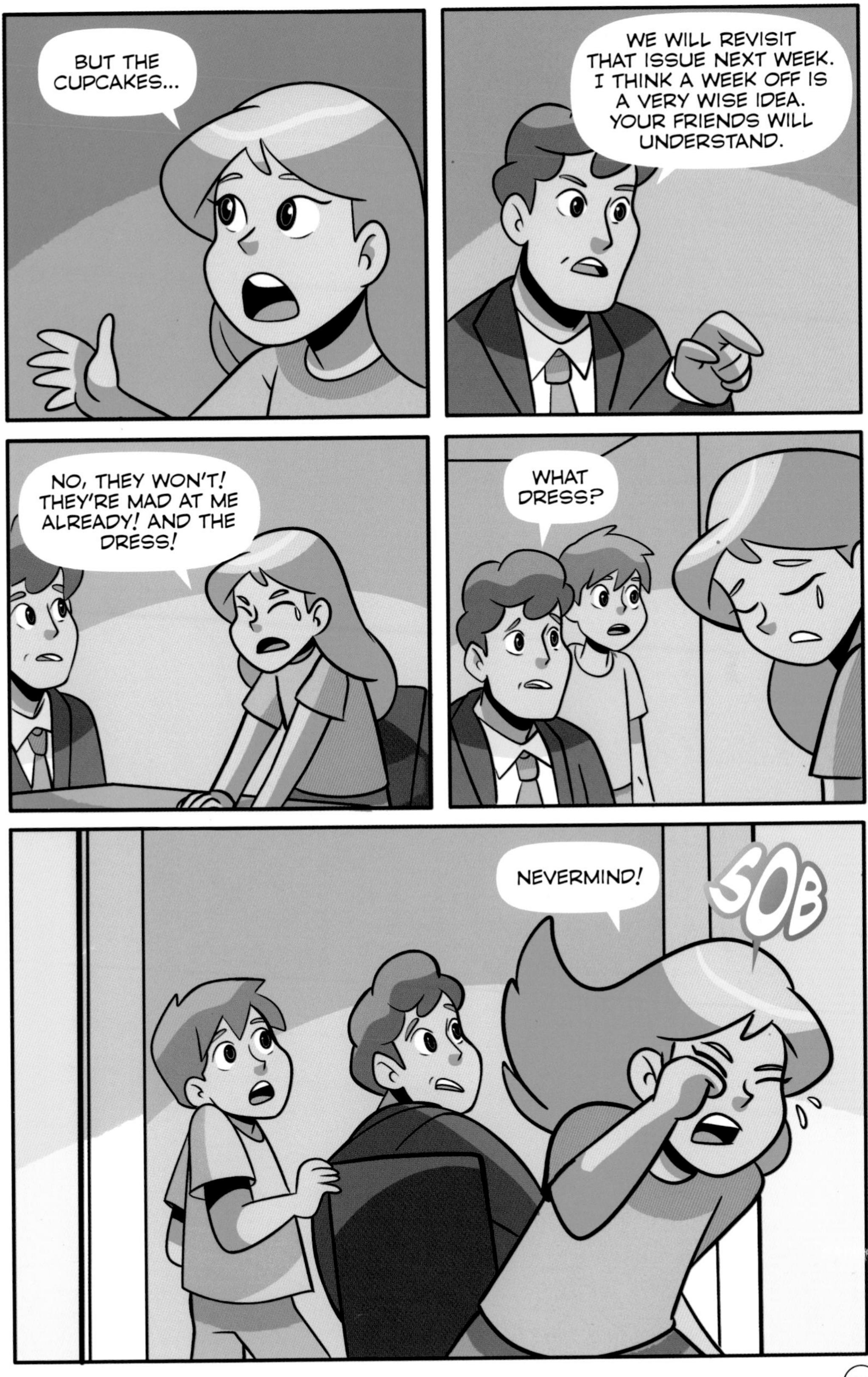
BUT THE CUPCAKES...
WE WILL REVISIT THAT ISSUE NEXT WEEK. I THINK A WEEK OFF IS A VERY WISE IDEA. YOUR FRIENDS WILL UNDERSTAND.
NO, THEY WON'T! THEY'RE MAD AT ME ALREADY! AND THE DRESS!
WHAT DRESS?
NEVERMIND!
SOB

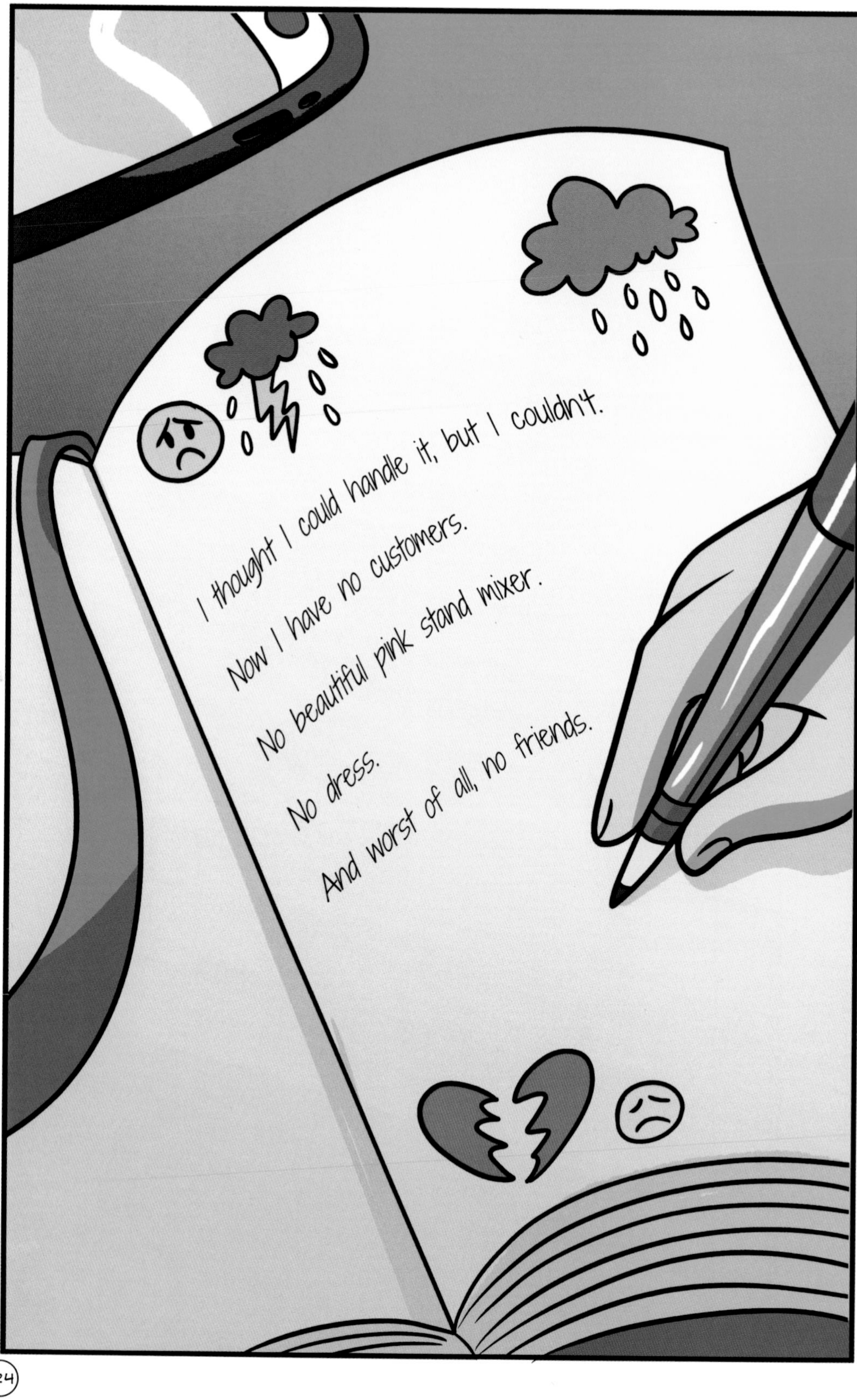
I thought I could handle it, but I couldn't.
Now I have no customers.
No beautiful pink stand mixer.
No dress.
And worst of all, no friends.

Chapter 10

THAT SOUNDED LOVELY, EMMA.

KNOCK!

I'M ONLY DOING SCALES.

HONEY, DAD TOLD ME EVERYTHING. AND I JUST WANT TO SAY THAT I'M SORRY I HAVE TO PUT ALL THIS RESPONSIBILITY ON YOU RIGHT NOW. IT MIGHT NOT BE FOR TOO MUCH LONGER, THOUGH. I FOUND OUT THAT THE LIBRARY MIGHT BE ABLE TO BRING ME BACK.

GREAT.

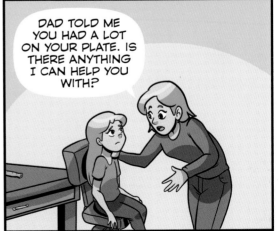

DAD TOLD ME YOU HAD A LOT ON YOUR PLATE. IS THERE ANYTHING I CAN HELP YOU WITH?

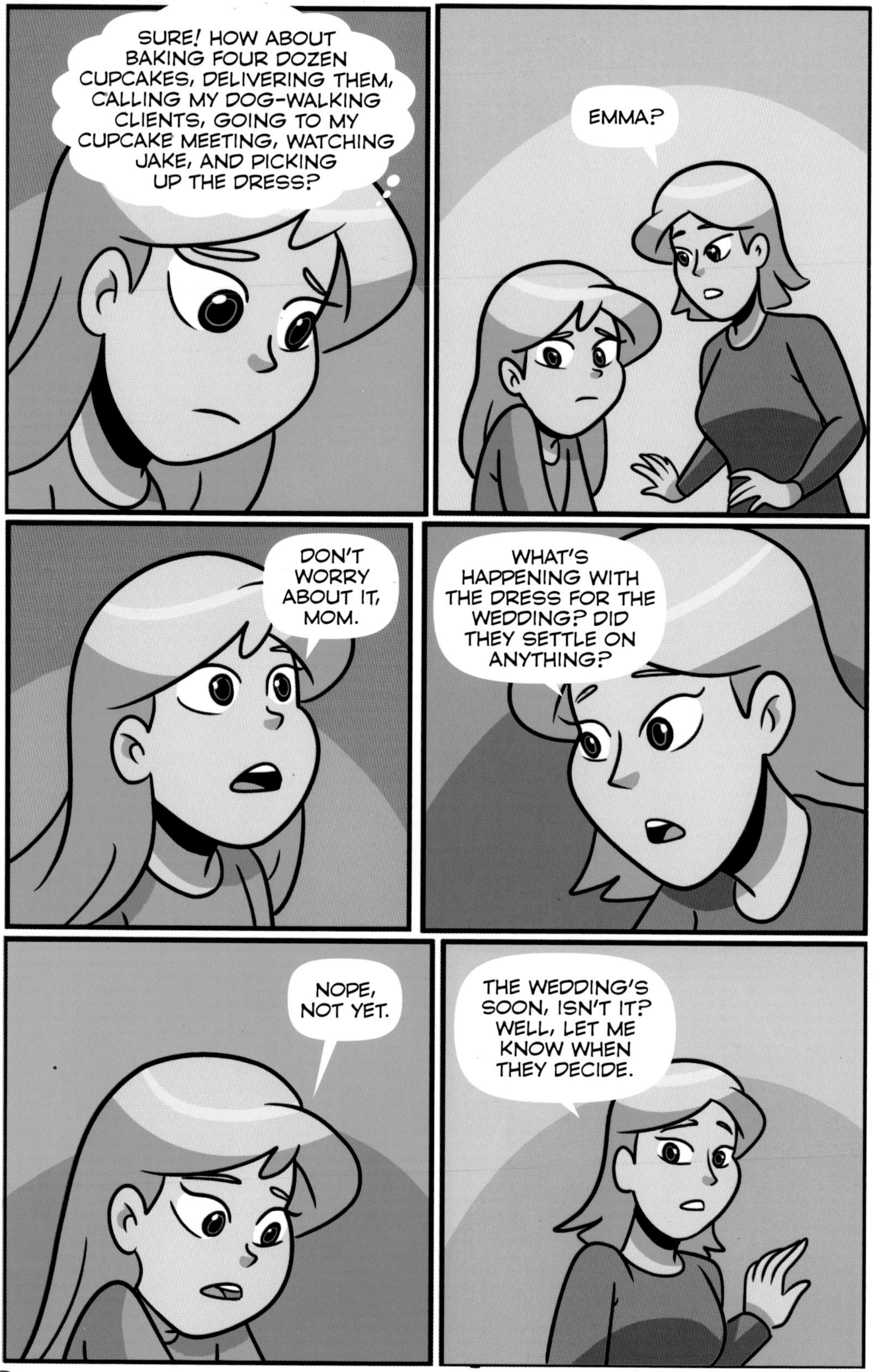
SURE! HOW ABOUT BAKING FOUR DOZEN CUPCAKES, DELIVERING THEM, CALLING MY DOG-WALKING CLIENTS, GOING TO MY CUPCAKE MEETING, WATCHING JAKE, AND PICKING UP THE DRESS?
EMMA?
DON'T WORRY ABOUT IT, MOM.
WHAT'S HAPPENING WITH THE DRESS FOR THE WEDDING? DID THEY SETTLE ON ANYTHING?
NOPE, NOT YET.
THE WEDDING'S SOON, ISN'T IT? WELL, LET ME KNOW WHEN THEY DECIDE.

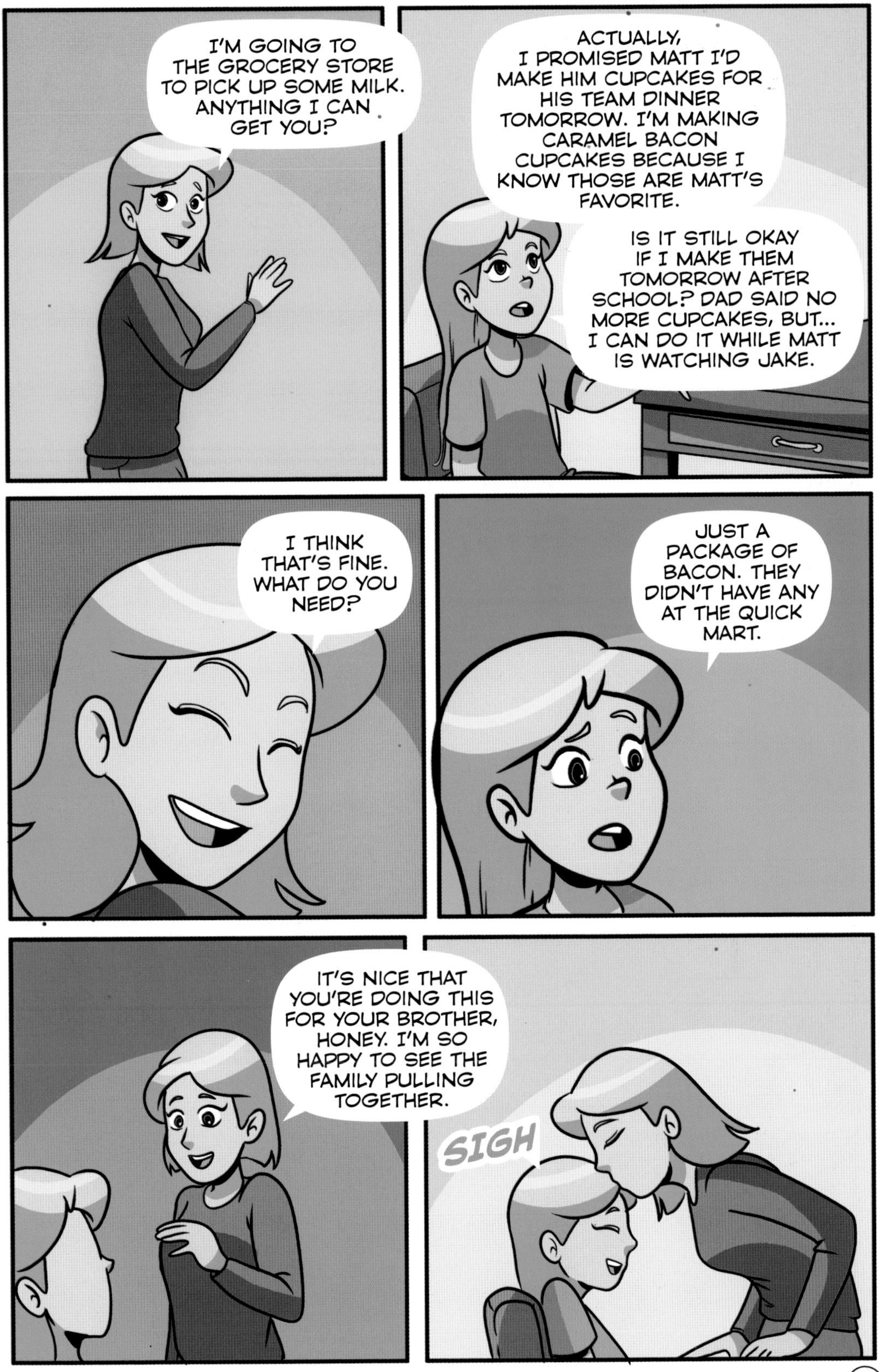
I'M GOING TO THE GROCERY STORE TO PICK UP SOME MILK. ANYTHING I CAN GET YOU?
ACTUALLY, I PROMISED MATT I'D MAKE HIM CUPCAKES FOR HIS TEAM DINNER TOMORROW. I'M MAKING CARAMEL BACON CUPCAKES BECAUSE I KNOW THOSE ARE MATT'S FAVORITE.
IS IT STILL OKAY IF I MAKE THEM TOMORROW AFTER SCHOOL? DAD SAID NO MORE CUPCAKES, BUT... I CAN DO IT WHILE MATT IS WATCHING JAKE.
I THINK THAT'S FINE. WHAT DO YOU NEED?
JUST A PACKAGE OF BACON. THEY DIDN'T HAVE ANY AT THE QUICK MART.
IT'S NICE THAT YOU'RE DOING THIS FOR YOUR BROTHER, HONEY. I'M SO HAPPY TO SEE THE FAMILY PULLING TOGETHER.
SIGH

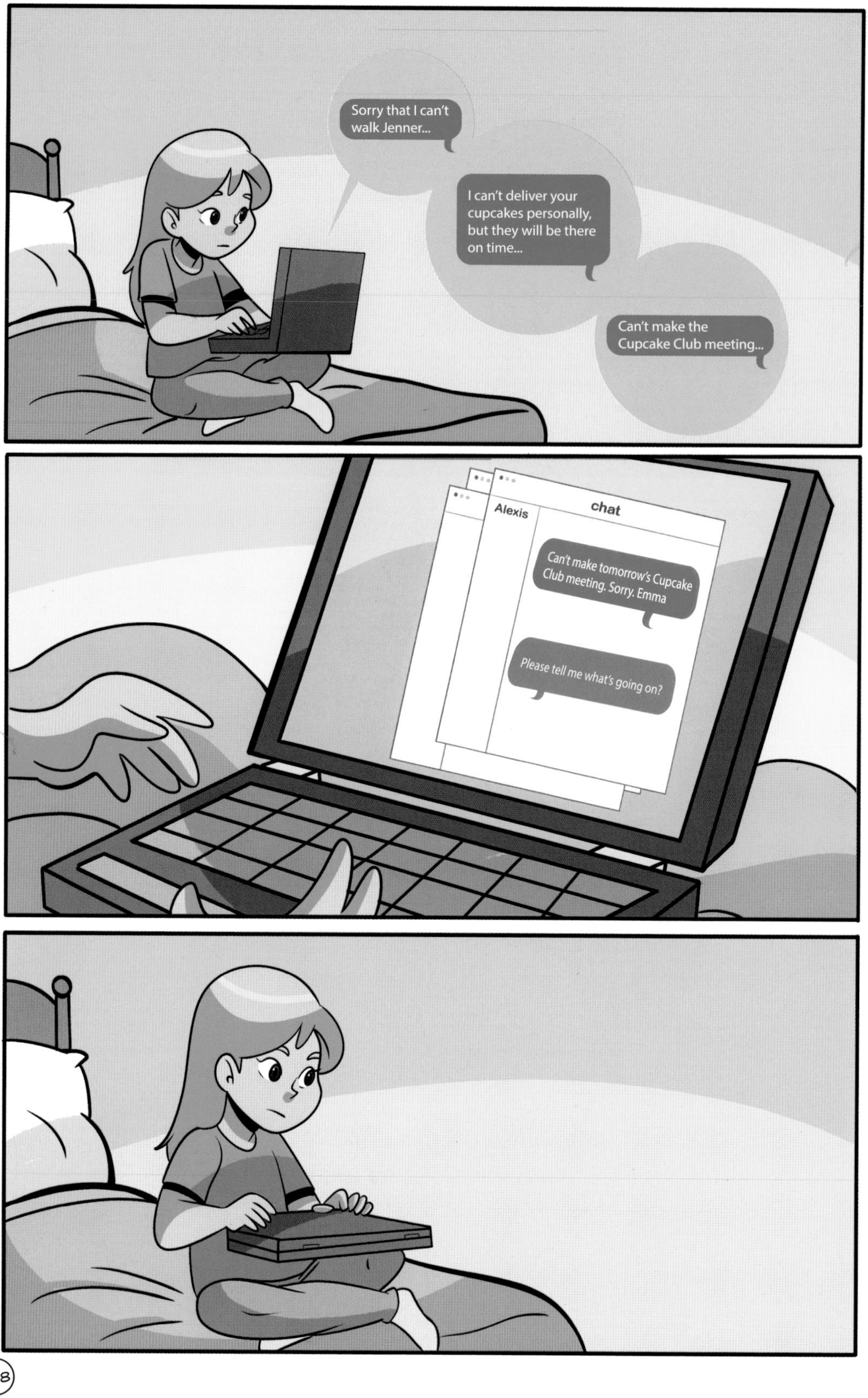
Sorry that I can't walk Jenner...
I can't deliver your cupcakes personally, but they will be there on time...
Can't make the Cupcake Club meeting...
Alexis
chat
Can't make tomorrow's Cupcake Club meeting. Sorry. Emma
Please tell me what's going on?

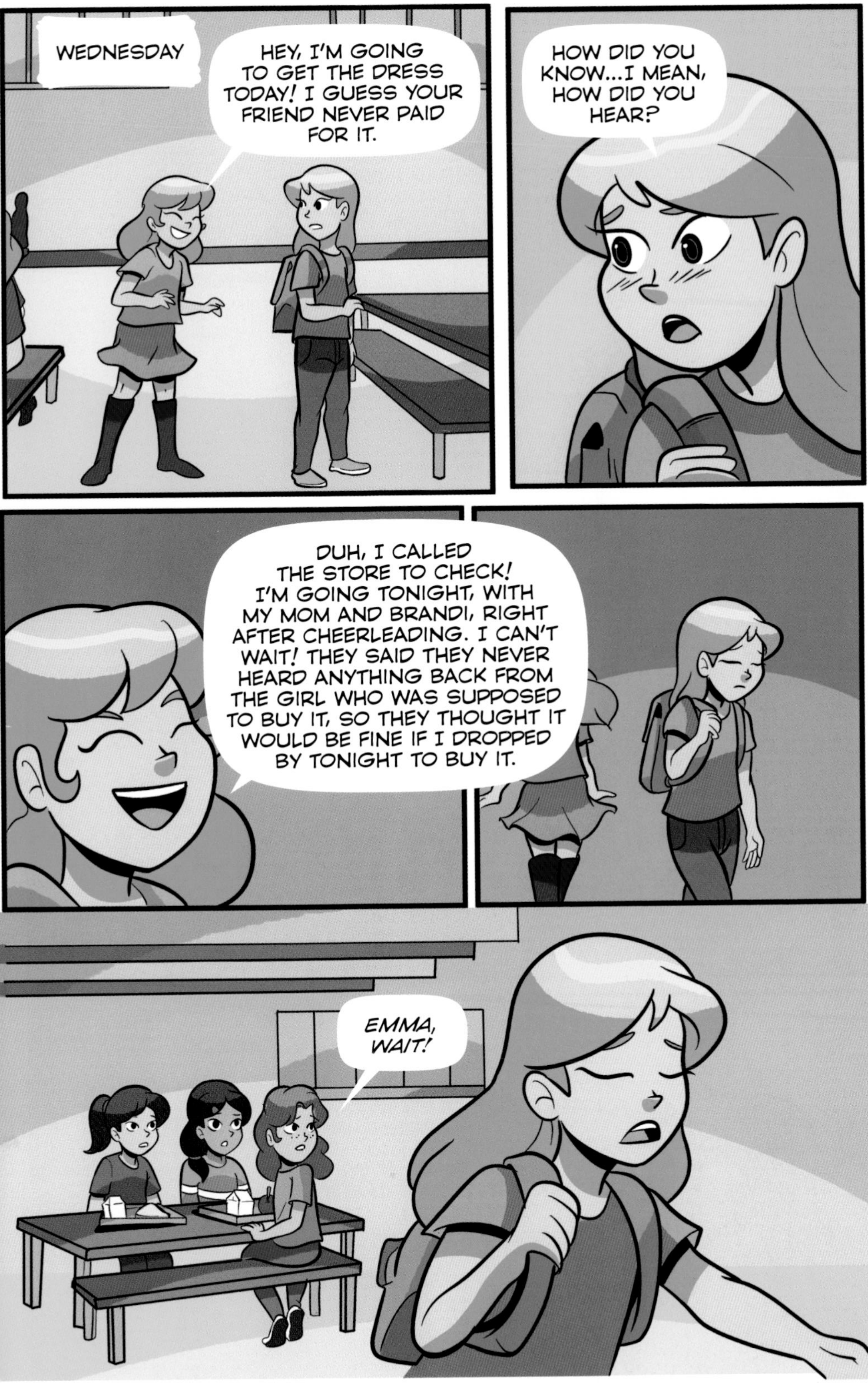
WEDNESDAY
HEY, I'M GOING TO GET THE DRESS TODAY! I GUESS YOUR FRIEND NEVER PAID FOR IT.
HOW DID YOU KNOW...I MEAN, HOW DID YOU HEAR?
DUH, I CALLED THE STORE TO CHECK! I'M GOING TONIGHT, WITH MY MOM AND BRANDI, RIGHT AFTER CHEERLEADING. I CAN'T WAIT! THEY SAID THEY NEVER HEARD ANYTHING BACK FROM THE GIRL WHO WAS SUPPOSED TO BUY IT, SO THEY THOUGHT IT WOULD BE FINE IF I DROPPED BY TONIGHT TO BUY IT.
EMMA, WAIT!

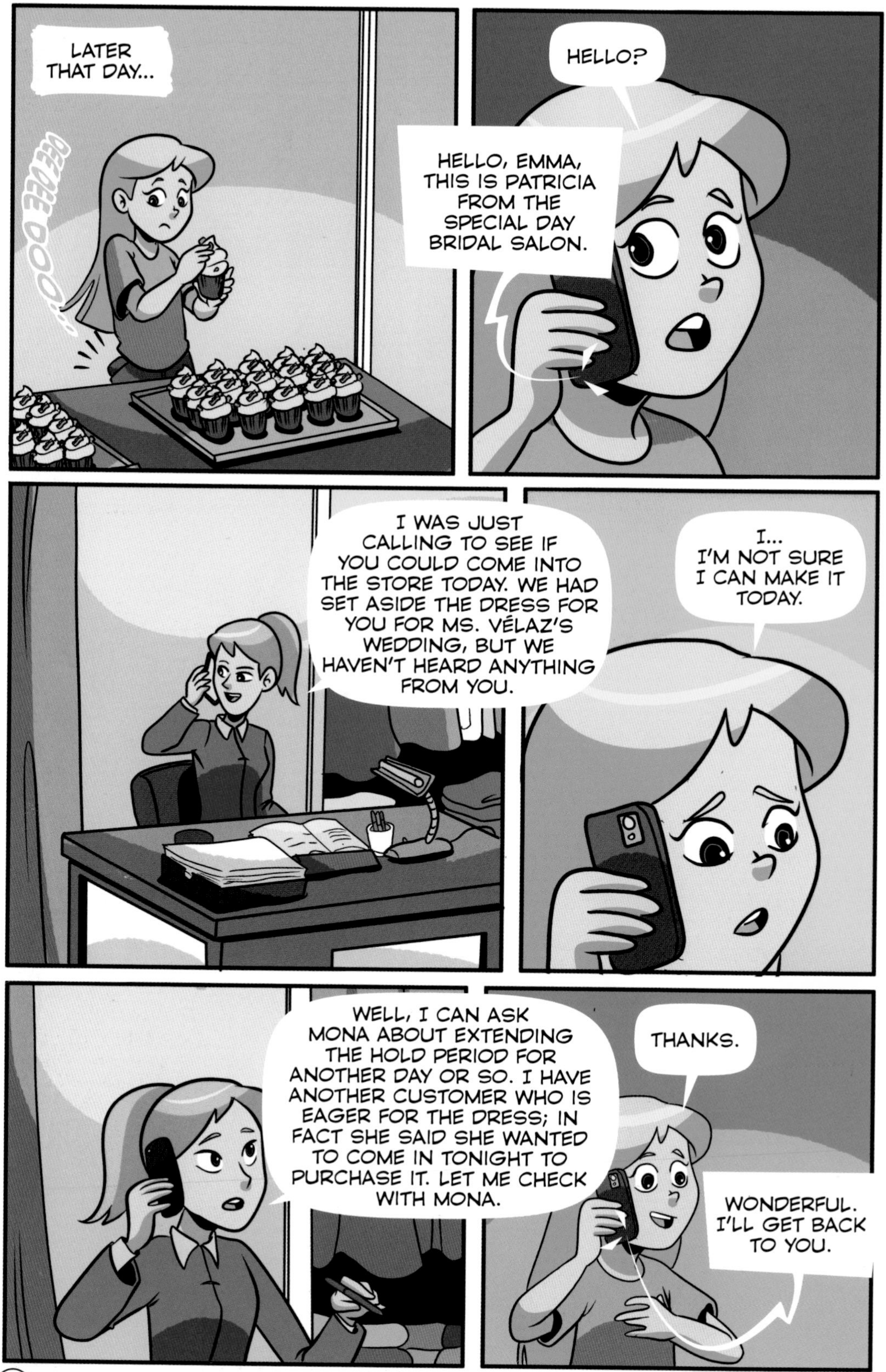
LATER THAT DAY...
DEEDEE DOO!!
HELLO?
HELLO, EMMA, THIS IS PATRICIA FROM THE SPECIAL DAY BRIDAL SALON.
I WAS JUST CALLING TO SEE IF YOU COULD COME INTO THE STORE TODAY. WE HAD SET ASIDE THE DRESS FOR YOU FOR MS. VÉLAZ'S WEDDING, BUT WE HAVEN'T HEARD ANYTHING FROM YOU.
I... I'M NOT SURE I CAN MAKE IT TODAY.
WELL, I CAN ASK MONA ABOUT EXTENDING THE HOLD PERIOD FOR ANOTHER DAY OR SO. I HAVE ANOTHER CUSTOMER WHO IS EAGER FOR THE DRESS; IN FACT SHE SAID SHE WANTED TO COME IN TONIGHT TO PURCHASE IT. LET ME CHECK WITH MONA.
THANKS.
WONDERFUL. I'LL GET BACK TO YOU.

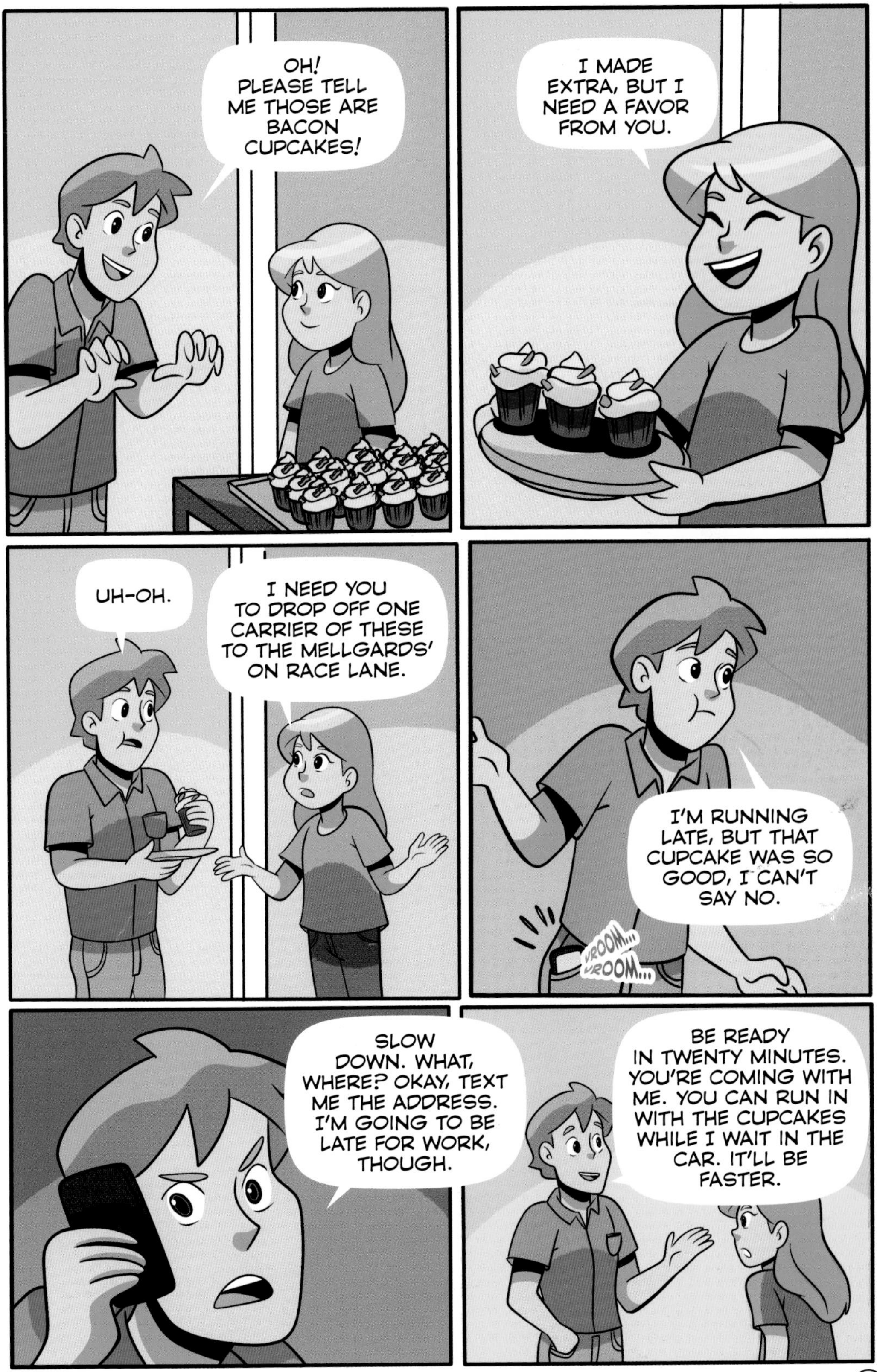
OH! PLEASE TELL ME THOSE ARE BACON CUPCAKES!
I MADE EXTRA, BUT I NEED A FAVOR FROM YOU.
UH-OH.
I NEED YOU TO DROP OFF ONE CARRIER OF THESE TO THE MELLGARDS' ON RACE LANE.
I'M RUNNING LATE, BUT THAT CUPCAKE WAS SO GOOD, I CAN'T SAY NO.
VROOM... VROOM...
SLOW DOWN. WHAT, WHERE? OKAY, TEXT ME THE ADDRESS. I'M GOING TO BE LATE FOR WORK, THOUGH.
BE READY IN TWENTY MINUTES. YOU'RE COMING WITH ME. YOU CAN RUN IN WITH THE CUPCAKES WHILE I WAIT IN THE CAR. IT'LL BE FASTER.

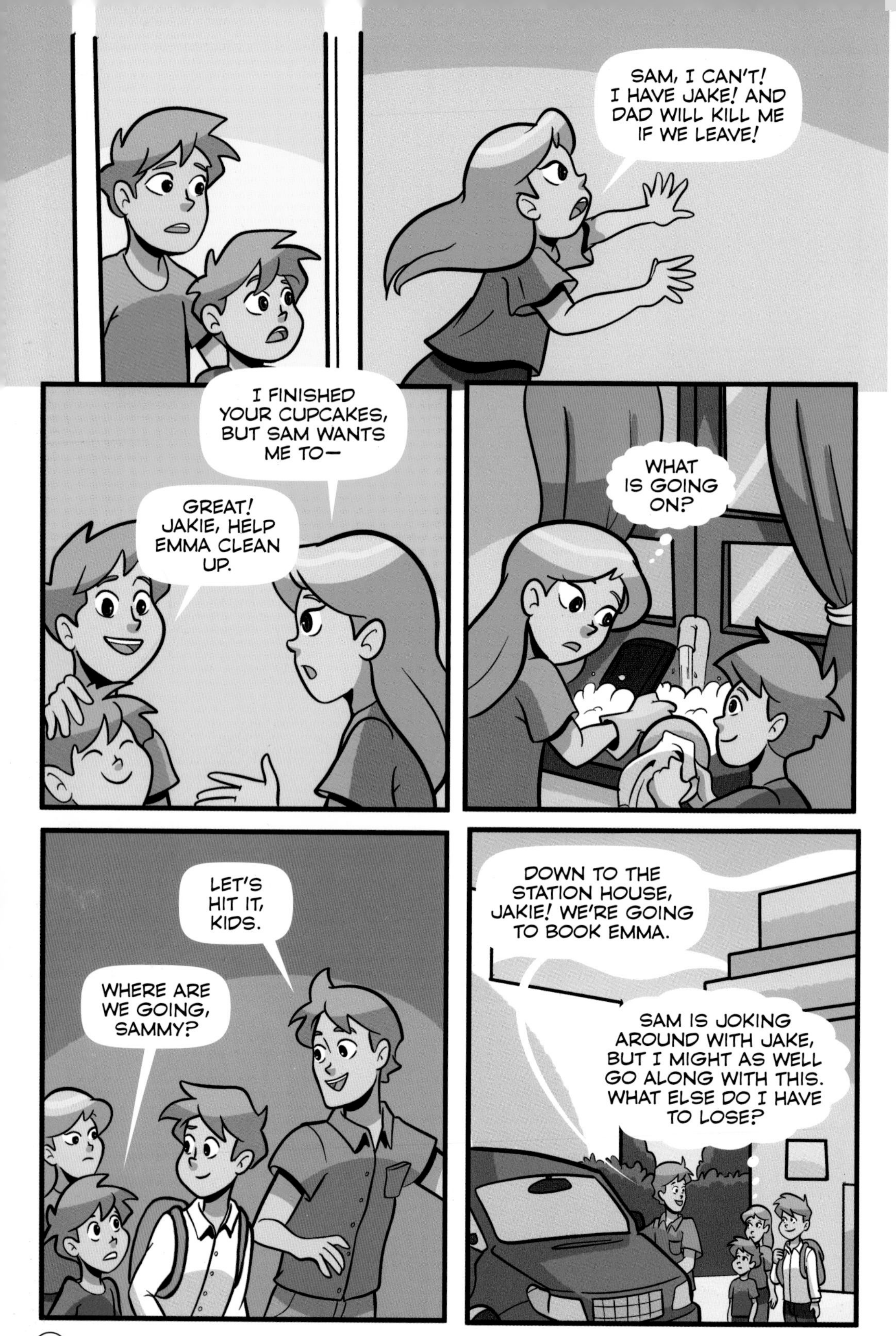
SAM, I CAN'T! I HAVE JAKE! AND DAD WILL KILL ME IF WE LEAVE!
I FINISHED YOUR CUPCAKES, BUT SAM WANTS ME TO—
GREAT! JAKIE, HELP EMMA CLEAN UP.
WHAT IS GOING ON?
LET'S HIT IT, KIDS.
WHERE ARE WE GOING, SAMMY?
DOWN TO THE STATION HOUSE, JAKIE! WE'RE GOING TO BOOK EMMA.
SAM IS JOKING AROUND WITH JAKE, BUT I MIGHT AS WELL GO ALONG WITH THIS. WHAT ELSE DO I HAVE TO LOSE?

Chapter 11

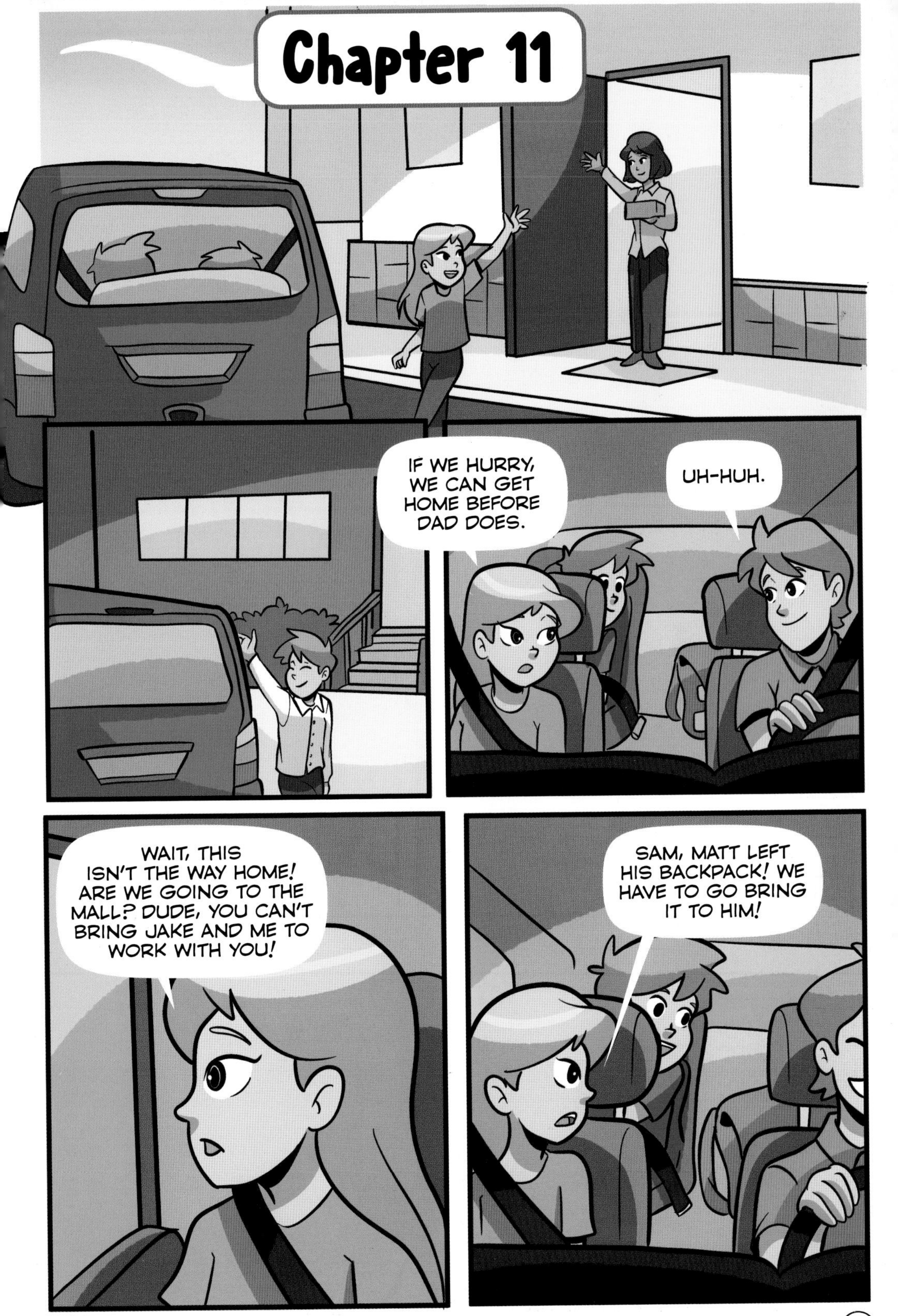
IF WE HURRY, WE CAN GET HOME BEFORE DAD DOES.
UH-HUH.
WAIT, THIS ISN'T THE WAY HOME! ARE WE GOING TO THE MALL? DUDE, YOU CAN'T BRING JAKE AND ME TO WORK WITH YOU!
SAM, MATT LEFT HIS BACKPACK! WE HAVE TO GO BRING IT TO HIM!

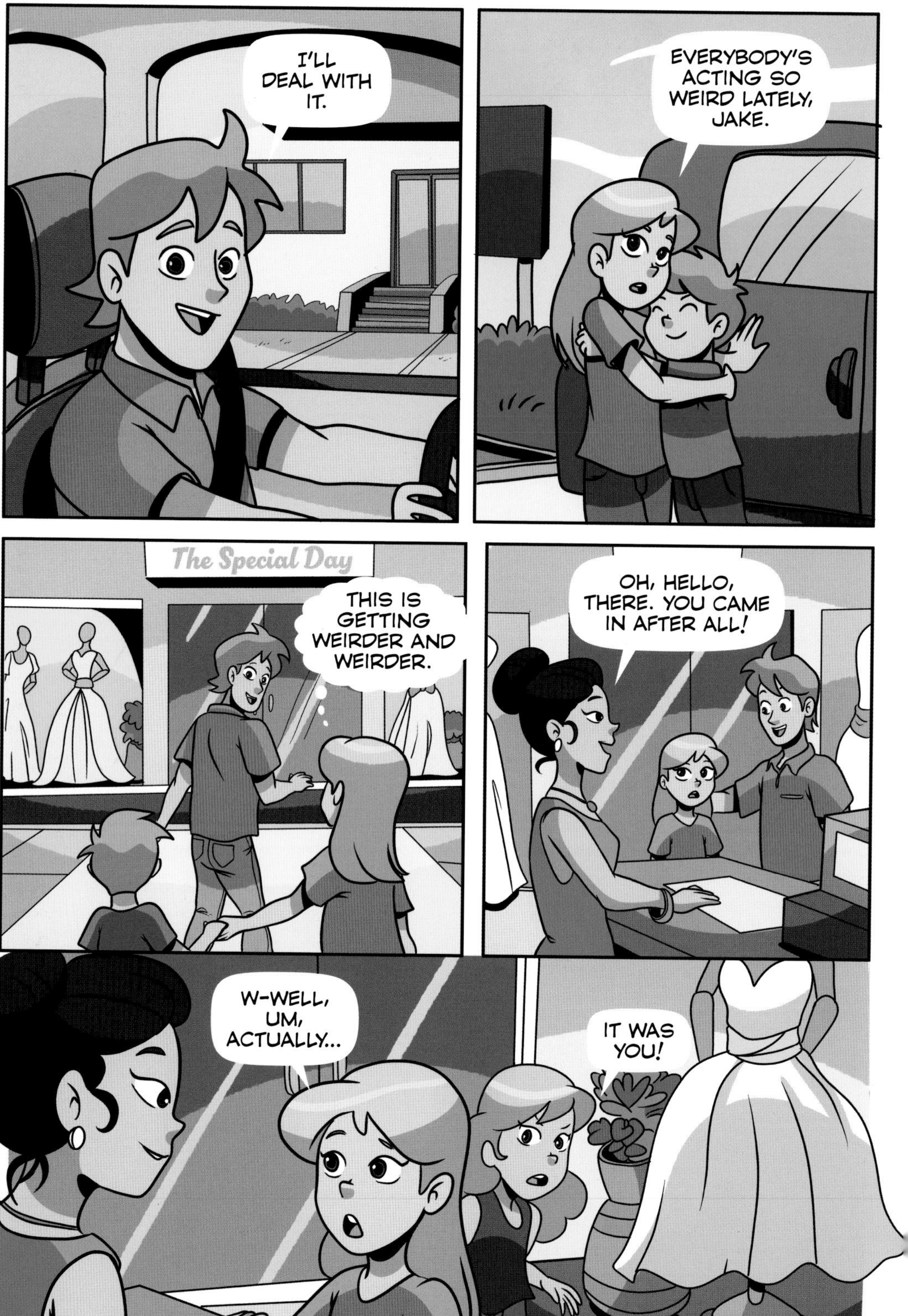
I'LL DEAL WITH IT.
EVERYBODY'S ACTING SO WEIRD LATELY, JAKE.
The Special Day
THIS IS GETTING WEIRDER AND WEIRDER.
OH, HELLO, THERE. YOU CAME IN AFTER ALL!
W-WELL, UM, ACTUALLY...
IT WAS YOU!

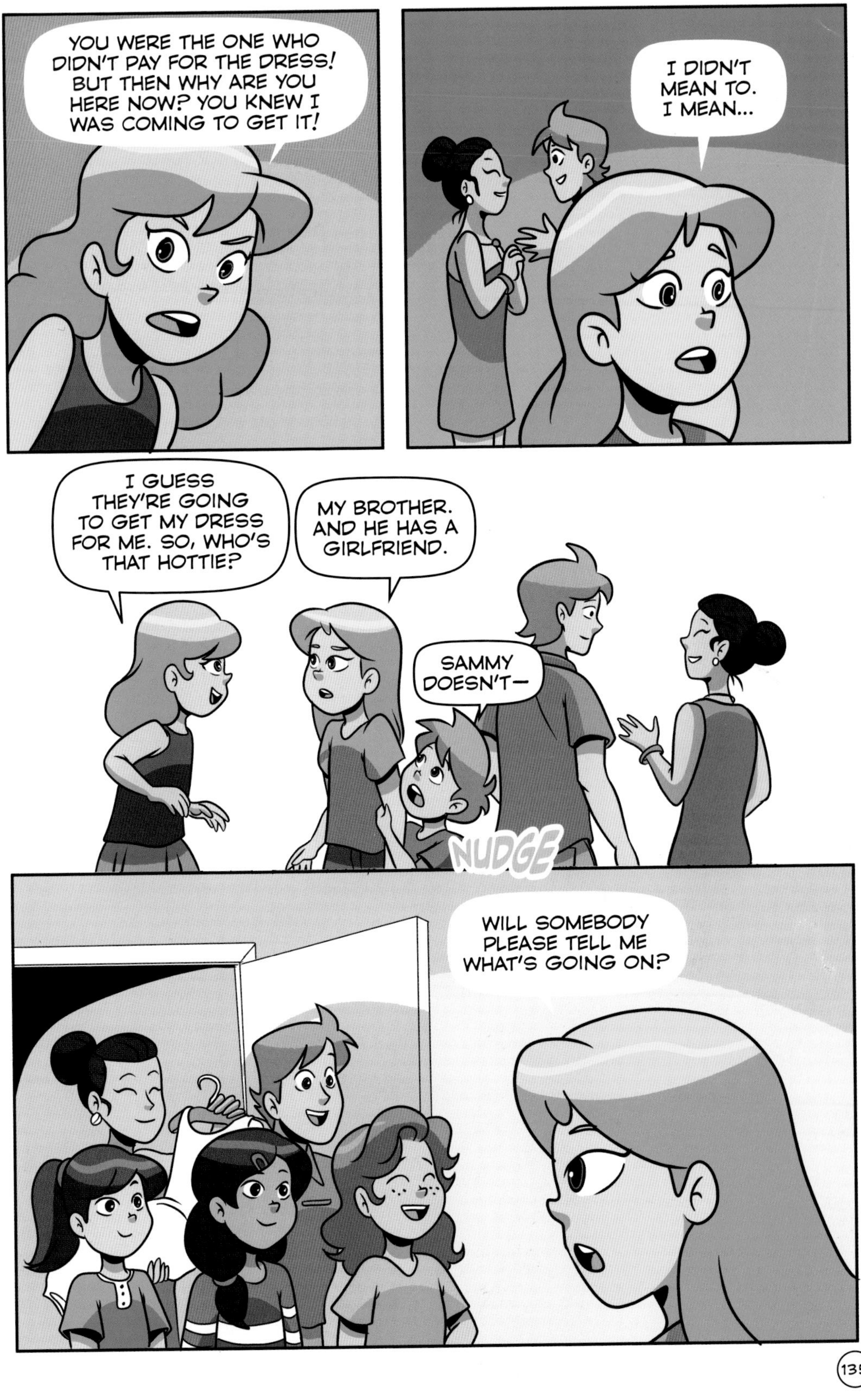
YOU WERE THE ONE WHO DIDN'T PAY FOR THE DRESS! BUT THEN WHY ARE YOU HERE NOW? YOU KNEW I WAS COMING TO GET IT!
I DIDN'T MEAN TO. I MEAN...
I GUESS THEY'RE GOING TO GET MY DRESS FOR ME. SO, WHO'S THAT HOTTIE?
MY BROTHER. AND HE HAS A GIRLFRIEND.
SAMMY DOESN'T—
NUDGE
WILL SOMEBODY PLEASE TELL ME WHAT'S GOING ON?

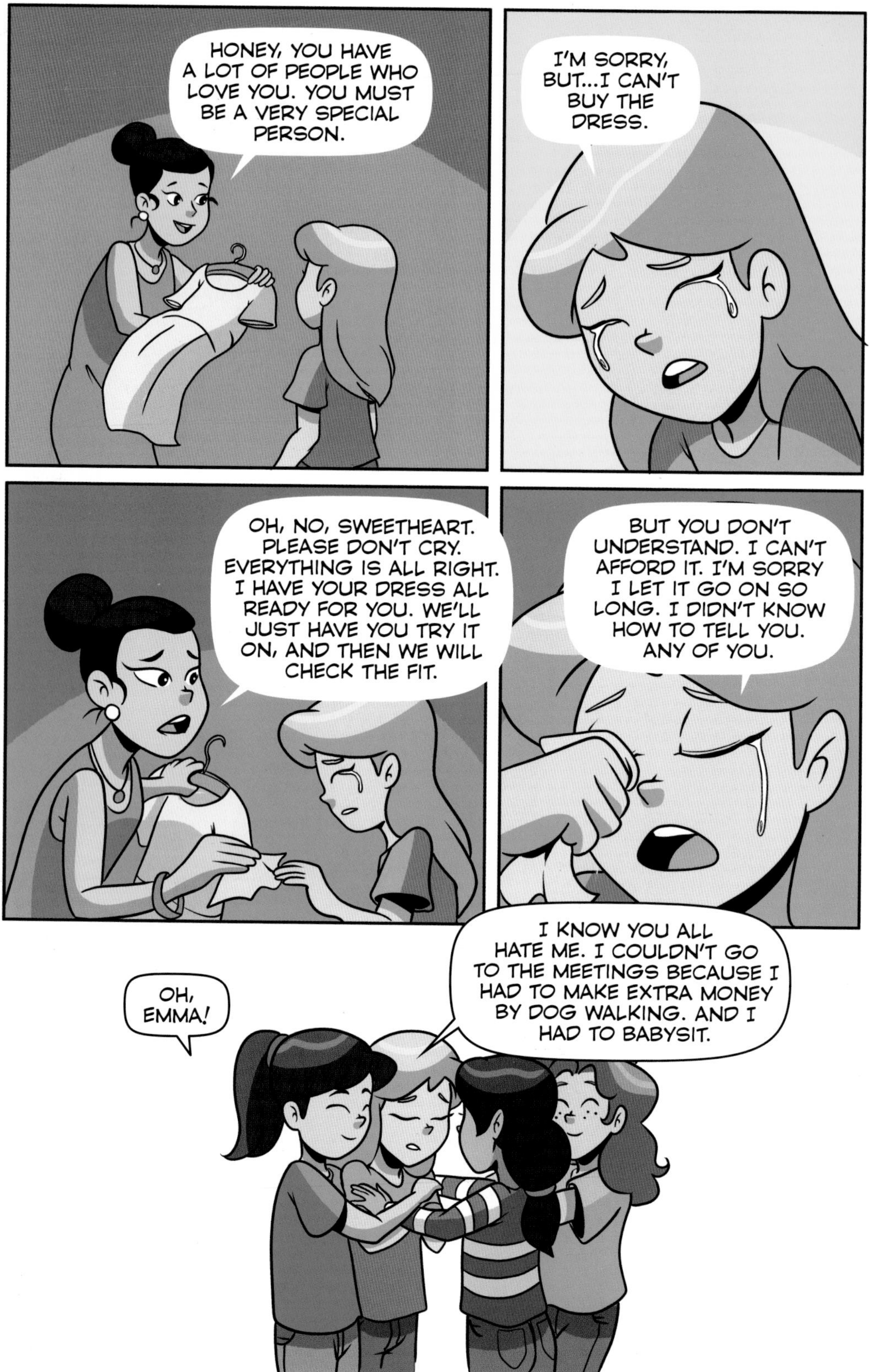
HONEY, YOU HAVE A LOT OF PEOPLE WHO LOVE YOU. YOU MUST BE A VERY SPECIAL PERSON.
I'M SORRY, BUT...I CAN'T BUY THE DRESS.
OH, NO, SWEETHEART. PLEASE DON'T CRY. EVERYTHING IS ALL RIGHT. I HAVE YOUR DRESS ALL READY FOR YOU. WE'LL JUST HAVE YOU TRY IT ON, AND THEN WE WILL CHECK THE FIT.
BUT YOU DON'T UNDERSTAND. I CAN'T AFFORD IT. I'M SORRY I LET IT GO ON SO LONG. I DIDN'T KNOW HOW TO TELL YOU. ANY OF YOU.
OH, EMMA!
I KNOW YOU ALL HATE ME. I COULDN'T GO TO THE MEETINGS BECAUSE I HAD TO MAKE EXTRA MONEY BY DOG WALKING. AND I HAD TO BABYSIT.

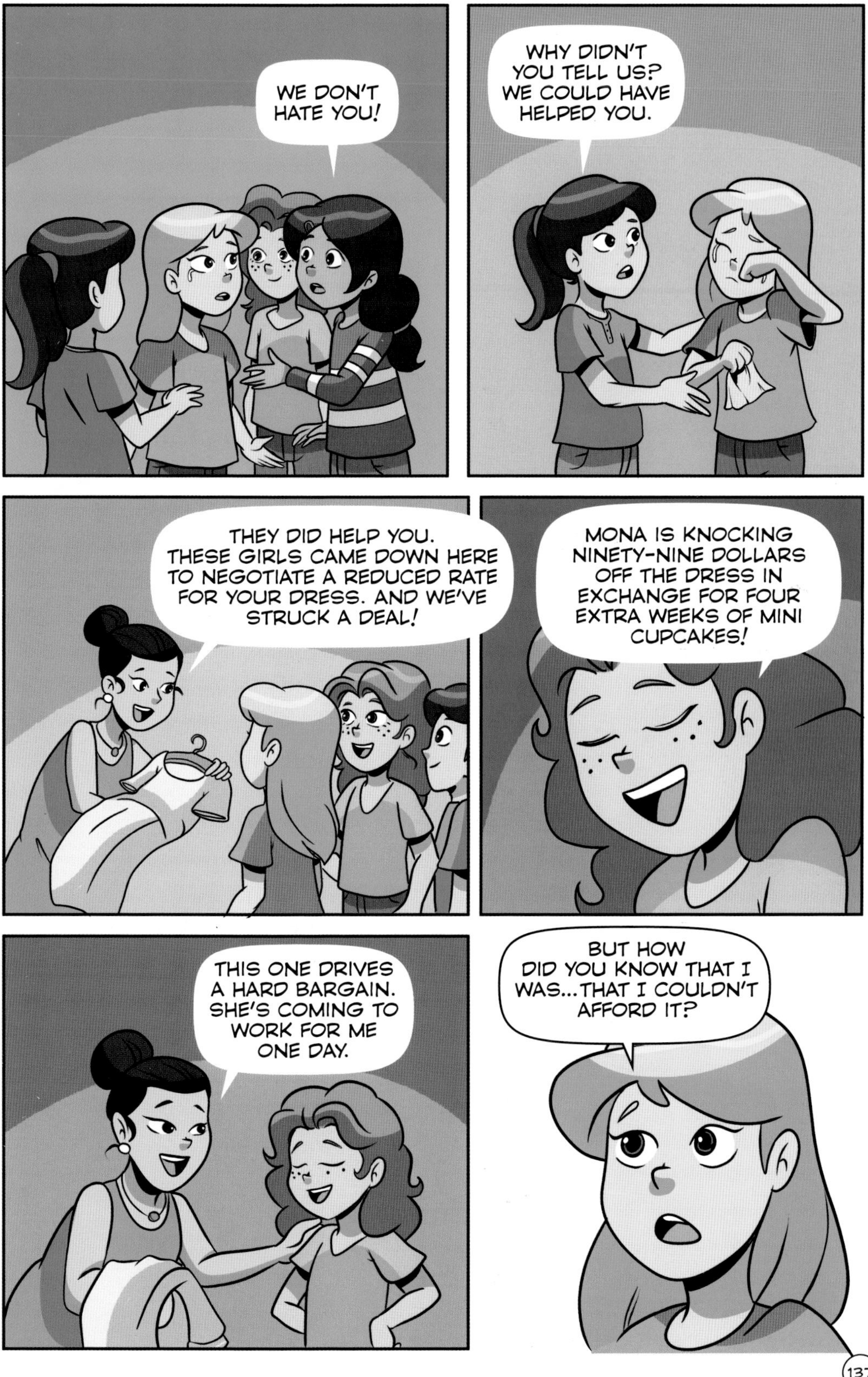
WE DON'T HATE YOU!
WHY DIDN'T YOU TELL US? WE COULD HAVE HELPED YOU.
THEY DID HELP YOU. THESE GIRLS CAME DOWN HERE TO NEGOTIATE A REDUCED RATE FOR YOUR DRESS. AND WE'VE STRUCK A DEAL!
MONA IS KNOCKING NINETY-NINE DOLLARS OFF THE DRESS IN EXCHANGE FOR FOUR EXTRA WEEKS OF MINI CUPCAKES!
THIS ONE DRIVES A HARD BARGAIN. SHE'S COMING TO WORK FOR ME ONE DAY.
BUT HOW DID YOU KNOW THAT I WAS...THAT I COULDN'T AFFORD IT?

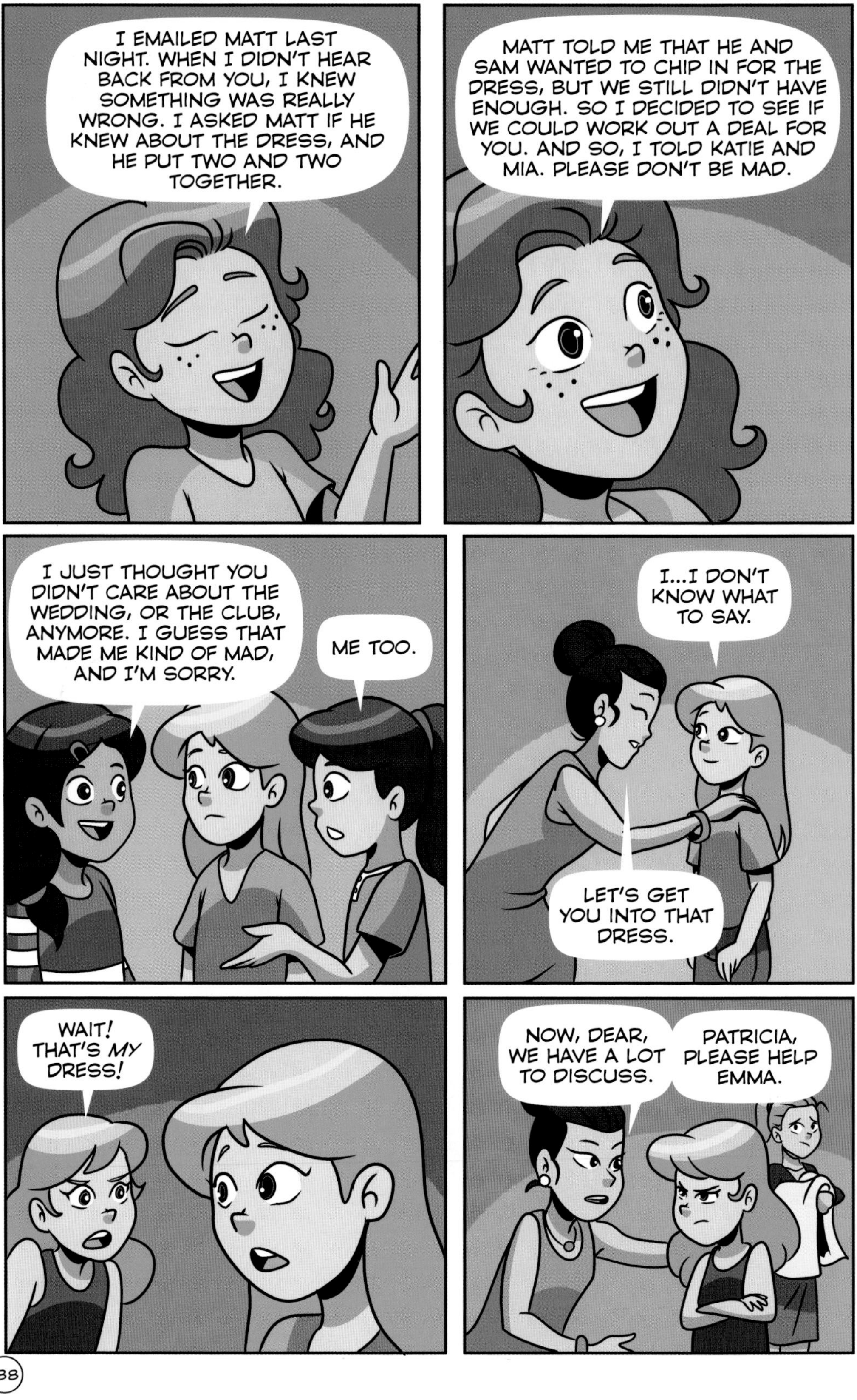
I EMAILED MATT LAST NIGHT. WHEN I DIDN'T HEAR BACK FROM YOU, I KNEW SOMETHING WAS REALLY WRONG. I ASKED MATT IF HE KNEW ABOUT THE DRESS, AND HE PUT TWO AND TWO TOGETHER.
MATT TOLD ME THAT HE AND SAM WANTED TO CHIP IN FOR THE DRESS, BUT WE STILL DIDN'T HAVE ENOUGH. SO I DECIDED TO SEE IF WE COULD WORK OUT A DEAL FOR YOU. AND SO, I TOLD KATIE AND MIA. PLEASE DON'T BE MAD.
I JUST THOUGHT YOU DIDN'T CARE ABOUT THE WEDDING, OR THE CLUB, ANYMORE. I GUESS THAT MADE ME KIND OF MAD, AND I'M SORRY.
ME TOO.
I...I DON'T KNOW WHAT TO SAY.
LET'S GET YOU INTO THAT DRESS.
WAIT! THAT'S *MY* DRESS!
NOW, DEAR, WE HAVE A LOT TO DISCUSS.
PATRICIA, PLEASE HELP EMMA.

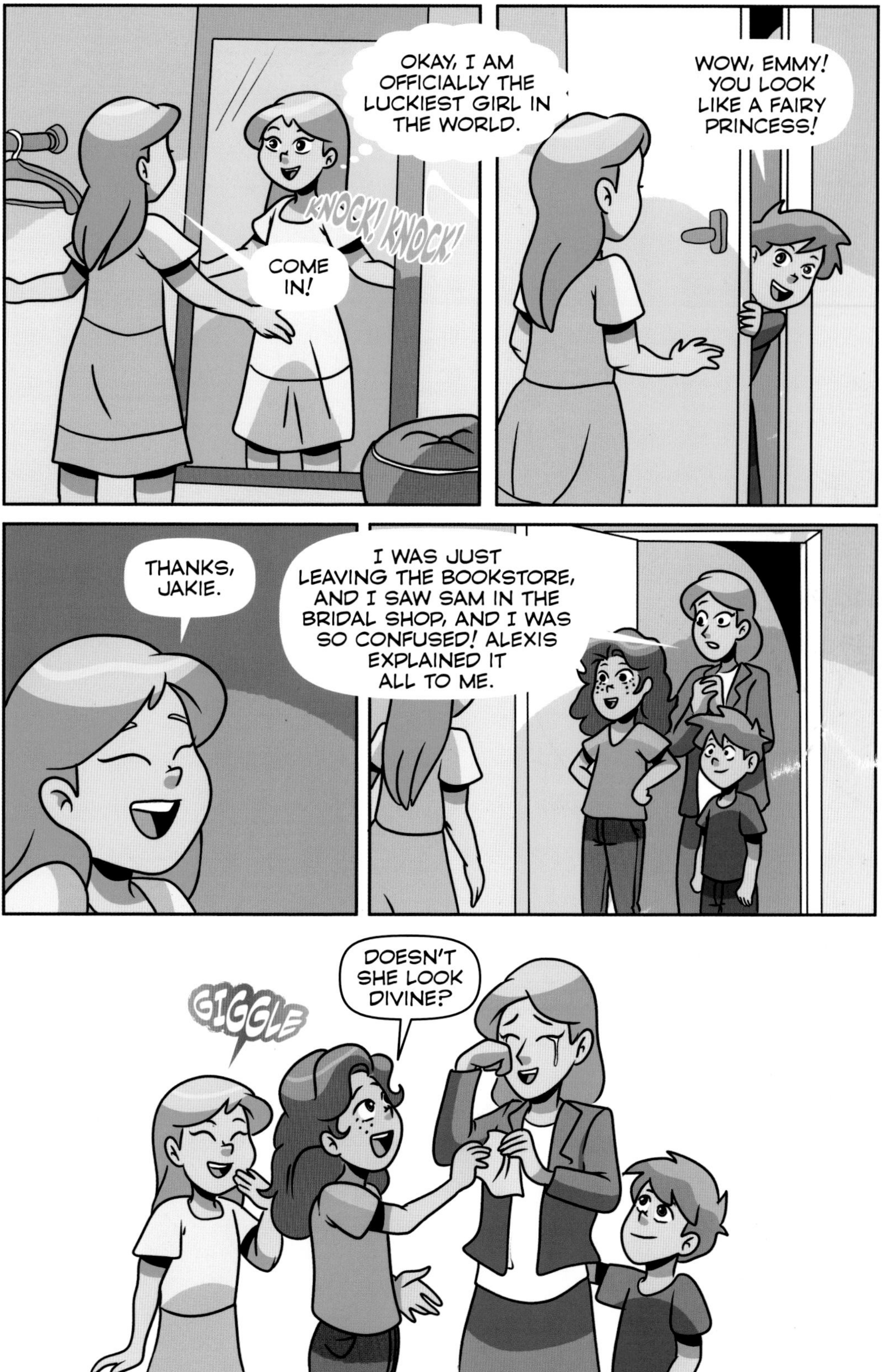
OKAY, I AM OFFICIALLY THE LUCKIEST GIRL IN THE WORLD.
KNOCK! KNOCK!
COME IN!
WOW, EMMY! YOU LOOK LIKE A FAIRY PRINCESS!
THANKS, JAKIE.
I WAS JUST LEAVING THE BOOKSTORE, AND I SAW SAM IN THE BRIDAL SHOP, AND I WAS SO CONFUSED! ALEXIS EXPLAINED IT ALL TO ME.
GIGGLE
DOESN'T SHE LOOK DIVINE?

Chapter 12

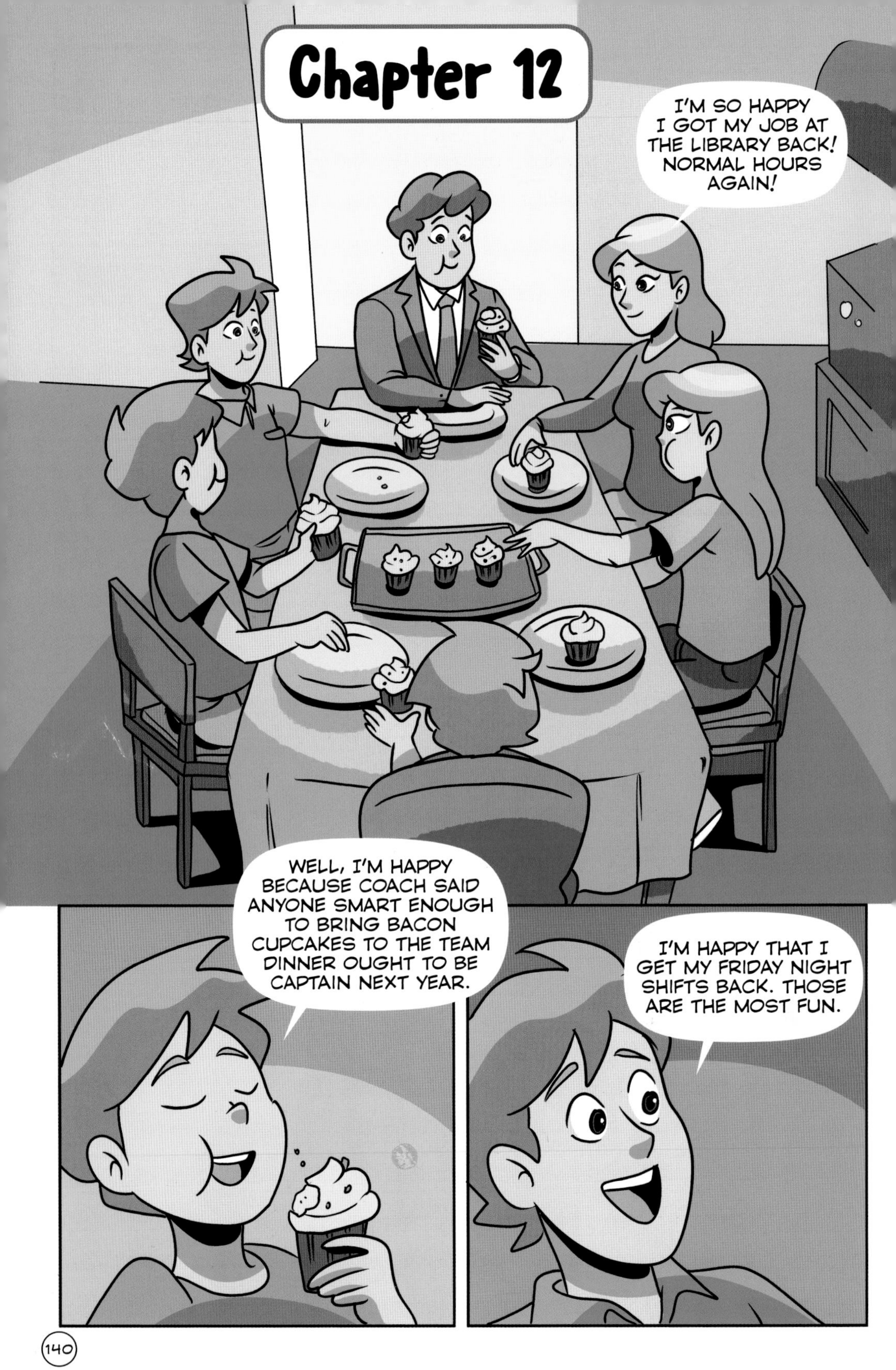
I'M SO HAPPY I GOT MY JOB AT THE LIBRARY BACK! NORMAL HOURS AGAIN!
WELL, I'M HAPPY BECAUSE COACH SAID ANYONE SMART ENOUGH TO BRING BACON CUPCAKES TO THE TEAM DINNER OUGHT TO BE CAPTAIN NEXT YEAR.
I'M HAPPY THAT I GET MY FRIDAY NIGHT SHIFTS BACK. THOSE ARE THE MOST FUN.

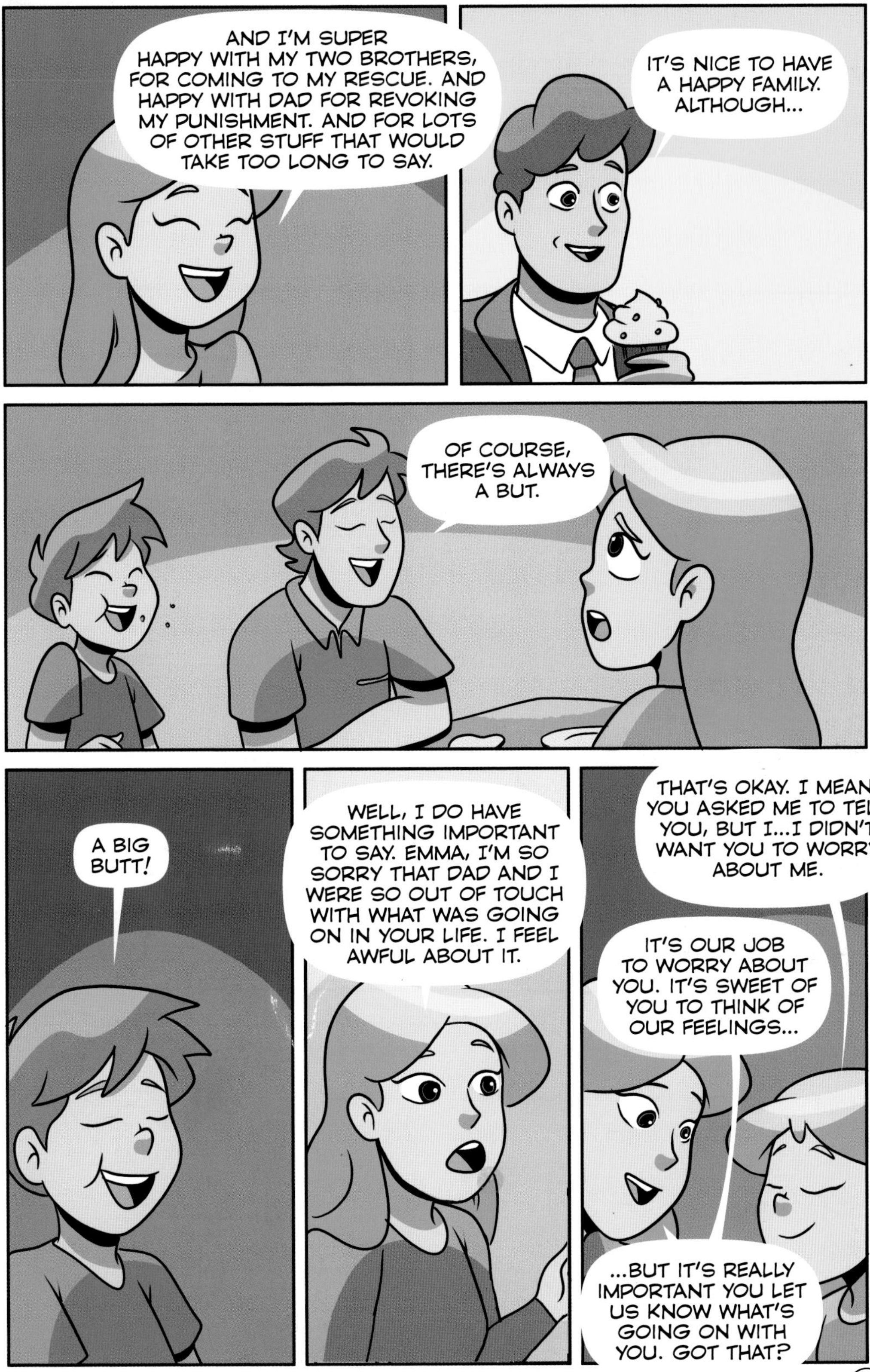
AND I'M SUPER HAPPY WITH MY TWO BROTHERS, FOR COMING TO MY RESCUE. AND HAPPY WITH DAD FOR REVOKING MY PUNISHMENT. AND FOR LOTS OF OTHER STUFF THAT WOULD TAKE TOO LONG TO SAY.
IT'S NICE TO HAVE A HAPPY FAMILY. ALTHOUGH...
OF COURSE, THERE'S ALWAYS A BUT.
A BIG BUTT!
WELL, I DO HAVE SOMETHING IMPORTANT TO SAY. EMMA, I'M SO SORRY THAT DAD AND I WERE SO OUT OF TOUCH WITH WHAT WAS GOING ON IN YOUR LIFE. I FEEL AWFUL ABOUT IT.
THAT'S OKAY. I MEAN, YOU ASKED ME TO TELL YOU, BUT I...I DIDN'T WANT YOU TO WORRY ABOUT ME.
IT'S OUR JOB TO WORRY ABOUT YOU. IT'S SWEET OF YOU TO THINK OF OUR FEELINGS...
...BUT IT'S REALLY IMPORTANT YOU LET US KNOW WHAT'S GOING ON WITH YOU. GOT THAT?

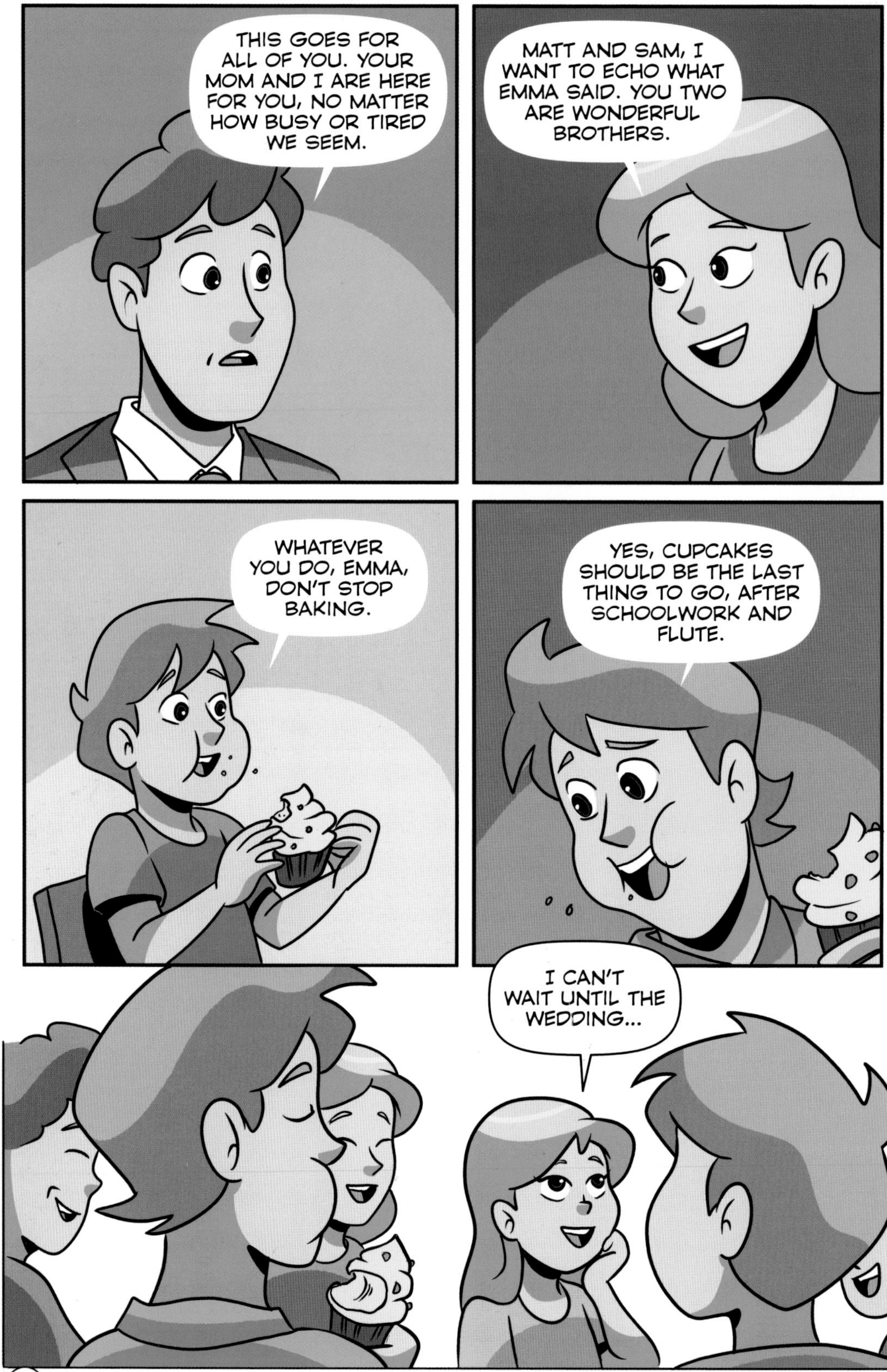
THIS GOES FOR ALL OF YOU. YOUR MOM AND I ARE HERE FOR YOU, NO MATTER HOW BUSY OR TIRED WE SEEM.
MATT AND SAM, I WANT TO ECHO WHAT EMMA SAID. YOU TWO ARE WONDERFUL BROTHERS.
WHATEVER YOU DO, EMMA, DON'T STOP BAKING.
YES, CUPCAKES SHOULD BE THE LAST THING TO GO, AFTER SCHOOLWORK AND FLUTE.
I CAN'T WAIT UNTIL THE WEDDING...

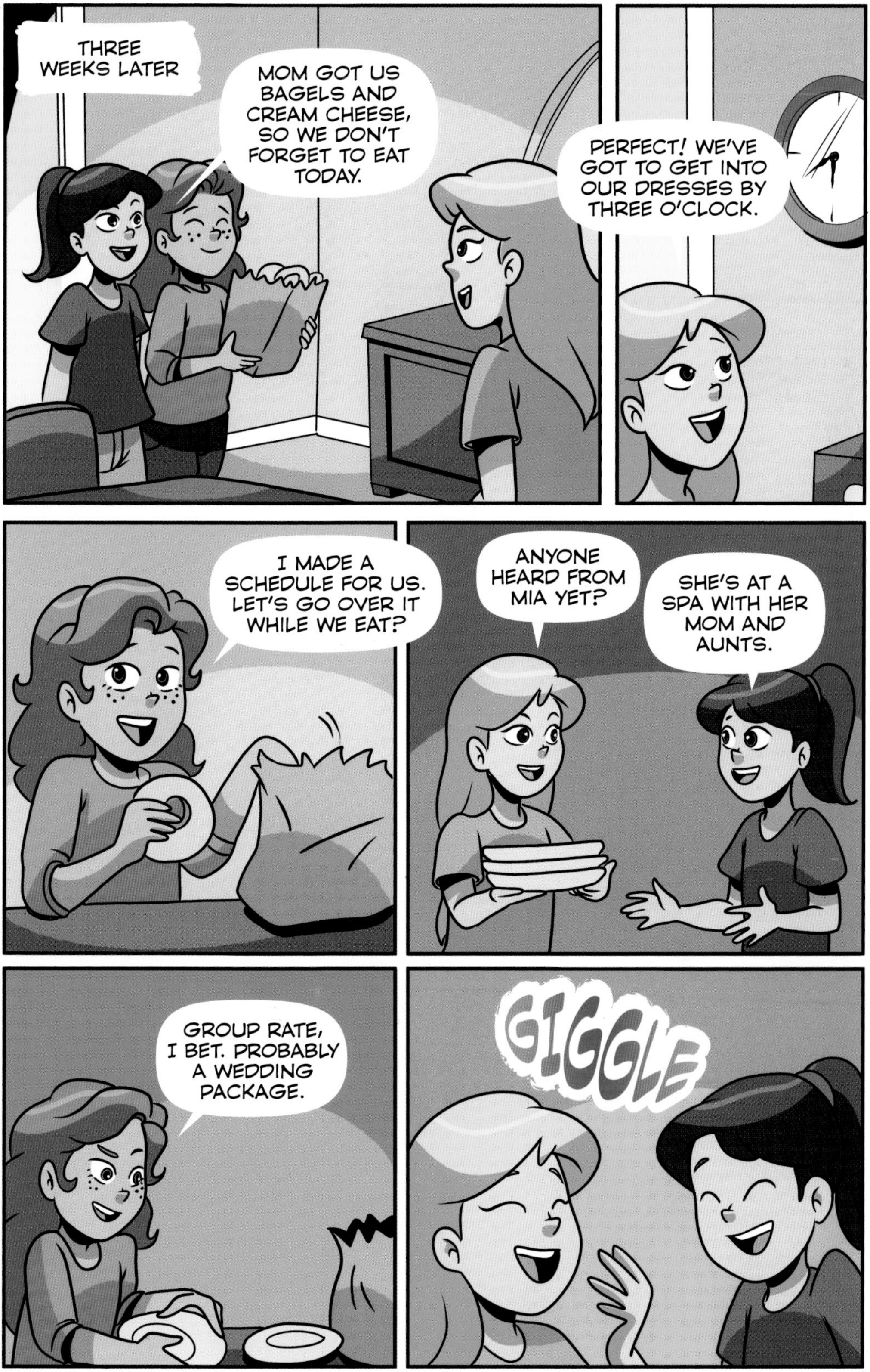
THREE WEEKS LATER
MOM GOT US BAGELS AND CREAM CHEESE, SO WE DON'T FORGET TO EAT TODAY.
PERFECT! WE'VE GOT TO GET INTO OUR DRESSES BY THREE O'CLOCK.
I MADE A SCHEDULE FOR US. LET'S GO OVER IT WHILE WE EAT?
ANYONE HEARD FROM MIA YET?
SHE'S AT A SPA WITH HER MOM AND AUNTS.
GROUP RATE, I BET. PROBABLY A WEDDING PACKAGE.
GIGGLE

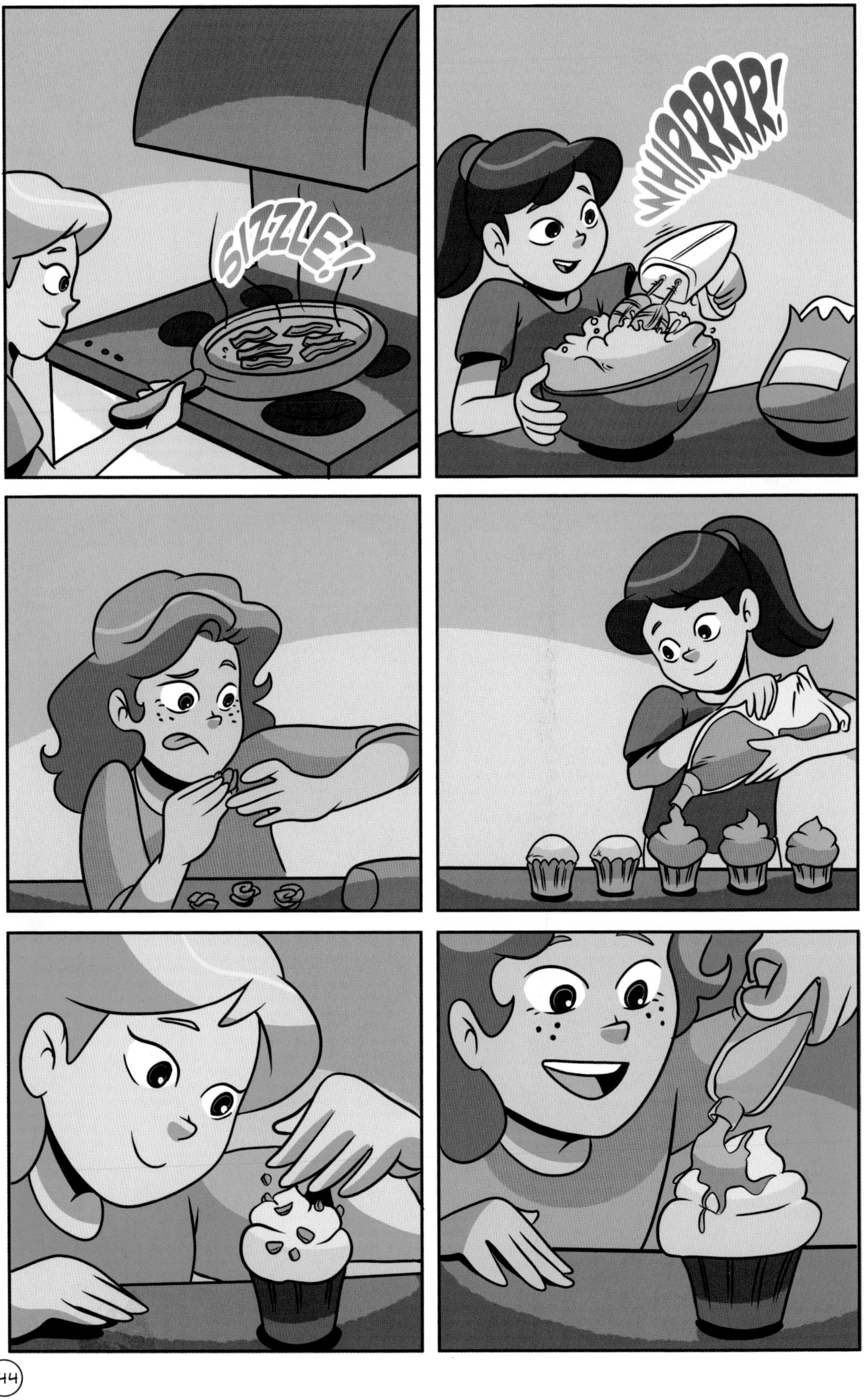
SIZZLE!
WHIRRRRR!

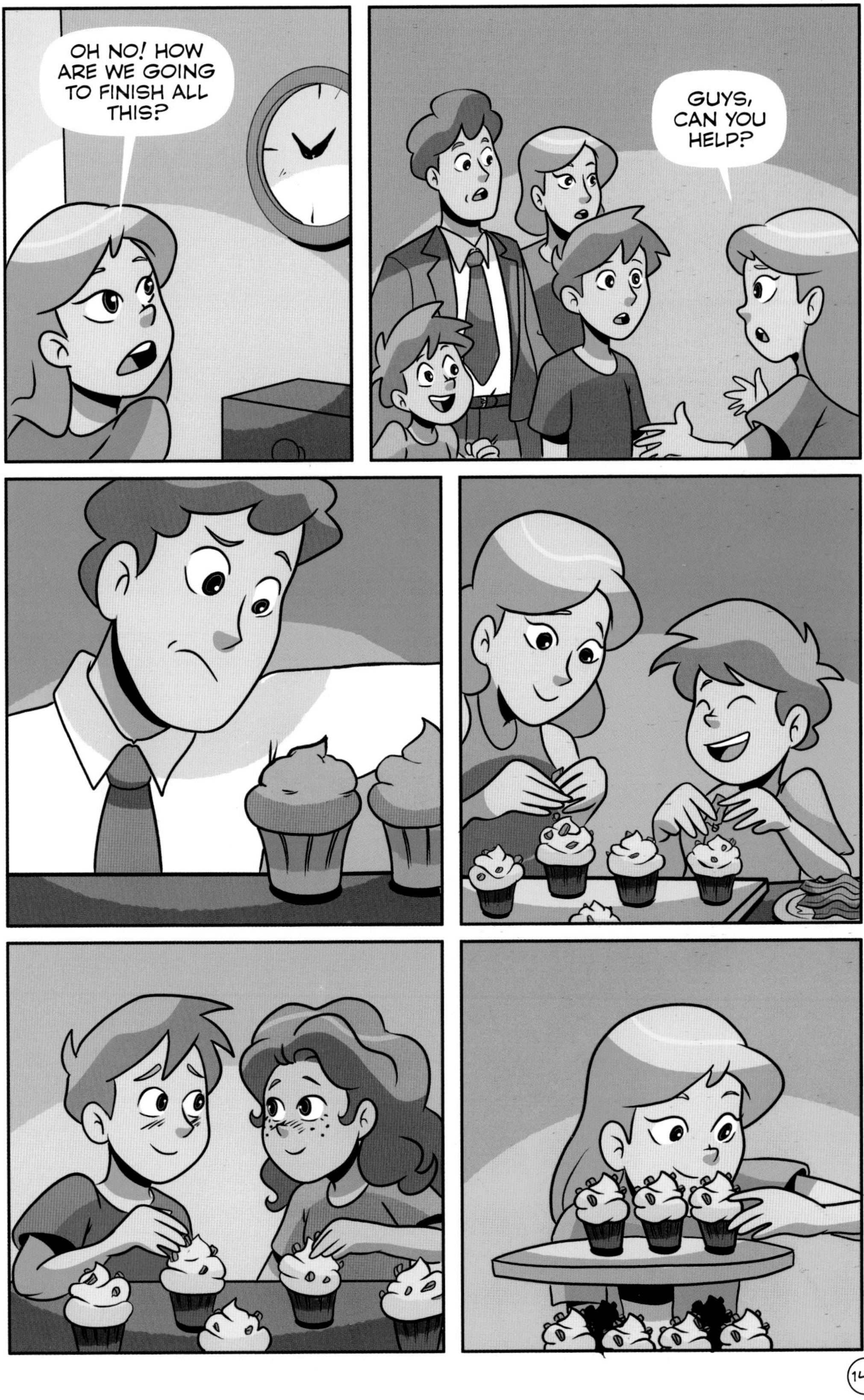
OH NO! HOW ARE WE GOING TO FINISH ALL THIS?
GUYS, CAN YOU HELP?

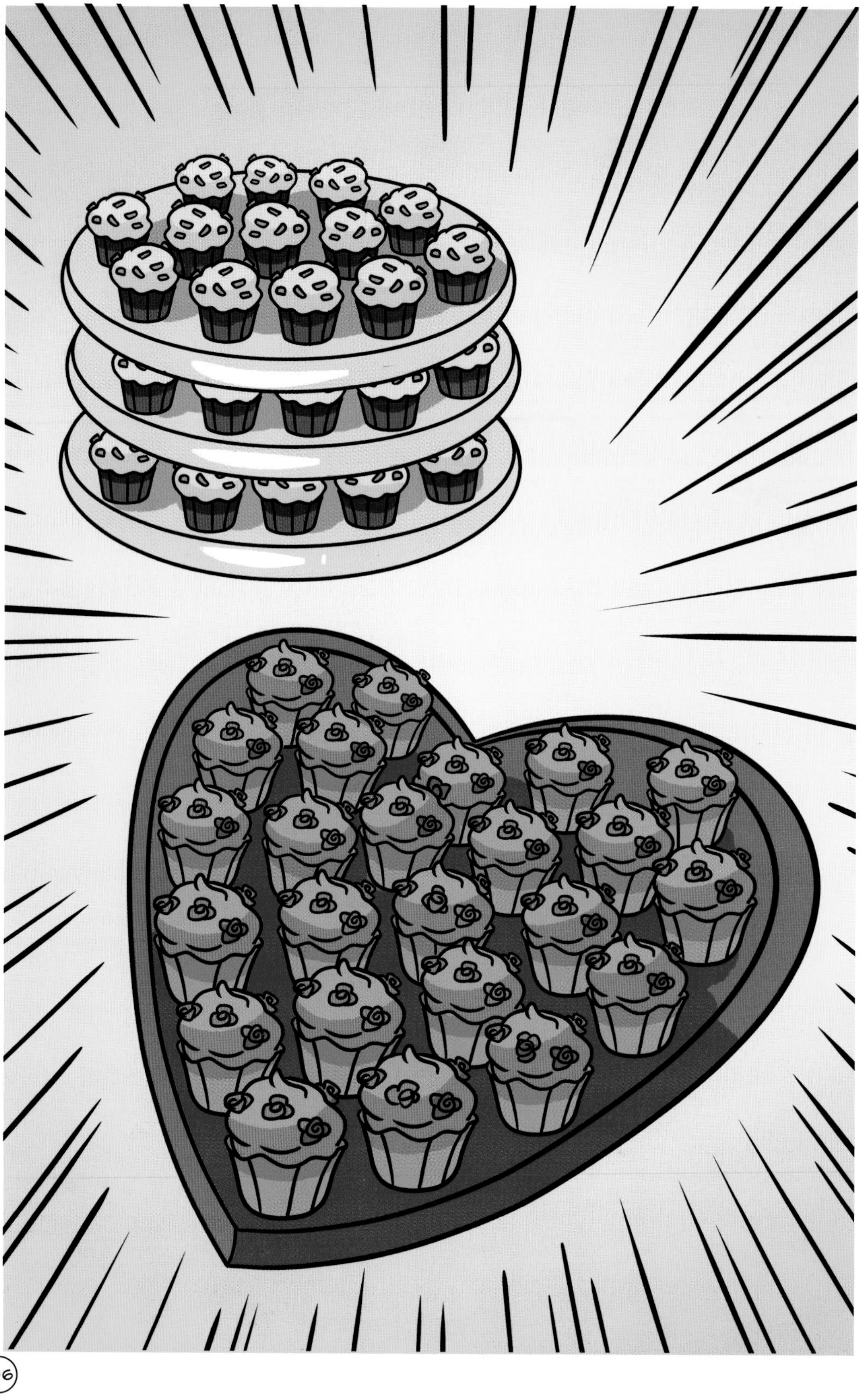

Chapter 13

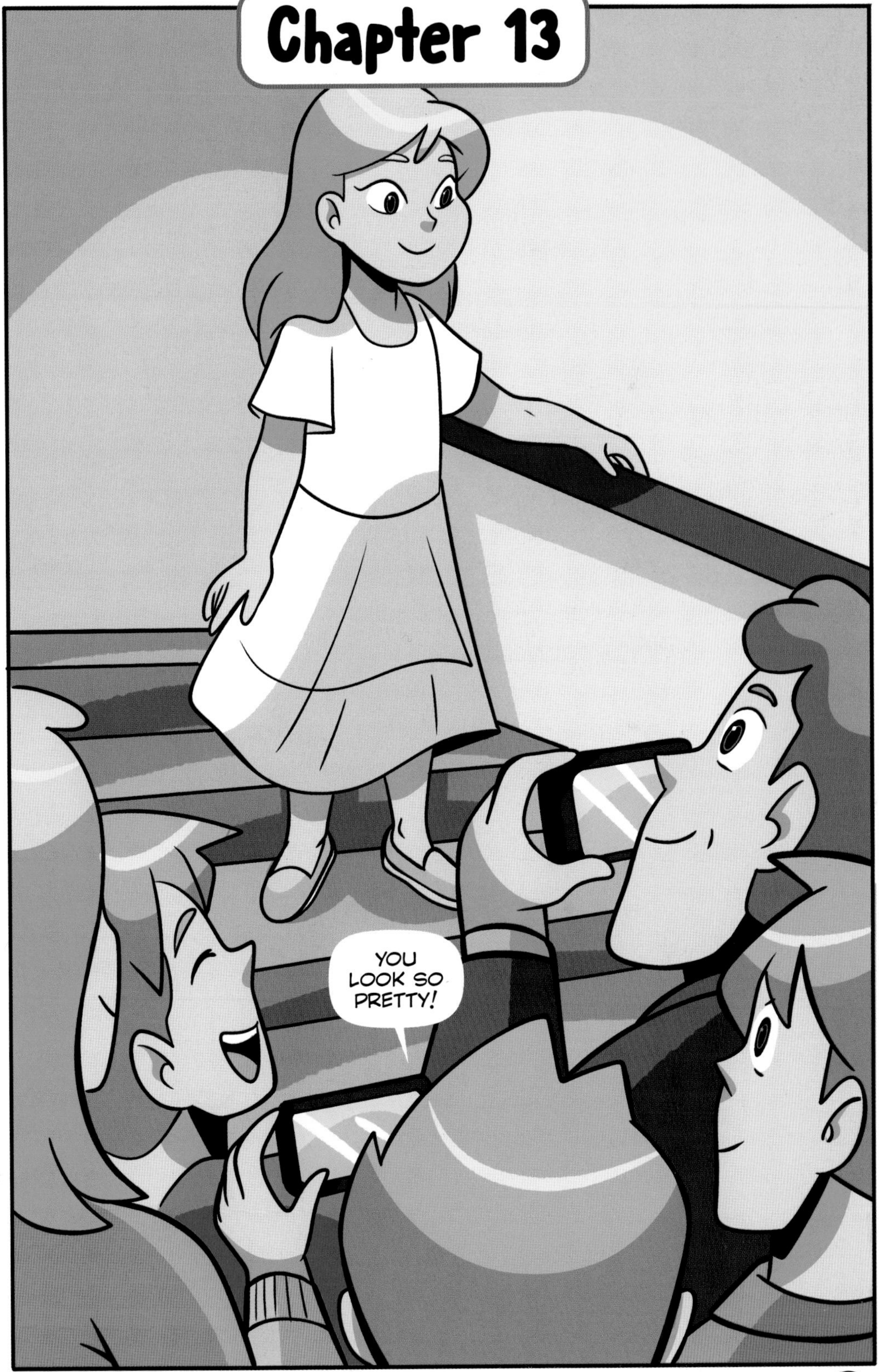
YOU LOOK SO PRETTY!

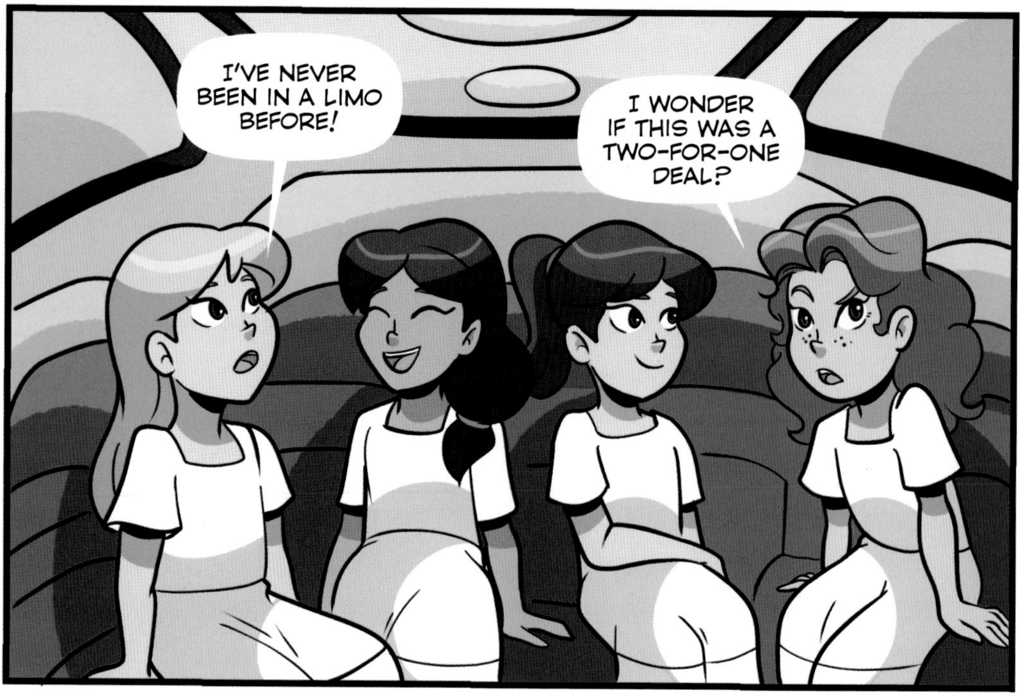
I'VE NEVER BEEN IN A LIMO BEFORE!
I WONDER IF THIS WAS A TWO-FOR-ONE DEAL?

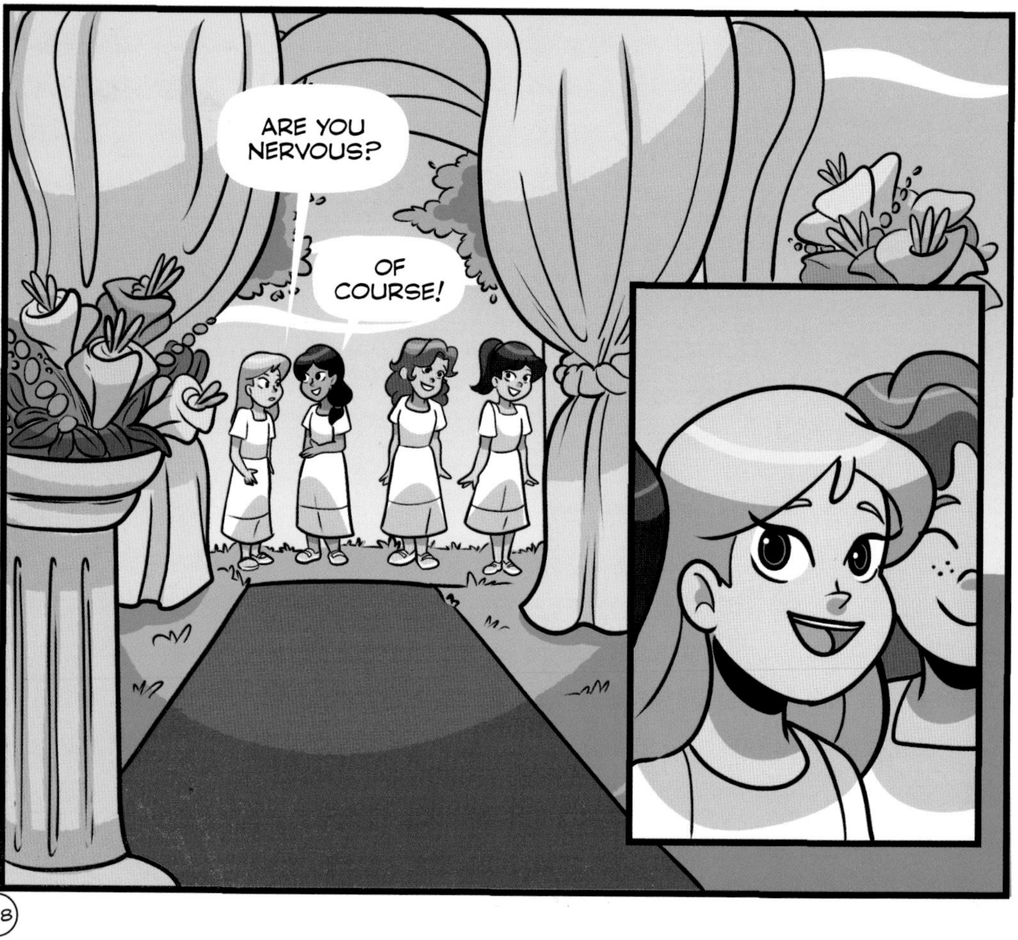
ARE YOU NERVOUS?
OF COURSE!

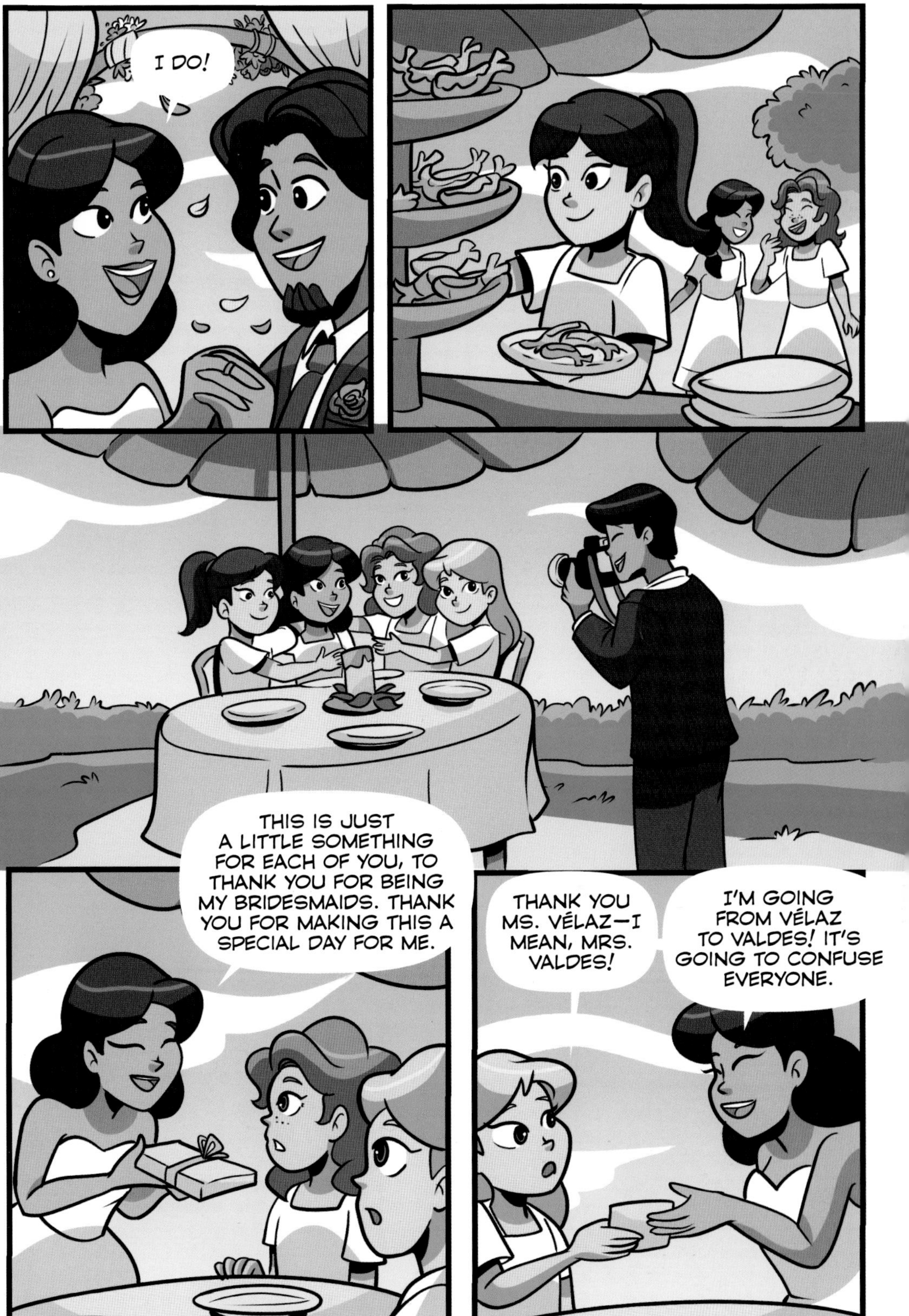
I DO!
THIS IS JUST A LITTLE SOMETHING FOR EACH OF YOU, TO THANK YOU FOR BEING MY BRIDESMAIDS. THANK YOU FOR MAKING THIS A SPECIAL DAY FOR ME.
THANK YOU MS. VÉLAZ—I MEAN, MRS. VALDES!
I'M GOING FROM VÉLAZ TO VALDES! IT'S GOING TO CONFUSE EVERYONE.

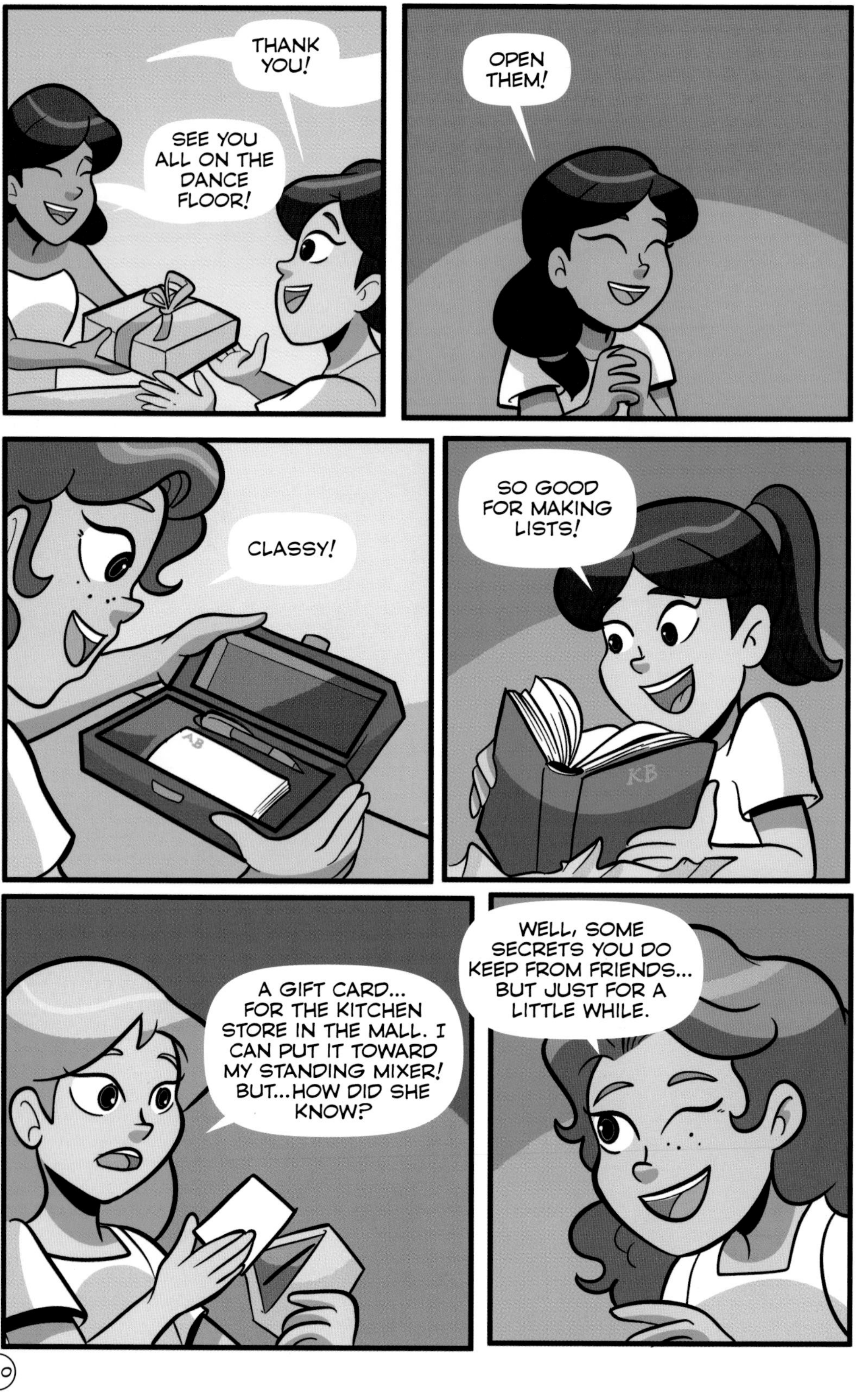
THANK YOU!
SEE YOU ALL ON THE DANCE FLOOR!
OPEN THEM!
CLASSY!
SO GOOD FOR MAKING LISTS!
A GIFT CARD... FOR THE KITCHEN STORE IN THE MALL. I CAN PUT IT TOWARD MY STANDING MIXER! BUT...HOW DID SHE KNOW?
WELL, SOME SECRETS YOU DO KEEP FROM FRIENDS... BUT JUST FOR A LITTLE WHILE.

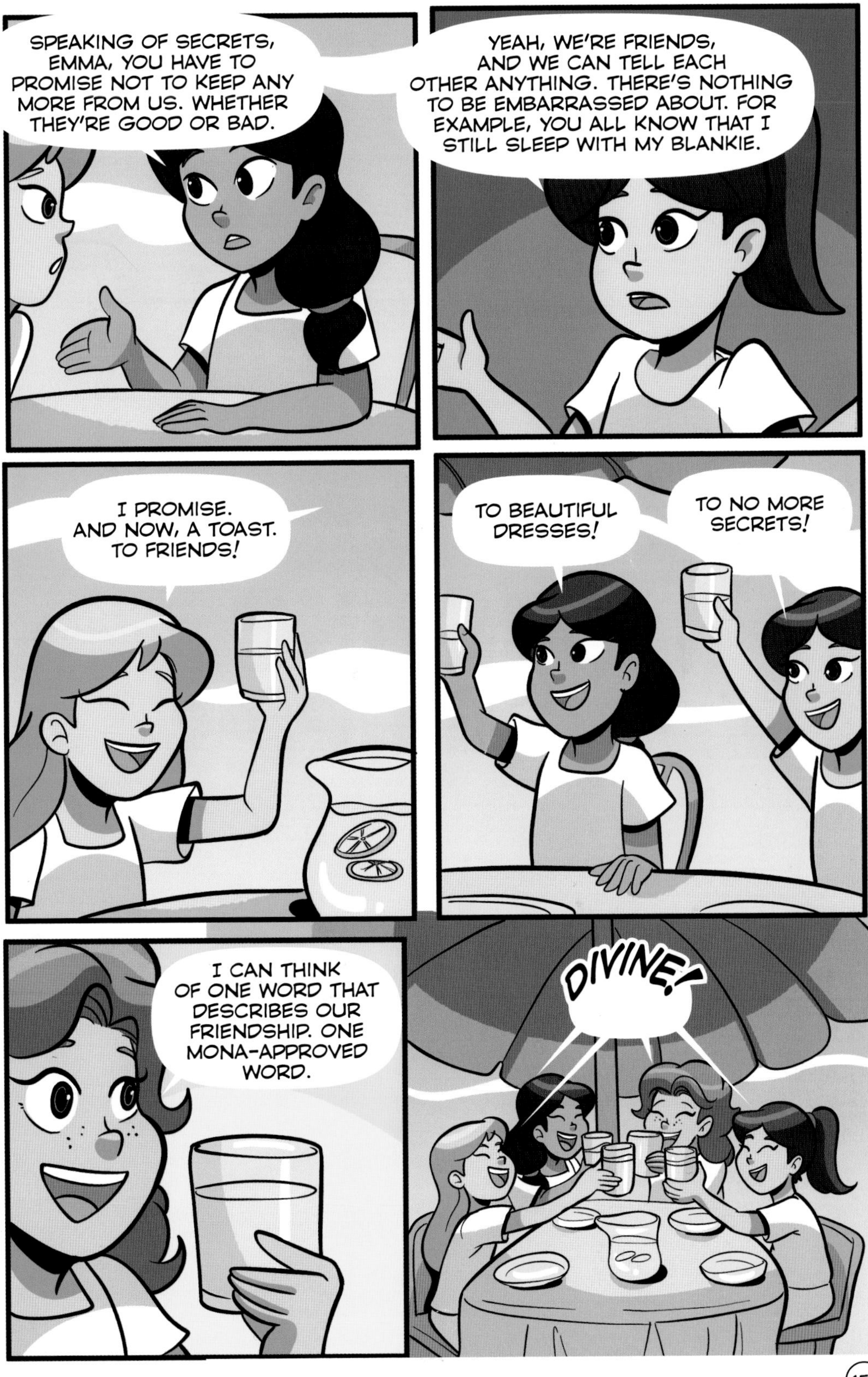
SPEAKING OF SECRETS, EMMA, YOU HAVE TO PROMISE NOT TO KEEP ANY MORE FROM US. WHETHER THEY'RE GOOD OR BAD.
YEAH, WE'RE FRIENDS, AND WE CAN TELL EACH OTHER ANYTHING. THERE'S NOTHING TO BE EMBARRASSED ABOUT. FOR EXAMPLE, YOU ALL KNOW THAT I STILL SLEEP WITH MY BLANKIE.
I PROMISE. AND NOW, A TOAST. TO FRIENDS!
TO BEAUTIFUL DRESSES!
TO NO MORE SECRETS!
I CAN THINK OF ONE WORD THAT DESCRIBES OUR FRIENDSHIP. ONE MONA-APPROVED WORD.
DIVINE!

Make sure you read them all!

Cupcake Diaries

Mia in the Mix

From the bestselling author of Cupcake Diaries Coco Simon
Cupcake Diaries
#2
The Graphic Novel
Mia in the Mix

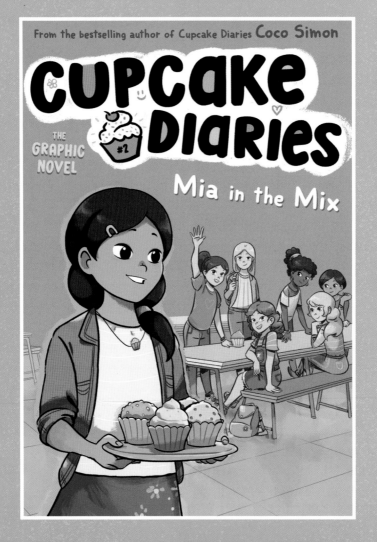

Chapter 1

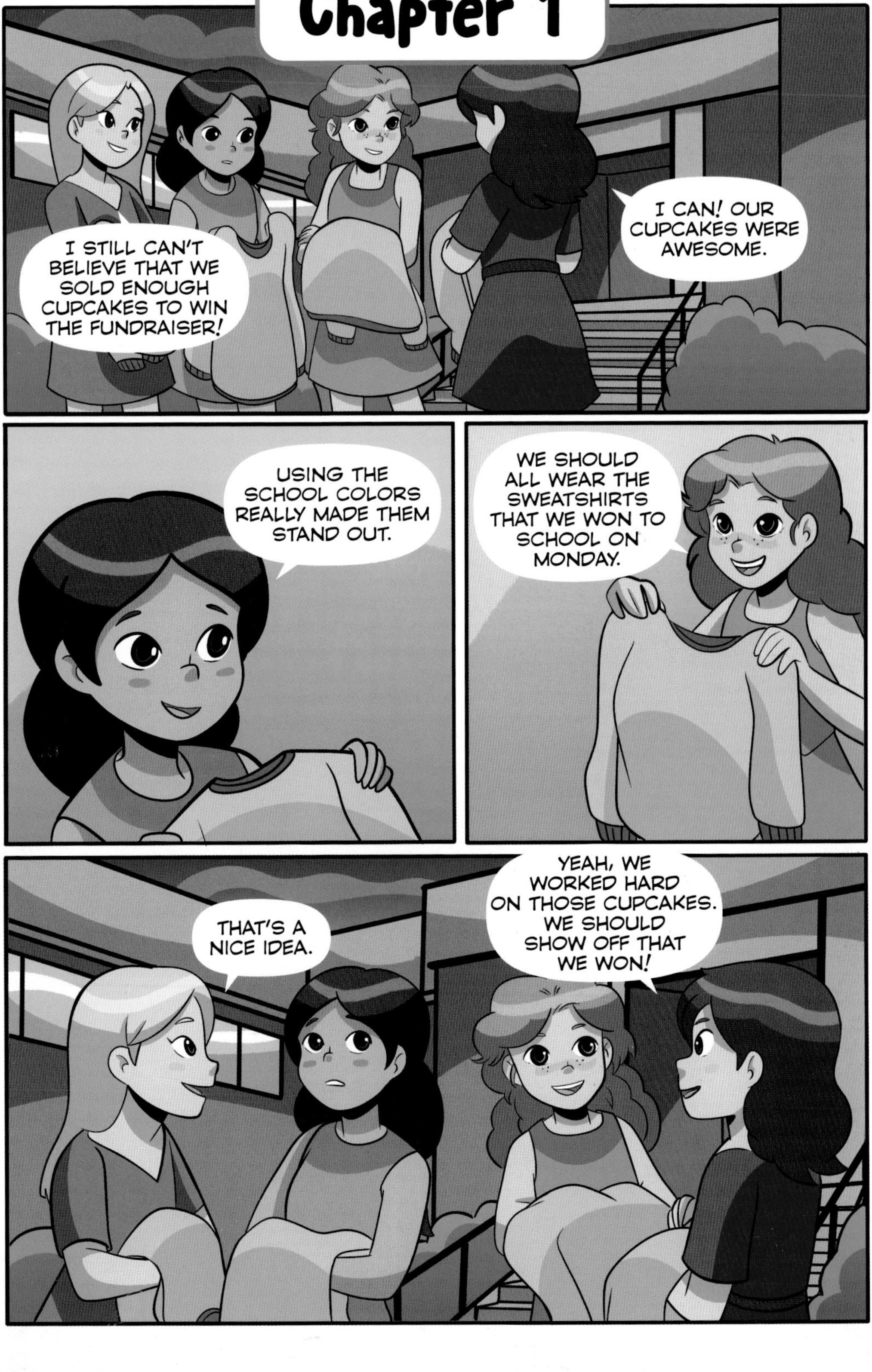
I STILL CAN'T BELIEVE THAT WE SOLD ENOUGH CUPCAKES TO WIN THE FUNDRAISER!
I CAN! OUR CUPCAKES WERE AWESOME.
USING THE SCHOOL COLORS REALLY MADE THEM STAND OUT.
WE SHOULD ALL WEAR THE SWEATSHIRTS THAT WE WON TO SCHOOL ON MONDAY.
THAT'S A NICE IDEA.
YEAH, WE WORKED HARD ON THOSE CUPCAKES. WE SHOULD SHOW OFF THAT WE WON!

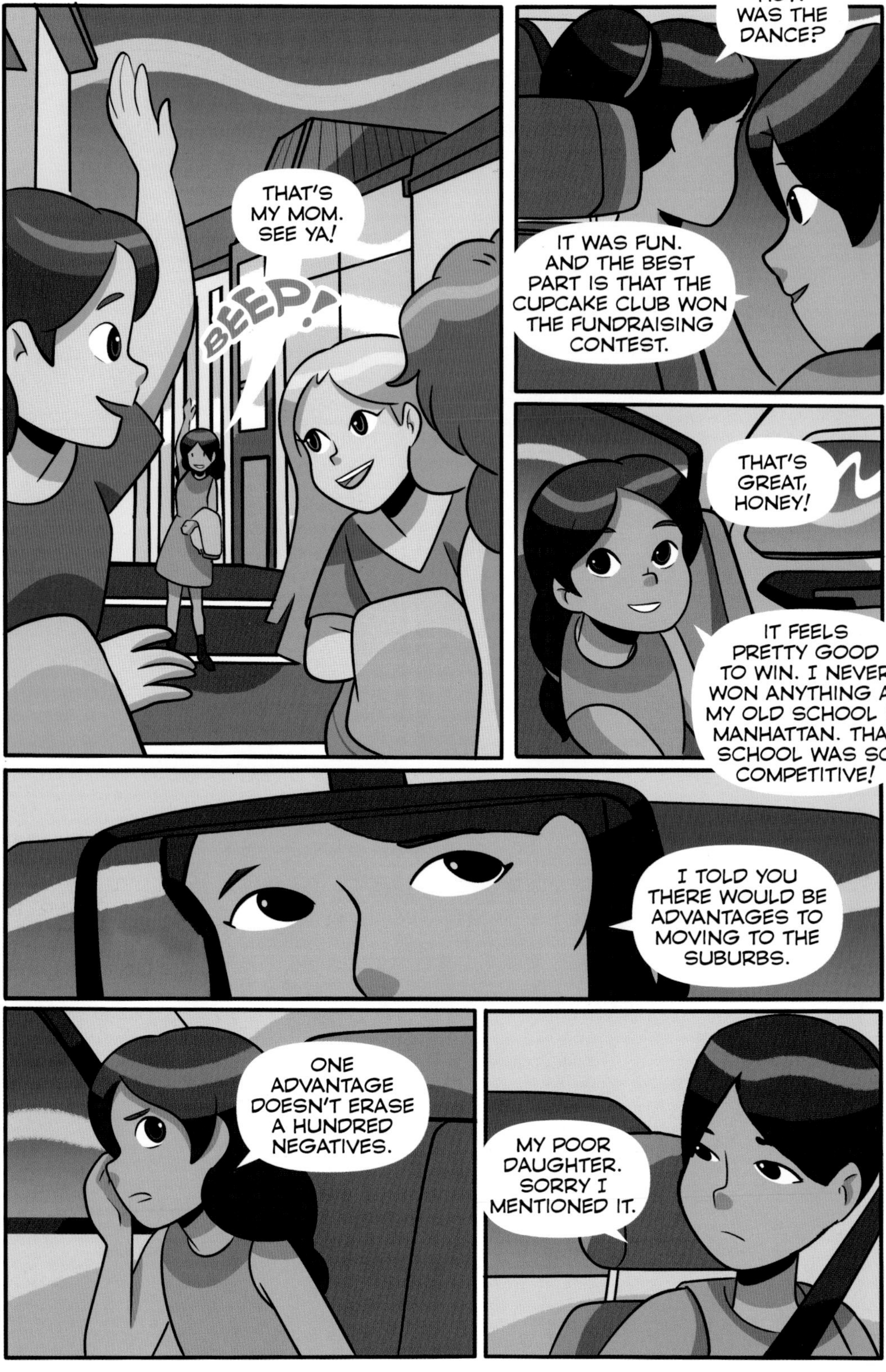
THAT'S MY MOM. SEE YA!
BEEP!
HOW WAS THE DANCE?
IT WAS FUN. AND THE BEST PART IS THAT THE CUPCAKE CLUB WON THE FUNDRAISING CONTEST.
THAT'S GREAT, HONEY!
IT FEELS PRETTY GOOD TO WIN. I NEVER WON ANYTHING AT MY OLD SCHOOL IN MANHATTAN. THAT SCHOOL WAS SO COMPETITIVE!
I TOLD YOU THERE WOULD BE ADVANTAGES TO MOVING TO THE SUBURBS.
ONE ADVANTAGE DOESN'T ERASE A HUNDRED NEGATIVES.
MY POOR DAUGHTER. SORRY I MENTIONED IT.

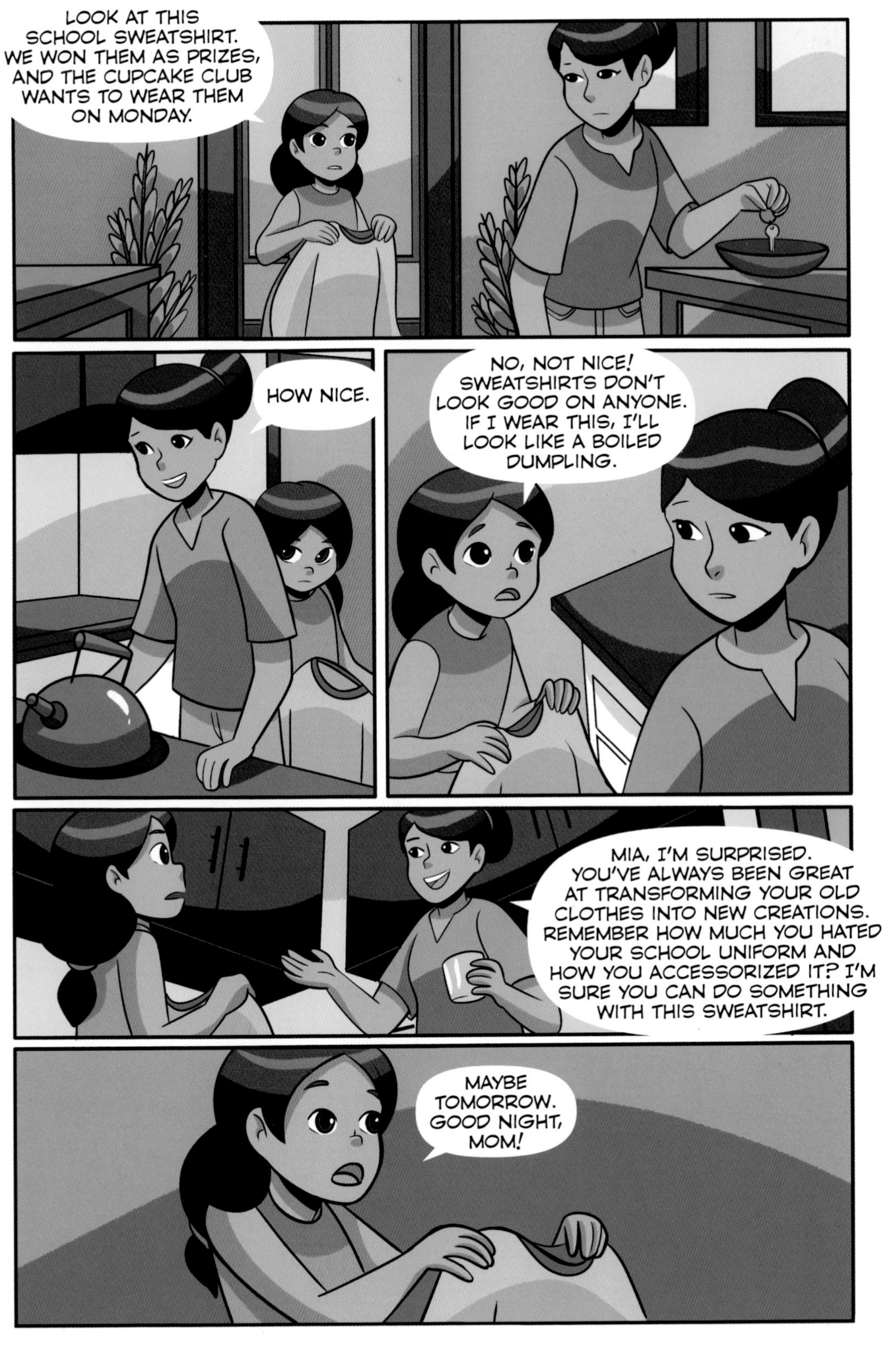
LOOK AT THIS SCHOOL SWEATSHIRT. WE WON THEM AS PRIZES, AND THE CUPCAKE CLUB WANTS TO WEAR THEM ON MONDAY.
HOW NICE.
NO, NOT NICE! SWEATSHIRTS DON'T LOOK GOOD ON ANYONE. IF I WEAR THIS, I'LL LOOK LIKE A BOILED DUMPLING.
MIA, I'M SURPRISED. YOU'VE ALWAYS BEEN GREAT AT TRANSFORMING YOUR OLD CLOTHES INTO NEW CREATIONS. REMEMBER HOW MUCH YOU HATED YOUR SCHOOL UNIFORM AND HOW YOU ACCESSORIZED IT? I'M SURE YOU CAN DO SOMETHING WITH THIS SWEATSHIRT.
MAYBE TOMORROW. GOOD NIGHT, MOM!

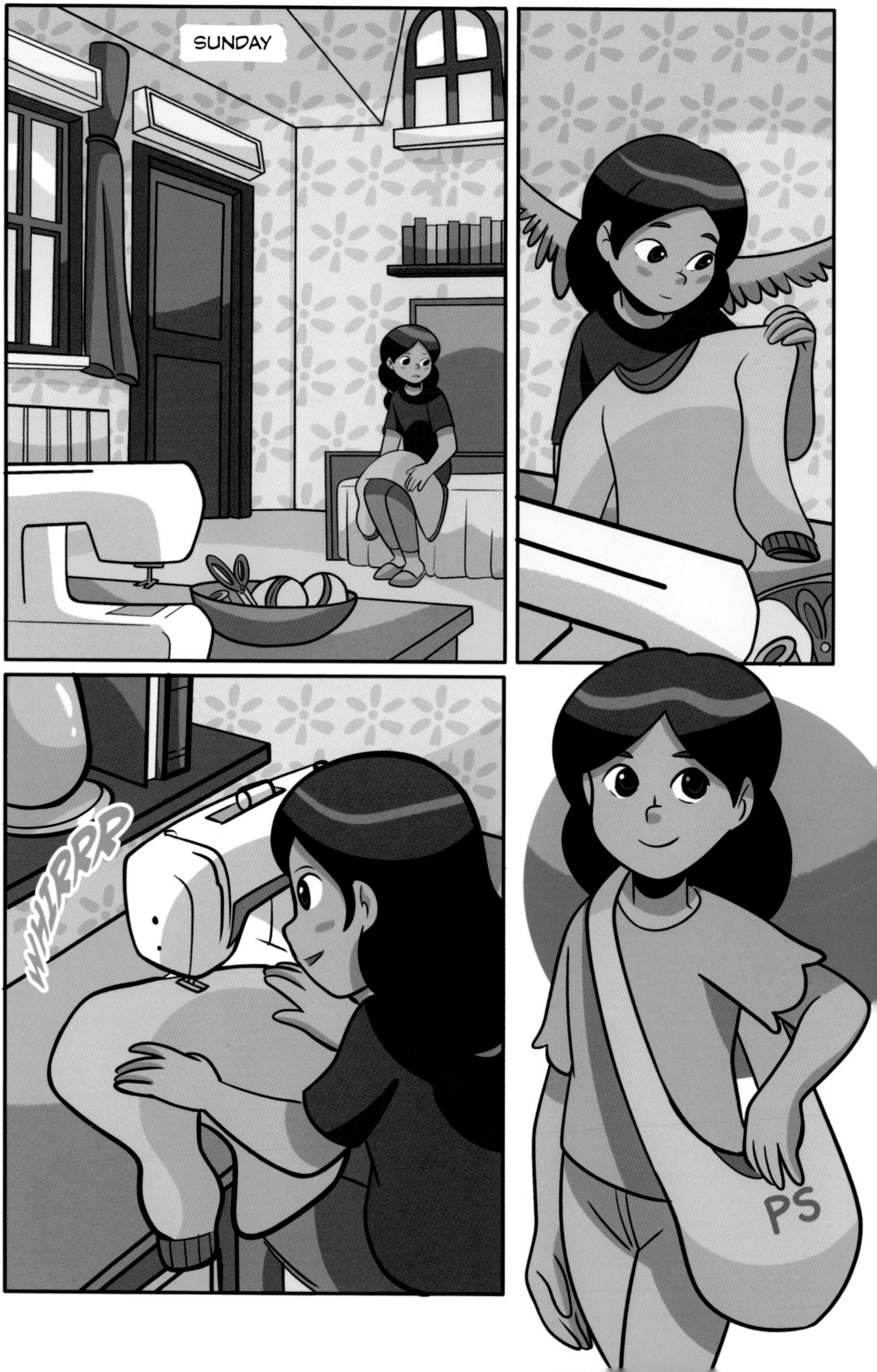
SUNDAY
WHIRRRP
PS

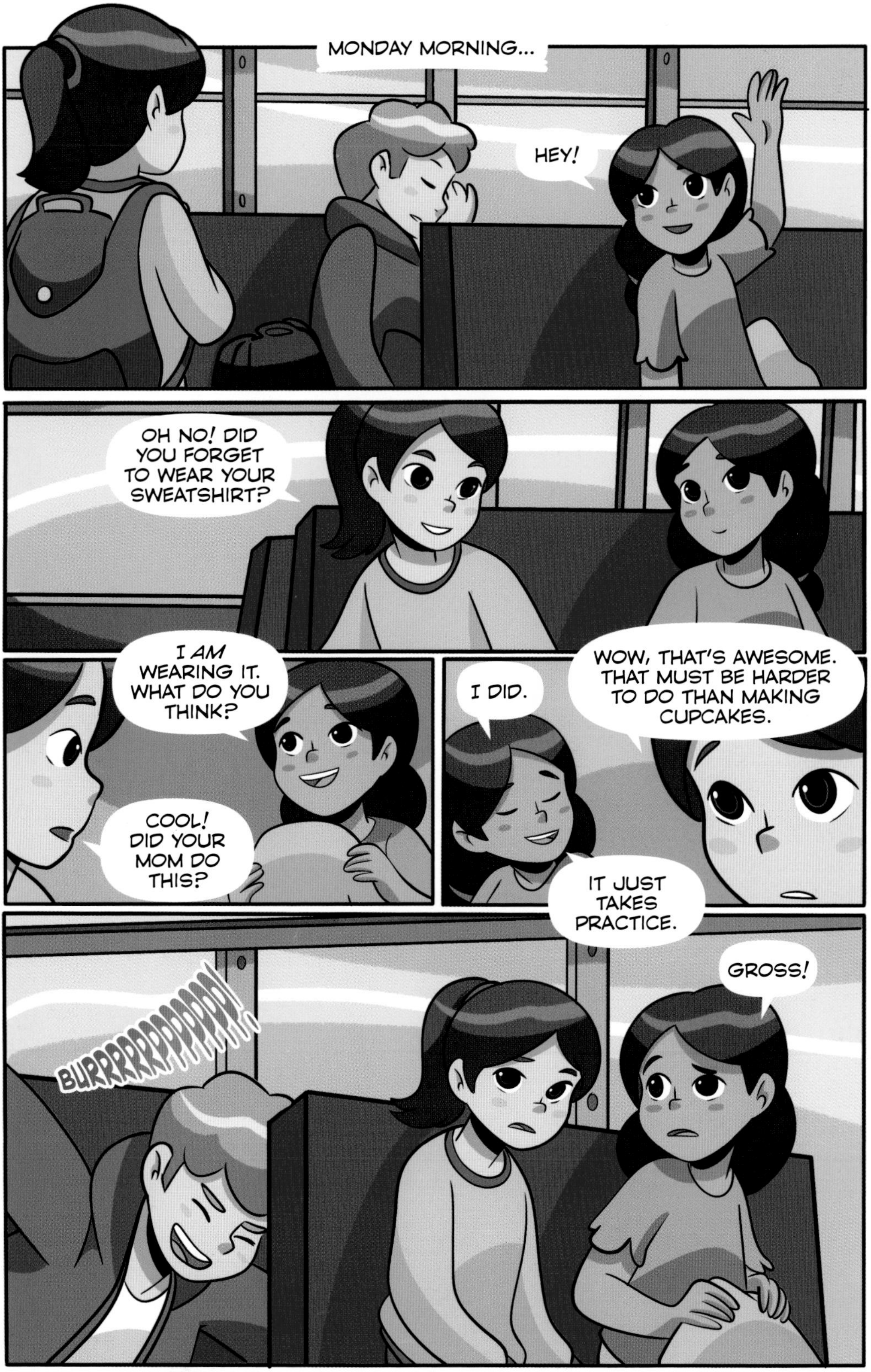
MONDAY MORNING...
HEY!
OH NO! DID YOU FORGET TO WEAR YOUR SWEATSHIRT?
I AM WEARING IT. WHAT DO YOU THINK?
COOL! DID YOUR MOM DO THIS?
I DID.
WOW, THAT'S AWESOME. THAT MUST BE HARDER TO DO THAN MAKING CUPCAKES.
IT JUST TAKES PRACTICE.
BURRRRRPPPPPP!
GROSS!

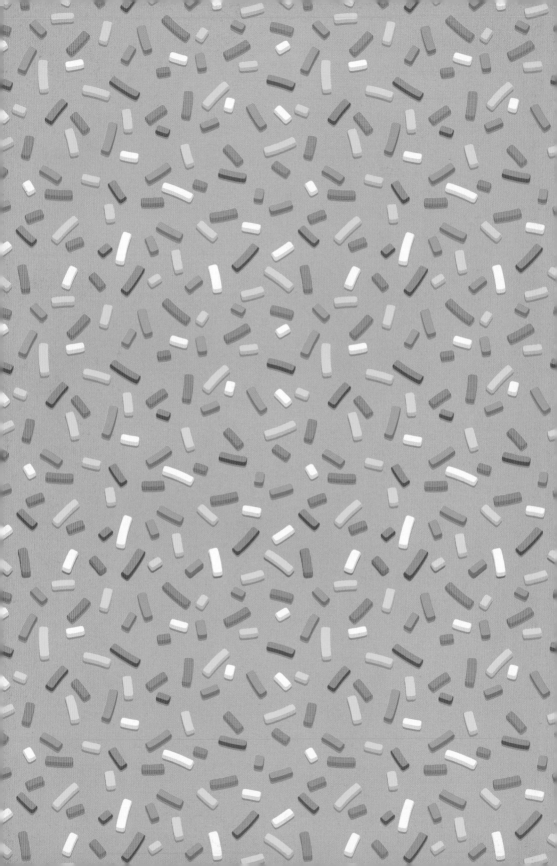